THE LAMB CART

A novel by Richard Hooton

1st WORLD PUBLISHING

THE LAMB CART

A novel by Richard Hooton

© Richard Hooton 2009

Published by 1stWorld Publishing
1100 North 4th St., Fairfield, Iowa 52556
tel: 641-209-5000 • fax: 641-209-3001
web: www.1stworldpublishing.com

First Edition

LCCN: 2009930654
SoftCover ISBN: 978-1-4218-9103-3
HardCover ISBN: 978-1-4218-9102-6
eBook ISBN: 978-1-4218-9104-0

All rights reserved. No part of this book may be reproduced or utilized in any form or by any means, electronic or mechanical, including photocopying or recording, or by any information storage and retrieval system, without permission in writing from the author.

This material has been written and published solely for educational purposes. The author and the publisher shall have neither liability or responsibility to any person or entity with respect to any loss, damage or injury caused or alleged to be caused directly or indirectly by the information contained in this book.

The characters and events described in this text are intended to entertain and teach rather than present an exact factual history of real people or events.

Cover photography by Michael Edminster

THE CONTENTS

Chapter One—THE CHOICE 9
Chapter Two—STORM CLOUDS 23
Chapter Three—ALICE AND JUNE. 37
Chapter Four—SANCTUARY. 55
Chapter Five—LOST AND FOUND 69
Chapter Six—FENCE MENDING 87
Chapter Seven—WINTER SOLSTICE. 111
Chapter Eight—PANDORA'S ILLS. 135
Chapter Nine—WILD MUSTANGS. 147
Chapter Ten—COOPER'S WAY 161
Chapter Eleven—SPRING THAW 175
Chapter Twelve—MUTTON BUSTERS. 193
Chapter Twelve—GARDEN HARVEST 219
Chapter Twelve—DOG DAYS. 225
Chapter Twelve—THE SHEEP BRIDGE 235
Chapter Twelve—A FATHER'S FURY. 257
Chapter Twelve—THE UMBRELLA STAND. 269
Chapter Twelve—BUS STOP BILLY 277

PROLOGUE

The life of Jennifer Barnett had entered a time of uncertainty, complicated by an unplanned pregnancy, and worsened by the ongoing conflict with her disapproving father. Burdened unexpectedly with the obligation of supporting four orphaned children, Jenny was forced to swallow her pride and turn to her parents for help.

Cooper Barnett wanted nothing more than to be left alone to work his sheep ranch in Camas County, but unforeseen events compelled him to protect his daughter from her brewing legal trouble with the State of Idaho. He argued that she should turn the children over to the Child Welfare Services Agency for placement in foster homes, and move back home to the ranch until her baby was born.

Jenny refused to accept her father's argument. She vowed to keep the children together, and promised never to abandon them. She was a fierce protector, and she was prepared to risk everything—including her freedom.

So she gathered all her cubs
She was a lioness on the prowl
Little Joseph wore a hat
And Brother Danny wore a scowl

Mother Jenny led the way
As they walked out into the night
Fretful Alice stayed the course
And tiny June just held on tight

'cross the sheep bridge there was refuge
'cross the bridge and homeward bound
Every child will be protected
When the Keeper comes around

CHAPTER ONE
THE CHOICE

Mountain Home, Idaho—1973

Jenny Barnett was lost. She stood outside Harry's Diner and waited for a bus to arrive, shivering uncontrollably. The rain came down hard and the wind picked up again. It was after dark—exactly what time she wasn't sure. The whole place looked deserted—there were no cars left in the parking lot, and the gas station next to the diner was already closed for the night. She walked inside and found a booth next to the window so that she could watch for a northbound bus.

Harry's Diner had been the official bus stop for Greyhound and Sun Valley Stage Lines for as long as anyone in town could remember. During the daytime, buses stopped in intervals of two or three hours, making their runs to Boise and points north, or to Twin Falls, and south to Salt Lake City. A few small local buses operated less frequently, and were not as reliable.

"You look half-frozen. How did you get here?" the middle-aged waitress asked, stopping to fill Jenny's coffee mug.

"My boyfriend dropped me off," Jenny answered, averting her eyes to look out the window.

"I didn't notice a car pull up—I must have been in the kitchen."

Jenny's eyes brimmed with tears. Her pale face was etched with sadness and regret. She didn't want to offer any more details. The older woman recognized the signs—she knew a young woman in distress when she saw one.

"I'm guessing that you've got yourself into some trouble, haven't you?" the woman asked, and then pressed a little further. "Where is he—your boyfriend, I mean?"

"A few miles down the road, I guess," Jenny answered quietly, her eyes downcast.

"Something happen between you two? You have a fight?"

"Sort of," Jenny answered briefly.

"Either you did or you didn't," the waitress responded. "You must have had a real tiff for him to just leave you. You got family here?"

"My folks don't live far from here," she answered, hoping to put an end to the woman's questioning.

"Where are your things, honey?" the older woman asked, noticing that Jenny didn't have any luggage. "Don't you have a suitcase?"

Jenny's face fell, and she cast a glance out the window to the spot where Roger dropped her off, just in case there was a chance he had thrown her suitcase out when he ejected her without a second thought. She had left her suitcase in the trunk of Roger's car, and she had nothing but her purse and the clothes on her back.

The older woman let it go. She knew the stranded young traveler had enough trouble without being badgered for any more information about her personal life. She put the coffee pot down on the table and slid into the booth across from Jenny.

"What's your name, honey?"

"Jennifer Barnett," she replied. "Jenny."

"I'm Donna—my husband and I own this joint. I know it's none of my business, Jenny," the waitress continued, "but a man doesn't just drop a woman off at a bus stop and leave her there, argument or no argument. It must have been something serious."

Jenny had been humiliated by her no-good boyfriend, and she was embarrassed to talk about it, but she yielded to the older woman's insistent questioning. Sometimes, she thought, it was easier to talk to a total stranger than it was to confess something so personal to family or friends.

"He got mad and dropped me off here when I told him that I was pregnant. He said I was stupid for not being more careful and then he told me to go back to my parents."

"So is that where you're going?" Donna asked. "Back to your parents?"

"Oh my gosh, no! My father would kill me—he would absolutely kill me."

"Fathers always talk tough, Jenny, but when it comes right down to it, they can be very understanding in situations like this."

"You don't know my father," Jenny insisted. "He'll never forgive me for getting myself into this mess."

She looked Donna directly in the eye to make her point.

"He never liked Roger—from the first time he met him, he didn't trust him. Dad told me from the very beginning that he was no good, and that he would never treat me right. I should have listened to him."

"Where do your folks live, Jenny?" the understanding older woman asked.

"They have a ranch over in Camas County. That's where I grew up," Jenny answered wistfully. "I was always so bored hanging around the ranch with nothing to do, and couldn't wait to get out of there after high school. It seemed like we never went anywhere except into Fairfield or Gooding for groceries and livestock feed a couple of times a month. Now I'm almost thirty years old, and all I wish for is that I could just go home and stay there."

"Life couldn't have been all that bad, could it?" Donna asked. "I know a lot of people who would love to experience life on a ranch."

"They only think so," Jenny replied quickly. "Getting out of bed an hour before sunrise every morning in the cold of winter to go out with my dad to feed sheep wasn't exactly a holiday, and then helping my mom in the kitchen every afternoon and evening to keep the ranch hands fed. Every spring it was the stink of the lambing pens, and then the smell of wool and lanolin in the shearing sheds. In the summer, I had to listen to my dad every morning at breakfast, talking about alfalfa crops, water rights and grazing rights, and in the fall the conversation was all about getting the lambs to market. Nothing ever changed—it was all so boring."

"Didn't you have any friends?" Donna questioned.

"The only ones who stayed close to home didn't seem very happy either, so I didn't go out of my way to see any of them after graduation. It seemed that all that was left were old people and kids, so I finally moved away from home and got a job cooking at a truck stop in Pocatello. I was able to save up enough money after a couple of years to start taking some classes at Idaho State."

"How long did you go to school?"

"Five years—I finally finished school last year and got my teaching certificate. I thought that I might get a job in Hailey or here in Mountain Home, but all that's ruined now."

"Why do you say that?"

"There's no way a school district is going to hire me when I'm single and pregnant."

"So where will you go now?"

"I don't know—maybe Pocatello, or maybe Boise. I just know that I can't go home and face my parents."

"It's hard to know exactly what will please parents, Jenny," the older woman consoled. "I remember that my own mother and father only wanted to see me get married and raise a family, but when I married Harry and discovered that I couldn't have kids, my dad still wasn't happy for me. I guess all he really wanted from me was to see some grandchildren."

"My dad has five grandkids already," Jenny said. "It's not as though I'd be giving him anything he doesn't have, but I suppose he wouldn't mind a few more, as long as I was married to a man he considered to be a worthy son-in-law."

Donna understood, and nodded her head as she watched Jenny dry her reddened eyes with a paper napkin.

"Fathers are a hard bunch to please," she said knowingly, in an attempt to show Jenny that she understood.

"*Tell* me about it," Jenny said, ruefully.

"Why don't you go talk to your folks, Jenny?" Donna asked. "It can't hurt, and you may be surprised at how willing they are to help you."

Jenny thought about it for awhile, and decided that it would not be a good idea to show up on her parents' doorstep after nearly seven years on her own—pregnant and unemployed. Besides, the last Sun Valley Stage Lines bus had left more than an hour earlier, and there wouldn't be another until the next day. It was the only bus line that provided daily service to the small Idaho towns in the rural counties west of Mountain Home, and it only came through once daily, in the middle of the afternoon.

"He'll kill me," Jenny murmured to herself, looking down into her coffee mug again. "He'll *really* kill me."

She wrestled with the idea of facing her parents and confessing to her pregnancy, but decided that it would create an enormous rift between her mother and father. It would be better if she stayed away until after the baby was born.

"When does the next bus to Boise come through?" Jenny asked.

"Not until ten—sometimes later," Donna answered. "We don't close until after the Boise bus comes through, so take your time."

Jenny went back outside to be alone with her thoughts, and waited for the bus. She wasn't aware of the time that passed while she sat on the bench under a canopy, watching the rain water drizzle off and run across the concrete in tiny rivulets. She barely noticed the approaching bus until it pulled off the highway and slowed to a stop on the platform.

Jenny settled into a window seat of the Greyhound passenger coach and opened the copy of Life Magazine that Donna had given her to occupy her time during the two-hour bus ride north to Boise. There would be a few brief stops along the way, but only to drop off passengers and pick up a few new travelers for the trip into the state capital.

If she could just find a job and a place to stay in Boise, she thought, everything would probably work out. And she couldn't afford to be picky, she decided—most of her money was spent on the bus ticket and food, with very little left over to rent a room. She would have to accept the first job she could find.

Jenny stared out through the window into the rain, wondering whether to write to her parents once or twice a month and tell them that she was doing well. Maybe she could telephone them once in awhile, just to talk to her mom. She was determined to keep the baby a secret until after it was born. It might be easier for her parents to love a little grandchild than a wayward daughter with a big belly, she thought.

At least her father should be happy to hear that she was no longer together with her old boyfriend. He had despised Roger from the outset, and told her that he was a jackass and that he had no respect for women. It seemed to Jenny that she and her dad were always at odds with each other ever since she had become a young teenager, and it annoyed her to think that she had to admit he was right this time.

Roger *was* a creep—there was no denying that now. But she had no one else, and didn't consider herself to be a great catch for any man. Maybe that's why she had been so easily taken in by his smooth-talking ways—no one had ever paid much attention to her before.

She had always been tall and gangly as a kid, and she believed that her appearance hadn't changed much as she matured. Her feet and ears were too big, she thought, and she looked more like her dad than her mom—bad luck. A saddle of freckles on the bridge of her nose made her self-conscious—she always thought it made her look like a tom-boy. She envied the girls in school who were petite and feminine—they were always being asked out by boys. Jenny looked like a rancher's daughter—like she was born to ride a horse and work outdoors.

She flipped through the pages of the magazine, browsing through the fashion advertisements and artist's stylized conceptions of the latest automobiles from Detroit. She couldn't concentrate long enough to read any articles. The harsh reality of her predicament sank in, and Jenny's thoughts turned to the dilemma of becoming an unwed mother with no home and no means of support. She had always possessed a fiercely independent nature, and had learned from her parents how to take care of herself, but this was different. This time she was alone. She closed the magazine and dropped it onto her lap, then turned to gaze out the rain-streaked window into the darkness as she wept.

It was late evening when the big silver and blue motor coach pulled into the bus depot in Boise. A chill northern breeze pushed dark rain clouds over the town, blanking out the stars in the night sky. Light rain pelted Jenny's cheeks with its cold wetness as she stepped down from the bus and walked inside the depot. She was exhausted. A ticket window was still open, and she asked the station clerk if he knew where she could find a cheap motel or the YWCA.

She needed a place to sleep, and she was nearly broke. She could probably afford to hang out at the YWCA for few days before she ran out of money. It was only a half-mile walk from the bus depot, she learned. Jenny was happy to discover that it had a small reading room, cafeteria, and a pay phone in the hall. More importantly, it had hot showers and a warm bed, even it if was in a shared room.

She knew that she only had a day or two to find a job before she was destitute. If she could find work, maybe she could persuade the manager to wait another week for the room rent, just until she got her first paycheck.

In the morning, Jenny went straight to the reading room to find a newspaper so that she could look through the help wanted section of the classifieds. Several cook positions were available at a handful of short order joints, but none of them paid very well. She knew this was no time to be fussy about where she worked. A housekeeping job was listed, too, and a home tutor was wanted for some rich family's kid. Neither job would last very long, once her pregnancy began to show. She decided her best chance was to go back to work in the kitchen of a greasy spoon cafe.

Jenny called a couple of phone numbers, only to be told that the cook positions were already filled, but kept trying until someone told her to come in and fill out an application.

"How soon can you start?" a man's voice on the other end of the line asked.

"Right away," Jenny said eagerly. "Today, if you need me to."

"Well, come on in and talk to me," the man said. "Ask for Joe." He hung up abruptly, leaving Jenny feeling cast off and unimportant. Funny how a little thing like being homeless, unemployed and pregnant can affect a girl's emotional state, Jenny thought, with wry introspection.

Jenny walked to the front desk and asked about the bus schedule for downtown Boise. She learned that a bus stopped approximately every half hour on the corner near the front of the building. She took the newspaper with her, just in case she wasn't successful on her first interview, and waited on the bench at the bus stop.

She began to worry about what she was going to do as the time for her baby to be born drew nearer. She tried to push it out of her mind for the moment, realizing that there were more pressing problems, like food and rent.

It was only a twenty minute ride to the northern junction where the truck plaza was located, and Jenny stepped off the bus and walked across the street to the cafe next to the plaza. A big, two-sided metal sign in front of Idaho Joe's Cafe rose up nearly ten feet above the mansard roofline, painted with large navy blue letters, outlined with neon tubing. Jenny heaved a sigh of resignation. It looked identical to the truck stop cafe where she had worked in Pocatello—where she had worked to put herself through school. Only the name on the sign was different. She had hoped for something better.

"Can't ever seem to keep good help," Joe Bannock explained from behind the lunch counter after Jenny approached him and introduced herself. "Waitresses always runnin' off and gettin' married, and my fry cook's a drunk. Haven't seen him since last Friday. If he ever shows up, I'll fire his butt."

"I'm very reliable," Jenny insisted. "I can give you a good reference from the Junction Cafe in Pocatello. I worked there for nearly five years while I went to school."

"You a college graduate?" Joe asked, eyeing Jenny with a little suspicion. "Why you wanna work here?"

Jenny was sorry she mentioned going to college. "There aren't any good teaching jobs available right now," she lied. "And besides, I really like to cook," she lied again. "I always show up early and prepare soups and any specials you want for the day, and can stay as late as you need me on your busy days."

"We don't serve up anything too fancy here," Joe replied. "Just meatloaf and chicken fried steak and lasagna occasionally," he added. "My customers just want to leave with a full belly, and they want to be able to taste what they eat."

Jenny smiled at Joe Bannock's unintended humor. He seemed like a decent man, and she wouldn't mind working for him. A United States Marine Corps insignia was tattooed on his left arm, and he wore a white short-sleeved shirt so that it would not be concealed.

"I'm sure your customers won't have any complaints with my cooking," she said, smiling as she gestured toward the half-empty counter. "My meat loaf is always a hit with the customers, and I can make a lamb stew that beats anything they've ever had before."

"That good, huh? Did you say you could start today?" Joe asked gruffly, looking up from his task of wiping down the counter and replacing the ketchup bottles and salt and pepper shakers in their holders.

"Right now, if you want," Jenny said, trying not to seem too eager.

"There's a coat rack in the back next to the walk-in cooler," Joe said. "Put your stuff away and look around the kitchen and in the cooler to see what you've got to work with. I think you'll find everything you need. Yell out if you can't find something."

Jenny hung up her coat and walked into the stainless steel cavern that would be her workplace for the next few months. At least until Joe figured out that she was pregnant and fired her. She walked over to the grill, counted the pans hanging from the overhead hook rack, and inspected the ovens. She smiled and said hello to a young teenage boy bent over the pot sink, scrubbing out the pans that Joe had dirtied during the breakfast rush.

Joe pushed his head through the pass-through window and handed Jenny a plastic covered, grease-and-ketchup-splattered menu. "Get familiar with this as quick as you can," he told her. "Lunch crowd will start to show up in a couple of hours. That pimply-faced kid with his head in the pot sink is my nephew, Donny. Kick him in the pants if he doesn't do what you tell him." The teen-aged boy looked up and gave the new cook a friendly grin.

"He ain't so tough," the affable boy said. "He just likes to talk that way."

Jenny retrieved a tray of ground beef from the walk-in cooler, made up a few hamburger patties in preparation for lunch, then chopped up some onions and bell peppers to begin a large pan of meatloaf.

"Let me know if you can't find something," Donny offered. "I'm pretty sure I know where almost everything is," he went on. "I've only been here a week, though, so I can't help you too much."

Jenny made it through the lunch rush without a problem, and then began preparing soup for the dinner crowd. She was surprised how busy the cafe had been, and how popular it was with the locals and area businessmen. A middle-aged woman showed up in a starched blue-and-white waitress uniform around four-thirty in the afternoon, and Joe turned the counter and tables over to her.

"How's it going back here?" Joe asked, walking back into the kitchen, where Jenny was just beginning to put away everything she had prepared for the dinner menu.

"Everything's good, I think," Jenny said. "We should be ready for tonight. I've been sending out large portions for your counter customers whenever they looked like a trucker or a hunter. Hope that's okay—I know how they like to eat."

Joe was impressed. The girl knew what it took to keep customers coming back. He walked to his small office next to the utility closet in the back of the cafe and came back with a job application form.

"You take this home with you and fill it out tonight," he instructed. "Bring it with you when you come tomorrow, if you still think you want to work here," he said. "Can you be here by seven?"

Jenny agreed, and went to fetch her coat. She was relieved that Joe was pleased with her work. She was exhausted from the first hectic day at her new job, and ready to get back to the YWCA and clean up.

"Cook's pay is $3.75 an hour," Joe said, as Jenny came through the doorway from the kitchen, pulling on her calf-length woolen coat. "I'll give you a raise if you're still here in two weeks," he offered. "You make a real good meatloaf. All the customers cleaned their plates."

It occurred to Jenny that she hadn't asked when payday would be. She hoped it was every couple of weeks, at least, but decided to wait until later to ask. She didn't want to seem presumptuous, and thought she could make her money last a few more days. Maybe she could even catch a ride to work and save bus fare.

"Payday's every Friday," Joe said. "In case you were wondering."

Jenny smiled and nodded, then left through the front door. She couldn't help fretting about her pregnancy during the bus ride back to her temporary lodgings. She wondered how long it would take for her belly to show, and whether Joe Bannock would allow her to keep working when her condition became obvious. She had been too busy to think about it all day, and decided to put it out of her mind until she could deal with it rationally. Worrying wouldn't change anything. A baby was on the way, and that was that. She was resolved to deal with it, come what may.

Jenny stopped in the lobby of the YWCA and told the desk clerk that she had found work, and would probably be staying for another week or two, but no longer. She asked for some writing paper, and found an empty table in the reading room where she could pen a letter to her mother. She wrote that she had found employment working in a department store while she waited for word of a teaching job at an elementary school. After considering it for a moment, she decided against telling her mother that she was staying at the YWCA.

She didn't like hiding the truth from her mother, but after four years of college she was back in a dead end job, cooking in a greasy spoon joint. Worse, she couldn't imagine how she would break the news of her pending motherhood. She had a long time to think about it—she wasn't planning on going home any time soon.

She carried the letter around in her coat pocket for more than a week before she mailed it. She regretted taking so long to contact her parents, and she knew they would be worried if they didn't hear from her soon—especially her mom. There was something about mothers that made them worry about their offspring long after they left the safety of the nest.

Each day seemed busier than the one before, and Jenny found herself working longer and longer hours to help out at the cafe. Joe had come to rely heavily on her skill and efficiency in the kitchen, and she had proven herself to be reliable. The customers always left satisfied, and that made Joe happy. True to his word, he increased her wages by fifty cents an hour after two weeks. She didn't get overtime pay, but Jenny didn't mind. She was making enough to save a little money every week, and it wasn't long before she was able to move into a small, modestly furnished cottage apartment a short distance from the cafe.

Jenny only took off one day a week—usually on Sunday. She occupied her time reading books she picked up from the city library, or taking long walks by herself to clear her mind. Occasionally, she would attend church services, just to feel more connected to her upbringing. When she lived at home she had attended church with her mom nearly every Sunday. It was a social event as much as anything—a means of getting away from the ranch once a week and a chance to escape the routine of daily chores and the tedious boredom that accompanied ranch life. It's funny how life had never seemed boring to her when she was a kid, Jenny thought. Not until she reached her teen years and developed a yen for more excitement—more fulfillment in her life.

She found the excitement she was looking for when she left home to attend college in Pocatello, but it had come at a price. She discovered the joys of booze, all-night frat house parties, and other hedonistic pleasures available to college students who were away from home for the first time—unfettered by parental supervision. She temporarily lost sight of her goals of getting an education and starting a career.

Her low point arrived during her first year at school when she was arrested for underage drinking. She went along for a ride with some guys who walked out the back door of a supermarket with a case of beer, and she was still with them when the police pulled them over. She was nineteen at the time, and had to call her parents to come and get her out of jail. It was embarrassing for her mother, and disappointing for her father. It reinforced his belief that college was unnecessary for most kids. To Cooper's way of thinking, it was simply an excuse for kids to party, and a place to waste hard-earned tuition money. Jenny rode in silence in the back seat of her mom's Ford station wagon during the entire trip back to Camas County.

She had never asked for her dad's help with tuition, so she only had to convince him that she was doing the right thing by going to school, and the rest was up to her. By the time she finally settled down and began to concentrate seriously on her goal of finishing school and obtaining her teaching degree, she had become a good cook, and had no trouble finding work in a restaurant. It was her skill in the kitchen that landed her the job at Idaho Joe's.

Jenny was grateful to Joe for hiring her on the spot, and without even asking for references. She understood that he was in a jam, stuck without a reliable cook in the middle of deer hunting season. Still, she thought it was generous of him to give her a chance.

"Is there anything else you need me to do before I go?" Jenny asked, poking her head into Joe's tiny, cluttered office.

Joe glanced at his wristwatch, and looked over the tops of his bifocal glasses at his new cook.

"Nope, thanks Jenny," he replied. He set down the meat and produce invoices he had been reviewing. "You're a great help—worth your weight in cookbooks and recipes," he added with a grin.

Jenny retrieved her coat and scarf from the wall rack and left through the back door. She cut through the alley and across to the next street—a shortcut that took ten minutes off the walk home. The small, two-room bungalow she rented from Dora Rolfson was ideal. It was neat and clean, furnished with a full-sized bed and nightstands, a small sofa and an easy chair, a coffee table, and a small black-and-white television. It wasn't much—but it was clean, and it was home.

She spent much of her spare time reading, mostly to keep her mind off the pregnancy that was going to complicate her life a great deal in the coming months. She sat down in the easy chair without taking off her coat, unbuttoned the front and ran her palms over her belly. The baby was beginning to show.

CHAPTER TWO

STORM CLOUDS

Cooper Barnett tossed the heavy bales of hay into the back of the old Ford flatbed truck with uncommon ease for a man whose sixtieth birthday was already behind him. He had performed the same hard work every day with his father and grandfather when he was a small boy—scarcely old enough and strong enough to perform a man's chores on the ranch. It never occurred to him to do anything else with his life. He and his wife had raised their three children on the ranch before sending them out into the world. It was a good life, he thought, even though he sometimes felt isolated and detached from the rest of the world in his remote and rural seclusion.

"How many bags of feed will you need today, Mr. Barnett?" the young feed store worker asked, eager to help with the loading so that he could stay out of trouble with his boss. Cooper Barnett never asked for help when he came in to buy feed and ranch supplies. The tall, rangy rancher had a powerful build, and could lift things that usually took two of the young loading dock workers to wrestle into a truck.

"About twenty should be enough for now," Cooper replied. A spool of heavy barbed wire, a metal gate, or a heavy bale of hay—it made no difference to Cooper. He never asked for help from the younger men. When the young workers stepped in to lend a hand, they knew enough to stay out of his way. He had little patience for men who were slow or lazy. His leather-gloved hands grasped another fifty pound bag by the corners and tossed it easily onto the truck bed.

Cooper worked his ranch year in and year out, in fair weather and foul, and never complained. His father had always told him that whining wouldn't get the work done—some days are warm, and some days are cold. He never forgot the lessons of his youth. His father was right. There was nothing to be done about the weather. The wool and lamb markets had declined the past couple of years, and there was nothing he could do about that, either. Some years were just better than others.

The aging rancher couldn't bring himself to admit it, but he needed the help of a younger man to help with the ranch business. He always had the help of a Basque sheepherder or two to follow the bands of sheep along their summer grazing range, and the shearers always came to take the wool off his sheep every year, but he needed more help during the spring lambing season, and it was becoming more and more difficult for him to keep the old place up since his sons had left home. The barn was missing some shingles off the roof, and the house was in desperate need of a coat of paint.

Betty never once complained about it—she asked him to fix the kitchen screen door or replace a board on the porch steps once in awhile, but never asked for anything else. She was a good and understanding wife, and Cooper thought she looked the same as the day they first met. He was one of a rare and dying breed of men who had found his life's mate early and remained devoted to her throughout the years. He had given her a small engagement ring at the end of their senior year in high school, and they married that same summer. He never felt a day's regret.

"I have to go into Hailey this morning, Betty," Cooper said over his first sip of coffee. "We need some help with the property taxes again."

"Well, have some breakfast first," Betty insisted, knowing that food was the last thing on her husband's mind. "You can't talk to a banker on an empty stomach." She looked down at her husband with an understanding smile, and pushed a plate of hotcakes toward him. Cooper reluctantly forked a couple of the hot breakfast cakes onto his plate and poured maple syrup over the top. He was never in the mood to eat when he had to go begging to a banker, hat in hand.

"I hate going into the bank for money every year," Cooper said quietly. "Seems like we ought to be able to build a surplus every fall, like my dad was able to do, and my granddad before him."

"Don't be hard on yourself, Coop," Betty said, as she stood behind him and briefly rested her hands on his shoulders. "Times are different now. Lamb and wool prices are down, and money doesn't go as far as it once did—almost everything costs more these days."

"I know," Coop acknowledged. "It's just humiliating, that's all. We shouldn't still be borrowing to keep operating nearly forty years after the mortgage was paid off. Well, maybe to buy replacement farm machinery once in awhile," he recanted. "But that's all." Cooper took a mouthful of hotcake and began to munch, looking up to make eye contact with his wife every few seconds.

"Do you want me to go with you?" Betty asked quietly.

"No," Cooper answered quickly. "No, I don't want you to have to sit there and listen to a know-it-all bank manager ask me what I did with the money we made from this year's wool and lamb sales."

"I'll give him a piece of my mind if he does," Betty said defiantly, raising her voice in anger.

"That's what I'm afraid of," Cooper replied. "That's why it's best that I go into the bank alone. It would be nice to have some company for the ride to town and back, though. Maybe you could do a little shopping, or visit your aunt while I'm at the bank."

"I don't need anything from town, but it would be nice to see Aunt Marie. She's all alone now, and it's been at least four months since our last visit."

Betty took only a few minutes to get herself ready, changing into a cotton print dress and pinning her hair back before going to the closet for her parka. It was a chilly morning, and it looked like snow was on the way. She knew that her husband didn't like waiting on anyone when it was time to leave. He had probably laid awake half the night, rehearsing the conversation he was going to have with the bank manager. He was anxious to be on his way, and Betty knew his moods all too well. Until he got the matter of begging for assistance from the bank out of the way, he wouldn't be able to focus his attention on anything else. Their financial situation had put him in a sour mood.

Betty made small talk during the thirty mile drive into Hailey, hoping to take her husband's mind off of what was worrying him. She avoided talking about the kids—it would only cause him to think about Jenny, and his daughter had been another major source of worry for him lately.

"It looks like they may have enough snow to open the ski resort before Christmas this year," she observed, as they passed the Highway 20 turnoff to the Soldier Mountain Resort. Cooper shrugged—he didn't care about skiing or resorts.

"Yeah, I suppose," he responded to his wife, politely. "Don't know that it will make much difference, though. Hardly anyone goes up there—all the young people want to drive over to Sun Valley now."

Betty changed the subject to her latest recipe for baked turban squash before Cooper could begin to dwell on any thoughts of Jenny. All of their kids had skied at one time or another, and they even had a couple of family outings on the ski hill around Christmastime when all the kids were still little.

They passed the Martin ranch, and Betty tried again to engage her husband in light-hearted conversation.

"You and Jack Martin haven't gone deer hunting together for a few years, have you?" she asked, already knowing the answer.

"No reason to—we have plenty of lamb and mutton to eat," Cooper responded sullenly. "I've never been partial to venison anyway. Hunting was mostly an excuse to take the boys out camping for a couple of days. It's the same for Jack Martin. I don't think he's gone deer or elk hunting since his youngest son moved away."

Betty gave up. No matter what subject she brought up, the conversation always had a way of drifting back toward their kids. She turned on the car radio and dialed in the farm report, then sat back in silence for the rest of the drive. That should keep Coop's mind occupied for awhile, she thought.

Cooper turned the station wagon off the main street in Hailey at the first traffic light and drove the short distance up the hill to Third Street toward Marie Sadler's home.

"I'll just drop you off and go, if you don't mind," Coop said to his wife. "If I get into the bank early it should be easier to see the manager without an appointment. There'll be plenty of time to visit when I get back. You'll need time to catch up on all the family news anyway."

Betty opened the passenger door and turned to speak her husband before she got out.

"Take whatever time you need, Coop," she said. "I'll be here." She stood in the driveway for a few moments and watched as her husband drove away. She worried about his meeting at the bank. Although he could sound convincing and be very persuasive among his own peers, Cooper wasn't the most eloquent speaker when he wasn't in his element. Business meetings always made him uncomfortable. He usually talked too loudly and often repeated himself—a sure sign of nervousness. Betty wished that she could go in his place. She sighed and stepped up onto the walkway that led to the front door of the tall, two-story brick house.

Cooper was still thinking about what he would say as he pulled into the bank parking lot. He walked through the front door, holding it open for a young woman in a waitress uniform who smiled and thanked him on her way out. Maybe she got a loan, he thought, removing his worn Stetson as he crossed through the doorway into the large foyer. He wondered why banks were always so damned intimidating.

"I'd like to talk to the manager," Cooper said to a woman at the first desk he approached, without waiting for her to ask how she could help him.

"Do you have an appointment?" she asked politely. It seemed to Cooper like the start of an interrogation.

"No," he replied, fidgeting with the brim of his hat that he held in front of him.

"Do you need to open an account today?"

He didn't recognize the woman, but then he hadn't been into the bank in at least two years. Betty always deposited the checks collected from wool and lamb sales, so his trips to the bank were rare. He occasionally sold some alfalfa hay for cash, and he kept it in a coffee tin in the freezer. He would rather not deal with a bank.

"No," he replied succinctly. "My name is Barnett. I'd like to talk to the manager, if you don't mind," he said again. Cooper didn't want to

The Lamb Cart

explain his business with the bank to anyone who couldn't make a decision.

He waited in a fabric-upholstered chair across from the teller windows while the woman went to a glass-paneled door in the back of the bank and disappeared for a moment. She reappeared with a young man in a gray suit who followed close behind. The young man walked straight to the seating area where Cooper waited, and introduced himself.

"I'm Ron Henson, Mr. Barnett." the young man began. "Mr. Sorenson is out of town for the rest of the week. Can I help you?"

"Well, I don't know," Cooper began, with some trepidation. He didn't want to explain his situation to some young kid who couldn't approve a loan for him anyway. "Maybe I should come back later."

"I'm the Assistant Manager," the young man said, with an air of confidence. "I have full authority to act on his behalf when the manager isn't here." The gray-suited kid appeared younger every time he spoke "Why don't you step into my office and we can talk privately."

Cooper followed the young man into a small office furnished with an oversized mahogany desk and bookshelves, and with scarcely enough room for the two chairs arranged in front.

"Please, have a seat," Henson offered politely. "Tell me what we can do for you, Mr. Barnett."

Cooper sat uncomfortably in the small office chair and leaned forward slightly, resting his elbows on his wide-spread knees as he nervously thumbed the brim of the dirty Stetson he held with both hands. He looked up at Ron Henson and began to speak, a little too loudly. "Well, we didn't do as well as we'd hoped this fall with our lamb sales, and the wool market's down again," he began, sitting upright in the chair in a show of confidence. "We sort of need some help with our property taxes," he continued, slumping back down to prop his elbows on his knees and look down to inspect his mud-caked boots. He regretted not dressing a little better before making the trip into town. He raised his head to look at Henson, expecting the kid to show him the way out and explain that full authority didn't mean that he could make a loan to a rancher in trouble. The young assistant manager had already taken a lined tablet out of his middle desk drawer and was busy scribbling some notes.

"How much are your property taxes this year, Mr. Barnett?" Henson asked, looking up briefly, and with no apparent concern that the old rancher was seated in his office with his muddy boots resting on the new carpet.

"A little over six thousand," Cooper replied, reaching up to the front pocket of his denim shirt to retrieve a folded envelope. He opened the envelope from the Camas County Tax Collector's office. and removed the bill, placed it on Henson's desk and slid it forward for the young man's inspection.

"According to this, six thousand dollars will take care of your first installment, and your next installment will be due next spring. Do you want to borrow enough to take care of all of it?" the young man asked, as if the loan was already assured.

I suppose so," Cooper answered, leaning forward to rest his forearms on Henson's big mahogany desk as he watched the young man scribble some more notes on his lined tablet. "If we can, that is—I guess you'll have to wait for the manager to get back before a loan this size can be approved, huh?"

Henson looked up and smiled broadly. "Mr. Barnett, I've only been at this branch for two years, and I haven't had the pleasure of meeting you in that time, but I do know that the Barnett Ranch has done business with this bank for at least three generations. I have the authority to grant a signature loan for up to twenty thousand, so if you need some extra to hold you over through the winter and to make any equipment repairs to your trucks and farm machinery in the spring, we may as well take care of that right now. You can draw it out as you need it, and you won't be charged interest on it until you do. How does that sound?"

Cooper was more than a little surprised at how easy it was. He remembered the last time he had to come in to the bank for a loan. It had been six years earlier, when his old tractor had refused to start up in the spring after the March thaw, and had lost its power to perform any more work when its sputtering old engine finally turned over. He had to buy a new tractor, and needed to finance it. Betty had to fill out a lot of paperwork, but it only took a day or two and the new John Deere tractor was his. He paid off the loan in three years.

He bent down and picked up the small, crumbling pieces of dried barnyard mud that had fallen off his boots and onto the carpet of Ron Henson's tidy office, collecting the evidence of his bad manners as he deposited the caked dirt in his shirt pocket.

"Don't bother with that, Mr. Barnett," Henson laughed, pleasantly. "That's why we have janitors. Hailey is a farm and ranch community, and if our customers didn't come into the bank with a little dirt on their boots once in a while, we would suspect they're not working."

Cooper Barnett was relieved. He didn't know how he would get through the winter without selling part of his herd if he didn't get the loan, and he knew that selling off his livestock would be a sure sign to every rancher and banker in the region that he was in trouble. He was a very private man, and didn't like being the subject of gossip.

Cooper's spirits were high when he left the bank. It was a good day to be a rancher, he thought. There was no work left for the day, other than evening chores and livestock feeding. He could pick up Betty and her Aunt Marie and drive them up the road to Ketchum for lunch. He could keep his mouth full, and not have to join in any conversation. All he would have to do is smile and nod once in a while. Betty would be happy. Suddenly, he had a tremendous appetite.

He took the wheel for the early afternoon drive home, and he stopped off at the County Assessor and Tax Collector's office in Fairfield on the way back to the ranch to drop off the check for the property taxes. It was a relief to have that out of the way for another year.

"Did you have much trouble convincing the bank?" Betty asked, after they dropped Betty's aunt at her home and began the drive back to Camas County.

"Nope. All I had to do was say my name and show him the tax bill," Cooper explained. "That young assistant bank manager took care of the rest." He had learned long ago that brevity was his best friend in any conversation—especially with his wife. The more he talked, the more he seemed to invite other questions, so he preferred to keep it short and sweet.

Betty decided not to press her husband for any more details. The important thing was that everything had worked out—their property taxes would be paid and they had money left to get through the winter. Cooper didn't always fare so well in business meetings, given his lack of finesse and his inability to pay attention to necessary details. Betty was pleased to learn that he hadn't tripped over his own tongue at the bank, and come away empty handed. She wasn't going to question his success. She reached into her purse and started to take out the letter from Jenny that had arrived in the mail a day earlier, but decided to save it for later. She took out a small package of mints instead, and offered one to her husband.

Cooper was never a man who worried about what might happen sometime in the future—he was too busy taking care of what happened every day, and he usually had his hands full with that. Still, he wondered how he could keep up the ranch without help. The old place was getting run down, and needed more than a few shingles and buckets of fresh paint. Several miles of fencing needed major repairs or replacement, the lambing sheds and pens were falling apart, and the equipment shed was in sad condition. Maybe he could trade a good supply of lamb or beef for a carpenter's time, and work out a similar arrangement with an electrician. The few skilled tradesmen he knew didn't have much work in the winter months, so it wouldn't hurt to ask, he decided.

"I think I'll call Warren Spencer and see if he and his boy can come out for two or three days a week and help rebuild the lamb sheds—maybe put in a few extra pens," Cooper announced over his dinner plate. "We spent as much time last spring wiring gate panels together and nailing loose boards back on the pens as we did taking care of the ewes and their newborns."

Betty was pleased, and a bit surprised, that Cooper was feeling renewed enthusiasm for making improvements to the ranch. He seemed to have lost interest a few years after their boys moved away from home, and even more so when Jenny went off to school in Pocatello. Nothing was ever the same without the kids around, she thought. She supposed that it was the same for all parents when they were left with an empty nest. It's just that their nest was awfully big.

"I haven't seen you in such an upbeat mood in a long time, Coop,"

Betty observed with an approving smile. "What brought this on?"

"I'm not really sure," Cooper admitted. "I started thinking about it on the drive back from Hailey, and it just seems to me that a good year is coming for us—we're overdue. It's just a feeling," he added, with raised eyebrows and a little shrug, hoping she would understand. She did. Anything that gave her husband reason to stay physically active and motivated through the long winter months was good enough for her. There were several thousand acres to maintain, and all of the barns and outbuildings. It took more than a little enthusiasm to take on the task.

Betty baked a lot during the winter months, and enjoyed reading books she picked up at the rummage sales and school fundraisers. She even drove into town to attend church a couple of times a month and catch up on all the local news. Cooper spent most of his day in the barn or shop, and never accomplished much, other than to keep himself busy. She often wondered what he thought about during all the time he spent in his self-imposed solitude. She decided to wait until the next day to tell her husband about the letter from Jenny. She would have to show it to him soon, she thought, or he would wonder why it took more than a week for a letter to arrive from Boise.

Cooper felt good when he woke just before dawn—he must have slept at least nine hours, and that was the best night's rest he could remember in a long while. He turned to see if Betty was awake yet, and discovered that she was already up and gone. The bathroom door was open, and the light had been left on. The smell of freshly-brewed coffee beckoned to him from the direction of the stairway. He hurried to wash up, and dressed in long underwear and heavy woolen socks before pulling on his heavy coveralls. It was going to be a cold day in southern Idaho, he thought. Winter was coming on fast.

"Are you dressed warm enough?" Betty asked, giving her husband's wardrobe a quick appraisal. "Porch thermometer says twelve degrees and the wind is picking up."

"I'm good," Cooper answered, casually. "I'll only be out long enough to feed and give the dogs a run. Thought I'd saddle the gelding and give him a little exercise, too. I need to see how far the cattle strayed during the night. Maybe it's time to confine them to the corrals near the barn. They can't be finding much to eat out there."

"A letter came from Jenny yesterday," Betty said.

"How's she doing?" Cooper asked, looking up from his breakfast.

"She's fine—working in a department store in Boise while she waits to hear about a teaching job."

"I thought she was going to try to find something closer to home."

"I guess she has her reasons—maybe she'll have a better chance of getting a higher-paying job where she is."

"Why did she leave Pocatello? Is she still following that drifter around, expecting him to do something with his life?"

"She didn't mention him, Coop." Betty didn't want to discuss Jenny's boyfriend. She knew it irritated her husband to speak of him.

"Well, I better get to work," Cooper grumbled, setting his unfinished coffee on the table as he pushed his chair back.

Cooper zipped up his mackinaw and pulled a wool-lined cap snug over his head and ears, then pulled on his heavy, fleece-lined gloves and pushed open the creaky screen door to the back porch. *I need to get that screen changed out for the glass-paneled storm door soon*, he thought.

Two excited Border Collies greeted him as he stepped off the porch onto the frozen ground. They were ready before the sun came up to lead the way and bring in the sheep. Cooper didn't bother to feed them in the morning—they were far too excited to eat. Once they began to hear human activity from inside the house, they knew that work was afoot. They always ate well in the evening, and their appetites were good.

Cooper paused halfway to the barn and turned to look up at the sky to the north. A familiar honking sound signaled the presence of migrating geese. He raised a hand to shield his eyes from the bright sun, and the large, near-perfect chevron of Canada Geese flew gracefully overhead, tracing a straight line southward along the Pacific Flyway along their migration route to warmer climes.

"Must be twenty-five, maybe thirty of 'em," Cooper said aloud. He watched until they began to fade in the distance, and their honking was barely audible, then he turned and looked at the looming storm clouds moving down from the north on a rising wind. He turned his collar up and walked quickly toward the barn, calling his excited dogs to follow.

Cooper thought about his daughter's letter while he saddled his horse. Something didn't seem right, though he couldn't put his finger on it. He was sure there was another reason that Jenny had moved to Boise so suddenly, and he didn't believe it was for a teaching job—she would have told her mother about it if that were true. He didn't trust her boyfriend as far as he could throw a Hereford steer, and he was certain the drifter had something to do with the sudden detour to Boise.

"C'mon dogs—let's get those sheep rounded up."

Banjo and Holly were way ahead of him. The Border Collies raced around the barn, past the corrals and across the lower pastures, bending wide around the main band of sheep to avoid disturbing them, then continued up the brushy hillside in search of missing sheep.

The few sheep that had wandered away from the lower pastures during the night were easily found and quickly rounded up by his sheepdogs, but the job of locating stray cattle would be more tedious. They had a tendency to wander off, alone or in pairs, and not stay with the main herd. He only kept about a hundred beef cattle, and it was always more trouble keeping them together than it was to keep track of his sheep.

The time always passed quickly for Cooper when he was working with his dogs, moving livestock to where they needed to be. Three hours were gone before he knew it. He rode back to the house to tell his wife about his misgivings over Jenny's letter.

"There's something that doesn't sound right about Jenny going to Boise and not telling you about it beforehand," Cooper insisted, leaning against the kitchen counter as he spoke to his wife. "I know she's all grown up now, but she's always told you when she made a decision like this. I thought she liked living in Pocatello."

"I don't know, Coop. It doesn't sound right to me, either, but you know she makes her own decisions."

"I know she used to, before she hooked up with that lazy jackass."

"Maybe you're being too hard on him, Coop" Betty advised, hoping to calm her husband. "It could be that he just hasn't found a job that suits him yet."

"Being a lazy jackass is what suits him—he isn't looking for a job."

Cooper became agitated every time he thought about Jenny's boyfriend. He was the kind of man who didn't know how to treat a woman. He had no respect—not even for himself—and Cooper could see it the first time he met the man.

"I don't like the way he talks to Jenny, and I don't know why she puts up with it. He cusses around her all the time, and treats her like she don't matter. If a man ever talked to you that way, I'd put my fist in his mouth."

"Young people are different today, Coop. They're pretty casual with their language."

"Yeah, well, he hadn't ought to talk like that to someone he pretends to care about, that's all I know."

Betty restrained herself from saying anything else. It would only aggravate her husband more. And besides, she knew he was right.

"She said in her letter that she would call us soon. Maybe I can learn something more when I have her on the phone," Betty said.

"Maybe," Cooper grumbled.

CHAPTER THREE
ALICE AND JUNE

"Can you work again tomorrow?" Joe Bannock asked, as Jenny put on her coat to leave for the day. "I hate to have you work on your only day off, but it seems we've been rushed every day for the past couple of weeks, and I'm having a hard time getting caught up with the ordering and paperwork."

"No problem, Joe," Jenny said with an easy smile. "I can use the extra hours anyway, and I like staying busy."

"You're a gem, kid," he replied, grateful for such a reliable employee as Jenny had become over the few weeks that she had worked for him. "I won't forget this."

"Don't mention it—I'll see you tomorrow morning," Jenny said, pulling the back door closed behind her as she began her short walk home.

She had found a few inexpensive framed pictures at Woolworth's to add some color and life to her apartment, and a bright yellow cookie jar adorned with a likeness of a rooster for her kitchen counter. It wasn't exactly like the home she grew up in, but it was better than living in the stark, Spartan surroundings that she first encountered when she rented the cottage.

Over time, she became better acquainted with her landlady, and on occasion, she stopped to speak with Mrs. Rolfson's two young granddaughters who lived with her. The girls spent a lot of time playing in the yard or taking turns riding an old fat tire Schwinn bicycle up and down the back alley. Mrs. Rolfson wouldn't allow them to ride their bike on the sidewalk or in the street, for fear they might be run over by a reckless driver. The girls were shy and always polite around Jenny. They seemed very well behaved, and Jenny never heard them argue with their grandmother or disobey her in any way. Sometimes, Jenny would bring them leftover cinnamon rolls from the cafe.

Before long, the girls began to watch for Jenny to come home from work in the evening, and would put their coats on to run outside and greet her as she came around the side walkway toward the rear cottage. Alice would take Jenny's hand and chatter about her day at school as they walked to the door of the cottage, and her little sister always followed close on their heels, never more than a step or two behind.

Jenny stopped to check her mailbox as she came up the walkway, and looked up to see the forlorn little face on June, as the younger of the two sisters peered through the front window of the main house from her perch on the arm of an overstuffed sofa. She was not smiling or waving, and her big brown eyes were sad. Jenny retrieved a letter and an advertisement flyer from the mailbox, and then looked up to smile and wave at the little girl in the window. June only raised her tiny hand to wave briefly, and did not return the smile. Maybe Alice had come down with a flu bug, Jenny thought, and their grandmother was keeping them both inside. It was, after all, a chill and windy day, and the cold and flu season was well under way.

The letter was postmarked from Fairfield, Idaho, and Jenny's spirits lifted as she turned her key in the lock and pushed open the door to the small apartment. She switched on the lights and dialed the wall thermostat up to seventy degrees before she took a seat at the table in her tiny kitchen and opened the envelope.

She read the usual greetings that began all of her mother's letters. Dad's fine, the weather is cold, I've been baking, and your old school friend, Donna, asked about you at the market the other day. It seemed to be just another ordinary letter from home—even the question about whether or not she would be able to make it home for Thanksgiving. It ended with an invitation to call collect, and a promise that her Dad would be more civil toward her boyfriend this year if they could drive down for the holiday.

Fat chance, Jenny thought. She didn't dare go home in her condition. It was easier to lie in a letter than it was in a conversation, she knew. And parents always seemed to know. Kids were caught lying so many times during their high school years that it was hard for them to slip one past their parents later, even after they were grown and more practiced. It would be easy enough to make up a story about why her old boyfriend didn't come with her, given her father's rude behavior toward him the previous year, but explaining the bump in her belly would be a different matter.

She had a couple of days to think it over before she placed a call to her mother—time enough to make up a believable story. At first she thought about telling her mother that the department store needed her on the day after Thanksgiving for the start of the big holiday sales, but on further consideration, she knew that wouldn't work. It was only a two hour drive back to Boise from the ranch, so it would be easy enough to drive down to Camas County for the day. She decided to tell a different lie.

"Hi, Mom," Jenny said as cheerfully as she could, after her mother accepted the charges for the collect call from Boise.

"Hi, Honey. We were getting worried when we didn't hear from you for a couple of months. Are you doing all right?"

"I'm fine, Mom. Everything's great. How's Dad?"

"You know your father—he's always the same. You just missed him. He rode out to do the feeding a little while ago, but I'll tell him you called. Are you going to make it down for Thanksgiving?"

"No, I don't think so. I'm stuck here without a car for a couple of weeks."

"What's wrong with your boyfriend's car?"

"His dad came down sick, and he had to drive back to Spokane to help his mom out for a few weeks," Jenny lied.

"There's always room at the table if you can find your way down here for the day. Only one of your brothers is going to make it this year."

"I'll try," Jenny lied again. "I have to get going, Mom. I don't want to be late for work. I'll write soon."

Jenny hung up the phone in Joe's office and stared blankly at the desk calendar for a few moments, wondering if her mother bought her story. She wondered what to tell her mother in her next letter, then shrugged it off with an audible sigh of exasperation, disgusted with herself for conjuring new lies to cover up the old ones. She hung up her coat and busied herself with lunch preparations in the kitchen, putting her personal problems out of her mind for the moment.

She arrived home just before dark, and didn't see any little faces in the window of her landlady's house as she made her way around the walkway to her cottage. It wasn't like Alice and June not to be there to greet her. She turned around before she reached her front door and walked quickly back to the front house, knocked on the door and called out to anyone inside who might hear her.

"Mrs. Rolfson, are you there?" she called, as she knocked repeatedly. "Alice? June, are you girls in there?"

A sad little face appeared in the picture window, straining to see who was at the front door. It was June. Jenny heard her jump down from the arm of the sofa, and a moment later she heard the sound of the latch turning. The door opened just wide enough for the tiny girl to push her face through.

"Grandma's real sick," the sad little girl said, a sorrowful tone in her tiny voice.

"Do you want me to come in and look at her, honey?" Jenny asked, pushing the door open wide enough to walk through.

June stepped back, pulling the door wider as she nodded her head in acceptance. "Will you help her, Jenny?"

Jenny followed June down the hallway toward the rear of the house, as the little girl led her by the hand and pulled her along. She was shocked by Mrs. Rolfson's appearance. The woman's face was gaunt and pale, her eyes were closed, and it looked as though she had lost weight since the last time Jenny had seen her—perhaps a week or two earlier. Alice was wringing out a washcloth in a metal bowl filled with cool water, folding it to place it on her grandmother's forehead. Alice looked up with relief as Jenny entered the bedroom.

"She's real sick, Jenny," Alice said. Jenny walked to the young girl's side and leaned down to inspect Mrs. Rolfson's clammy skin, and to feel the elderly woman's forehead and cheeks.

"She's burning up," Jenny said. "Have you told anyone, Alice? Have you called the hospital?"

"I didn't know who to call," the eight-year-old girl cried. "Grandma kept saying it was just a flu bug, and that she just needed rest. I brought her juice and water, but she didn't drink very much." Alice and June both began to cry.

"All right, all right girls. You come in and sit down while I call the hospital. You settle down now—just be calm while I call the doctor."

Jenny dialed directory assistance and asked to be connected directly with Boise Memorial Hospital. "It's an emergency, operator. Please hurry, will you?"

Jenny looked in on Mrs. Rolfson again to make sure she was covered and warm. She gave no verbal response when Jenny tried to speak with her. Jenny realized the woman was very ill, and desperately in need of medical help. She hurried back to the kitchen and made some hot cocoa for the girls to keep them occupied until an ambulance arrived.

The ambulance drivers only asked for Mrs. Rolfson's name and age, and if she was taking any medications. Jenny looked on the nightstand and in the bathroom medicine cabinet for any prescription bottles, and came back with a bottle that contained what appeared to be blood pressure pills. The men never asked to know Jenny's relationship to the woman or the children. They had the elderly woman loaded into the back of the ambulance and were gone in less than ten minutes.

"They'll take care of your grandma," Jenny assured the frightened little girls. "We'll call the hospital in a while and see how she's doing, okay?" Jenny led Alice and June into the kitchen and sat them at the table while she looked in the cupboards to find something to fix them for dinner, hoping to take their minds off their grandmother for awhile.

"What would you like for dinner?" she asked, looking toward Alice and June as she sorted through packages of noodles, flour and cake mixes.

"June likes macaroni and cheese," said Alice. "And I don't care."

Jenny kept talking to the girls while she pulled the leftover fried chicken out of the refrigerator and pushed it into the oven and began to boil water for the macaroni.

"I'll have your dinner ready in just a few minutes," Jenny said with a comforting smile. "What have you been eating since your grandma got sick?"

"Cereal," Alice answered. "We ran out of milk yesterday, so we just eat it without."

Jenny found what she needed in the cupboards and refrigerator to prepare a meal for the girls. She was resourceful in the kitchen.

"Now, why don't you tell me what you've been doing in school?"

"I didn't go yesterday," Alice said. "I stayed home with Grandma. I guess I'll be in trouble."

"You won't be in trouble, honey. You did the right thing," Jenny reassured. "Why don't we play a game for a while after we eat, and then we can call the hospital to see how your grandma is doing."

"I like puzzles," June's face lit up as she offered her suggestion. "You wanna see mine?" She ran to a hallway closet and came back with a colorful box. The lid bore the image of the puzzle picture—a princess in a beautiful blue gown and glass slippers. June held it up proudly for Jenny to examine. "It's Cinderella."

"Yes, I see. That's wonderful," Jenny praised. The box contained about fifty puzzle pieces—enough to keep the girls occupied for a few minutes, at least.

Jenny glanced at the clock on the oven from time to time, anxious to call the hospital to check on Mrs. Rolfson. She hoped the woman's condition would not be so grave that it would keep her in the hospital for more than a day or two. Alice and June were still fitting puzzle pieces into place, one by one, when Jenny walked to the telephone and called the hospital.

"Hello, I'm calling about Mrs. Dora Rolfson. She was taken to the hospital by ambulance about an hour ago," Jenny inquired. "Can you tell me how she's doing?"

"I'll connect you to the nurses' station in the Emergency Room, ma'am. If she came by ambulance, that's where she would have been checked in," the operator explained.

It took two more transfers and a considerable wait for someone in charge to finally come to the phone and tell Jenny what was going on. Eventually, she learned that Mrs. Rolfson was stable and resting in a hospital room, getting the care that she needed. She had suffered a mild stroke, apparently brought on by stress and her failure to take her blood pressure pills. Alice didn't know that her grandmother needed daily doses of the medicine that was kept in the cabinet above the bathroom sink, and Jenny wasn't going to say anything to the girls about it. Alice would have been devastated if she thought she was the reason her grandmother was in the hospital.

"Your grandma is very sick," Jenny told the sisters as she sat down with them at the kitchen table. 'But she's going to be all right. She just needs some rest, and the doctor wants to keep her there at the hospital for a few days until she gets a little better."

"Who's going to take care of us?" Alice asked with some alarm.

"I will, of course," Jenny said, feigning surprise that Alice should question the arrangements. "Who did you think would stay with you, silly?"

Alice was immediately relieved, and the obvious feeling of relief was not lost on her little sister. June relaxed her sad face and replaced her own worried look with a smile. "Can we play some more games?" she asked.

"I think we've had a long day, honey," Jenny said. "Alice has to go to school in the morning, and I have to go to work."

"Where do I have to go?" June asked.

"You'll come with me," Jenny said, poking at the little girl's nose with her index finger. "You're still too little to go to school, and you don't have a bus ticket to Disneyland, so you might as well spend the day with me."

Jenny bathed the girls and got them into bed, then made herself a cup of hot tea and waited for the girls to go to sleep before going to her apartment for a quilt and a change of clothes. She spent the night on Mrs. Rolfson's sofa, tossing and turning to get comfortable on the narrow couch as she worked out a plan to take care of Alice and June for the next few days. She suddenly realized that she knew nothing about the whereabouts of the girls' parents, or why they weren't with them.

The following morning brought a flurry of activity, getting the girls fed and dressed, rounding up Alice's school books and a coloring book for June. They all walked the three blocks to the elementary school together, said goodbye to Alice, then walked back in the direction of Idaho Joe's Cafe, about four blocks to the west.

Jenny arrived for work a few minutes late. Joe was only slightly concerned when the best cook he ever had didn't show up on time, and he was sure she had a good reason. When Jenny came through the back door with June in tow, her boss didn't even raise an eyebrow. He knew that he was looking at the reason for his cook's tardiness.

"Counter's already full—looks like a busy morning," Joe said flatly, turning to walk back out to the counter to take care of his customers.

Jenny hurriedly pulled off her coat and tossed it across the back of a chair in Joe's office, then parked June in a chair with a coloring book in her lap.

"You stay here and color, honey," Jenny instructed. "I'll bring you something to drink in a little while." She rushed to the kitchen to wash her hands and take her place at the grill without stopping to put on an apron until all the breakfast orders were caught up.

"You hire an apprentice?" Joe asked, casting a sideways glance toward his office door and the tiny girl seated at his desk with crayons in hand.

"Joe, I'm sorry," Jenny apologized. "My landlady took ill and had to be rushed to the hospital last night, and there's no one to take care of her granddaughters. She looked toward the open door of the office, and the little girl who was coloring contentedly.

"Where's her mother?" Joe asked.

"I don't know," Jenny replied with a sigh. "It never occurred to me to ask. June and her big sister were already living there when I rented my cottage. Her sister is in school today, but this one's only three years old."

"Well, we can't have a three-year-old kid wandering around in the snow alone all day, can we?" Joe smiled. "Guess we'll just have to figure out something." He didn't say what that something might be—he just walked back out to the counter and took up his place with coffee pot in hand.

It's none of my business, anyway, Joe thought. If she wants to help out a family in need for a few days, it surely wouldn't be any trouble. The cafe was nearly empty of patrons by late morning, so Joe poured an orange soda over ice and carried the glass to his office.

"You want something to drink?" Joe asked the little girl seated in his chair, extending his hand to offer her the soda. The tiny girl looked up at the man in the coffee-stained apron and nodded.

Joe watched the little artist sip the fizzy drink from the glass, and then redirected his gaze to admire his freshly-adorned desk calendar with its colorful artwork. The square boxes on the calendar that outlined each day of the month had been redefined with nearly every color in the rainbow, and a few crayon stick figures stood along the outside borders. June looked up and smiled proudly, her upper lip stained a bright orange.

"That kid's a pretty good artist," Joe mumbled as he walked past Jenny toward the counter to post the day's lunch specials on his chalkboard.

"I'm sorry about your calendar, Joe," Jenny apologized, as she put on her coat to leave for the day. "And I'll make sure she understands that she has to confine her work to her own coloring books," she promised. "I'll come in early tomorrow, but I'll have to bring Alice with me, too. She can walk to school from here, and walk back afterwards. They won't be any trouble, I promise."

"I can't remember ever having such a pretty calendar," Joe replied." Girls aren't any trouble. They just busy themselves with their own pastimes and don't bother anybody else. Boys are a different matter."

"Sounds like you have first-hand experience, Joe," Jenny said. "You have kids?"

The Lamb Cart

"Yep. Grown up and moved away," he answered, succinctly.

"Any daughters?" Jenny was interested to know how where he got his insights and opinion of girls, and his patience with June's crayon graffiti.

"Just one—Debbie—she's my youngest. Got married last year to a deputy sheriff from Horseshoe Bend up on the Salmon River," Joe answered. "They seem to be real happy, and she loves living in a small town. Seems like it was just yesterday that she was four years old, and now she's grown and gone." He picked up a handful of extra menus and walked out of the kitchen to keep an eye on the front door of the cafe in case any customers came in

Jenny called the hospital as soon as she got home with the girls. She let them watch television while she fixed dinner—it was too cold to play outside. Besides, she was their safety line and they preferred to stay with her. Jenny had an engaging way with children—she was a regular Pied Piper, and the girls would follow her anywhere.

"Your grandma is very tired," Jenny explained, after speaking with a nurse at the hospital. "And she's still sick, so she needs more rest at the hospital where doctors and nurses can take care of her. Maybe we can go see her tomorrow."

Alice and June accepted everything that Jenny told them, without question. They trusted her, and they were happy that she was staying at their grandmother's house to take care of them and watch over them.

Jenny made herself a cup of hot tea after the girls were put to bed, and sat down at the kitchen table to ponder her dilemma. The news from the hospital was grim. Mrs. Rolfson was very ill—she had a very weak heart, exacerbated by the influenza. Jenny hoped for the best, but she was worried. Other than staying with the girls, she didn't know how she could help.

The girls were both out of bed early, dressed and ready to go to the hospital to see their grandmother. Jenny fed them a quick breakfast of cold cereal before they donned their coats and began the short walk to the bus stop.

"Do you think Grandma will be surprised to see us?" June asked, her upturned face and big brown eyes searching for reassurance from Jenny as they all sat down near the front of the bus.

"Of course she will, June-bug," Jenny answered, with all the enthusiasm she could muster. "And I'm sure she misses you a whole bunch."

The sisters' faces both lit up with big smiles, and they settled back to look out through the window, chattering and pointing when they passed the city park and the tall buildings in the center of town. The bus ride took them farther and farther away from their own familiar neighborhood and closer to the hospital on the other side of town.

They stopped at the hospital gift shop on their way to the elevators, and Jenny let the girls select a small bouquet of flowers for their grandmother. Alice picked out a magazine and a get well card that they all signed. Jenny took an extra minute of time to help June print her name—it was a little ragged, but her grandmother would know who signed it.

They waited by the nurses station on the third floor for someone to check to see if Dora Rolfson was awake, and then followed one of the nurses down the hallway. June tugged at Jenny's coat sleeve.

"It smells funny in here," June complained, wrinkling her nose in disgust.

"Shh—that's disinfectant," Jenny explained quietly, picking up her pace to keep up with the nurse as she pulled the little girl along with her.

"What's disfeck-tunt?" June asked in a loud whisper. "It smells funny."

"They have to use it to kill all the germs and keep the hospital clean," Alice whispered to her little sister. "Now hush."

"Well, it smells funny," June protested again, sourly. "Why do they have to use so much?"

The nurse walked into Mrs. Rolfson's room ahead of the girls, announcing the visitors and removing the breakfast tray on her way out. Alice moved to her grandmother's side and held up the bouquet of flowers.

"Hi Grandma—look what we brought you," she said, hoping her grandmother would be pleased.

Dora Rolfson tried to smile, but a crooked smile was all she could manage—she had little feeling in the left side of her face or her left arm. She hoped her appearance would not alarm the girls. She took the bouquet from Alice with her right hand and placed it in her water carafe.

"They're lovely, Alice. Thank you," Dora said with a slight slur, reaching up to stroke her granddaughters hair. "Have you been doing everything Jenny asks you to do?"

June quickly jumped into the conversation. "Uh-huh. We always do what she says. And I get to go to work with her." She held up the envelope with the get well card and presented it to her grandmother. "Everybody signed it, and I signed it, too, Grandma."

Dora let the girls chatter away and inspect the room and the view from the window while she spoke quietly with Jenny.

"I can't thank you enough for looking after the girls, Jenny," Dora said, sincerely. "I'm sorry this burden fell to you, but I'm the only family they have—there's no one left to take care of them."

Jenny had learned from her parents when she was growing up to stay out of other people's business. If someone wanted you to know something about their private lives, they'd tell you. She had been curious why Alice and June lived with their grandmother, and wondered why their parents were never around, but she never asked—she didn't want to appear nosey. Dora Rolfson read the questioning look in Jenny's eyes, and gave the younger woman the answer she was waiting for.

"My son and daughter-in-law left the girls with me last winter and drove up to Spokane so my son could look for work. The whole time they lived here, he was in and out of jobs the way a stage actor changes costumes. Before long, nobody around here wanted to hire him—he wasn't reliable. He blamed his employers, and never once looked to himself as the reason he couldn't fit in with other employees or do his job properly. He figured a new start in another town would give him the break he was looking for," Dora continued. Jenny had an uneasy feeling from the sound of Dora's voice and the sorrowful look on her face. She was sure this story did not have a happy ending.

"He called after four days and told me he found a good job at a lumber mill in Post Falls, just across the Idaho border from Spokane. He sounded so excited, and I was truly happy for him. I thought that a fresh start with a new job in another town might make him try harder to change his life for the better. His wife was a good girl, and a wonderful mother," Dora reminisced.

"Was?" Jenny asked.

Dora sighed and looked at her little granddaughters; their noses pressed against the cold window as they watched the busy street below and tried to count the cars and buses going by. She turned her attention back to Jenny, and spoke in a soft voice.

"My son was anxious to get back and tell his girls about where they would be moving, and how much they were sure to love it up there around all the mountains and lakes and pine forests, so they left that same afternoon to drive back to Boise. They didn't make it home. It was already dark when they started up White Bird Hill into Grangeville—and there's nothing but hairpin turns on that road all the way from top to bottom," Dora lamented, staring off into space as she remembered the phone call she got the following morning, and the panic that had seized her when she heard the news of her son's death.

"It had been raining nearly all day, according to the sheriff's office, and got real cold right after the sun went down. They must have hit some black ice, that's all the sheriff's deputies could figure. They said they could see where the car slid off the road about halfway up to the plateau, and the car tumbled all the way down to the river," Dora went on, her raspy, emotion-choked voice almost a whisper. "That was less than a year ago."

"Dora, I'm so sorry."

"I can't walk, Jenny," Dora said to the younger woman, reaching out with her right hand to grasp Jenny by the wrist. "They have to put me in a wheelchair to take me to the bathroom. I never thought I'd be the one to have heart trouble. It was my husband's side of the family that always had bad hearts."

Jenny placed a comforting hand on top of Dora's hand and tried to console her. "Don't you worry about a thing—and especially not the girls—they'll be fine with me," Jenny assured. "The doctors do amazing things these days, and I'm sure that with good therapy you'll be up and walking in no time."

Jenny called the girls over from the window so they could spend a few minutes with their grandmother before they had to leave. A stern-looking, middle-aged nurse came into the room and explained that the girls were too young to be in the ward, and that they would have to leave right away.

"We were just leaving," Jenny said, wondering why such ridiculous rules were put into place to keep children and grandchildren from visiting their parents. "Get your coats, girls."

Alice and June waited near the door while Jenny went back to their grandmother's bedside and leaned down to speak to her.

"Don't worry about anything, Dora," Jenny reassured the older woman. "I'll take good care of them, I promise. You just get better."

The girls felt better after their visit with their grandmother. Jenny was relieved to know that Mrs. Rolfson was getting the best care available, and would be coming home soon. She walked hand-in-hand with Alice and June as they left the hospital. They made a detour on the way to the bus stop, and walked into the Woolworth's store for hot soup and cold chicken sandwiches at the busy lunch counter. Jenny let the girls buy new coloring books before they took the short walk back to the corner to wait for the bus.

A cold wind began to blow in from the north, and the girls huddled close to Jenny as they waited for the bus, pressing their little faces against the front of her woolen coat to stop the icy wind from nipping at their cheeks and noses. June began to shiver, and clasped her mitten-clad hands under her chin as she pressed even tighter into the warm folds of Jenny's long coat.

"We'll have to see if we can get you some warmer coats soon," Jenny said. "It looks like you're outgrowing these, and we could be in for a long winter."

The truth was, the coats were large enough, but the fabric was a thin polyester material with very little lining. The coats barely kept the wind off their backs, much less protect against the bitter cold. Alice smiled at the prospect of going shopping with Jenny, and June mimicked her big sister's actions, smiling broadly at Jenny. A warm coat would be something new for her—she had never owned one before. Grandma Rolfson never spent more money than was absolutely necessary—a trait she had acquired from her husband.

Jenny could see the bus coming down the street in the next block, and it was just in time. A few snowflakes were beginning to fall, and were already sticking to the domed metal top of the trash can that stood next to the uncovered bus stop bench. The trunk of an elm tree rose up through a square cut in the cement sidewalk a few feet away, but the canopy of leafless branches offered no protection. Jenny hated having to depend on public transportation—it was always such an inconvenience. Missing the bus by minutes and having to wait too long for the next one, or being caught in rain or snow—there was always something to contend with, it seemed. And the bus rarely ever got her to where she needed to go—if she got within a mile of her destination she felt lucky. She missed having her own car.

The next week went by quickly—Jenny stayed busy at work and at home, taking care of the girls. They made two more trips to the hospital to visit Dora Rolfson, and Alice and June didn't understand why their grandmother couldn't come home. Her condition was unstable, and she experienced another stroke just as her doctor thought she might be able to go home. She died in her sleep before her granddaughters could visit her again.

It was hard for Jenny to explain to the frightened little girls. Three-year-old June's memory of her mother and father was already fading, thankfully. But now the girls had lost the only other family they knew.

"Will you stay with us, Jenny?" Alice begged, through a flood of tears.

"Will you, Jenny?" June pleaded, sorrowfully, though less frantic than her older sister. Tiny June had already bonded closely with Jenny, spending every minute of every day near her side, and took it for granted that Jenny needed them as much as they needed her.

"Of course I'll stay with you," Jenny assured. "I'll always stay with you. I'd be sad and lonely every day without you."

Jenny felt a stab of fear in her belly as she pledged to take care of the girls. She wasn't even sure how she would be able to take care of herself and the baby that was on the way. Life was hard, and it got more complicated every day.

She was sure that her old friend, Lorraine, would know how to handle her situation. She had become close friends with Lorraine when they worked together at the cafe in Pocatello during her college days. Lorraine had three little boys, and still worked part time, the last Jenny had heard. She had moved to Twin Falls a few months earlier, and got a job as a waitress at the Five Points East truck stop. Her youngest boy wasn't yet two years old, and her truck-driving husband left her at home most of the time to take care of the boys by herself. If anyone knew how to work and take care of kids, it was Lorraine. Jenny made a mental note to call her old friend soon for a long chat, and seek her advice.

In the meantime, she decided, she would have to focus on what to do with the girls on a more immediate basis. Alice had been attending the same school for more than a year, so it shouldn't be difficult to leave everything status quo for the time being. When the school needed to talk to a parent or guardian, or if a signature was required on a permission slip or report card, Jenny would simply pretend that she was Alice's aunt, filling in for her grandmother. No one would be looking for June at school, and as long as Joe didn't mind that she spent her days adorning his office with her crayon artwork, there was no need to worry about hiring a babysitter.

Jenny worked hard for the next few weeks, and saved every spare dime so that she could buy a used car—she was tired of going by bus every time she and the girls needed to travel more than a few blocks from home. Her thrift paid off—she was able to find an old sedan offered for sale in the want ads of the *Idaho Statesman* newspaper. It had been languishing, unused, in the garage of an elderly couple for the past two years. Neither of them could drive any longer, and they only asked $400 for it so that they could make room for storage in their tiny, one-car detached garage.

"I ran an extension cord out to plug in the battery charger this week," the old-timer told Jenny when she arrived at the couple's house to look at the car. "I know it don't look like much, but it's reliable, and it don't use much gas—just a little oil once in a while."

"Are the tires okay?" Jenny asked, in her one attempt to sound knowledgeable about automobiles.

"See for yourself," the old man gestured with his foot, kicking the sidewall of a front tire to prove its durability. "I have to tell you, though—the heater acts up once in a while. Sometimes it's good, and other times it just doesn't want to give up any warm air."

Jenny thought she couldn't find a better deal anywhere else, and she was determined not to stand in the freezing cold at a bus stop any more—she made the deal and gave up her hard-earned cash. She was no mechanic, but the old car seemed to run well enough. If the old-timer said the car was reliable, who am I to argue with him, Jenny thought.

CHAPTER FOUR

SANCTUARY

Jenny needed desperately to get away for a couple of days, and a visit with Lorraine Fuller might help her to gain a new perspective on her dramatically-changed life. She could learn from the lessons of another woman's experiences, and it might help to calm her fears about the responsibilities of motherhood—especially if she could learn from a woman she trusted and admired so much. Lorraine dealt with the joys and trials of motherhood every day, and made it look easy, Jenny remembered. She couldn't think of a single time when Lorraine had come into work complaining about her boys, or about how hard it was to take care of them by herself with little or no help from her husband.

"You're taking a lot on yourself, aren't you?" Joe Bannock asked, solemnly, as Jenny settled Alice and June into the passenger side of the old Studebaker.

"I know," Jenny responded with a sigh. She couldn't think of anything else to say in her own defense. It was crazy—taking on two orphaned girls when she could scarcely take care of herself in her present condition. "Thanks for giving me an extra day off, and for letting me leave early today. I'll be here first thing Monday morning."

The old sedan purred in overdrive as Jenny steered it along its way, south toward Twin Falls, and to a reunion with her friend. The car could certainly have used a better heater, she thought, but there was still tread left on the tires, and the six-cylinder engine didn't use much oil. She dialed the heater up to high and told the girls to leave their coats on.

"Is it warm in Twin Falls?" Alice asked, hopefully, after Jenny made the turn onto Highway 20 at Mountain Home, and continued the journey that would take them very close by the Barnett Ranch. "I hope it's warmer there."

"So do I," her little sister said, hopefully, mimicking her sister. "I hope it's warm, too. Don't you, Jenny?"

From her spot on the fabric-covered bench seat, wedged snugly between Jenny and Alice, the three-year-old could barely see over the dashboard to the road in front of them. It was easier to peer through the side passenger window and keep track of the buildings and treetops that passed by.

"Yes, I hope so, too," Jenny responded, somewhat detached and distracted. If she could work up her nerve, Jenny decided, they might stop on the way home Sunday afternoon and pay a short visit to her parents. She had no idea how to explain her blossoming pregnancy, or why her boyfriend was no longer with her. She dismissed the notion almost as quickly as it entered her mind.

It had snowed several inches during the early hours of morning, and it was beginning to drift along the side of the highway, banked deeper by the cold wind blowing down from the north. The temperature dropped to well below freezing, and it began to snow again. Jenny hoped they could make it into Twin Falls before the storm got much worse.

She pulled the car into a gas station in Shoshone, and called Lorraine from the pay phone inside while the attendant filled her tank and checked the oil. There was no answer at the Fuller house. Maybe she's at the market, Jenny thought. When the two friends spoke on the previous day Lorraine was very excited to hear Jenny's voice, and even more excited to have her bring the girls for a visit. Jenny thought it best not to wait any longer to call again—the weather might get worse, she worried, and the Studebaker didn't have snow tires or chains. She decided to press on, and to call her friend as soon as they arrived in Twin Falls.

"Are we lost?" June asked, in her small, meek voice. She was frightened by the sound of icy snow crystals being whipped against the windshield by the worsening weather. "Where are we?"

Even at forty miles per hour, the blizzard-like conditions made it difficult for Jenny to see the road for more than a few yards ahead of the car. Headlights reflected off snowflakes, obscuring the roadway ahead. Several inches of fresh snowfall collected on the pavement and covered the center line of the highway. Jenny was getting nervous. Alice remained silent and transfixed as she stared through the windshield into the darkness beyond the headlight beams.

"We'll pull off the road as soon as I can find a safe place," Jenny comforted. She kept her voice low and calm, her eyes on the road ahead and her mind on her driving. "We should see some lights before long."

The whine of a big diesel engine came at them from somewhere in the darkness behind, and the faint reflection of headlights appeared in the rear view mirror. The girls turned around and kneeled up on the seat to peer through the back window at the approaching headlights.

"It's a big truck, Jenny," Alice said, timidly, worried that they may be run over. "What if it can't see us?"

"He can see us, honey—don't worry. Turn around and sit down, so I can drive," Jenny ordered firmly. The girls obeyed, and watched intently through the side window as the big livestock-hauling rig downshifted and moved slowly to the inside lane to overtake the Studebaker, flashing its headlights as it passed.

The brightly-lit rear of the trailer was a billboard of red taillights and reflectors. Jenny accelerated to keep up, staying a safe distance behind, but never allowing the well-lighted truck to get too far ahead. It was a beacon in the night, lighting their way down the long stretch of road ahead.

"See how easy that was," Jenny said, happily. "We'll just follow that big old truck right on into Twin Falls. I'll bet it takes us right to a truck stop, and we can all go inside and have hamburgers."

"Yay!" June trilled, bouncing up and down on the seat as she gripped the dashboard with both hands. "I want french fries."

"Jenny, don't get too close," Alice fretted, reaching across her little sister to place a hand on Jenny's leg as she asked her to ease up on the accelerator.

"Don't be nervous, Alice. There's plenty of distance between us,"

The Lamb Cart

Jenny responded, softly.

Jenny wasn't sure if it was just her imagination, but it seemed that the storm was abating and that visibility was improving. She could see the lights of a town far off to the right, and then more lights shining through the veil of falling snow on the road ahead, as the sedan rolled down the long, straight slope of highway toward the valley floor below. The lights of Twin Falls came into full view amid the broad expanse of darkness, spreading out across the Magic Valley to send a twinkling sign of welcome to the grateful travelers. The old sedan slowly followed the lights of the big diesel rig downhill and onto the long span of the Rim-to-Rim Bridge that crossed over the Snake River Canyon to the north edge of town.

Jenny turned the car into the Five Points Truck Stop behind the tractor-trailer rig that had been her guide on the final miles of their trip. Her young passengers had fallen asleep—June slumped against Jenny's side, and Alice with her head rested on her sister's shoulder.

"That didn't take long," Jenny mused aloud, smiling down at the angelic faces. She woke the sleepyheads and led them inside, all three shivering from the cold night air. The noisy cafe was bustling with the late-night activity of motorists and truckers alike, all trying to get fed before the town closed its doors for the night. Even the truck stops closed early when the winter storms sent people indoors for the night.

Jenny settled the girls into a booth and ordered hot cocoa to keep them busy while she went to the pay phone to call her friend. There was no answer, so she went back to the table and ordered hamburgers for everyone. Alice and June were having trouble keeping their eyes open, and even more trouble finding their appetites. Neither of the girls could finish her meal, and even Jenny began to lose her appetite after making two more attempts to call Lorraine without success.

Jenny noticed a Slumberland Motel sign down the street when they came into town—it would be as good a place as any to bunk for the night, she thought. She could try to reach Lorraine by phone again first thing in the morning. It wasn't like her friend to be unreliable. Jenny had told her the previous day that she was driving into town tonight with the girls.

She bundled the girls back into the car for the short ride down the street. It was a quiet Friday night for the motel, and luckily for Jenny, it was easy to rent a room with two beds. The girls were asleep almost before their heads hit the pillows, but sleep didn't come so easily for Jenny.

She woke before dawn and read the time on the radio alarm clock. It was a little after six o'clock—still too early to call Lorraine. Jenny waited a little longer, not wanting to dress and go downstairs to use the pay phone in the lobby, just in case the girls woke up and wondered where she had gone. She lay awake, wondering if something had happened to Lorraine. She shrugged it off, and got up to take a shower and get dressed before the girls woke. The hot water blasted from the shower head and temporarily soothed away Jenny's concerns. She dressed and waited a few more minutes for the sun to come up before she opened the window shades and woke the girls.

"I'm hungry," June said, less than a minute after her eyes opened. "Are we going to have breakfast?"

Alice looked at her little sister, then at Jenny, wondering what their day's itinerary might be. She was less concerned with thoughts of food than her little sister was, and more curious about what events the day held in store for them.

"Are we still going to your friend's house?' Alice queried.

"We'll have breakfast first—so why don't you hurry and get yourselves ready so we can leave," Jenny instructed. "June-bug, come here and let me brush the tangles out of your hair while Alice takes a shower—then you can finish getting ready."

The snow had stopped falling during the night, but the morning dawned cold and breezy. The engine of the old Studebaker turned over reluctantly, sputtering weakly at first before it finally roared to life after four or five failed attempts to start. Jenny left the heater turned on high, though little good it did to warm the interior of the old sedan for the short ride back down the street to the truck stop.

She ordered waffles for the girls, and let them eat while she made another call to Lorraine from the pay phone.

The Lamb Cart

"Hello?" Jenny said, loudly, as she heard the barely audible whisper on the other end of the phone line. "Hello, Lorraine?" she repeated.

"Yes, it's me," Lorraine whispered a little louder into the mouthpiece. "I can't talk very loud—Bud's still asleep. Are you in town? Can you come over?"

"Sure," Jenny answered with some concern for her friend's odd behavior. "Are you all right, Lorraine? Is anything wrong?"

"Please hurry, Jenny," Lorraine pleaded, her voice a frantic whisper. "I need to talk to you before Bud wakes up."

Jenny hung up the phone and rushed back to the cafe booth for the girls. "Eat up, girls," she commanded. "We have to go."

"I'm still hungry," June protested. "I'm still eating my waffle."

"Break off a piece and bring it with you," Jenny said abruptly, as she gathered their coats and headed toward the cashier counter.

Alice was fearful—she understood that any time they were in such a frantic rush, it probably wasn't for any reason that she would like.

"What's the matter, Jenny?" Alice fretted, as she jumped up from her seat and followed Jenny toward the front door.

"We have to hurry, that's all," Jenny explained. "Here, June-bug, put your coat on—we don't have much time." Jenny had a bad feeling about Lorraine—something was wrong.

Jenny read the directions she had scribbled on the lined note paper two days earlier, and followed Blue Lakes Boulevard toward the center of town before tuning off onto Third Avenue. The neighborhood was slightly run down, populated with small houses and sporadic store fronts with paint peeling off the cracked and weathered stucco and brick exteriors. She pulled the car over to the curb when she recognized the house number displayed on a faded blue porch post. The tiny house was a shanty compared to Lorraine's home in Pocatello, Jenny thought. She turned off the car engine and told the girls to wait in the car.

Lorraine was waiting for her at the front door when Jenny stepped up onto the front porch, and opened the door to step outside, closing the door quietly behind her.

"Lorraine, what's wrong?" Jenny asked.

"Bud came home early yesterday—he got fired from Simplot for drinking on the job, and he probably won't find another truck driving job now. He's been drinking a lot—he stayed up half the night drinking beer and yelling at me and the boys. I'm afraid." Lorraine trembled uncontrollably as she explained her situation to Jenny.

"Maybe he'll regret it when he wakes up," Jenny suggested. "Maybe he'll sober up and feel sorry about it."

Lorraine shook her head emphatically as Jenny attempted to find a possible excuse for Bud's bad behavior. "You don't know him, Jenny. He acts normal when other people are around, but when he drinks, he's a monster."

"What do you want to do?" Jenny asked, feeling helpless as she struggled to think of a solution for her friend.

"Will you take my boys?" Lorraine asked bluntly. "Just for a couple of weeks, I promise—just until Bud can find another job, and things can get back to normal."

"Oh, Lorraine, I don't know," Jenny began. "I think the boys would be much better off with their own mother, and I already have these girls to take care of now."

"Jenny, please, you don't understand. I wouldn't ask if it wasn't important."

Jenny succumbed to her friend's frantic pleading. There must be something more that Lorraine wasn't telling her, she thought.

"Wait here—I'll be right back," Lorraine spoke urgently, and in a hushed tone. She disappeared inside and came back in less than a minute, carrying a brown paper shopping bag filled with clothes and pushing two little boys ahead of her.

Jenny greeted the boys, expecting them to be excited to see her. They had always been happy to see her come for a visit when they lived in Pocatello, but today they were sullen and quiet. She and Lorraine had become good friends in the time they had worked together at the cafe, and Jenny spent at lot of time at Lorraine's home. She had grown attached to the boys, and missed them after she moved to Spokane with her boyfriend. Those had obviously been much happier days for Lorraine, she thought.

Danny and Joey didn't appear to have slept well—they both had dark circles under their eyes. Little Joey wore an old army cap several sizes too big for his head, and his cheeks were tear stained. His big brother had a sober, stoic look about him, and stood rigidly, waiting for further instruction from Jenny or his mother. Lorraine thrust the paper shopping bag into Jenny's hands, urging her to go.

"You have to go, Jenny," Lorraine insisted. She pushed a handful of one-dollar and five-dollar bills into Jenny's coat pocket. "That's all I have. You take it, and call me in a few days. I put some of their clothes in the bag." She pushed Jenny toward the porch steps to send her on her way.

Neither of the boys wore coats, Jenny noticed, and they clung to her as she led them to the car. Frozen snow crunched under foot as she opened the back door of the old sedan to put the boys inside. Joey climbed in first, and Jenny placed a hand on Danny's back to guide him into the back seat and out of the cold wind.

"Aaahh," Danny cried out, arching his back away from Jenny's hand.

"I'm sorry, honey, but we need to get you out of this wind," Jenny said, placing her hand on his back again to coax him inside the car.

"Ow," the boy cried out again. It suddenly occurred to her that something was wrong with the boy's back—something uncomfortable—perhaps something painful. She dropped the paper bag filled with clothes onto the crusted snow and stepped closer to the boy.

"Come here, Danny," she said, softly, pulling him toward her by his arm. "Come here."

She reached for the boy's shirt at his shoulder, careful not to touch his back. Pulling the youngster close, she bent over his shoulder and lifted up the back of his shirt, raising it higher as she spun the boy around to get a better look. His small back was covered with reddish-blue welts from side to side—welts the width of a large belt. Dried blood was beginning to scab along the edges of the overlapping wounds where the belt strap had repeatedly cut through the tender skin. She saw that six, maybe seven, deep welts had been laid across the seven-year-old boy's back. Jenny flew into a rage.

"Get in the car, Danny," she ordered.

The injured boy climbed in through the rear door, careful not to lean against the seat back and cause more pain to his sensitive, damaged skin. The children all stared mutely through the side windows as Jenny stormed across the snow-covered yard in long, deliberate strides, and onto the front porch, clearing two steps at a time. She didn't pause for a second to consider the delicacy of her own physical condition—she was a guided missile. Lorraine opened the front door and stepped outside to intercept her friend and to beg her not to interfere, but Jenny refused to be deterred. She pushed Lorraine aside and barged through the doorway, screaming as she began her search for Lorraine's husband.

"Bud Fuller, you come out here!" she screamed, in a voice resembling that of a shrieking harpy more than a human. "Get out here, you miserable excuse for a man!"

Jenny was seething. She started toward the hallway, but Lorraine reached for her arm to stop her. Bud appeared out of a bedroom doorway—his hair was mussed and he wore nothing but boxer shorts and a dirty tee shirt.

"What the hell's going on?" he demanded, slurring his speech through the drunken haze of a hangover, as he stumbled into the small living room. "Can't a man sleep?"

"This is what's going on, you evil bastard!" Jenny spat through gritted teeth, as she snatched up a heavy ash tray from the coffee table and hurled it at the man's head.

Cigarette butts and ashes scattered across the carpet as the heavy glass object flew at Bud's face, missing its mark by inches as it sailed into the kitchen and shattered against a cabinet door. Shards of broken glass sprayed the linoleum floor, and the half-naked man stood speechless.

"Please, Jenny," Lorraine whispered hoarsely, stepping between Jenny and the target of her unbridled fury. She leaned in closely, hoping that her words would not be overheard by her husband. "Please,

please don't do anything—just take the boys and go." Lorraine's eyes were pleading—begging Jenny to understand the danger.

Jenny knew that something terrible had been happening at the Fuller house—and more than just once. She feared for her friend, but suddenly realized that it would be wise to defer to Lorraine's judgment, and get the children away as quickly as possible.

"Where's she goin' with those boys?' Bud demanded, exposing more of his surly nature, as he tried to appear like a man in charge.

"She's just taking them downtown to see the Christmas decorations, that's all," Lorraine said, meekly, praying that Jenny would take the hint and get out of the house immediately.

"It's none of your damn business, that's where I'm taking them," Jenny fumed, with all the venom she could muster. She leaned defiantly over Lorraine's shoulder, and glared at the man she had suddenly come to hate. She turned again to walk out the door, though reluctant to leave her friend alone with her despicable husband.

"What the hell's she goin' off about?" Bud snarled at his wife, indignantly, before aiming his insolence at Jenny. "Them boys ain't none of your business."

Jenny's fury erupted again, and she whirled to unleash more of her anger at the drunkard in the dirty boxer shorts. She cast her eyes about the room, searching for anything that she might use to inflict bodily damage, and opted for a ceramic table lamp that rested on a small stand next to the sofa. She grabbed it by its base and yanked its cord from the wall outlet, then raised it over her head like a javelin and pitched it at Lorraine's husband with all her strength. Bud's arms flailed in an attempt to deflect the lamp's impact, but the large lampshade slapped him across the face in spite of his drunken effort to defend himself. The lamp bounced off his chest and broke against the coffee table. He was caught off guard once again by his female assailant who faced him down, unflinching, and read him his rights.

"If I ever hear of you raising a finger to a kid again, I'll call the sheriff myself," Jenny threatened, vehemently. "And you'll go to jail, where you belong."

Jenny marched stiff-legged out through the front door and down onto the snow-covered walkway, then whirled around to level more verbal abuse at the object of her contempt.

"And if you touch Lorraine or the baby, I'll come back with my dad's Winchester and I'll shoot you!"

Her face reddened to a deep scarlet as her anger continued to overflow, and she picked up a fist-sized chunk of frozen snow and flung it at the closed front door. Jenny tried frantically to think of something else she might do to help Lorraine, but was only frustrated by her state of anger. She clenched her fists and tried to imagine how good it would feel to knock Bud Fuller on his butt.

"If I were a man, I'd beat his ass into the dirt," she hissed through gritted teeth, as she stomped through the snow toward the car.

Neighbors peered through half-opened window shades as Jenny unleashed her tirade—onlookers drawn by their curiosity to the early-morning commotion in the front yard of the Fuller house. Some of them had heard the terrified screams in the night from a defenseless little boy.

Jenny walked around to the driver's side and climbed in behind the wheel, then turned the ignition key and hit the starter button on the floor. She dialed the heater up to high and turned to look at the startled faces of the four frightened children, trying to change her demeanor and hide her wrath.

"You kids okay?" she asked, in a voice she hoped would sound sweet and calming to the ears of the upset children. The kids stared in awe at their protector, wide-eyed and mute. Danny and Joey were shivering, but filled with gratitude, nonetheless.

"Where are your coats, boys?" Jenny asked, glancing through the rear-view mirror at the inadequately-clothed brothers. Neither boy spoke—Danny was worried about his stepfather far more than the cold weather, and wished only for Jenny to keep the car moving along the snow-covered street, far from his unhappy home. She glanced again into the mirror. The boys were wearing old, worn-out clothes, and were badly in need of haircuts.

She pulled the car off the road at the north end of Blue Lakes Boulevard, and set the hand brake, leaving the motor running to keep warm air coming from the heater. She reached into the back seat for the brown paper bag and fumbled through its contents, extracting a pair of cotton sweaters. She helped Joey to pull the sweater over his head and get his small arms into the sleeves. Danny was unable to raise his arms, and Jenny's blood began to boil again.

The sky had cleared and the snowplow trucks had plowed and sanded the highways throughout the night, making travel easier for the motorists who ventured out after the winter storm. Jenny stopped at the Five Points Truck Stop on the way out of town and picked up snacks and drinks for the drive north. She purchased a tube of first aid cream and took Jimmy into the restroom, where she applied the soothing cream generously over the injured skin on his small back, then got him back into the car and carefully wrapped her coat around his small body.

The drive north was very quiet. Danny and his little brother fell asleep in the back seat, and the girls remained silent, sensing that Jenny was doing some hard thinking and didn't want to be disturbed. June's curiosity finally overcame her, and she turned to kneel up on the seat and look at the sleeping brothers in the back seat before blurting out her first question.

"What's wrong with him?" she asked, looking at the boy wrapped in Jenny's heavy winter coat. "Is he sick?"

"Never mind," Jenny replied, softly. "You turn around and sit down."

"Are we going home now, Jenny?" she queried.

"No, June-bug," Jenny answered patiently. "We're going to the ranch."

Jenny didn't know what else to do. It wasn't an easy decision, and definitely not what she wanted, but she needed her parents' help—and she needed their advice.

"Where is the ranch?" June asked, wanting to know how her day had been planned for her. "How far is it?"

"It's not far—maybe an hour. We'll be there before you know it."

June processed the information she had been given before she formed more questions in her young and inquisitive mind.

"Who lives there?" June asked.

"Grandma and Grandpa live there," Jenny answered. "Now just sit back and relax—we'll be there soon enough."

"Are there cows?" June continued.

"Yes," Jenny answered patiently.

Alice remained silent throughout her little sister's endless litany of questions—she was still uneasy with the disturbing events of the day. She had endured the pain of losing her grandmother only two weeks earlier, and she was now thrust into another difficult situation that upset her delicate sense of order. She longed for a safe refuge.

The old sedan rolled along the highway for a few more miles before it turned onto a gravel road next to a sign that read: *Ranch Access*. Jenny slowed the car to a stop and paused for a few moments to reconsider her decision, then shook her head and accelerated the car down the snow-covered road toward the Barnett Ranch. She was resigned to the only place she could go.

Jenny pulled up in front of the old, two-story farm house and stepped out of the car to a raucous chorus of excited Border Collies. The dogs ceased their barking the instant they recognized Jenny, and greeted her with raised forepaws and nuzzles to her hands, begging for attention. The excited sheepdogs offered the same greeting to the children as the tiny travelers tumbled out of the car and lined up next to Jenny.

Betty and Cooper Barnett appeared together on the front porch, and Betty was still drying her hands on her apron after washing up in the kitchen. They tried to grasp the meaning of what stood before them—a band of shivering gypsy children, chauffeured by their prodigal daughter—their pregnant, prodigal daughter.

"I thought you said she was working in a department store," Cooper said, turning his head to cast a suspicious glance in his wife's direction—a glance that implied she had kept something from him. He wondered if she had told him everything that was in Jenny's letter, or if she had begun to keep family secrets from him after so many years of honesty.

Betty Barnett continued to stare at the troupe of gypsies as they shivered in the cold, posed for inspection as they stood in a line next to the old Studebaker. She reached a hand over to grab her husband's forearm and grip it tightly—a signal that he should be silent and allow her to handle the situation. She thought she had a better question than the one her husband asked, but nothing came to mind.

"I thought you said you were working in a department store," Betty said to her pregnant daughter.

"I'll go bring in some more firewood," Cooper muttered to no one in particular. "I expect we'll be up late tonight."

CHAPTER FIVE
LOST AND FOUND

"I know one of them is yours," Cooper said to his pregnant daughter, pointing a leather-gloved finger at her belly. "But what about these other kids—where did they come from?" he asked, gesturing with his thumb toward the four small children who were warming themselves by the fire.

Jenny drew a deep breath and pondered how to begin. It was all so complicated, and the events of the past two weeks had happened so fast, it was all a blur. She didn't know how to explain to her father that she had taken four children under her wing without any legal guardianship. Her father had always been a law-abiding man, and he was sure to be critical of her poor judgment.

"I don't know where to start," she said.

"Start at the beginning—that's what I'd do."

Jenny looked up at her father with imploring eyes and took another deep breath. She couldn't find the words to explain all that had happened, and she hardly knew where to begin. She hoped her dad would not press her until she could have time to think about how to solve her dilemma. She had done what she had to do—nothing more. She was certain her father would understand, once she explained. Cooper could see his daughter was stalling for time.

"Dad, do you remember what you used to say to us when we were kids?" Jenny asked, reminding her father of the wisdom he had shared when she and her brothers were growing up on the ranch. "You always said that life was unpredictable. One day life's a bore, and the next day it can be a tightrope walk over a raging river—do you remember?"

"I don't remember saying that—but I may have," her father allowed. "I remember telling you a lot of other things, though," Coop responded, eyeing his daughter's belly. "I remember telling you not to get pregnant unless you got married first. Are you married?"

Jenny didn't answer.

"We drove down to see my friend Lorraine in Twin Falls, and she was having some family trouble, so she asked me to look after her boys."

Coop thought that he could see where his daughter was trying to go with her explanation. She was in a predicament, and he decided to let it go before it all got so complicated that it gave him a headache. He knew that women had their own special way of talking all around a subject before they came to the point, and he didn't want any part of this one. Betty was better equipped to handle the matter, he thought.

"You've had a busy day," he remarked, without criticism. "I think I better go check on the horses."

Cooper donned his heavy mackinaw and pulled on his rubber boots, then walked out the back door and across the short span of frozen ground to take refuge in the barn and stables. His dogs followed him into the barn, curious to see if there was work to be done. He checked the feeders of the two Clydesdale draft horses, then crossed to the other side to check on his gelding and mare. The gelding pawed at the straw-strewn stall floor with one hoof, asking to be let out for some much-needed exercise. The mare whinnied, anticipating the customary carrot that often accompanied a visit from the man.

"You animals are all spoiled," Cooper grumbled, as he parked himself on a short wooden bench and fumbled through his coat pockets to find his gloves. "Those kids are gonna be spoiled, too—Betty and Jen will see to that."

His two sheepdogs, Banjo and Holly, sat on the floor in front of him, listening patiently with their heads cocked to the side and ears raised as they waited for instructions. Whenever their master put on his coat and gloves, it usually meant they were going to work, rounding up sheep to fetch them to the lower pasture, closer to the barn. Sometimes it meant that they were going for a run, to follow along while their master rode out on horseback to check the sheep and cattle. Either way, it would be something the dogs liked doing. Today, their master just sat on the wooden bench and talked to himself. Banjo and Holly took turns yawning, first one and then the other, until they finally dropped onto their sides for a winter snooze in the barn.

Cooper went back inside the house after giving his wife and daughter some time to talk in private, and found the kids all seated around the big breakfast table in the kitchen. He got a closer look at the four children as Betty fed them the last of the apple pie that he thought would be his after dinner. The girls appeared to be well-cared for, but the boys looked a little rag-tag. They all looked up at him, curious and unsmiling, as they devoured the last of his dessert.

Betty helped her daughter put the boys to bed in the room Jenny's older brothers had shared until they moved away from home. They carefully washed and applied more ointment to Danny's tender back, then dressed the damaged skin with gauze bandages and helped him to lie down on his stomach to fall asleep. The boys had been awake most the previous night, and were exhausted. Joey got into bed, but refused to take off his army hat. Jenny didn't push him to give it up—she knew its history.

Betty made coffee and sat at the kitchen table to listen to Jenny's tale of the four orphans, and how they had come to be in her care. Alice and June sat with them and listened intently.

"The girls lost their grandmother two weeks ago—she was my landlady," Jenny began to explain.

"She just up and died," Alice said, innocently, her hands clasped together under the table and held in place between her knobby little knees. She leaned forward against the table and gave her own explanation to Betty about what happened to her grandmother. "She had a bad heart."

"She was in the hospital and she died," June said, nodding her head as she affirmed her big sister's explanation.

"They didn't have any other family," Jenny continued. "I promised them and I promised their grandmother that I wouldn't let anything happen to them. I'm not sure how we're going to work it out, but they're staying with me."

Alice and June looked at Jenny's mom to see if she was accepting her daughter's explanation. Somehow, they sensed that if Grandma Barnett gave her permission, everything would be all right. At a very young age, they had already learned that it was the matriarch in the family who usually got the final say in all important decisions. Betty decided that it could wait until after the girls went to bed to discuss it any further. They settled the girls in Jenny's old room, and left the door open a crack, with a light on in the hallway so they could find their way to the bathroom during the night.

"What about the boys?" Betty asked, after she returned to the kitchen to continue their conversation. "Tell me exactly how they came to join your brood."

"It happened this morning," Jenny answered. "Do you remember me talking about my friend, Lorraine, who worked with me at the cafe in Pocatello? Well, she moved to Twin Falls with her husband a few months ago. I took an extra day off from work to go and visit her, and she was having big trouble with her husband. He lost his job, and he's drinking a lot. I'm sure this isn't the first time he strapped Danny—you saw all the belt marks on his back."

Betty was aghast. She slowly shook her head in disbelief as she struggled for words.

"Why would a man do that to a child—and especially his own son?" she asked, horrified that men like that existed in the world.

"They're not his boys, Mom. Lorraine was married once before. Their dad was killed in Vietnam three years ago."

"Then you think he resents them?"

"Oh, I don't know, Mom," Jenny said, exasperated with the questioning and speculation. "But he's a mean devil, that's for sure, and I think he's been like that for a long time. I tried to throw half the furniture at him on my way out of their house."

Betty gave her daughter a brief, wry smile. She knew where Jenny got her toughness—she was her father's daughter, for sure.

"Why don't you go talk to your dad while the girls help me start breakfast," Betty suggested. "I imagine he's out in his office, doing a lot of brooding and thinking right now."

Jenny put on her heavy coat and bundled up with a scarf, then lifted one of her father's wool-lined hunter caps from the rack next to the kitchen door. She pulled it down snugly over her ears, and turned to look at Alice and June. They stayed seated at the table with her mom, waiting obediently for instructions from Jenny.

"You girls stay here with Grandma and help her, okay?"

"We'll be fine," Betty said.

"I expect this will take awhile," she said to her mom, as she pulled the back door open and stepped outside and ducked her head into the chill wind.

"Is she in trouble with her dad?" the astute eight-year-old Alice asked, after Jenny pulled the door closed behind her. "Is it because of us?"

"It's nothing they can't work out, honey," Betty answered, shaking her head as she smiled pleasantly at the girls. "How would you girls like to help me bake some fresh bread?"

Jenny rolled the barn door back enough to walk inside, and allowed her eyes to adjust to the dim light. She was greeted immediately by Banjo and Holly, tails wagging and muzzles pushing at her mitten-clad hands. Her father looked up as she walked over to where he was seated.

"Hi, Dad," she said, quietly and respectfully.

He gestured with a gloved hand toward several bags of horse feed, stacked evenly on a wooden pallet a few feet away. Jenny perched atop the bags, and got as comfortable as she could in the cold, drafty barn. She looked at her father, and he stared back at her, silently. Jenny knew the conversation would not begin unless she spoke first.

"I got myself in a real fix, Dad," she began.

"I see that," Cooper responded, nodding his head in blunt acknowledgment of his daughter's admission. He waited for the rest of the news.

"Roger's gone—he left when I told him that I was pregnant," Jenny confessed, hoping that her dad would not be too critical of her bad judgment and poor taste in men.

"You're better off—he was nothing but a drifter—a damn tumbleweed," he stated, flatly. "And a jackass," he added, with absolute certainty. He stopped short of saying I told you so.

Tears welled up in Jenny's eyes as she accepted the truth of her father's words. All she wanted now was his understanding.

"What am I going to do?" she asked, in a small, plaintive voice. "I've got all these kids, and I can't just let them go. They've got no one else."

"We can talk it over with your mother tonight, after the kids are all in bed," Coop said, confirming his willingness to help his daughter to find a way out of her dilemma.

"And you might want to think about being honest with us from now on, if it's not too much trouble," he added. "You're not working in a department store, are you?"

"How did you know?" Jenny asked, amazed that her father could guess so easily that she had lied about her job.

Cooper lifted his big frame off the bench and reached to give his daughter a helping hand, pointing toward the barn door with his free hand to signal that their private father-daughter conversation was adjourned for the time being.

"You'd be wearing better clothes," he said. "And so would those two girls."

Jenny held onto her father's arm as they walked back to the house, and thought about the many times she had gone to the barn for private conversations with her dad when she was a kid. That's where all the private talks were held with Cooper's kids, and Jenny's older brothers went there far more often than she did. They were always the ones who got into trouble when they were growing up, or needed their dad's help in some way.

Cooper Barnett was a patient and understanding man. When his children needed to talk—or needed a talking to—he always made himself available for a conversation. It was usually one-sided, with Cooper doing most of the talking while the offending child endured long minutes of scolding and tough love. The kids eventually learned to do what was right, just to avoid those long sessions in the barn.

It wasn't always scolding and discipline, Jenny recalled, on her walk back to the house with her dad. Sometimes she and her brothers asked to meet with their dad in the barn to discuss their most private concerns—like what to do about bullies at school, or failing grades in chemistry class, or their plans for a future beyond the boundaries of the Barnett Ranch as they neared the end of their high school years. Cooper Barnett always listened to his kids; and he always tried to do what was best for them.

"Everything all right?" Betty asked her husband and daughter as they came through the back door. Father and daughter stomped the snow off their boots, and shed their heavy coats.

"Sure," Cooper said to his wife, as he hung up his hat and kicked off his boots on the mud porch. He stepped inside the kitchen to inhale the aroma of bread baking in the oven.

"Did you know it was Alice's birthday tomorrow?" Betty asked, looking up from her task of scrubbing potatoes in the sink to gauge the reaction on Jenny's face. "She's going to be nine years old"

"I never even thought to ask—we've been so busy. Alice, I'm so sorry," Jenny apologized. "We'll do something special for your birthday tomorrow," she promised.

Alice basked in the attention she was getting from Grandma Barnett and Jenny, and was equally pleased to see the kind, smiling face on Grandpa Barnett. He had looked so stern—even angry—when they first arrived at the ranch.

"I'm going to be four," June blurted.

She looked up at Grandpa Barnett's softened features and waited for him to be impressed.

"Four?" Coop responded, in mock surprise. "Is that all? I'll bet we've got stuff in the refrigerator that's older than you." The girls giggled, and Betty threw a wet dish towel at her husband.

"She was born in June," Alice said. "That's why Mom named her June. But I'm not sure what day."

June was suddenly downhearted when she realized that she might miss her birthday if no one knew exactly what day it was. She looked at Betty, and then to Jenny, hoping one of them would know the answer. Jenny quickly came to her rescue.

"Don't you worry, June-bug. We'll find your birth certificate when we get home, and then we'll know when your birthday is," Jenny assured. "And we'll have a big party, just like the one we're going to have for Alice tomorrow."

"Can I have my party here?" June asked, wanting assurance that her birthday status was equally as important as her big sister's.

"Of course you can," Betty answered. "Where else would you have it?"

June was satisfied, once that her birthday plans had been resolved, and beamed a happy smile to all in the room. Her eyes came to rest on Jenny's father—he seemed so much kinder than the grumpy old man who stepped out of the house to meet them when they first arrived.

"Do you have cows?" she asked.

"Well, yes, we do—lots of them—and horses, too," Cooper admitted. "We can go and see them today if you want to."

June grinned and nodded.

Jenny woke the boys to get them washed up for breakfast, and was relieved to find them calm and well-rested. They finished their breakfast—hearty appetites and good moods restored. Betty allowed Joey to keep his army cap on his head during his morning meal.

"Were you in the army?" Cooper asked Joey, as they got up from the table and carried their plates to the sink. Helping to clear the table after a meal was the single chore that Betty expected everyone in the family to share.

Joey looked up at Cooper and shook his head as he handed his plate up to the man. He never considered whether the old rancher was serious when he questioned his enlistment in the military.

"It was our dad's hat," Danny offered, standing in for his little brother, who was usually very shy. "It helps him to be brave when he wears it—like our dad."

Cooper noticed the double chevron insignia on the front of the olive drab cap.

"Your dad was a corporal?" he asked the older brother.

"I don't know," Danny replied. A sad expression crossed his young face. He had little understanding of ranks or insignias. "He was in the infantry, that's all I know."

Cooper didn't press the boys for any more information. Their father had served in the army, and had died in Vietnam—that's all he needed to know for now.

Cooper banked more wood onto the fire, and everyone sat in the living room and caught up on family news until the children became drowsy in the warmth that radiated from the crackling fire.

Betty was relieved to know that her daughter had a steady job at a cafe, and a place to live, but felt uneasy about how Jenny was going to deal with the problem of the orphaned girls. Caring for the sons of her friend was another matter. It was obvious that Jenny had taken a great deal upon herself, and with no apparent plan for how she was going to manage it all. Betty was deeply concerned for her daughter—and for the children.

"Are you going to try to find out if the girls have any other family?" Betty asked, after the kids had all been put to bed.

"I will, Mom," Jenny said. "But I don't expect to find anyone. Dora Rolfson said she was the only family they had, and the girls don't remember having any aunts or uncles. I know Alice remembers her parents, but she doesn't talk about them much. June only remembers her grandma. She was only two years old when her parents died last year."

Cooper listened intently, but he asked no questions and gave no advice. It was well outside the realm of his expertise to offer suggestions about obtaining guardianship of minor children. His daughter seemed intent upon keeping the girls, but how she would accomplish that, he did not know. He spent the rest of the day outside, taking care of his chores and feeding livestock. He waited until it was almost suppertime before he came into the house.

"You were gone a long time—you must have had a lot to do," Betty said.

"Yeah."

"Is everything all right?"

"Yeah." He didn't come back to the house for conversation—he only came inside because he was hungry.

"Why don't you go wash up—supper will be ready in a minute."

Cooper passed through the living room on his way to the hallway bathroom. The children were busy sorting through the pieces to a picture puzzle on the coffee table, trying to make them fit into place. He didn't stop to help—he was never very good at fitting puzzle pieces together. He had no patience for it.

He said good night to the women after dinner, and went to bed, leaving them to stay up late and solve the world's problems.

Jenny and her mom talked late into the night about Alice and June, and about how to help the two mistreated boys. They came up with a temporary solution before they said goodnight and went off to bed. Jenny tried once more to reach Lorraine by telephone, but there was no answer at the Fuller home.

The kitchen was bustling with activity when Cooper came in from his early morning chores. It seemed to him like the old ranch house was alive again, filled with the sounds of breakfast chatter and familiar conversations between his wife and daughter—conversations that were generally of no interest to him. He overheard one remark that he thought might concern him, and interrupted to be certain he heard them right.

"Did I hear you say that the boys were going to stay here for another week?" Cooper inquired of his wife. "When was that decided?"

"Last night, after you went to bed," Betty declared. "It will be good for you to have some boys around to keep you company and help out with the chores."

If he had an opinion on the matter, he kept it to himself, but

Cooper wondered how his wife always seemed to know what would be good for him, and he was particularly curious to learn what help he might expect to get from two little boys who were weren't much taller than a yardstick. As far as he could tell, the boys had never even been on a ranch before yesterday. He hung up his coat, pulled an empty chair up to the table, and sat down to wait for his breakfast while four curious kids gave him the once-over.

The boys stayed inside with the women after Cooper finished his breakfast and went back out to the barn to escape the endless chatter that accompanied the preparations for Alice's birthday party. Danny had no experience being around a man who wasn't mean-spirited and abusive. He had little memory of his own father; and his ordeal with his stepfather was one that he didn't care to relive. Nevertheless, the memory would undoubtedly be with him for a long time.

While her mother kept the kids busy in the kitchen, Jenny called Lorraine again, and was relieved when her friend finally answered the phone.

"I'm sorry to put this on your shoulders, Jenny," Lorraine said.

"I didn't plan it, I swear. I didn't know before you came down to see me that Bud was going to behave the way he did."

"Has he done that to Danny before?" Jenny questioned, certain that she already knew the answer.

Lorraine was silent for a long moment.

"Yes," she whispered, meekly, with the shame that followed her regret for not doing more to protect her son from harm. "He usually took Danny out to the back yard for a strapping. I kept Joey and the baby inside with me, because I was scared he'd hurt Joey, too."

Jenny's anger rose to the surface again.

"Why don't you just leave him, Lorraine? Why don't you just take the baby and leave?"

"I've got no place to go," Lorraine uttered, with total resignation. "I don't have a car, or any money or any place to live."

"You can live with me, Lorraine—we'll make room."

"Most of the time he doesn't act this way," Lorraine excused, ignoring Jenny's offer of help. "And I'm afraid he might take the baby if I try to leave. I've got no way to support myself or the baby."

Jenny was no psychologist, but it wasn't difficult for her to see that her friend was in a fragile state of mind. Lorraine had surrendered control of her life to an overbearing man who had shown nothing but scorn for her, and abuse and brutality toward her sons.

"Do you want to talk with your boys?" Jenny asked, expecting an eager response.

"No, I better not. Just tell them that I'm sorry, and that I love them—I don't know what else to say," Lorraine answered in a voice tinged with hopelessness. "I better hang up now—Bud's probably awake."

Jenny felt a cold chill as she returned the phone to its cradle. She didn't understand how anyone could be trapped in such a terrible situation and not simply pack up and leave.

A day back at home on the ranch had given her a brief respite from the cold, harsh realities of life. Wrapped in the comfort and protection of her family, and surrounded by all the familiarities of her childhood home, Jenny felt safe again. She wished desperately that she could share her refuge with her longtime friend.

She had to think about making the trip back to Boise with the girls soon, and about how to deal with the matter of guardianship, leaving the boys to be cared for by her mom and dad. It wasn't fair to her parents, she knew, but she had no one else to turn to for help.

"It can't be much different than having your own grandkids around for a week," Betty suggested to her husband, as she finished icing the devil's food cake for Alice's birthday party. Jenny kept the kids busy in the living room while her mom finished wrapping up a knit scarf and tam in colorful paper. She had intended the gift for one of her granddaughters for Christmas, but there would be plenty of time to replace it.

Cooper remained silent—an obvious sign that he wasn't entirely pleased with the prospect of having to help to babysit two small boys for a week.

"Coop, that oldest boy has been taking a beating from his stepfather." Betty said. "He's been protecting his little brother, and taking a beating for both of them. Apparently, it happened almost every time their stepdad would get drunk. It's as if it was his favorite pastime," she finished, with disgust.

"How do you know that?" Cooper asked, his face contorted into a mask of anger and revulsion.

"Jenny told me about it last night—and I've seen the strap marks on his back," she answered, not feeling the need to elaborate any further for her husband.

Cooper sat unresponsive for a long moment. He got up from the table and put on his coat, opened the back door and walked out to the barn, forgetting his hat and gloves as he stepped out into the cold air. He waited in his sanctuary next to the horse stalls so that no one would see his dark mood. His reservoir of feeling was deep—fathomed only by those closest to him—and his empathy for helpless and mistreated children was boundless.

It was mid-afternoon when the party festivities broke up, and Jenny rounded up the girls and their things for the drive back to Boise. She wanted to get home before dark—Alice had school in the morning, and she had promised Joe she would arrive at work early.

"I'm sorry the boys didn't have any coats, Mom," Jenny apologized, giving her mother a hug at the front door before guiding the girls down the steps and into the car.

"Don't worry about it—we'll find something for them to wear," Betty said, waving to the girls in the car as she spoke. Betty rarely threw anything away; and the closet under the staircase held a decades-old collection of children's coats, hats, mittens and snow boots.

Cooper came out of the barn just long enough to wave a brief goodbye to his daughter and the girls, and then retreated back into the solitude of his lair. Jenny watched her father go, his shoulders stooped as he walked slowly back inside the barn to be alone. Her father spent a lot of time in the barn—a place where he could be alone to tend his horses and to think his thoughts. He was thinking hard about the injury done to the little boy called Danny.

Jenny tuned in her favorite local country station on the AM radio for the drive back to Boise, and turned her thoughts to what she was going to do about Alice and June. The girls entertained themselves on the long drive by watching for jackrabbits along the highway, and updated Jenny periodically on their total count.

She wondered what explanation Lorraine gave to Danny and Joey's school to justify their week-long absence. One thing at a time, she decided. First, she had to deal with the problem of guardianship for Alice and June.

The girls had no family that she knew of, and Alice was already attending school—happy with her teacher and her classmates, even though she had no friends outside of school. The fewer changes she had to make, the better off the girls would be, and the less scrutiny she was likely to get from the school district. If Alice told anyone at the elementary school that her grandmother had passed away, it probably wouldn't attract too much attention, since she was obviously being taken care of, and showing up for school every day.

She made a mental note to go through Dora Rolfson's mail and private papers after they got home and the girls were in bed. Jenny thought she had understood that the Rolfsons had owned their modest house with the rental cottage in the rear for many years, so perhaps there wouldn't be a mortgage payment to worry about.

She feared that if she contacted a lawyer to help secure the property in trust for Dora's granddaughters, she would most likely encounter a custody issue over the girls, and she had no idea how to deal with it.

Jenny had thought long and hard during the drive, and was stressed with worry by the time they reached the junction at Mountain Home. She resolved to stay in the Rolfson home and take care of the girls as she had promised, so payment of monthly rent would not be an issue. She would need her paycheck to pay for food and winter clothes for the girls.

She was relieved that the roads were clear—no snow had fallen for at least two days. It was after dark when they reached the city limits of Boise, and the sisters were still chattering about all the things they had done and seen at the ranch.

"Is your mom our grandma now, Jenny?" Alice asked, hopefully.

"I'm pretty sure that she would like it if you called her grandma."

The girls had discovered an instant affection for Jenny's mother in the short time they spent on the ranch, and they assumed that they would always be with Jenny. It never crossed their innocent young minds that they could be rejected, or that they might be taken away to be placed into foster homes.

"I didn't get to see cows," June remembered suddenly.

Jenny was sleepy after the long drive, and exhausted with worry, so she put off going through Mrs. Rolfson's papers until later. She followed Alice and June to bed only minutes after the girls were safely tucked in for the night.

The next morning, Jenny woke early and called Lorraine to talk about what to do about the boys.

"They're staying with my mom and dad at the ranch," Jenny explained to her friend. "They seem to really like it, and they'll be safe there—but I don't know what to do about school."

"I told the school that I had to go and take care of my parents for a week, and they said the boys could make up their schoolwork when they got back. I don't know what to do after this week," Lorraine worried.

"I know it's asking a lot of your folks, but do you think the boys could stay there until I can figure out something else? I'll sign whatever they need to get the boys into school, and I promise I'll send whatever money I can," Lorraine pleaded. "I don't know where else to turn."

Jenny was silent and crestfallen. She had dumped the boys at the ranch and promised to be back for them in a week, and now she was being asked to keep them indefinitely. She was not even remotely prepared for such an overwhelming obligation of parenting, and didn't know what she was going to say to her parents. It would be completely unfair to expect them to provide a home and full-time care to the boys. She was out of ideas, and she was going to be late for work.

"Okay, Lorraine, I'll see what I can do," she relented.

Joe Bannock was happy to see Jenny when she arrived for work a few minutes late. He was relieved that she had shown up at all, given all the recent turmoil in her life.

"Glad to see you made it back okay," Joe said, taking Jenny's coat to hang it on the rack next to his office.

"Hi, Joe—I'm sorry to be late, but I'll get you caught up with your customers as fast as I can."

"Morning, girls," he greeted the two rosy-cheeked sisters who followed Jenny through the back door of the kitchen. "Did you have fun last weekend?"

The sisters smiled and nodded at Jenny's friendly boss, and June showed her big sister the office where she worked with crayons all day while Alice was at school.

The early breakfast crowd cleared out quickly, and Alice left on her brisk morning walk to school, leaving time for Jenny to sit down for a minute for a cup of coffee with her boss.

"I think I bit off more than I can chew, Joe," Jenny confessed, uncertain about how she should begin to explain the events of the past few days. She had to ask for another Saturday off during the upcoming weekend, and she was afraid that Joe's patience would wear thin."

"Are you talking about holding down a full-time job and taking care of the girls?"

"No, it's not the job—and the girls are okay," Jenny said.

Joe was relieved she wasn't talking about quitting. He was not typically a selfish man, but his self-interests were important, nonetheless. He couldn't remember when he had such an efficient and reliable cook, and he didn't want to lose her.

"Why don't you tell me what the trouble is—maybe I can help," Joe offered.

"I drove down to Twin Falls for the weekend to visit a good friend of mine, and to see if she could give me some helpful advice about taking care of kids. Turns out she's the one who needed help. I was just hoping for some reinforcement from her, but she didn't tell me that her own life was a mess."

"Have you been able to find out if the girls have any other family?" Joe inquired, thinking that perhaps Jenny could escape the bonds of her self-imposed child custody.

"Alice can't remember anyone, and June is too young to know," Jenny answered, slowly shaking her head.

"Have you called anyone at child services?" Joe asked plainly, believing that he already knew the answer.

"No. I'm afraid the girls will be split up, or be taken into a foster home with other kids, where they won't be treated special, you know?"

Joe decided to let it go for the time being—he was sure that Jenny was aware of the difficulty she could be facing if she didn't contact the state child services people fairly soon.

Jenny stayed busy during the week, at work and at home, and the girls fell comfortably into their daily routine. They were happy and content to have Jenny there to care for them. Friday morning came, and she realized that she had let the week go by without even giving a thought to contacting child services. She was procrastinating out of concern for Alice and June. She wasn't convinced that contacting the state agency would result in the best outcome for the girls.

"Why don't you bring what you want to take with you for the weekend, and we'll leave right after work to go and visit Grandma and Grandpa Barnett at the ranch," Jenny announced.

"Yay!" the girls chorused, gleefully.

June was bouncing up and down, excited to spend another weekend in Grandma Barnett's kitchen, where she was certain there was always something sweet to eat.

Jenny busied herself throughout the work day with advance preparation for the weekend meals at the cafe, making sure that Joe wouldn't have to bear the burden of her absence by doing everything himself while she was gone.

"Joe, I really appreciate you for letting me take this extra time off while everything is so unsettled. You can't know how much it means to me," Jenny said.

"Don't worry about it Jenny—just go and take care of what you need to," Joe replied. "You do enough work around here for two people."

Jenny ushered the girls out the back door of the cafe as soon as Alice got out of school, and they climbed into the car for the ride south to Camas County.

They made good time, and passed Mountain Home before dark, so the girls were able to take up their favorite highway pastime of counting jackrabbits along Highway 20 before the daylight was gone.

Their earlier excitement turned to exhaustion before they reached the turnoff to the Barnett Ranch. By the time Jenny's old sedan pulled up in front of the two-story ranch house to be greeted by her dad's sheepdogs, the sleepy headed girls had already nodded off.

CHAPTER SIX

FENCE MENDING

"Where's Dad?" Jenny asked, as she walked into the kitchen to find her mother was seated at the table, going through a pile of mail to sort the bills and letters from the junk mail.

"He's down on the east creek bank, fixing the fence along the stand of willows," her mother answered. "He lost a few cows in there last week, and it took him most of the day to roust them out."

"Are the boys with him?"

"No, I think they're in their room."

The kitchen was the epicenter of the Barnett Ranch. It was where every conversation of any importance took place between the Barnett women. It was where the family meals were prepared and eaten, and where the bills were paid. It was usually where the newspaper got read, and where the Barnett kids got help with their homework when they were young. It was where the family gathered on every important occasion, and where every day would begin and end.

Betty got up and walked to the wood stove and pulled an iron skillet down from the overhead rack.

Jenny poured herself a cup of coffee and walked over to the counter next to the old stove. "What can I do?" she asked, offering her expert culinary services.

Her mom began to crack eggs into the heavy, black frying pan until she had enough to feed all the hungry mouths in the house, then scrambled them with some diced onion and green pepper.

"You might want to think about doing a little fence mending of your own," Betty suggested, without taking her attention off her work. "You haven't convinced your father yet that you're using sound judgment by taking on so many kids—you better talk it over with him."

"I told Dad I was sorry when we talked in the barn last week," Jenny said, attempting to get herself off the hook—free of any further explanations about her unwed motherhood.

"It's going to take a bit more work than that to smooth things out between you and your dad," Betty insisted. "There's still four other kids besides your own to be considered, and as far as I can see, you'll have your hands full trying to take care of Alice and June. Oh, and did I mention—it doesn't appear that any of them belong to you."

"I was hoping that I might be able to leave the boys here a little while longer—I'm sure Lorraine will sign anything you need to get them into school," Jenny suggested, meekly.

"That's why you better go and talk with your dad," Betty said. "He needs to hear it from you if you're not going to take the boys home to their mother. Enlighten him as to why you felt the need to open your own private orphanage."

Danny and Joey heard the women's voices in the kitchen, and came out of their room to greet the new arrivals.

"We didn't hear you come in, Jenny," Danny said, rushing up to give Jenny a hug.

"Why don't you boys come and sit down so I can trim those mops of hair?" Betty instructed. "Jenny has to go talk to her dad for a few minutes." She pulled a wooden chair away from the kitchen table and gestured for Danny to sit down, then opened a cabinet drawer and retrieved a pair of scissors and electric clippers. She was sure it had been a couple of months, at least, since the last time the boys had gotten haircuts, and Betty was an experienced home barber. She had trimmed hair for her husband and sons for many years.

Ordinarily, Jenny would have saddled her dad's mare and followed the fence line down to Willow Creek and along the stream bank until she found the spot where her father was repairing fence. Today, the cold

December wind precluded a winter horseback ride, so she took her dad's pickup and followed the hoof prints in the light snow until she saw her father's horse tied to a fence post near the edge of the willow stand.

Cooper had his back turned when Jenny drove up, and he was using a stretcher to pull an extra strand of barbed wire taut across the span between two rough wooden posts. The added barrier should be enough to deter the steers from pushing their way through the fence to get into the willows, he thought.

Jenny waited until her dad finished fastening a heavy steel staple to secure the wire in place before she spoke. She knew that he must have seen her approaching from a distance—and he couldn't have missed hearing the familiar rumble of his old Chevy pickup engine when it pulled up behind him.

"I guess you saw me coming, huh?" Jenny asked, opening the conversation with her father in her usual small-talk way. She stood next to him while he assessed his work.

"My horse did," Cooper answered, without looking up

His gelding was always the first to raise its head and turn its ears toward anything moving in the distance. Deuce was a good sentry, and a reliable mount for any chore around the ranch, or for the ride up through the Sawtooth Mountains to and from the summer grazing range.

Jenny didn't wait to gather her thoughts—it never impressed her dad much when anyone had to think for very long about what they were going to say. He had always believed that any conversation that had to be prepared in advance was probably dishonest.

"Dad, I'm so sorry about all of this," she began, trying desperately to contain her emotion. "I didn't mean to drop those boys in your lap, but I didn't know what else to do."

"Those boys aren't the problem—we can watch them all right, as long as there's no trouble with the law," Cooper responded,

"I had no choice with Alice and June, either," Jenny defended. "I promised their grandmother I wouldn't let anything happen to them.

You would have done the same."

"That's not it, either," Cooper replied, gruffly.

"Oh," Jenny answered quietly, reaching a hand up and pressing a palm to her belly. "You mean this—I thought we talked about this last week."

"You might have at least told your mother about it," Cooper insisted.

"I was ashamed of what you would think of me, Dad. Besides, anything I tell Mom—she's just going to tell you anyway."

"Then you *should* have told your mom, so she *could* tell me," he added, hastily, scolding his daughter for her unnecessary secrecy. "What difference would it have made if I knew?"

Jenny's chest and shoulders heaved with a big sigh, as she realized the truth of her father's words. Her pregnancy was bound to become known sooner or later, she knew. It was foolish of her to keep it from her parents, even though she thought they would be angry with her.

"I won't keep anything like this from you again, Dad," Jenny promised, respectfully.

"There better not *be* anything else like this again," Cooper said, his voice and eyebrows raised, as he turned to square off with his daughter, and look her straight in the eye. "At least not until you're married."

Jenny smiled, understanding her dad's remark perfectly. It was the kind of comment that was the closest he ever came to making light of a tough situation.

"You know what I mean," she said, reaching around her dad with both arms to embrace him. The world felt safe again to Jenny—at least for the moment.

"I think that will hold," Cooper said, turning to look over his fence mending work. He looked at his daughter and gave her a nod and a smile—evidence that he was satisfied with his work, and satisfied with his daughter for driving out to the fence line to talk with him. "We better get back to the house now, before it gets too dark."

He tied his horse to the back of the pickup and helped Jenny climb into the passenger side. Banjo and Holly jumped into the back of the truck for the short ride to the house, now certain that there was no livestock work for them to do. Cooper drove slowly on the bumpy dirt road that led to the ranch house so that his horse could keep up, and so that his sheepdogs wouldn't bounce out of the back—or Jenny's baby come too soon.

Jenny let her thoughts wander back to her childhood as they drove the maze of old dirt roads, following the fence lines and irrigation ditches that led back to the house and barn. The world was such a carefree place then, she thought—but often lonely. She wondered why her dad and grandparents had chosen to scratch out a life in such a desolate place. Camas County never had more than a thousand residents in the whole county—mostly ranchers and farmers eking out a living on the prairie, and a few hundred others living and working in town at the county seat of Fairfield.

"Did you ever think about doing anything else besides sheep ranching?" Jenny asked her dad.

"What, like hog ranching, you mean?" Cooper responded, in all seriousness. "Never could stand the smell."

"No, Dad," Jenny smiled, feeling like she was a ten-year-old again, being teased by her father. "You know what I mean."

Cooper steered the wheel with both hands and steadied the truck as it picked its way through the ruts in the old dirt road. The occasional brush that grew up through the soft dirt in the middle of the untended road scraped along the undercarriage of the truck.

"I thought about being a movie star once," Cooper replied with a grin, tossing an amused glance in his daughter's direction. "I think that I could have made a pretty good swashbuckler—or a ladies' man. Wouldn't have been fair to put Doug Fairbanks or Clark Gable out of a job, though—and they probably didn't know a danged thing about ranching, so I couldn't have offered to trade them my job for theirs."

Jenny smiled broadly at her father's clever remarks—he always had a way of pointing out the absurd instead of simply saying no.

"I mean something else—something more practical,"

"A millionaire," he said. "I always meant to be one—just never got around to it."

Cooper gripped the steering wheel with both hands and stared straight ahead through the cracked windshield as he pondered what it might have been like to live life as a rich man.

"Doesn't the heater work in this truck?" Jenny asked, holding her coat collar snugly under her chin.

"Not since you were twelve."

Betty had supper prepared, and nearly devoured by four hungry kids by the time Jenny and her dad came through the back door of the kitchen.

"You're lucky you got back in time for some table scraps," Betty said. "This pack of wolf pups almost picked this table clean."

The boys sat at the table, sporting their tight, new haircuts, as they grinned self-consciously and munched on man-sized bites of meatloaf sandwiches.

Cooper pulled up a chair and sat down next to Danny, then took a moment so smile at all the kids to put them at ease before he began the task of building himself a giant sandwich. He took another moment to give an approving nod to the brothers to acknowledge their neat appearance.

"Sittin' still for a haircut all morning is hungry work, isn't it men?" he said to the boys. Danny and Joey nodded in unison, never taking their eyes off of the old rancher.

"Looks as though they really have picked this platter clean. Did you eat all this?" he asked, looking directly at little June with a smile, as he continued to fill his plate.

June shook her head emphatically and pointed a tiny finger across the table at Danny, who looked up at Cooper again and grinned—proud of his good appetite.

"The weather news says there's a big storm moving in tomorrow, Coop," Betty advised her husband. "Think you'll need any help?"

"Nothin' the dogs and I can't handle," Cooper replied plainly.

"We'll just move the sheep down closer to the barns and corrals, so I can get to 'em with the feed team."

"I can come with you in the morning, Dad," Jenny offered. "If you think I can help."

"What would *you* do?" Cooper asked. "Besides cause me to worry, I mean."

"I could look for strays out in the brush," Jenny answered. "Seems like there's always a few that wander off, doesn't it?"

"You're not as fast as Banjo, I don't think—and Holly's got a better nose than you do for finding a couple of lost ewes, I expect."

Jenny smiled wanly. Her dad always had a flair for stating the obvious in the most ridiculous sort of way.

"I didn't mean that I'd run alongside your horse, Dad. I meant that I could saddle up your mare and ride along."

"Thought you'd take your baby out for a bumpy horseback ride, did you?" Cooper said, with just enough of a frown to let his daughter know he didn't think much of her judgment. "You stay off that horse."

"I'm not so far along that I'm waddling, Dad. I can sit a horse as good as my brothers ever could."

Cooper looked up and caught his daughter's attention with a steely stare. He wanted her to know he meant business.

"And if your horse stumbles in a ditch or a badger hole and throws you, then what?" Cooper answered, growing more impatient with his daughter's persistence. "No, you stay off that horse," he repeated. "Don't even go near a saddle—then maybe you won't be tempted."

Jenny gave up and went to the girls' bedroom to get Alice started with her homework for Monday, and to occupy June for awhile with a picture book. The boys stayed with Cooper at the kitchen table and waited to see if any pie or cookies might come their way.

"She's got a stubborn streak," Cooper observed aloud, after Jenny left the room.

"Gee, where did she come by that, do you think?" Betty asked.

"I don't know," Cooper answered honestly. "But she sure is stubborn."

He had been thinking about riding out that afternoon to round up the sheep and bring them down close to the barn and corrals, but decided the job would keep until morning. They could wait until then to be fed, and the hay would keep them from straying off again.

Cooper went back outside and untied his horse from the back of the pickup, then led it into the barn and relieved it of its saddle and bridle. The horse walked quietly into its straw-strewn stall and sniffed its feeder for any leftover hay from the morning feeding.

"It's not time for your dinner, Deuce," Cooper explained to his saddle horse. "You just wait a minute."

He spent nearly two hours tending to his horses after their feeding, brushing manes and tails, and scratching the underside of their hooves with a steel pick to clean any packed dirt and manure, and any tiny rocks that might have wedged onto the underside to irritate them. He cleaned and filled their water troughs and raked out their stalls, then gave a final pat on the neck and shoulder of his big Clydesdale mare.

Cooper sat on a bale of straw and pulled a saddle onto his lap, opened a can of saddle soap and used an old cotton rag to apply the paste generously onto the aging leather. Deuce and Blue and the big draft horses eyed him from their stalls as he absentmindedly rubbed the nourishing treatment deeply into all the stitching and tiny crevices of the decorative tooling, giving the well-worn leather extended life. He enjoyed nothing better than the time he spent going about small chores in the barn and stables, or working with his animals—and knowing that his wife was busying herself in a house full of children again. Cooper Barnett was a wealthy man.

Light snow was beginning to fall—a little early according to the weather report. Maybe it wouldn't last, Cooper hoped. The region hadn't yet been hit with a big storm that winter—nothing more than five or six inches of snow. He only needed half a day to round up the bands of sheep and drive the herd over two or three miles of brush land, so that he could bring them in near the barn and corrals so that he could keep a closer eye on them from the house.

Betty had the boys entertained with a board game at the kitchen table when Cooper came in and hung up his coat. He poured himself a cup of coffee and stood at the counter to talk with his wife.

"I heard they brought in a few of those big, white European-bred guard dogs over at the Flat Iron Ranch near Carey—Pyrenees, or somethin' like that," Cooper said to his wife. "They say there's nothin' better for keepin' predators away from the sheep."

"*Who* says?" Betty asked, without looking up from her spot next to the sink, where she perched on a tall stool—elbows on the counter—as she leafed through her Betty Crocker cookbook.

"Well, John Parker, for one," Cooper explained, not expecting to be cross-examined for his comments. "His family has been running bigger herds of sheep than we have for a lot of years out there on the Flat Iron, and their livestock is exposed to quite a few mountain lions and coyotes up there against the Sawtooth Range. Maybe even a few wolves, if there's any left."

"You thinking about getting some more dogs, are you?" Betty asked, looking up from her recipe page to peer at her husband over the tops of her reading glasses.

"No, I was just thinking," Cooper said, feeling a little like he was being interviewed for a loan at the bank. "Just thought it might be something worth looking into, that's all."

He took his coffee and sat down with Danny and Joey at the table, and watched as they took turns rolling the dice and moving their pieces along the winding path of Uncle Wiggly's rabbit trail.

"You wanna play?" Danny asked.

"No," the old rancher was quick to respond, sitting back in his chair and raising his eyebrows in surprise at the invitation. "No, I've never been very good at this kind of sport."

"You might have learned if you had ever taken the time to play it with any of your own kids," Betty chided softly, so as not to chase her husband back to the barn.

"We'll teach you,' Danny offered, handing the leather-faced old sheepman a painted wooden board piece. "You can be green."

Cooper shook the dice vigorously in a clenched hand—then let them fly—sending one banging into a salt shaker as the other one rolled off the table and onto the linoleum floor.

The boys laughed and squealed at the old man's over-exertion, and rushed to retrieve the dice, encouraging him to try again. Cooper shook the dice lightly inside his big paw, then turned his palm over and let them spill out onto the table top next to his coffee mug.

"Three," Joey pronounced confidently, after quickly adding the two black dots to the single one poised in the center of the other cube.

Cooper hesitated—then realized the boys were waiting on him—and picked up his green wooden game piece to advance three spaces along the rabbit trail. *No wonder I never played this with my kids*, he thought.

Betty grinned from the sidelines, almost reading her husband's mind. He squirmed a bit in his chair and watched the boys make their next moves. Betty decided to let the boys finish the game before she rescued her husband from his predicament. He hung in until a winner was proclaimed, while working on a plan to excuse himself before the boys could trap him in another game.

"Do you need to bring in some firewood?" Betty asked of her husband, letting him off the hook with the boys.

"Yeah, thanks for reminding me," Cooper answered gratefully, pushing his chair back quickly to make his escape. "I'll bring in a good supply—we may be in for a big storm."

Cooper carried in several large armloads of split firewood and stacked it neatly along the hearth, piling it as high as he dared, without risking that it might tumble forward onto Betty's carpet. He thought it would be enough to keep the fire going steadily for three days or more. He went back outside and covered the woodpile with a large canvas tarp to keep it dry.

A chill wind was beginning to blow in from the west, and the light in the sky was dimming as low-hanging storm clouds moved in, bringing with them a dusting of light snow. *So much for the weatherman's predictions*, Cooper thought. *The storm is either early, or it misses the region altogether.*

Cooper fed the horses before their usual feeding time, and made sure the barn doors were battened securely in case the wind picked up. The snow was coming down harder by the time he reached the back door of the house, and it felt as though the temperature was dropping rapidly. He left his coat on as he stepped into Betty's kitchen, trying to think whether there might be something else he could do to prepare before the daylight was lost.

"Does it look like a bad one?" Betty asked, seeing her husband leaning against the door jamb, looking a bit pensive as he stared at the floor in deep thought.

Cooper broke from his concentration, looked up at his wife, and nodded briefly.

"It may be—I better move the pickup into the equipment shed," he said, turning to go back outside. "Get Jenny's car keys, will you? I'll put it under cover, too."

Danny and Joey stared, first at Cooper and then at Betty, as they listened to the conversation and noted the concern in the voices and mannerisms of the adults.

"Is everything going to be okay?" Danny asked.

"Yes, of course it is," Betty assured. "We just have to think about everything that needs to be done when a storm moves in, that's all. There are a lot of animals to worry about."

She knew that her husband was probably wishing he had brought the sheep in closer to the barn and hay storage sheds sooner, but there was nothing more to do about it now until morning. The hundred or more Hereford cattle wouldn't have any trouble making the trek across the pastures to their source of winter feed next to the corrals, even if they had to plod through a foot or more of snow.

"Do you think the sheep will freeze?" Joey asked, worried that the animals might not have enough wool on their backs to keep warm in a blizzard. He thought of them more as pets than livestock.

"They have thick, warm coats of heavy wool, Joey—don't you worry," Betty said. "And they'll huddle together to keep warm."

The boys read her face, and were both satisfied that she was giving them an honest assessment of the sheep's chances of survival—staying outdoors all night in the wicked cold of a winter storm.

She got Jenny's car keys out of her daughter's purse and went to the back door to wait for Cooper's return. The snow was coming down harder, driven near horizontally by the increasing wind from out of the west. Danny and Joey stood close behind her, one on either side, and tried to peer through the ice-coated storm door.

Cooper came back to the house at a brisk pace, holding his coat collar up against the cold as he leaned into the wind. Betty opened the storm door and stepped outside to hand him the keys to the old Studebaker. The cold wind took her by surprise, nearly ripping the door out of her grip and causing the boys to huddle closer to her sides. They buried their faces against her cotton house dress as they felt the stinging bite of wind-driven snow crystals against their cheeks.

Cooper came to the bottom of the steps and cupped his gloved hands together, making a bowl for Betty to drop the keys into. He hurried to start the old sedan, and gave it a minute or two to rev and warm up the motor before moving it to the tractor shed and parking it under cover alongside his pickup. He wasted no time in rushing back to the house, taking only a moment to check the barn door on the windward side, just to be certain that it was secure.

"Banjo! Holly!" he called out into the wind and snow. "Here, dogs!"

The two Border Collies came out from under the wooden porch steps when they heard their master's call. They had sensed the impending storm long before Cooper saw it coming, and had already curled up out of the cold, taking cover as close to the back door as they could get.

"Come on," he coaxed, inviting his dogs in out of the storm.

They quickly accepted their master's invitation, and slipped quietly inside while Cooper held the storm door for them. They found a spot out of the way, next to the washing machine, and curled up on an old rug to wait for their dinner.

Cooper built a blazing fire in the living room fireplace, putting a few extra pieces of firewood on to warm the room up more quickly. Jenny and the girls had come out of the bedroom when Cooper looked up from his task of fire building and saw that he had a room full of spectators. The girls sat on the hearth and enjoyed the flicker and crackle of the warm blaze.

"I'll start supper in a few minutes," Betty said, in answer to the familiar question that was written on her husband's face—a look of hunger that came around at the same time every evening. "Jen, why don't you get out some records and find something the kids might like to listen to for awhile."

Cooper settled into a big easy chair and lifted an old National Geographic magazine out of the rack under the lamp stand, then watched for a moment as his daughter kneeled with the kids in front of the stereo console and pulled several LP's out of the oak laminate cabinet.

"Do you need to feed your dogs?" Betty called out from the kitchen, reminding her husband that he had one last chore to do. "That's not like you to forget them."

Cooper got up from his comfortable chair and dropped the magazine onto the seat cushion, a little surprised with himself that he could be so easily sidetracked from one of his daily routines.

"I reckon they'll still be hungry when I get there," he said, excusing his tardiness.

He walked through the kitchen to the enclosed back porch, and scooped the daily portions of dry dog food into metal bowls for his herding dogs. They were still chowing down hungrily when Cooper came back from the kitchen sink with their filled water bowl.

"You don't think you'll have any trouble rounding up the sheep in the morning?" Betty asked, as Cooper came back into the kitchen. "Do you want to call and see if someone can come out from town and help out for awhile tomorrow?"

"No, everyone else dealing with the same weather, I expect," Cooper declined. "They're probably going to have to clear driveways and thaw frozen pipes in the morning. Besides, no one could get here before I leave with the dogs. We'll take off before the sun's up."

Cooper went back into the living room and banked the fire with a few more pieces of wood, then settled back into his big easy chair and took up his National Geographic magazine to read an article about the Spanish Mustangs of the American West. He had read the same article at least three times, but he never tired of it. It didn't take long for the warmth of the fire and a few pages of reading to cause him to nod off—Betty had to wake him from his nap when supper was ready.

The luminescent face on the bedroom alarm clock told Cooper it was almost six o'clock—he should have already been on his way to find his sheep. He rolled out of bed quietly and pulled on his jeans, taking a flannel shirt with him as he headed out through the bedroom door and down the stairs. Banjo and Holly heard him coming, and waited at their invisible barrier—the threshold of the open doorway between the kitchen and the back porch. They pranced in place and nuzzled their master's hand to urge him to hurry. Cooper pulled on a pair of insulated coveralls and sat down to lace up his boots. The dogs were ready and waiting at the back door when he zipped up his heavy mackinaw and a pulled a woolen cap with ear flaps snugly over his head.

The wind had died down during the night—but a light snow was still falling—and Cooper saw that nearly a foot of new snow had piled up on the porch steps and blanketed the landscape during the night. He knew that it had drifted much deeper on the wind-swept brush land where his sheep were likely to be found.

He rolled back the barn door with some difficulty, struggling against the snow that was pressed against the bottom of the door. There was just enough room to bring a horse through the opening. He fed his gelding first—a scoop of oats and a flake of Timothy hay. His horse would need some energy for the work ahead. He let the horse eat while he went about feeding the other horses, and then carried a few bales of grass hay out to the corrals and broke them open for the cattle. He left the gates swung wide so the cattle would be tempted to venture into the corral when they smelled the feed. He decided to wait to fill the feeding troughs with silage until more of the cattle came in—there would be more than sheep to round up after the storm, it seemed.

He saddled Deuce while the horse finished eating its ration of hay—waiting until the animal could fill its belly a little more before putting on its bridle. Deuce was still chewing a mouthful of hay when

Cooper led the horse out of its stall and through the partially-opened barn door into the freezing morning air. His mare raised her head and whinnied when Cooper left without her.

He saw a light go on in the kitchen as he rode out, but didn't go back to the house for coffee or a slice of toast. He needed to bring his livestock in, and there was no time to waste. If more snow fell, or if the wind picked up again, the drifting snow could trap some of his sheep. If they couldn't move, they would soon freeze to death, or become easy prey for predators.

He set out toward the southwest at a good pace, his energetic Border Collies leading the way as they bounded through the drifted snow. His reliable dogs would locate the herd—he had no doubt. His concern was whether they would be in time to avoid losing any of his livestock to the storm.

They traveled in a nearly straight line toward the area where Cooper last saw the bands of sheep on a grassy hillside not far from one of the stock ponds. He counted on the wooly animals to stay near the water hole, and the dying grass that was still a source of nutrition for them. Though covered in snow, he believed the sheep would stay close to the spot where they last found something to eat—at least for a little while.

Banjo and Holly ran out ahead as they came within a quarter mile of the pond—they could smell the sheep long before they could see them. Cooper reined in his horse and scanned the horizon, searching for the familiar clusters of white wool bunched together against a white background of drifted snow and sagebrush. The lightly-falling snow limited his visibility, and he had to squint to make out the distinct shapes of his ewes. He finally caught a glimpse of something moving. A band of at least seven or eight hundred sheep by Cooper's reckoning— their backs covered with fresh snow as they moved down the long slope toward the spot where Cooper sat on his horse—being driven by two of the best herding dogs in the county.

The count was still nearly two thousand shy of the total number that were out on the hillsides, wandering in the snow-covered brush, and searching for something to eat.

Cooper whistled for his dogs to leave the band of woolies where they were—just a few yards from the shallow, ice-covered pond—and to follow him as he gently kicked his mount in its flanks and urged it up the hillside so he could get a better look around. Sunlight streamed through a break in the dense cloud cover, and visibility improved as the snow began to let up. There were too many to count, he thought, but the sheep were spread out over such a wide area on the windward side of the hill that it appeared to Cooper that he had found the bulk of the herd—or as many as could be found.

A number of sheep were trapped in snowdrifts more than belly deep, struggling weakly to free themselves from their icy prison—too dim-witted to have found their way onto the wind-protected leeward side of the hilltop, away from the worst of the drifting snow.

The sheepdogs waited and listened for their master's command, carefully eyeing the sheep that were spread out over at least a half-mile, as the woolly-clad animals tried to move through the snow, following in the footsteps of whatever trailbreaker was bold enough to take the lead. He sent both dogs—one in each direction—to flank the large herd and gather them in, urging them to move together in the direction of the snow-covered pastures near the barn and corrals. He waited until the first sheep came near and passed him on its way over the crest of the hill and down the leeward side toward home. As they moved past, the snowbound ewes struggled to free themselves from the drifts that held them, trying in vain to join the rest of the herd. A few managed to escape, but most were either too weak or too stubborn to move, and would have to wait until Banjo and Holly could move the main herd over the top of the hill before they could return to coax the stragglers out of their snowy trap.

In the end, Cooper had to unfasten his lariat from his saddle and throw a noose over five or six of the ewes—one at a time—and pull them free of the deep drifts. He sent Banjo out to the west one more time, just in case any more stragglers were lost in the brush. He waited ten minutes or more before deciding that any missing ewes were probably beyond help—or would find their own way back if they were lucky enough to have survived. He reined his horse around and called his dogs to start the sheep down the long slope to the northeast—back to the safety of the barn and corrals. Banjo came over the crest of the hill, driving a small flock of stragglers ahead of him. Once gathered into the lower pastures, the sheep could be fed and watched over day and night.

The snow had stopped falling altogether by the time the old sheepman pushed his herd across the wide vale and onto the broad, snow-covered pastureland near the barn. He left his dogs to watch the sheep, and to keep them from straying, while he rode to the barn and put his horse away in its stall. Deuce went immediately to the feeder after the saddle was removed, to finish the hay he had begun to eat a few hours earlier. Cooper walked back to the house to get a bite of food, and to talk with his wife before starting his next task. Jenny and the kids were gathered around the kitchen table, where they all waited anxiously for his return.

"How did it go?" Betty asked, as she poured a cup of strong, black coffee into Cooper's favorite mug and set it on the table.

"I think we got 'em all—most of 'em, anyway," Cooper said, hopefully. 'If there's any left out there in the brush, I don't know where they are—and neither does Banjo."

He pulled out his chair and sat down, rubbing his hands together vigorously, allowing the friction to warm his cold flesh.

"Got anything I can eat fast, before I hitch up the feed team?" he asked.

"I got up to fix your breakfast, but you were in a big hurry to get out the door," Betty complained. "How about a scrambled egg and bacon sandwich—it's already warming in the oven."

"Sure, that's fine," Cooper answered gratefully, taking a sip of hot coffee as he waited for his wife to feed him.

"The kids want to come out with you when you feed, Dad," Jenny said, prompting her dad to remember how much fun it had been to feed when the whole family was involved.

"I don't see why not," Cooper answered. "Plenty of room on the hay sled—everybody who wants to can go."

He finished up his sandwich, gulping down big bites, then pulled on his coat to go back into the cold air and bring his team of Clydesdales out of the barn. His big draft horses were waiting for him in their stalls, where they had stood idle for the past several weeks, except for an occasional trot around the corral. They were ready when he lifted their harnesses off the wall rack and placed the big, leather-clad and brass-knobbed collars over their massive heads—then began the work of fastening and adjusting their harnesses so that they could pull the weight of the wagon in unison—each gentle giant sharing the load evenly.

He rolled the big barn doors open wide, and took up the reins to guide his feed team out to the equipment shed where the winter hay wagon, equipped with heavy sled runners, had sat idle since the previous winter. The matched pair of shaggy-hoofed draft animals backed obediently into place, one on either side of the long, wooden wagon tongue, and stood quietly while the old rancher connected their harnessing into place for the day's work ahead. There was a lot of hay to be scattered—for sheep and for the cattle.

The steel-covered runners scraped across the gravel lined equipment shed as the big horses tugged the hay wagon out from under its cover and onto the open, snow covered ground. Cooper drove his team expertly around to the open end of the hay barn and slid it in close to the stack so that he could easily transfer the fifty pound bales onto the flat bed of the hay sled.

Betty and Jenny and all of the kids came out of the house, bundled warmly in heavy winter coats—ready to climb aboard for the first ride of the winter with the feed team. Cooper hurried to finish loading another twenty bales onto the wagon, stacking them in staggered tiers to provide seating for everyone.

Betty helped Jenny to climb up onto a bale of hay and get comfortable, then lifted little June up onto the wagon to sit beside Jenny as the older kids clamored aboard. Danny and Joey stood up front, one on either side of their driver, and took a good grip on the boards. They hung on tightly, leaned back far enough to see behind Grandpa Barnett's big body, and grinned at each other.

Cooper took up the reins, looked back to see that all the ladies were safely seated on their chosen bales of hay, then turned to his big horses and snapped their reins.

"Hang on, men," he instructed the boys, as the big Clydesdales leaned into their harnesses, and the heavy wagon lurched forward on its runners, making a crunching sound as it pressed its evenly-spaced tracks deeply into the new snow. The bells on the harnesses jingled and jangled, reminding the children of the sounds of Christmastime. Betty and Jenny each hugged a little girl tightly and smiled as they began their winter ride out onto the snow-covered pastures to help the old sheep rancher with his feeding chores.

"Get up, Road—get up there, Snow," Cooper called out to his big draft horses. They were the most powerful workers on his ranch by far, and he gave the giant horses the names of Roadblock and Snowplow when they first came to work on the Barnett Ranch twelve years earlier—proper names for horses that were almost as big as his pickup. The horses tossed their massive heads and bent their necks as they plodded up the gentle slope, pulling their heavy load toward the large gathering of hungry sheep.

It was the biggest adventure so far in any of the children's young lives—one that they would never forget—and one that none of them ever imagined they would have experienced.

The children stared in wonder as the big horses moved into the near edge of the herd, watching with rapt attention as the sheep parted to let the hay wagon slide into their midst. Betty stood up and pulled a large pocket knife from her coat pocket and began cutting the strands of heavy twine that bound the bales of hay together. All the children followed Jenny's lead, and joined in to help separate flakes of hay from the bales and toss them onto the snow-covered ground, where they were instantly surrounded by pushing and shoving animals—each one jostling for position—eager to get its rightful share.

"Grandma, look!" little June squealed. "They're eating it!"

The children continued to toss the hay onto the snow as more and more of the woolly animals surged forward to crowd around the feed wagon. The sheep followed along behind the wagon whenever they could not push their way into the center of a flock of hungry sheep that were already gathered tightly around a small pile of hay. Cooper urged his feed team on as they carved a wide circle in the snow, and his helpers dropped the small parcels of hay all along the broad arc of sled tracks as they laid down feed across the pastures.

When the bales had all been opened and the hay tossed to the ground, Cooper turned the sled back toward the barn and coaxed the big draft horses to pick up the pace, leaving the sheep behind. He pulled the wagon alongside a haystack and tied off the reins, allowing his horses to take a rest. It was the first time they had worked in nearly two months—since the first early storm of the winter season. The big, noble animals bobbed their heads and tossed their manes as they blew large puffs of steamy, warm breath through their nostrils and drew fresh air into their lungs.

The stallion pawed the gravely earth beneath the snow with its huge front hoof, loosening the frozen earth and releasing the odor of dirt mixed with manure into the open air.

Betty helped the girls climb down off the wagon and then offered a hand to help Jenny to steady her so that she wouldn't slip and fall as she slid down onto the snow-covered ground. The girls followed the same trail that they had broken through the snow from the house to the hay barn as they retreated back to the warmth of the house while Cooper loaded the wagon for the next trip out to the pastures. Danny and Joey were cold, too, but they stuck it out with the old rancher, nevertheless. They worked together to roll and tumble bales of hay toward the wagon—one at a time—so that Cooper could lift them into place. When Cooper was satisfied that he had enough feed to take care of the entire herd, he jumped down and invited the boys to come back into the house with him to warm up for a few minutes, and maybe get a hot drink in their bellies, before going out to finish the feeding.

Betty had a freshly-brewed pot of coffee ready, and hot cocoa for the kids, when the trio of hay buckers came through the back door. They left their coats on and drank their warm drinks as fast as they could, warming their hands on the porcelain mugs. When they were finished, Betty put her coat on again and followed her husband and the boys to help with the last of the feeding.

Jenny stayed behind with the girls, who had enough adventure for one day. It was a good day for Jenny—the kind of day that caused her to miss her life on the ranch.

"That was fun, wasn't it, Jenny?" Alice said, happily, her nose and cheeks still rosy from the cold winter air.

"It was fun," June added, enthusiastically, nodding her head at Alice and Jenny, as she kicked her dangling feet under the table and sipped her warm cocoa.

"Yes, it was," Jenny agreed, as she removed empty mugs from the table and set them in the sink, then watched through the window as her father took up the reins and urged his feed team forward again.

Her mom and the boys stood up front with her dad, hanging on to the top board on the front panel of the big hay wagon as it slid smoothly over the snow and moved back out toward the pastures.

It took the little ranch crew less than an hour to complete their second feed run and return to the barn.

The girls watched through the window for the hay sled to come into view, and they put on their coats to run back outside when Grandpa Barnett drove his team around the end of the hay barn and reined them in next to the long equipment shed. Betty stayed with the kids when they followed her husband into the barn to witness the unharnessing of the giant draft horses. June stood safely behind Betty, holding on to her arm, as she watched the huge Clydesdales being led back into their stalls.

Danny and Joey helped to coil the long harness reins for Grandpa Barnett so that he could hang them on their heavy wooden pegs.

"I hope it snows a lot," Joey said.

"Yeah? Why's that?" Cooper asked his little helper.

"So we can go on the hay sled every day," Danny answered for his little brother.

Jenny waited in the house, and thought about her afternoon drive back to Boise. She hoped all the highways would be plowed clear of snow and well sanded. The weekend had gone by too quickly again, and she caught herself thinking about her potential legal dilemma—she didn't know how she was going to deal with the issue of guardianship of Alice and June. She did know that she had been putting off any action to resolve it, and that it probably wouldn't help her in the end. The matter of Danny and Joey was not resolved, either, although she knew that

Lorraine would sign anything that was necessary to leave her boys on the ranch so they could be cared for by her parents—safely out of reach of their abusive stepfather.

She decided that she would have to have one last private conversation with her father before she left the ranch to make the afternoon drive home. She put on her heavy coat and walked out to the barn to spend a few minutes alone with her dad.

"Why don't you boys go on inside now," Jenny said to Danny and Joey, who were still hanging out in the barn with Cooper while he finished tending to his horses. "Grandma has your lunch ready, and I know you must be hungry after all that work."

Danny and his little brother looked to Cooper for permission to leave before starting toward the door, thinking that they must now be indispensable to him.

"That's a good idea, men—you go ahead, and I'll be along in a minute," Cooper said, supporting his daughter's instructions.

The boys left together, feeling some hunger pangs after the morning of hard work with Grandpa Barnett and the feed team. The two sheepdogs showed up just as Danny and Joey crossed the snow-covered ground to the house and waited by the back porch steps as the boys went inside.

"Has Mom talked to you about keeping the boys here for a little while longer?" Jenny asked her father.

Cooper nodded, looking carefully at his daughter's face and reading the concern that was written on it.

"They're no problem," he said. "They're as much help as your brothers were at that age, and more enthusiastic about it, I think. But we'll have to be sure we get everything signed that we need from their mother to get them into school next week. I suppose you and your mom will work that out, huh?"

"Yes, I'll call Lorraine tonight or early in the morning and let her know we'll be sending some papers," Jenny answered, a dejected look still etched onto her pretty face.

"You're worried about those girls, aren't you?" her father said.

"I don't know exactly what to do about them, Dad. I don't even know how to begin filing papers to get custody—especially since I'm not even a blood relative."

Cooper faced his daughter and held eye contact, making certain she was listening carefully and understood that he was very serious.

"You can't just hang onto those girls indefinitely, and not let the authorities know you have them, Jenny," he admonished. "If you can't find some legal help next week, you better let the child welfare people know you have them, and let them decide what's best."

Jenny bristled. She had heard too often about kids who had been bounced around from one foster home to another—brothers and sisters separated from each other—sometimes never to see each other again. She pushed her hands deep into her coat pockets and looked down at her feet, shaking her head solemnly.

"No, I won't do it, Dad. I promised them and I promised their grandmother—I'm going to keep them, no matter what it means."

"If you run off with those girls, you could risk getting put in jail—you know that," Cooper said, grimly.

"I know," Jenny acknowledged. She looked up at her father, her eyes brimming with tears. "I can't help that."

"I think you're asking for trouble."

"And I think that you would do the same thing if you were in my shoes. I think you're only telling me to give them up to the child welfare people because you're worried about me getting into trouble. And I also know that if you had them, there's not a chance that you would let anyone come here and take them away—that's what I think."

"How are you going to take care of them?" Cooper knew his daughter was as resolved as she was stubborn, and that she would not be dissuaded.

"I don't know—how am I going to take care of my baby when it's born?"

Cooper pushed the barn door open for his stubborn daughter, and Jenny walked quietly back to the house, arm-in-arm with her stubborn father.

CHAPTER SEVEN

WINTER SOLSTICE

Cooper Barnett was a reluctant mentor. He was more than happy to teach anyone what he knew about ranching, but when it came to formal schooling, he was lost—he had nothing to offer. He had always considered himself very lucky to graduate from high school in Fairfield at the end of his senior year. He always believed that his teachers knew he was never going to be anything but a sheep rancher—just like his father and grandfather—so the school just gave him a diploma out of sheer mercy for his classmates and teachers, and sent him home. Betty had always told him that the school wanted to get rid of him because he was too big and hungry to allow him to have another year of lunches in the school cafeteria—he was a one-man strain on the school budget.

In any event, Cooper learned to read pretty well, and to write just enough to get by, but his numbers had always been lacking. If it wasn't for Betty's mathematical skills, the ranch wouldn't operate and their bills would never get paid—much less ever show a profit.

Cooper wasn't the best example to Danny and Joey of how to get through school with a sense of pride intact—he was certain of that.

"Can you help me with this multiplication?" Danny asked, seated next to Cooper at the kitchen table after his third day at his new school.

"Um, maybe you better let Grandma help you with that," Cooper deferred. "I have to go check on the horses right now—she's better with numbers than I am."

"Can I come with you?" Danny asked.

"No," Cooper refused quickly. "No, you better stay here and finish your homework first. There's a lot to learn, and you need to give it all the time it deserves to make the best of it."

"How many years did you have to go to school," Joey asked, resting his elbows on the table next to his big brother. Joey's one-page homework assignment consisted of upper and lower-case alphabet letters, and nothing more.

"Not as many years as you're going to, that's for sure," Cooper said, trying to imagine each of the boys with a college education. "Now you get your work done, and I'll be back in a little while."

Cooper stayed busy in the barn as long as he could. He finally gave up and came back inside with an armload of firewood when it got too cold for him, and after it seemed that enough time had passed for Betty to help the boys finish their homework. He regretted that he could not be more help, but he decided that he would make up for his lack of tutoring ability by helping the boys learn a few practical things around the ranch. Maybe they would like to go horseback riding sometime, he thought. They seemed to really enjoy going out with the feed team in the morning to drop hay for the livestock.

"You look cold, Coop," Betty said. "Why don't you get a hot shower and a change of clothes—supper will be ready in half an hour."

Cooper was glad that his wife had taken care of everything to get the boys enrolled in school. He always felt outmatched whenever he had to talk to a school teacher or anyone in the administration office. Even when his own kids were going to school, it was Betty who dealt with everything from registration to helping with their homework, and reviewing their grades at the end of each term.

He only took fifteen minutes to shower and change, so he waited in his easy chair when he came back downstairs, and thumbed through the National Geographic Magazine he had already read many times.

"Supper's ready," Betty called from the kitchen.

"How did you do?" Cooper asked Danny, a bit self-consciously, when he sat down at the table next to the boys. "Homework's all done?"

"Yep," Danny answered, simply. "It's good."

"Grandma's real smart," Joey observed, adding his share to the conversation.

"Yep, she's always been real smart," Cooper agreed.

When she arrived back in Boise, Jenny delayed her attempts to make contact with a lawyer or anyone at the state child services office—she was still at a loss over what course of action might have any chance of success. It was near the middle of the week when she came home from work and found a business card from an attorney wedged into the front door jamb of Mrs. Rolfson's house. Her heart climbed into her throat as she considered every possible reason that a lawyer might have to come to the house, and decided that none of those reasons could be good. She stayed up late that night, wondering what would happen to her if she just took the girls and ran. It became obvious to her that she had no other place to go except back to the ranch in Camas County—and she wouldn't be hard to find there. Her only other option was to call the attorney who left his business card stuffed into a crack by the door—a card that left cryptic notice of the trouble that lay ahead. She gave up worrying and went to bed—it had been a long day and she was exhausted.

"You don't seem yourself today, Jenny," Joe Bannock observed, with some concern. "You havin' some trouble at home?"

"Sorry, Joe—I didn't know it was obvious," Jenny replied.

"That last breakfast order for a short stack and eggs over medium came out with four pancakes and scrambled eggs—didn't matter, though," Joe said, unperturbed. "The customer is a regular who doesn't really care how he gets his eggs—and he was grateful for the extra pancakes."

"I'll pay attention, Joe," Jenny promised. "I've just been too worried about the girls."

"Maybe it's time you got in touch with a lawyer," Joe advised, not knowing what else to say. "It couldn't hurt."

"A lawyer left his business card stuck in the door at my landlady's house yesterday. He wrote on the back that it was important that I contact him immediately. I'm afraid he may be from the state."

"What's his name—do you remember?" Joe inquired.

"It's right here," Jenny answered, pulling the business card from her blouse pocket, and turning the card so she could read the name. "Alvin Harker, Esquire it says."

"I remember a lawyer named Harker," Joe said, sounding upbeat at hearing the familiar-sounding name. "Used to come in here for lunch with some of his co-workers or colleagues, or whatever they call each other—don't think he ever did any work for the State."

"Do you think it's safe to call him?" Jenny asked, a bit fretfully.

"Let me ask around first—see if somebody knows anything about him," Joe said, suddenly feeling more helpful. "I'll let you know tomorrow morning—one more day shouldn't hurt."

"I don't know anyone," Jenny responded. "I'll have to find someone affordable—but someone who still knows what they're doing. I can't afford to wait any longer and risk the future of Alice and June on some incompetent shyster."

"I'll ask some of my customers about him," Joe offered. "We get all kinds of professional people who stop in here for lunch and breakfast."

Jenny felt better when she walked home with Alice and June after work. It was a comfort to the girls—and for Jenny, too—just to have the girls hang around at the cafe after Alice got out of school in the afternoon. Alice usually sat down in Joe's office with her little sister, and worked on any homework she might have for the day. Joe never seemed to mind. He was more than her boss—he was an ally—ready to step in and help her find the legal assistance she was going to need if she expected to have any chance of keeping the girls.

When she reached the front door, Jenny saw another card stuck in the door, and pulled it free as she unlocked the door to swing it open for the girls. It was from the same lawyer who came by the house the day before. She turned in over and read a short note on the back. *Jennifer Barnett—please call me as soon as possible. Very important. A.H.*

Jenny laid awake yet another night—catching an hour or two of sleep here and there—worrying about the dilemma she was caught up in, and with no easy way out. She got up early and woke the girls to get

Alice ready for school and get June dressed to spend the day coloring old menus at Idaho Joe's Cafe.

"Maybe I should take a couple of hours off today, and see if I can find a lawyer who can help me," Jenny suggested half-heartedly to her boss, hoping for his agreement and support—or a better suggestion.

"Maybe you should call the attorney who left his card on your door—that Harker fella," Joe returned, with a look of confidence on his face. "I found out he's a probate attorney—maybe he knows something about the girls' grandma and can offer some good advice."

Jenny perked up a little. She poured herself a cup of coffee and sat down with Joe at the end of the counter. The cafe was nearly empty—it was after the breakfast rush, and snow mixed with sleet was starting to come down hard, keeping people off the streets and driving them indoors.

"You don't think he came around to cause trouble, do you?" Jenny asked, hoping Joe might know more than he had told her.

"Well, you can't avoid him forever, and at least you know he doesn't work for the State, so why not give him a call?"

Jenny went into Joe's office and dialed the number from his phone, feeling some fear well up in her chest as she listened to the rings and waited for an answer. A woman's voice answered, and Jenny identified herself.

"Yes, Miss Barnett—Mr. Harker has been expecting a call from you," the pleasant woman greeted her cheerfully. "Hold for just a moment, please."

Alex Harker came on the line momentarily, and Jenny listened carefully for the next ten minutes or so, as the lawyer explained the reason for his visit to the Rolfson house. She hung up the phone, not yet fully comprehending everything she had heard.

"Is everything all right?" Joe Bannock asked when Jenny came back to the counter and sat down.

"I think so—I'm not sure," Jenny replied, numbly.

"Well, what did he say?"

"He said that Mrs. Rolfson called him when she was in the hospital and he went to see her—he's her attorney. He said she told him that she wanted her granddaughters to be left with me," Jenny explained, still stunned and unbelieving.

"Then it's as good as settled, isn't it?" Joe said, feeling triumphant for his part in urging Jenny to make the call.

"Not exactly—he said Dora Rolfson made out a crude, handwritten will and explained it to him when he visited her at the hospital. She even signed it—but he was never able to complete a formal will before she died, so a probate court will have to decide how to put her property in trust for Alice and June. The problem is, he says, that the probate court isn't where the custody issue for the children will be decided—he has to notify child services and let them know where the girls are now. I'm not sure what's going to happen next."

"Don't worry, Jenny. I've heard that Harker is very good at what he does. You're doing the right thing by putting your trust in him."

"I never really had any choice, did I?" Jenny capitulated.

Alex Harker arranged for a meeting on the following Monday morning at his office with a representative from the State of Idaho Child Services Agency. Jenny was to be there early with Alice and June, so that he could prepare her and make certain the girls were calm and unafraid. He assured Jenny that he would do everything possible to help her and Dora Rolfson's two granddaughters. In the meantime, he urged Jenny to go about her life as usual, and to make sure that Alice continued to go to school.

Jenny promised Joe that she would stay in town and work on Saturday so that she could take the day off on Monday to meet with Mrs. Rolfson's attorney and the child services people. She didn't know what to expect, and she really wanted to drive home to Camas County for the weekend and talk with her parents. There was no way to know how the meeting would go until it was over. Jenny stayed busy at work and at home for the next few days and hoped for the best.

She called her mother on Friday night and explained what was happening, knowing that her mother would offer her the best advice she could.

"I've never had to go through anything like this myself, Jenny," her mother began. "But your common sense should tell you that you should look your best, and make sure the girls are in their best dresses and shoes. And do their hair."

"Thanks, Mom," Jenny said, trying her best to sound appreciative.

She had hoped for something a little more substantive from her mother than simply being told to always wear clean underwear. It did make good sense, though, Jenny thought. Whoever was coming from the State to talk to the girls would probably have a sharp eye for things like scuffed shoes and dirty fingernails. It certainly wouldn't hurt to make sure they all looked their best. She had bought them new coats a month earlier—maybe it was time for new shoes and some special attention to their hair.

Monday morning came soon enough, and Jenny had the girls looking their best. As an afterthought, she had Alice bring her last few papers and test scores to impress the state worker with her good grades. They arrived at Alex Harker's office fifteen minutes earlier than he had asked—just in case they needed more time to be prepared for the meeting ahead.

"Thanks for being on time," Attorney Harker said, courteously, and with an air of genuine confidence, as he came out of his office to greet Jenny and the girls for the first time. "You all look very nice—why don't you come in and sit down. Mrs. Sorenson should be here in about thirty minutes."

He ushered his three clients into his spacious office, where Jenny and the girls settled into three of the four straight-backed office chairs arranged in a semi-circle around the front of his big mahogany desk.

"Now then," Harker began, drawing in a deep breath as he sat back in his high-backed swivel chair and straightened his shoulders. "I want you to just relax and let me take the lead in our conversation with Mrs. Sorenson. This is just a preliminary meeting today—so that she can see for herself that Alice and June are doing fine and in good hands."

Jenny nodded tentatively—trying to maintain her composure and not give away her nervousness. She kept her heavy woolen coat buttoned, hoping that her pregnancy would not be obvious.

Harker counseled Jenny for a few minutes—mostly to remind her to only answer the state worker's questions—nothing else. Too much said would create a disadvantage—Mrs. Sorenson would ask about the things she wanted to know. It wouldn't help to offer anything further.

When Vera Sorenson arrived, Jenny was a bundle of nerves, but she did her best to conceal it. She held the lawyer's words of advice foremost in her mind—she kept her mouth shut after saying hello, and waited until she was asked a question. From the expression on Mrs. Sorenson's face, she was not displeased with the appearance of the girls, or with the obvious affection they felt toward Jenny. Alice and June flanked Jenny's chair, both leaning in close to maintain contact with the foster mother of their choice.

The meeting lasted no more than twenty minutes, but it seemed an eternity to Jenny. Fortunately, there were no questions that Jenny found herself at a loss to answer. If Mrs. Sorenson asked a question that Harker believed was unfair to ask of his new client, he quickly intervened with an appropriate answer. It became clear before the interview had ended that this was not the first meeting between Alex Harker and Mrs. Sorenson. There was a mutual respect between the two—a professional courtesy that each had grown accustomed to extending toward the other.

Jenny was relieved beyond words when Mrs. Sorenson ended the interview and showed herself out, bidding a courteous goodbye to Alex Harker, and to Jenny and the girls. She wasn't sure what had just happened, but her feeling of desperation had vanished—at least for the moment. Alex Harker waited until he heard the outer door close that led from the reception and waiting room to the hallway before he spoke.

"That went well enough for a first meeting," Harker said, sounding upbeat and satisfied with the early results of the first contact with the State. He was clearly pleased.

"A first meeting?" Jenny asked, puzzled about what process might be involved to secure her appointment as a foster parent.

"Yes," Harker explained. "There will be a lot of paperwork to submit—information about you and the girls—and more meetings, background checks, reviews and interviews. Meanwhile, I'll talk to a judge about the handwritten, holographic will that Dora Rolfson prepared before she passed. It may carry some weight when a decision is made—it can't hurt."

Jenny didn't want to ask what might happen if the handwritten will was set aside by the courts and Mrs. Rolfson's wishes ignored. She especially didn't want to bring it up in front of Alice and June. She decided it would be best left in the able care of Attorney Harker.

"I can tell you that it made a difference that the girls were clean and well dressed," Harker added. "And it helped to bring along some of Alice's school papers—I should have thought to suggest it. And good performance in school is taken as a sign of discipline and stability in the home."

"Will you let me know when we need to come in again?" Jenny asked, waiting for Harker to excuse her before standing to leave.

"Of course," he answered. "And don't be surprised if Mrs. Sorenson shows up at the house some afternoon, just to look in on you and the girls—she'll be looking for a clean living environment, and to make sure there is food in the house."

"That's okay with me," Jenny said. "We eat well—and we keep a tidy house, don't we girls?"

Alice and June both agreed, nodding first at Jenny, and then at Alex Harker to affirm the claim of cleanliness and adequate food supplies.

Jenny felt enormous relief when she and the girls crossed the parking lot and climbed into the old Studebaker. The worn fabric upholstery and familiar interior comforted them like a second home. Funny how familiar surroundings gave a person a feeling of safety, Jenny thought, as she fired the ignition and turned the heater on to high.

"Girls," Jenny began, "what do you say we stop at home and fix some lunch, then Alice can go to school for the afternoon while June and I go into Idaho Joe's and see if we can get some cooking and coloring done?"

Jenny called her mother that evening and gave her the news about the meeting with Dora Rolfson's attorney and the lady from the child services agency. She was no more than a minute into the conversation when she wished that she had waited for the weekend to explain to her mother what transpired in the first meeting to discuss custody of the girls. Her mother asked more questions—then more after that—wanting to tie up all the information into a neat little bundle to satisfy herself that everything was in good order.

"Mom, the lawyer told me to relax and let him do his job—so that's what I'm going to do," Jenny finished, with a tone of finality. "I have to check on Alice to see if her homework is done—I'll talk to you tomorrow."

"I suppose that's best," Betty capitulated. "I'm sure he knows what he's doing."

"We'll try to get there Friday night—not too late, I hope. How are Dad and the boys doing?"

"The boys are in school," Betty said. "I'm not sure if they like it yet, but at least they haven't said they don't like it. I nearly have to drag them off the hay sled in the morning to get them ready for school—they follow your father around all the time. I'm surprised he hasn't stepped on one of them."

"That must make Dad feel good, huh?" Jenny reminisced, thinking about all the winter mornings she and her brothers would go out with her dad to feed the sheep together. "I'll bet he's glad to have help again."

"He enjoys it as much as the boys do," Betty confessed. "And they firmly believe that they're indispensable to him now."

"They're probably right." Jenny smiled into the phone. It could have turned out much differently, but as it was, her father was pleased to have kids around the ranch again. Maybe he wouldn't spend so much time in his easy chair now—reading and rereading old magazines.

The rest of the week passed quickly for Jenny, and without the constant worry that had plagued her days and interrupted her sleep at night. When quitting time came on Friday afternoon, she already had the car packed with the things they would need for the weekend, and they left straight from work so they could arrive at the ranch before bedtime. Jenny wanted to spend some time talking with her folks and the boys before they turned in for the night. She couldn't remember the last time she had been so eager to go home for a visit—other than Thanksgiving or Christmas. The children had altered her life and the lives of her parents so dramatically, that nothing would be the same.

Alice and June watched the illuminated highway ahead, counting every jackrabbit that crossed the road through the beam of the headlights until they got bored and began reciting children's poems they had learned from their grandma—just to pass the time. A two-hour drive took much longer for young kids than it did for adults. The miles seemed longer and the car seemed so much slower with every trip—it had been that way for Jenny, too, when she was a little girl. She was relieved that she didn't have to listen to Alice and June drive her crazy with constant appeals of "are we there yet?" the way she and her brothers had pestered her parents when they were kids.

Alice and June had so little stability in their young lives—first losing their parents a year earlier, and now their grandmother. They were content to spend all their time with Jenny and Grandma Barnett. The ranch was their refuge—their place of safety and reliability—it was their happy place.

The time passed quickly for Jenny—if not for Alice and June—and before long she turned the old sedan off the highway south of Bellevue, and onto the snow-packed gravel road that led west to the Barnett Ranch. After a few minutes, the beckoning lights of the old house glowed in the distance. Alice and June leaned forward, peering into the night and watching for Grandpa Barnett's dogs to come out and welcome them. Banjo and Holly were there at the end of the drive—worthy sentinels that they were—to bark a greeting and guide the old Studebaker up the drive to the two-story ranch house with its brick chimney that spouted wood smoke and filled the air with the familiar aroma of burning pine.

Betty was waiting at the back door, and swung it wide to allow two excited boys to bounce down the steps and across the frozen ground to greet Jenny and the girls as they exited the old sedan. They chattered nonstop as Jenny rushed all of the children up the steps and into the house—out of the freezing night air. Jenny's father waited in the background—just inside the kitchen doorway—where he stood and smiled approvingly at his daughter as she and her mom ushered the children into the warmth of the kitchen. Jenny reached out and tugged on her father's shirt sleeve—their equivalent of a father and daughter embrace.

"How ya doin', Dad?" Jenny asked, standing shoulder to shoulder with her father as they watched the kids jockey for position at the table to sample Betty's lemon meringue pie. Her sideways greeting to her dad was less intrusive—and more traditional among some ranch families—than the overly affectionate hugs and kisses that were so common among city folk and their suburban neighbors. He welcomed the tempered show of affection from his only daughter—it was just enough for the grisly old sheepman. He returned a faint, but genuine smile, and nodded—he was fine, thanks.

"Alice, do you want to go out with us and feed the sheep tomorrow?" Danny asked, excitedly. "There's still enough snow on the ground, so we use the big hay sled."

"Uh-huh, it's fun."

"I want to go, too," little June protested, thinking that her sister's invitation from Danny somehow excluded her.

"Don't worry, June-bug—everyone can go," Jenny assured, calming June's worries that she might be left behind. "But you'll have to get up early—Grandpa leaves with the feed team before the sun comes up."

"That means everyone into bed," Betty instructed. "Morning comes early."

Every child scrambled to carry their plates to the sink and be off to bed so that they wouldn't run the risk of being left behind in the morning. It was remarkable what an incentive a little thing like a hay ride could be to motivate a child to go to bed on time.

Jenny sat down at the kitchen table with her parents after the children were all tucked in for the night, and tried to explain all that had happened with the Boise lawyer and the woman from the State Child Services Agency. It gave her father enormous relief to learn that his daughter's future, and the welfare of Alice and June, was now in the hands of someone so capable and experienced in the law. Betty, however, wanted more details.

"When do you have to meet with the child services woman again?" she asked.

"I don't know, Mom," Jenny said. "Next week, I suppose—sometime after Mr. Harker finishes the paperwork she left for him to complete."

"Does she know you're not married?" Betty asked.

"I don't know, Mom—maybe."

"Well, what does she know about you?" Betty prodded. "Does she know you're pregnant?"

Jenny's face darkened, and wrinkled into a frown. She had deliberately covered her growing belly with a heavy winter coat while she was in Harker's office. She wasn't sure if he had noticed her condition, either.

"I guess you better go and see this lawyer fella again when you get back to Boise," Cooper advised, offering his first opinion of the conversation. "Tell him everything you can think of that might be important."

"That's right, Jen," her mom added. "You don't want that woman to think you're hiding something."

"I am hiding something, Mom," Jenny resigned. She couldn't imagine a scenario where the State of Idaho would welcome the chance to grant custody of two minor children to an unwed, pregnant fry cook with no home of her own, or a recent job history longer than two months.

"I'm going to bed," Cooper muttered, excusing himself from the table.

The giant Clydesdales were harnessed and hitched to the wagon before the sun rose, and Cooper had the hay bales stacked as high as he dared without jeopardizing the safety of his passengers and helpers. He didn't mind the extra time it took to go back into the house to swallow a slice of toast and swill down some hot coffee before helping to herd the kids out the door and get them loaded onto the hay sled. The sheep would still be waiting—they didn't have a better offer of a free meal anywhere else.

The sleigh bells filled the air with a metallic, resonant tone when Roadblock and Snowplow shook their handsome heads—forelegs prancing in place as they waited impatiently and anticipated the moment when their driver would start them on their way around the barn and onto the snow-covered pastures. It was an experience that Alice and June had been looking forward to all week long, and one that was becoming a tradition for Danny and Joey—one that bonded them closer to Grandpa Barnett a little more each day.

The weekend went by so quickly for Jenny that she almost couldn't believe that Sunday afternoon had already arrived and that it was time to drive home to Boise again. Alice and June sat quietly at the kitchen table with Grandma Barnett when Jenny began to gather her belongings and set them on a chair next to the back door—they knew the time was drawing near when they would have to carry their things out to the car and reluctantly climb inside for the ride home. If children were allowed to make all the decisions—rather than adults—life would be way different, Alice thought.

"Can't we wait and go home tomorrow, Jenny?" Alice pleaded.

"I wish we could, Alice," Jenny said, fully understanding the young girl's reluctance to leave so soon. "It seems like we just got here, doesn't it?"

"There's only one more week of school before the Christmas break," Betty cheerfully reminded the children. "Then you can spend the whole week here, if Jenny can stand to be without you for a few days while she goes back to work."

Alice was all smiles. It was a fantastic idea, and she welcomed the suggestion of a winter holiday at the sheep ranch. June was more concerned for Jenny's feelings, and thought she might be sad if she were left alone for too long.

"I'll stay will you, Jenny," the precocious child assured. "You need somebody to color the menus, so they'll be pretty for your customers, and I'll help you buy Christmas presents for everybody."

"Come on, you two," Jenny laughed. "Go get your things together and let's get ready to go home. I don't want to have to drive after dark again."

Almost from the time Jenny turned the car onto the blacktop and began the drive north, the girls started to fuss, and remained in their difficult moods all the way home. Jenny felt much the same way—she didn't relish the idea of having to meet with Mrs. Sorenson again, and of having to disclose all of the gritty details of her personal life. The thought of having to answer all of the woman's prying questions put her in a bad mood. It didn't seem fair that she would have to undergo so much scrutiny. After all, who else would be better to take care of Alice and June, she wondered.

Jenny appeared tired when she showed up for work on Monday morning. The dark circles under her eyes told of yet another sleepless night—one of worry and concern. She took a break after the breakfast crowd left the cafe, and retreated to Joe's office to place a phone call to Alex Harker.

Harker picked up his phone immediately upon learning that the incoming call was from Jenny Barnett. He seemed to be in an extremely good mood.

"Hello, Jenny—thanks for calling," Harker began. "I have some good news for you."

"Yes?" Jenny inquired, perking up at the sound of her lawyer's upbeat tone.

"Our case worker called me late Friday afternoon—I tried to call you but I guess you had already left for the weekend," the lawyer continued. "She told me she was taking two weeks of her vacation through the holidays—she'll call after the first of the year."

"That's great," Jenny responded, truly relieved that the next two weeks would be free from the prying eyes and harsh judgments of state workers like Vera Sorenson—no matter how well-meaning they thought they might be. She was feeling guilty, however, for not coming clean with Alex Harker about her pregnancy.

"Mr. Harker," she began to apologize, "I don't know if I ever told you that I'm expecting a baby," she abruptly confessed, knowing full well that she had not.

"Yes, I did know that," Harker replied, matter-of-factly. "Mrs.

Rolfson told me—and she told me that you weren't married."

"That's not going to matter to the State?" Jenny asked, somewhat surprised.

"Oh, it may," Harker said, answering honestly and practically. "But let's cross that bridge when we come to it, shall we? Let's show them all the positive things about you first."

"Is there anything that I should be doing until we hear back from the State?" Jenny queried.

"Just go home and have a nice Christmas holiday with your family, that's all," Harker replied, pleasantly. "There's no need to worry about anything until we know if there's something to actually worry *about*—that's what my grandmother used to tell me, anyway."

"Good news?" Joe Bannock asked, leaning against the doorway to his office with a fistful of colored menus in his hand.

"I hope so," Jenny said, breathing a big sigh of relief. "I didn't tell the lawyer that I was pregnant, but he said he already knew."

"You didn't tell me, either," Joe said with a little smirk. "But I figured it out all by myself—I've got eyes. Most of your body was slender and your belly was growing, but I never saw you eat very much while you worked. Most of the cooks I've hired in the past used to stuff their faces during their work shifts—some of them used to waddle out of here like danged hippos."

"I can't imagine anyone having the time to eat all day when they're working at Idaho Joe's," Jenny laughed. "We're usually too busy to eat."

"It's busy now that you're here," Joe praised. "I haven't always been proud of some the slop that's come out of my kitchen—and my customers haven't always found it as tasty as it is now, or even palatable, for that matter."

Jenny gave Joe a smile of gratitude. She knew how lucky she was to have a good job—the economy was reeling from the beginnings of a recession, and a lot of hard-working people were being laid off from their jobs.

"I hate to ask this, Joe," Jenny uttered meekly, "but I wonder if I might have a couple of days off around Christmas—just so I can take the girls down to the ranch for the holidays. They're counting on it so much."

"And you're not?" Joe said, chuckling a bit to see how concerned his cook was about leaving him short-handed during the holiday week.

"Of course," Jenny admitted with a disarming smile. "I'm looking forward to spending some time at home with my folks, too."

"Well, if you wouldn't mind working this weekend, and up until noon on Christmas Eve, you can take off the rest of the week and come back after New Year's. How does that sound?" Joe bargained. "We usually get a pretty good crowd of Christmas shoppers, so if you can help me out until then, I can get by until you get back."

"You've got a deal!" Jenny quickly agreed, beaming at the prospect of telling the girls that they could count on a whole week at the Barnett Ranch over Christmas.

She forgot to mention to Joe that Alice would be out of school for the holidays beginning Friday afternoon, and that she and June would have to occupy their time in his office for the next few days.

"And don't worry about the girls," Joe said, seeming to read her mind. "They won't be in the way, and I'm sure they'll find plenty to do. Maybe we can plug in a small television and let them watch cartoons in the office on Saturday morning."

Saturday turned out to be a slow day at the cafe after the breakfast and lunch crowds came and left, so Jenny was able to take off early and do some Christmas shopping. It was a bit tricky, keeping the girls distracted while she whispered to a sales clerk, asking for her purchases to be wrapped up before Alice or June could see them. Even the gifts for her parents and the boys had to be kept hidden from view—Jenny knew what a temptation is was for young mouths to blabber, and she didn't want the boys to have their Christmas ruined because Alice and June couldn't keep a secret.

"Today is winter solstice," Jenny told the girls after dinner, as she checked the magnetic calendar on the refrigerator door. "It's the shortest day of the year—and the longest night. You won't have to wake up too early, and I don't have to go to work until nine."

The Lamb Cart 127

The girls grew more excited by the day as they counted down to Christmas Eve, always eager to bounce out of bed in the morning and tell Jenny how many more days were left before they could make the drive back to the Barnett Ranch and the warmth of Grandma Betty's brightly decorated kitchen. They could almost smell the cinnamon rolls baking in the oven.

The big day arrived none too soon for Jenny—the girls had nearly driven her crazy with their constant daily chatter about Christmas at the ranch, and how much they hoped there would still be a few ornaments left for them to hang on the tree. Jenny had spent a few Christmas holidays away from home during the past five or six years, and had nearly forgotten how much it meant to be with family at this time of year. She was looking forward to the trip home as much as the girls were—maybe more.

The drive to the ranch on Christmas Eve went by quickly, with Jenny and the girls all chattering like magpies for the entire trip—their excitement couldn't be subdued. For Jenny, it was like being a child again.

There was plenty of daylight left when they rolled into the ranch in the early afternoon. Dogs and kids surrounded the old Studebaker as Jenny opened the door to get out, and all the children were talking at the same time—too fast to be understood.

Jenny settled into the kitchen with her mom while the kids all bundled up and rode with her dad on his afternoon feeding rounds. She couldn't remember the last time she felt so much at home. It must be a part of growing up, she thought. Her parents acted much the same as they always had—unchanged over the years—so it must have been her own perceptions that changed, Jenny decided.

She took advantage of the time the kids were out with her dad and the feed team, and accepted her mom's offer of help to wrap up gifts for the kids and hide them away on a shelf in the broom closet. She checked the trunk of her car again to be sure the gifts for her parents were out of sight, and would not be discovered before morning.

Betty found a box of old-fashioned Christmas ornaments and set them aside for Alice and June to hang on the tree when they returned from helping Grandpa Barnett with his afternoon chores.

"Thanks, Mom," Jenny said, sincerely. "They were hoping that there would be something left for them to decorate."

"It wouldn't be Christmas without helping to decorate the tree, would it?" Betty acknowledged.

Jenny knew that her mother was dying to hear any news of her progress in securing guardianship of the girls, so she didn't keep her waiting. She explained that the case worker took two weeks of vacation time and had postponed any further meetings until after the first of the year.

"Mr. Harker said that it was a good sign—the woman couldn't have been too concerned for the girls' welfare if she was so willing to put off any further contact for a few more weeks. It was almost as good as an endorsement of my parenting skills, he told me."

Betty accepted her daughter's explanation—at least for the moment—and didn't press for any more information. Besides, it was Christmas, and no time for unnecessary worrying.

Alice and June came bounding through the back door, so excited to talk about how the sheep were so hungry they crowded up close to the hay sled and the some of the hay the kids tossed to the ground landed on top of the sheep and covered their woolly backs and heads with alfalfa leaves. Betty and Jenny listened patiently until the girls ran out of steam and asked if there was something to eat.

"We're hungry, Jenny," little June announced, hoping something tasty would appear on the table, simply for the asking. It usually did. The girls were still snacking on Christmas cookies and hot cocoa when Danny and Joey came through the back door, stomping snow off their oversized rubber boots.

"Wash up first," Jenny said.

The three older children all rushed to the kitchen sink and bathroom wash basins to soap up their faces and hands, but little June held her ground.

"I'm clean," she stated flatly, reluctant to give up her place at the table as she looked first to Jenny and then to Grandma Barnett, and then back again to Jenny. "I washed yesterday."

Betty soaked a washcloth at the kitchen sink and brought it to the table to wipe June's hands, face, and ears, so that the three-year-old wouldn't have to surrender her claim on her favorite spot at the table.

"Where's Dad?" Jenny asked her mother, after the children had been inside for the better part of an hour.

"He was in the barn—he told us to come inside," Danny said.

"He'll be along in a minute, I expect," Betty said. "He takes his time when he's taking care of his horses."

"Should we go get him?" Joey asked.

"No, you stay here, Joey—he'll be here soon."

Cooper finished saddling Deuce and rode out without saying anything to his wife—he had noticed a dead ewe when he was out with the feed team—lying among the brush on the hillside above the pasture, and he saw the crows beginning to gather. It was too cold for the carcass to rot and begin to stink—if it hadn't been for the circling birds, he might not have seen it at all. If he didn't get it buried, it would certainly draw coyotes in, and that was the last thing he needed when his sheep were all gathered into one open pasture like a giant predator's buffet.

"Let's go, dogs—stay with me." Cooper gave his familiar command to his sheepdogs and they ran out ahead of him, turning to look back from time to time, just to be certain he hadn't altered his course as he spurred his horse up the long hillside. He had his Winchester in his saddle scabbard and he carried a shovel in his hand—equally prepared for coyotes and a burial. He located the spot where the crows were gathering—it wasn't hard to spot the big, black birds with their wide wingspans, new arrivals circling overhead as three or four were already vying for position as they picked at the eyes and tongue of the unfortunate ewe.

"Get 'em, Banjo! Get 'em outta there!" Banjo and Holly made quick work of chasing the reluctant crows away from the carcass. The birds hovered overhead and crow-hopped around on the snow a few yards away, waiting for the dogs to get bored and go away. The circling birds were going to be too much of a nuisance for Cooper to dig in the hard, rocky soil and bury the sheep on the hillside, and they were certain to attract the attention of any predators in the area.

Cooper uncoiled his lariat and tied the lasso around the sheep's hind legs, then let out about fifteen feet of rope and wound the other end around his saddle horn to drag the dead animal back down to the barn. The trail in the snow would be easy to follow for any hungry coyote, but it would have to be very hungry to venture close to the house and barn—it wouldn't like the smell of horses and dogs and humans and wood smoke. It would probably lose its nerve and look elsewhere for a meal. He could bury it behind the barn, in soil that would be easier to get his shovel into.

"Where have *you* been all day?" Betty asked her delinquent husband when he came back into the house.

"Outside."

"I know that—but what were you doing out there all day?"

"Chores."

"It's starting to snow," Danny said, smiling as he delivered his brief weather report. "Just in time for Christmas, huh, Grandma?"

"Just in time," Betty agreed. "Let's get cleaned up now—and then it's off to bed for all of you—Santa doesn't come if any child is awake."

The boys hurried to put on their pajamas and climb into their bunk beds—Joey on the top bunk and Danny on the bottom. Jenny allowed the girls to stay up a little longer, just so they could help Grandma Betty hang the last of the tree ornaments—tiny wooden rocking horses, carved wooden polar bears and penguins with hand-painted red neckties, and a miniature gingerbread house adorned with tiny candy canes on either side of its entry door. It was almost more excitement than Alice and June could bear.

"Can we stay up and wait for Santa?" Alice asked.

"We'll be real quiet," June whispered. "We'll hide—he won't hear us and we won't say anything."

"He'll know you're awake, June-bug," Jenny said, scoffing at the notion that two little girls could trick the jolly old elf. "He always knows—you can't fool Santa—now scoot."

Christmas morning dawned clear and blue, and with four inches of new snow on the ground, roof, haystacks and treetops—creating a winter wonderland as beautiful as any scene that ever graced the front of a Christmas card. Cooper was up early, and built a blazing fire in the living room fireplace before going out to make his feeding rounds an hour early. The boys wouldn't be disappointed for long, once they saw their presents under the tree—and Cooper knew they wouldn't miss the afternoon ride with the feed team.

Jenny couldn't remember a happier time than the Christmas day she spent with her folks and four very lucky children at the Barnett Ranch. Even the best holidays she could recall from her youth were no better, and the kids were thrilled with their gifts of books and games and cap guns and tea sets. They even liked their gifts of new winter apparel—Joey was ecstatic when he unwrapped a three-pack of new woolen socks.

The next days slipped by so quickly that no one could remember what happened to the time. Alice and June were unhappy about loading their things into the car for a trip to Boise.

"Can't we stay one more week?" Alice implored, hoping that Jenny would come to her senses and decide to stay with her parents for a while longer. "There's nothing to do in Boise."

"You have school in Boise," Jenny retorted, firmly. "And I have to work, so we can eat."

"Grandma has lots of food," June attempted to reason. "She'll let us eat here if we stay with her."

"We have to go home, June-bug," Jenny said with a sigh. "I don't want to leave any more than you do, but we have to go."

The girls began to shed tears of protest—first Alice, and then June. They didn't understand why adults didn't have more control over their own decision making. Reluctantly, they climbed into the car with Jenny.

The car battery was drained low from several days of sitting idle in the cold weather, and the engine refused to turn over from the weak jolt it received from the ignition system. The girls cheered when the car failed to start, and were crestfallen when Grandpa Barnett pulled a set of jumper cables from behind the seat of his pickup and raised the hood of the old Studebaker.

They were quiet for the entire trip home—reveling in their fresh memories of a wonderful Christmas—content as they relived the adventures and joys of the past week on the ranch. There was no place on earth that they would rather be. It was the safest place they had ever lived—and the happiest.

CHAPTER EIGHT
PANDORA'S ILLS

Vera Sorenson wasn't pleased when she learned about Jennifer Barnett's pregnancy soon after she returned from her vacation.

"How is she going to manage a job, and a new baby, and take care of two young girls at the same time?" she demanded, sitting across the desk from Alex Harker as she voiced her displeasure at having such an important matter concealed from her during the earlier interview. "And all without the help and support of a husband. What kind of home life will that be for those girls?"

"She takes very good care of those girls, Mrs. Sorenson, and you know it," Harker rebutted.

"Where do they stay when she's at work? Who takes care of them?" She insisted upon learning every detail now that she knew she had been kept in the dark about several critical details of the case.

"They go with her—they have a little day care office set up where she works, with books and television and everything," Harker responded. "She doesn't work on weekends, and she spends all of her time off with them."

"So the three-year-old goes to the cafe with her every morning, and spends her entire day in the back of a kitchen—is that what I am to understand?" the self-righteous and ill-tempered social worker charged. "This isn't going to be allowed."

"First of all, she isn't going to need a husband for financial support," Harker defended, regaining his composure after being so sternly berated. "She'll have ample financial assistance from the trust, and a home to live in as long as she cares for the girls until the youngest one turns eighteen—maybe longer."

"What about the baby that's on the way? Who's going to help with that, and who's going to take care of the girls while she's dealing with a new infant?"

Vera Sorenson had always believed in the possibility of a perfect world—one in which every difficulty that might arise in the day-to-day challenges of family life would be met with a predetermined course of action, outlined by the State and imposed upon its citizens whether they liked it or not. A mandatory solution imposed by her department is what was needed here, she thought—one that would bear a stamp of approval from State of Idaho. A government guideline for every occasion was her answer to everything that was wrong in the world.

Alex Harker saw things quite differently, and he met the case worker's criticism with stubborn defiance.

"Now you listen to me, Vera Sorenson," he said, pointing his finger into the air to make his point, but stopping short of poking it in the direction of her reddening face. "If you try to take those girls before the probate court can finish its work and give its ruling, I'll have the story on the front page of every paper from Boise to Twin Falls—and you and your department will be vilified for it. Your boss might not think much of your judgment then."

"Those two orphans are the responsibility of the State of Idaho now, and custody is a separate issue," the indignant case worker insisted. "They're my responsibility."

"Those girls are better off where they are than they would be in a foster home, and they're in no danger. You know that as well as anyone. Just leave it alone for awhile, will you?"

"We'll see," Mrs. Sorenson answered, stiff-lipped in her resistance to the lawyer's sensible suggestion.

Sorenson abruptly got up from her chair and saw herself out, appearing every bit like a woman who was prepared to launch a personal crusade—or at least to engage in a test of wills and the knowledge of the law with Alex Harker.

Harker stared blankly at the door that closed behind the irascible woman, and realized that he would have to brace himself against a potential onslaught of challenges from the State. He would have to be very careful to avoid any missteps in his procedures, or any lacking in Jennifer Barnett's ability to care for the Rolfson girls. He picked up his phone and pressed a single button to summon his secretary from the outer office.

"Call Jennifer Barnett, would you, Susan," he requested. "Check my calendar and set up a meeting as soon as possible."

There was nothing that Attorney Harker wanted more than to put the overbearing case worker in her place. It was true that they had enjoyed a mutual respect over the years—but now she was flexing her authoritative muscle and it was going to make his work more difficult.

Jenny left for the ranch with the girls immediately after her Friday afternoon meeting with Alex Harker. He had advised her strongly not to let the girls out of her sight, and to be gone as much as possible from the house in Boise until he could try to arrange for a temporary custody hearing. Jenny had no problem heeding his advice. She preferred to be with her family, and to spend some time with Lorraine's boys. Traveling to Camas County every weekend and coming home late Sunday was fine with her—and more than fine with Alice and June.

"I suppose we may as well leave some of your clothes at Grandma's house, since we'll be spending so much time there—what do you think?" she asked the girls.

"Yay!" the sisters chimed. "Does that mean we're going to live there all the time?"

"No, it just means we'll leave a few changes of clothes there," Jenny answered, sensibly, hoping to keep the girls from getting too excited. "We'll come every weekend that we can."

"Okay," Alice said. She was happy with the arrangement, and hoped they could always spend their weekends at the Barnett Ranch.

Betty Barnett warmed up supper for the three travelers when they arrived at the ranch after dark, and they spent the rest of the evening talking while the kids watched television for a couple of hours before bedtime.

"The baby is due in less than eight weeks, isn't it?" Betty asked her daughter. "Have you thought about where you're going for the delivery?"

"What hospital, you mean?" Jenny replied. "I was thinking about the Blaine County Hospital in Hailey. It's as good as any, and the closest to the ranch."

"Your dad will be glad to hear that you'll be staying here for awhile," Betty said. "You'll be glad, too, once you realize how much help you're going to need."

Jenny took some time for herself on Saturday, and left the kids at the ranch while she drove into Fairfield to visit some old school friends and pick up a few things at the market for her mother. She avoided the stares of some women in the market, and on Main Street outside the beauty salon. She knew that no one could keep a secret in a town the size of Fairfield, and she knew that her pregnancy was more grist for the local gossip mill.

The Wild Rose Hair Salon was gossip central for the women who lived in and around the small town of Fairfield. The sign in the window offered expert manicures and pedicures, in addition to cut, curl, color and perms, but Phyllis Hanson only gave a few manicures a month, and always to the same customers. Her last one was for the mayor's wife, and the one before that was for the county clerk. No one in town could recollect if she had ever given a pedicure. Most of the ranch women who lived around Fairfield had hard-worn, calloused feet, and wouldn't think of letting anyone see them, much less touch them—not even their own husbands. Still, it was a good place to catch up on all the latest town news and gossip.

"I don't understand why that woman doesn't move her hair salon to a bigger town, so she can have a larger audience to listen to her gossip," Betty said to her husband, who was barely listening out of one ear.

She walked to the table, filled his coffee cup, and stood next to him, waiting for a response.

Cooper finally looked up from his newspaper when his wife wouldn't go away. "What? Oh, Phyllis Hanson, yeah. Well, what's so surprising about gossip in a hair salon? You always said she's been a storyteller since High School," he added, looking up at his angry wife as she loomed over him with a pot of hot coffee in one hand.

"Why can't you just ignore her?" Cooper suggested, leaning back a little more in his chair to escape his wife's disapproving glare. It was the only thing he could think to say.

"Because she's talking about our daughter, Coop—*your* daughter. Don't you care?"

"Of course I care, Betty, but you can't stop people from talking—even if they do twist the facts."

"*Twist* them? Phyllis Hanson *fractures* the facts. She has an amazing talent for it. The woman only needs to speak two words to tell three lies."

Cooper chuckled. "That *is* a special talent."

"It isn't funny, Cooper," Betty chastised.

"No," he agreed, solemnly, as he folded his paper and left it on the table. "No, it isn't." He was trying hard to take his cues from his wife's mood, but he wasn't sure that he could keep up.

"I wish someone would put her in her place."

"Well, what do you want me to do about it?" Cooper defended. "I've never been able to stop gossips and liars."

Betty walked to the kitchen table, drying her hands on a cotton dish towel, as she hovered over her husband again. Cooper had to lean back in his chair to look up into his wife's fierce blue eyes.

"I want you to get involved in Jenny's predicament, and see what you can do to help her" Betty replied sensibly. "She's going to need some help when the authorities get more involved and start questioning where all these kids came from," she added, placing both hands on her hips as she continued to look down on her husband, just to keep him locked in place until she finished making her point.

"Well, it does look like a danged orphanage out here ever since she came home" Cooper admitted. "But the kids seem to like it here, and I expect it's the first time in their young lives that they haven't had to miss a meal, or wonder whether they'll have a warm bed to sleep in at night."

Betty was exasperated with her husband.

"That's not the point, Coop. Sooner or later someone from Child Welfare Services is going to show up here, and what will we tell them?"

"We could tell them that we have plenty of kids, and that we don't need any more," Cooper responded, believing he had arrived at a clever, if not practical, solution.

Betty draped the wet dish towel over his head and walked out of the kitchen. It was the best weapon in her arsenal against her husband's insensibilities and lack of good judgment. A wet towel over his head always worked to render him helpless.

"You don't have to be so casual about it," Betty scolded as she walked out of the room.

To his enormous relief, his wife changed the subject when she came back to the kitchen, and began to talk about Danny and Joey.

"There's a parent-teacher meeting at the elementary school Wednesday night—do you want to come with me?" Betty asked, hoping that Cooper might show an interest in the boys' schooling.

"No, I don't suppose I will," Cooper declined.

"It wouldn't kill you to go to a function at the school once in a while, you know," Betty chided. "You haven't been asked to go in a very long time."

"That's because our kids haven't gone to school in a very long time," Cooper retorted. "That's why."

"Well, we've got some more kids in the house now, so you might want to learn how to take an interest again."

Cooper could sense a confrontation brewing, so he decided to leave it alone and try to get past the middle of the week without being asked again. He despised the functions at the school—he never liked them when he was a student, and he liked them even less as an adult. All except for the Christmas plays, which could be entertaining if one of the wise men lost his beard or tripped on his robe. He liked to listen to the kids sing, too—he knew they practiced hard to memorize all the lyrics to so many Christmas carols. Other than that, Cooper didn't care if he ever saw the inside of a school again.

Another weekend sped by and Jenny was gone again with the girls. She was moody on her drive back to Boise, and wanted badly to find a simple solution to the problem of custody over Alice and June. She thought it was about time to give up her job at Idaho Joe's and spend all her time at the Barnett Ranch, but she knew that it wouldn't be fair to her parents to bring five hungry mouths to the table—soon to be six—and not contribute to their financial support. There was no possibility that she could get work in Fairfield—the town was simply too small. Working somewhere closer, like Ketchum or Sun Valley, was out of the question, too. At least until after her baby was born. She realized that she was going to be asking a lot of her mother—and her father—to expect that they should help her with so many children, and only one of them her own.

Some good news came on Monday morning when Alex Harker called and said he had been granted an order shortening the time for a temporary custody hearing, and that the hearing was scheduled for the following Thursday. Jenny would have to take the morning off work—it seemed like she was doing that so often lately. She was nervous all week in the time leading up to the hearing, and near panic whenever she imagined that the judge might order that the girls be turned over to the State.

Mr. Harker had her drive to his office first, rather than meet him at the court house. He asked her to ride with him so he could talk to her along the way, and put her and the girls more at ease. Alice understood why they were going before a judge that morning. If her little sister understood any of it, she didn't seem the least bit worried—June believed that Jenny could take care of everything and never let anything bad happen.

Jenny wished that it were that easy. The judge seemed to be a fair and thoughtful man, and asked Alice and June how they liked staying with Jenny. When the State's attorney and Mrs. Sorenson laid out their opposition to granting temporary custody to Jenny, citing her advanced pregnancy and marital status, and soon she would have no job or other visible means of support. Jenny's heart sank and she began to lose confidence. There would be no denying the allegations.

To Jenny's surprise and delight, Alex Harker immediately rebutted the case worker's assertions and urged the judge to allow the children to stay with Jenny long enough for him to conclude his probate work on Dora Rolfson's estate.

"There is a very good chance, your honor, that Jennifer Barnett will have a home and all the financial support she needs for the foreseeable future, once the disposition of Dora Rolfson's assets has been adjudicated," he assured the child custody court. "Her handwritten will made clear her express desire for Miss Barnett to be the guardian and main caregiver for her granddaughters."

The judge agreed to take the State's urgings under advisement, but for the present, he ordered that the children remain with Jennifer Barnett.

"You understand, Miss Barnett, that you are not to leave the State of Idaho with the minor children, and must continue to see that the oldest girl stays in school—am I understood?" the judge questioned, prior to granting his order of temporary custody.

"Yes, your honor," Jenny replied, rising from her seat in a show of respect.

Vera Sorenson stopped Alex Harker and Jenny in the hallway outside the courtroom, with the State attorney by her side.

"We have the right to continue to stop by and see how the girls are doing, and to be sure they're being cared for properly," the woman insisted. "That means you can expect to see me every week or so."

"Not a problem, Mrs. Sorenson," Harker agreed, trying not to sound condescending. "You'll find Miss Barnett to be very cooperative."

He put his hand on Jenny's back and ushered her away from the woman and out of the courthouse quickly, before Jenny could attempt to say anything in her own defense to Mrs. Sorenson.

"The judge made his ruling, Jenny," Harker reminded her. "And here's the important thing—they can't just come and take the girls now, or they'll be in violation of the court order. They won't do that."

"Does that mean we're out of the woods?" Jenny asked. She began to breathe easier.

"It means that I have a lot of work left to do on this probate matter. The hand-written will by itself probably won't be adequate—it was only witnessed by me, and it required two witnesses. I'll have to publish notices in the newspaper for a month, and there's a lot of other stuff I have to do. I don't think anyone is going to challenge it, so it's mostly the law and formalities that I'm dealing with. I'll contact you when it's time to go back in for our next hearing."

"You've been right about everything so far," Jenny said. "I don't see any reason to start doubting you now."

"Wise choice, Jenny," Harker responded, smiling confidently. "You better get back to work now—wouldn't want you to lose your job."

Jenny didn't waste any time in going back to work. She took both girls with her instead of dropping Alice off for a half day of school. Vera Sorenson didn't waste any time getting back to work either—she called the State Attorney's office and conferred with one of the senior lawyers that she had worked with on many cases over the years.

"Tell me what constitutes a moral turpitude issue," she asked. "If a female petitioner for guardianship is seeking custody of minor children who are not blood relatives, and she is several months pregnant, *and* unmarried.—what kind of case can we make that she is unfit to be a foster parent?"

"A very good one," was the lawyer's succinct reply.

She was pleased—it seemed to block any avenue that Jennifer Barnett might follow to gain custody of the Rolfson girls. Few child custody judges would consider allowing unrelated minor children to be taken into such an environment, especially given the Barnett woman's short time on the job, and with no home of her own. Vera was confident that she could have the girls removed from their current home within a few weeks—when Alex Harker was least expecting it.

Jenny tried not to worry too much about her legal issues—there wasn't much she could do about it anyway. She kept herself and the girls as busy as she could every day so that there wouldn't be time to fret over things that were outside of her control. She hoped that Alex Harker could resolve the Rolfson probate matter quickly—not because she wanted access to Dora Rolfson's money—but because she would have to quit her job before long, and it was going to be very important that she be able to demonstrate that Alice and June could be cared for properly, and without financial strain.

The weighty problems of the outside world melted away when she was at home on the Barnett Ranch—it was a refuge from everything that troubled her, and from every person who threatened to take the girls away.

Betty hung up the telephone on the kitchen counter and turned to her husband, visibly troubled by the phone call.

"That was Sue Carver from the elementary school," she said, as Cooper looked up and listened intently. "There was someone at the school today who was asking all around town about Jenny and the girls—someone from the State—and they know all about the boys, too."

For the first time, Cooper felt a sense of urgency and vulnerability. His family lacked any means of protection against a raft of lawyers from the State of Idaho. He had always heard that the wheels of government turned slowly, but when they did, they ground everything beneath them to dust—there was no fighting it if the Child Services Agency was determined to take the children away.

When their Jenny arrived from Boise with the girls that night, Cooper and Betty were both anxious to talk with her about the snoops who came to town. Jenny calmed her parents with the news of the temporary custody order, and assured them that she had been granted temporary custody until she had a chance to demonstrate her ability to care for Alice and June on a permanent basis.

"I still don't understand it," Betty fretted. "If the judge granted you temporary custody, then why were those people here, asking questions all around town about you and the children?"

"They're just trying to find ways to discredit me, Mom—to show that I'm an unfit guardian. There's nothing we can do about it, so just relax. The attorney is working on it."

Jenny tried to put on a bold face, but she wasn't prepared for all the gossip that was circulating around the little prairie town of Fairfield, or for how difficult it might be to keep the children from hearing it. She couldn't prevent her parents from worrying about it—especially her mother. She was determined to stay away from the town until the reason for all the rumors could be dispelled—until she could be granted permanent guardianship of Alice and June. She would need good fortune on her side.

Betty didn't have the option of solitude like her daughter did. She had to go into town every school day to drop the boys off in the morning and then pick them up again later in the afternoon. She couldn't avoid contact with a number of townspeople, nor could she escape the rumors and stares that followed her around from the market to the post office and from the gas station to the church. There was nowhere in town that she could go without being recognized and talked about. She finally resolved to ignore all the stories about her daughter and the children—stories that had been stretched far beyond the truth. For the time being, at least, she would heed her daughter's advice and try to be patient. There was nothing that she could do about small-town gossip.

CHAPTER NINE
WILD MUSTANGS

February, 1974

"I thought I'd drive into Gooding today and pick up a few things at the ranch supply," Cooper said, over his first morning cup of coffee. "Maybe those boys would like to ride along."

"I think they would like that," Betty agreed, cheerfully. She was pleased to see that her husband was willing to take an interest in the boys.

"Are they up yet?" he asked.

"No, they're still sleeping. I think they like it here, Coop. I don't believe they've ever had a home that felt safe—not since their father died. I know it's just for a little while, but they may as well feel at home while they're here."

"Is that oldest boy's back healing up all right?" Coop asked. He was concerned that the boy might have some lasting physical scars.

"He's doing fine," Betty answered, softly. "And his name is Danny."

"I know his name," Cooper assured. "I know they haven't left the ranch without you by their side, except to go to school. I'll do my best to make them feel at ease."

"I know you will," Betty acknowledged. "I'll get the boys up and dressed while you do your feeding chores. They'll be ready to go by the time you get back."

"Can you make out a check for Broward's Ranch Supply before we go?" Coop asked. "I should pay them off for the past couple of months before I charge any more. And maybe an extra one in case I need to stop anywhere else."

He pulled on his heavy coat, and disappeared out the back door, greeted by the sheepdogs that shadowed him on his morning rounds. The daily routine of feeding and caring for his animals was something that Cooper had never considered work. It was simply what he did to survive in the world—every day of his life. He couldn't imagine ever doing anything else.

"Where's your G.I. Joe hat?" Betty asked when Joey and his big brother tumbled to the bottom of the stairs and rushed to the breakfast table.

"In my room," he answered politely, as he pulled out his chair and climbed into his usual seat, ready to put on the morning feed bag.

He looked up at Betty with trusting eyes, waiting for her acceptance of his sudden change in habit. It was the first time he had left the security of his father's army cap behind, and prepared to venture out into the world without his head cover. It had been his protective helmet against all things dangerous in the world for the past three years.

"Well, that's fine," Betty said, without making an issue of it. "The only hard and fast rule we have about hats is that you never go outside without one when it's raining."

She dished eggs and pancakes onto the boys plates, and urged them to eat up—it was going to be a busy Saturday.

"How would you boys like to ride into town with Grandpa Barnett today?" Betty said, presenting the brothers with the opportunity for travel and adventure.

"Are you going, too?" Danny asked immediately.

"Not this time—I have too much to do around the house," Betty said, smiling warmly to inspire confidence in the boys. "But you'll have a nice time with Grandpa, and he always stops at the Dairy Queen for ice cream on the way home. Would you like that?"

Danny hesitated, feeling a bit unsure about leaving the safety of the nest provided by Jenny's mother, but Joey instantly gave his big brother a look that said "don't turn this down—it's ice cream," and then waited for Danny to decide for both of them.

"Okay," Danny agreed, confident that Grandma Barnett would never send him off with anyone who might mistreat him or his little brother. The fact that the quiet, gray-haired man was also Jenny's father did much to vouch for his character, and in Danny's mind, that counted a great deal.

Betty bundled the boys up in a pair of old plaid coats that her own sons had worn when they were small. The coats were well-worn, but still usable, and had serviced many grandkids that had shown up at the ranch in the wintertime, ill-prepared for the cold weather and improperly dressed to keep out the chill prairie winds. She rummaged through the closet and found a knit cap for Danny—it would keep his head dry and his ears warm. His little brother still refused to part with his army cap when he went outside. It was on his head when he went to sleep at night, and if it happened to dislodge during his sleep, it was the first thing he located amid the rumpled sheets when he woke in the morning. It took a lot of courage to leave it on his pillow when he came downstairs for breakfast.

"Couldn't you find anything that fit them a little better?" Cooper asked as he came through the back door, stomping the snow off his boots before he stepped into his wife's kitchen. He looked the boys over, noticing the oversized coat that hung over little Joey's small body like a ragged tent, and the short sleeves on Danny's worn-out coat—a borrowed garment that failed to cover the bare skin between the end of his coat sleeves and top of his mittens.

"I thought *you* might do that when you're in town," Betty answered.

Cooper nodded—he had a clear understanding of what she had in mind.

"Well, let's get going, boys," he urged. "We've got a little drive ahead of us."

He led the boys out the back door and down the steps toward the old flatbed hay truck, and opened the passenger door to let the boys climb inside. Both boys trailed behind, slogging through the snow to catch up as they got used to walking in the oversized rubber galoshes.

"How would you like to go see some horses at the rodeo grounds while we're in Gooding?" Cooper asked, hoping to instill the boys with a sense of excitement about their outing to the feed store.

The brothers looked up and nodded in unison, smiling faintly at Jenny's kindly, gray-haired dad. Danny was beginning to feel a sense of trust, and was willing to give Cooper the benefit of the doubt. Joey was willing to do whatever his big brother wanted to do.

Cooper turned the old truck south at the end of the gravel road that led west off the ranch, and steered onto the blacktop that led toward the town of Gooding. He normally made the drive into town alone, riding in silence with his own thoughts, but today he had two young helpers along for the ride—boys who needed his reassurance to convince them that they were wanted.

"I thought we'd stop at the ranch supply and feed store first, just to pick up a few things we need," Coop suggested, in an effort to make the boys feel like they had a part in deciding what to do first. "How does that sound?"

The brothers nodded again, reluctant to speak, as a result of the past two years of negative conditioning by an uncaring and abusive stepfather. Being asked for their opinion about anything was a new experience for both of them.

Cooper kept talking for the remainder of the drive, mostly entertaining the boys with stories about Jenny and her older brothers when they were just kids, growing up on the ranch. It worked well enough to pass the time and put the boys at ease.

He pulled up in front of Broward's Farm and Ranch Supply and climbed out, inviting the boys to come with him.

"Let's go, men," he said, good-naturedly. "We need to get in there, buy what we need, and get out again before they sell all the best stuff to somebody else." Cooper knew before he invited the boys to come on the trip that he didn't need anything from the storage yard or rear loading dock, but he was sure that they would like to look around inside—most boys did.

Danny pulled on the door handle and quickly exited the cab of the truck with his little brother in tow, hurrying to keep up with Cooper, who was taking long strides toward the front door of the store.

Cooper held the glass-front door open and gently pushed the boys inside ahead of him. The smell of leather and animal feed permeated the air inside the store. He led the boys past the pallets stacked high with dog food and horse pellets, and through the displays of saddles and tack equipment to the back of the store. Men's and boy's boots, jeans and western wear were stacked neatly along several aisles of shelving, and hanging from sturdy garment racks.

A red-haired teenage girl came out of a back room carrying an armful of boot boxes. Her well-fitted western shirt and jeans showed that she was right at home in the western clothing department. She wore a custom-tooled leather belt and sported a shiny championship barrel racing buckle.

"Can I help you find something?" the young salesgirl asked, beaming down a radiant white smile at the young boys. Danny and Joey were immediately impressed with her black ostrich boots, and were in awe of her colorful shirt and bright red hair.

"Yes, ma'am," Cooper replied. "We're in the market for some warm new winter coats. Maybe you could steer us in the right direction."

Cooper removed his hat when he spoke—a conditioning he had received as a boy from his own grandfather. It was a proper demonstration of courtesy toward a lady, regardless of her age.

"Of course—are you looking for something dressy, or work coats?" she asked, looking back over her shoulder as she led the trio of ranch hands toward the coat racks.

"Work coats," Cooper said. "We'll be needing some shirts and jeans, too, and some new boots for these boys."

The boys looked up at Cooper, wide-eyed, as he ordered up a full complement of western wear for the poorly-dressed brothers. No one had ever shown them such kindness or generosity, and they had no understanding of why it was happening now. Their mother never had money to spend on them, and their stepfather was angry with her if she saved a little extra from her grocery money to spend at a shirt sale or for an occasional cheap pair of shoes to replace the old ones that they were wearing holes through the soles.

The red-haired young barrel racer made a fuss over the boys, and helped them pick out some flashy western shirts and new jeans, sized a little large to allow them room to grow for a year or so. They got fitted for Roper boots, round-toed and comfortable to wear, and with extra pairs of socks. The boys couldn't believe their good fortune.

Joey grinned from ear to ear as he stood in front of a full length mirror and admired his new outfit. Cooper helped them pick out wool-lined mackinaws, and chose one to replace the worn and faded old coat that hung on his own back—soiled and nearly in tatters from years of hard wear.

"How about some western hats for these boys?" the clever salesgirl asked. She realized that she had a generous buyer in the store, and may as well reel him in and ring up a hefty sale.

"Why not?" Cooper responded. "I've got one."

He walked to the tools section and picked up a new post-hole digger while the salesgirl carried their purchases to the front counter. He wanted to show that he had come to the ranch supply for more than clothes. Besides, his old rusty digger had been broken and unusable for more than a year, and he was tired of laboring in the rocky soil with a shovel every time he needed to replace a rotted fence post.

Cooper signed the sales slip and left the girl with the check that Betty had filled out and signed to take care of their old bill. The barrel-racing salesgirl complimented the boys as they followed Cooper out the door.

"You look like genuine buckaroos, now," she praised.

Joey smiled and hitched up his jeans as he tightened his new western belt another notch. Cooper tossed the big sack filled with old clothes into the back of the truck, and opened the truck door for his new ranch hands.

"What do you say we go and get us a bite to eat, and then we'll go and take a look at those horses at the fairgrounds," Cooper suggested.

The boys' spirits were lifted high, and they smiled in agreement with the generous old rancher, ready to follow wherever he wanted to lead. Cooper drove the old hay truck down the main street of town and into the parking lot of his favorite greasy spoon—a place where a man could eat with his hat on and not feel discourteous or out of place.

"C'mon men—let's go fill our bellies," he offered.

Danny didn't have to be asked twice. He pulled on the old door handle and jumped to the ground, his little brother right on his heels. The boys fairly strutted in their new western outfits as they hurried to keep up with Grandpa Barnett. Sometimes, all it took was a new set of clothes and a respectable hat to make a fellow feel new again.

Cooper settled into a booth with the boys and looked over the familiar menu, opting for the rib-eye steak sandwich, broiled medium rare and tasty. It was the only thing he had ever ordered off the menu at the Stockmen's Cafe, and they always made it just the way he liked it.

"You boys like some hot soup and grilled cheese sandwiches?" he asked.

A familiar waitress came to the table just as they agreed on lunch. She had overheard Cooper ask the boys what they wanted, and repeated the question for their benefit.

"Hi there," she greeted. "You cowboys gonna have a bowl of vegetable beef soup and a cheese sandwich?"

The brothers nodded eagerly, thrilled that they should be recognized as cowboys only minutes after getting their official uniforms. Danny opened his coat to show the waitress his new western shirt, and Joey followed his big brother's example.

"I never saw better-looking shirts on any rodeo cowboy. You boys look real sharp today," she praised, then turned to Cooper to get his order.

"You having the rib-eye sandwich today, Hoss?" the old, dyed-blonde waitress quipped, already scribbling the order onto her note pad.

"You takin' these boys over to the horse sale at the fairgrounds? I hear there's fair-sized crowd over there today," she said, performing her duties as a waitress by dispensing the local news, in addition to serving food.

Nobody who knew Cooper Barnett paid much attention to the fact that he had two boys along on his trip into Gooding. Like most farmers and ranchers in the area, he often came into town, trailing two or three grandkids behind.

"Eat up, men," Cooper urged. "Let's go and have a look at those horses."

Danny and Joey looked at each other and grinned when Cooper called them men for the third time that day. For the first time in their young lives, they were being treated with respect by a grown man.

A few other customers came and left, nodding their heads in greeting as they passed by the booth where Cooper and his men were finishing their lunch. Most of them he didn't recognize, and there were fewer still that he knew by name, but it would be rude not to be friendly in the small rural town.

The brothers walked out to the hay truck, side by side with Cooper, trying to match his long strides and do justice to their new images.

"We never had cowboy boots before," Danny said.

"Well, you've got 'em now, and they look good on you," Cooper praised. "Be sure to take good care of them."

"We will," Joey agreed.

On the short drive to the fairgrounds, the boys waved at every stranger they passed along the way, and nearly every one waved back. They reveled in their new-found confidence and popularity. It was remarkable how self-assured a fellow could feel with a new pair of boots and a cowboy hat pulled snugly over his head.

The boys stuck close by Cooper as he led the way into the large metal building that sat adjacent to the livestock exhibit buildings at the fairgrounds. The small arena was being used as a sale ring for the horses that had been brought from around Southern Idaho, and as far away as Utah, Wyoming, and Northern Nevada.

It was unusual to see a sale in the middle of winter, but a number of ranchers and horse breeders were selling off animals that were unwanted or no longer needed, just so they wouldn't have to feed them through the winter months.

No more than seventy or eighty buyers and onlookers sat in the spectator stands, scattered into small groups, or individuals sitting alone. Some stood along the arena fence, just to get a closer look at the horses when they were brought into the ring.

The ongoing auctioneering process was fairly informal, and a few horses were sold without ever being brought into the arena. Fewer than a hundred animals had been brought to the fairgrounds to be offered for sale. Most were older saddle horses that had become lazy since their young riders had grown up and left home. There were a few well-muscled, green-broke colts—mostly quarter horses—that garnered some interest from a couple of local cowboys who were looking for a new stock horse that could be trained into a hazer or a good cutting horse.

Most of the domestic stock had been sold, and a couple of miniature horses were trotted out into the sale ring on a halter and lead, to the delight of several youngsters and their parents. Two little paints—a mare and her two-year-old filly offspring—sold in the first round of bidding to an impulse buyer who wore a new Stetson and an expensive Pendleton jacket.

"Figures," Cooper muttered to himself.

He didn't have any desire to own a horse that wouldn't be useful in some capacity on the ranch.

The tiny horses were led away to be claimed by their new owner, and the arena fell silent while preparations were made to bring in the last of the horses—Spanish Mustangs from the high plateaus of Utah and Wyoming, and the mustangs from the brushy plains and wide valleys of BLM-managed federal land in Northern Nevada. The Bureau of Land Management had been working to keep the numbers of the wild horse herds reduced, blaming the horses for the overgrazing problems that occurred on public lands.

Danny and Joey stared in wide-eyed wonderment as the first of the Spanish Mustangs were driven in, their hooves pounding across the dirt floor of the arena. The spirited horses galloped around the outside of the small enclosure, tossing their proud heads and shaking their long manes as they looked for a way out of the small confines of the sale ring.

"Let's go and get a closer look, shall we?" Cooper said to his young charges, noticing that they had leaned forward in their seats, enthralled by the sight of the wild mustangs.

He led them down to the railing above the arena, where a number of spectators and bidders gathered to get a closer look.

Danny stared in awe at the captive horses. They seemed entirely out of place to him—trapped in a man-made enclosure instead of roaming, wild and free, on the open plains. As the youngster watched intently, the mustangs whirled and bolted back toward the gate where they had been driven into the arena, then balked when they discovered their escape was blocked.

They were the last of a breed of noble animals which centuries earlier had roamed the open plains of the Iberian Peninsula, and were brought to the Americas in the sixteenth century by the Spanish Conquistadors. They eventually migrated northward from the Yucatan Peninsula in Mexico, and their ancestors had first been ridden by the Indians of the Southwest. Over the centuries, the mustang became more common in the northern regions of Western America. Over the years, many of the horses escaped their human bonds to roam free in the high deserts and prairies of the West. The purest of the Spanish bloodlines had survived in remote pockets of mountainous land in Northern Utah and Wyoming.

The numbers of pure-bred Spanish Mustangs had dwindled into the thousands in recent years, most of them protected by a handful of caring ranchers and horsemen from the Mountain West, whose goal it was to keep the bloodlines intact.

It was from among these last descendants of the proud and noble animals from Spain that some remnants of a remarkable breed were driven into the sale ring and offered up to the highest bidders.

"They don't belong here, all closed in like that, do they Grandpa?" Danny asked, looking up at Cooper's weathered face. The kindly rancher was the only man besides his own father that he had ever come to trust.

"No, they don't, son," Cooper answered, solemnly, feeling a touch of sorrow at witnessing another vanishing emblem of the American West being offered for sale under the auctioneer's hammer.

"Can't we take some to the ranch?" Danny asked, innocently. "There's lots of room."

"Can we, Grandpa?" little Joey begged, believing in his heart that Grandpa Barnett could do anything he wanted—and would always be willing to do what was right.

Cooper was surprised to realize that he was actually thinking about it seriously, wondering what pasture on the ranch was well fenced, and large enough to give the horses room to run. Still, they would have to be tamed a bit—green broke so that a farrier would be willing to trim their hooves and a veterinarian could examine and treat them without being bitten or kicked half to death.

"Maybe," Cooper relented, in a one-word response. He watched as the bidding progressed on one or two horses at a time. Each mustang looked much the same as the next, except in color—colors that were more diverse than any he had ever seen in the more familiar breeds.

Impulsively, Cooper left the boys at the arena railing and walked down to the auctioneer with his request.

"I'd like to bid on that roan stallion, and any three mares, if you'll allow it," he requested.

Most of the mustangs went for between $200 and $300, and Cooper hoped that he wouldn't have to go any higher. It would be hard enough to explain to Betty what he had done with the check she sent with him to pay for animal feed.

Cooper walked back to the arena railing where the boys waited, and nodded his head with a wink and a smile.

"We'll see," he said.

More than half of the mustangs had been sold, and most of the bidders who showed any interest had already selected the horses they wanted. Only one other bidder tried for the roan stallion with a single low bid, but he quickly withdrew when the auctioneer modified his loosely-crafted rules to allow a single bid for the stallion and three mares. Cooper got all four horses for the price of eight hundred dollars. Now he had to explain it to his wife. He couldn't remember the last time he had done anything so impulsive, and he wondered if he was getting senile.

He saw a familiar old face among the group of men gathered by the pen railing below, and watched as the elderly man climbed the steps that led up into the stands from the holding pens. Cooper welcomed the old-timer with a broad smile.

"Hello, Petri," Cooper greeted. "How's your family?"

The old Basque sheepman stepped up and grasped Cooper's hand firmly, nodding in answer to the inquiry about his family's well-being.

"They're all good," Petri Beraza answered. "How is your wife?"

"Still in charge, and always telling me what to do."

"Yes, of course—nothing changes," the old Basque smiled. "My youngest boy tells me he enjoys working for you—taking care of your sheep on the summer grazing range."

"He's a good man, and I'm lucky to have him help me out," Cooper praised. "He knows his business, and I'm real impressed with those big white dogs of his. Great Pyrenees, aren't they?"

"Yes, Pyrenees, Petri confirmed. "My family has used them for many generations—long before we came to this country. You like the big guardian dogs?"

"I'd like to get a couple of my own, if they're as good as I've heard they are at keeping predators away," Cooper answered.

"Oh, they are the best, for sure," Petri acknowledged. "Maybe my son can bring some to your ranch sometime so you can see how they mingle with the sheep, and how they watch over them day and night."

"They don't get into disputes with the herding dogs?" Cooper asked. "No fights?"

"No, no," Petri emphasized. "There is no conflict—you will see. The guard dogs will leave the herding to your Border Collies—there is no competition for their jobs."

"I'll look forward to seeing them," Cooper said. "Have your son call me when he gets a chance."

"Yes, I will. I see you have some good men of your own helping you out today," Petri noticed.

"Yep—they're reliable helpers, for sure—don't know what I'd do without them."

"Did they help you pick out some good horses?"

"They sure did," Cooper admitted, looking down to smile on the boys. "I'm not sure how well our purchase will play to our audience back home, though."

Cooper bid a friendly goodbye to his old acquaintance and fellow sheep rancher—he marveled at how little Petri had changed over the years. The son of a Basque immigrant himself, Petri Beraza had grown up on the sheep trails of southern Idaho, and knew the land as well as any rancher in the Intermountain West. He was an educated man, too, but chose to remain in the same business as his father and his father's father before him.

Cooper arranged for the mustangs to be held overnight at the fairgrounds until he could return the next day with his stock truck, and made ready to leave for the ranch, so he could get home before dark and face the music with Betty.

"We better get home, before we get into any more trouble," Cooper said to the boys, only half in jest. He would need at least the time that it took to drive home to come up with a good reason why he had purchased four wild mustangs for a sheep ranch.

"Do you think Grandma will be excited when she sees the mustangs?" Joey asked, happily.

"Oh, she'll be excited all right," Cooper confirmed. "She'll be plenty excited."

Life had changed dramatically for the young brothers over the four months since they had been whisked away from their mother and an abusing stepfather. This morning they had left the Barnett Ranch wearing old and misfit winter coats on their backs; and by midday they were dressed in their new western outfits and recognized by all they met as the men from the Barnett Ranch—cowboys of the Camas Prairie and proud owners of Spanish mustangs. Their status among their classmates at school was sure to be elevated.

CHAPTER TEN
COOPER'S WAY

"Danny's teacher has given him some low marks," Betty complained, disgusted that he wasn't getting more help in the classroom. "If Madelyn Farmer spent as much time helping kids who were falling behind in their studies as she does running them down, they would all be honor students."

Cooper languished in his easy chair, trying to read the weekly paper before the news got too old to care about.

"Madelyn Farmer?" he asked, incredulous that the same teacher who berated his own children for not speaking perfect English was still allowed to have a key to the school. "Is that old dragon still there? She must love to torment kids."

Betty smiled, pleased that her husband was a sudden and willing ally, and was joining with her in her disdain of such an inept educator as the old crone who loved language more than she loved kids.

"Mary Hodges is the first grade teacher," Betty went on. "She gives Joey a lot of help, and he's doing well. He likes her, too—I can tell by the way he talks about her all the time and brings his papers home to show me. I think Danny is throwing some of his papers away before I can see them."

Joey sat in the bathtub, screeching out the high notes of the State Song of Idaho at the top of his lungs—rehearsing what he had practiced with his classmates all week, and admiring the sound as it echoed off the tile walls of his sound chamber and careened out of the bathroom and down the hallway.

And here we have I-da-ho,
Win-ning her way to fame
Silver and gold in the sun-light blaze,
And ro-mance lies in her name

Cooper lowered his newspaper onto his lap and listened for a moment—until he recognized the old refrain. It was clear to Cooper that the boy couldn't carry a tune any better than he could when he was that age—or at any time since. He got up from his easy chair and walked down the hallway to the bathroom to halt the incursion on his sensibilities.

"Come on and climb out of there now, before you get prune skin," Cooper ordered the offending child. "I'm about to bust into tears from your singing."

"It's pretty good, huh, Grandpa?" Joey called out from his sudsy seat in fifteen inches of soapy bath water—his enthusiasm unhampered by the old man's critique. He dunked his head into the bath water to rinse off the remaining shampoo and beamed with pride as he reveled in his newly-found talent.

"Yeah, it's pretty good," the old rancher acquiesced, as he turned and walked back down the hallway, muttering under his breath. "It ain't Johnny Cash—but it's pretty good."

He spent nearly the entire day on Sunday working around the barn, with two little boys under foot the whole time. It was a good day, even though not much work was actually done, and the horses got a few more oats than they needed. There were a lot of good conversations begun and ended, however. Talk of how important it was to take care of a horse's hooves, and what time of year the sheep got sheared—and what was done with the wool. Danny asked how much longer it would be before the snow all melted away and they could no longer drive the feed team out to the pastures, pulling the hay sled across the snow to feed the sheep.

All the really important things were talked over in the barn—it was where every problem that needed solving was solved. Cooper thought about his wife's admonition, and her insistence that he get more involved in his daughter's situation with the State Child Services people. He wasn't sure that any of his efforts on his daughter's behalf would result in any real benefit to her, but he decided that it was worth a try.

"I'll be gone for the day," Cooper announced to his wife early Monday morning, appearing quiet and thoughtful as he passed through the kitchen without stopping for coffee.

Betty didn't ask any questions. She could see by the way he had dressed in his only suit and tie—the same one he had worn on their wedding day—that he was embarking on a mission of some importance. He even had a new coat of polish on his boots to cover up the dirt and scuff marks as well as he could. He kissed his wife goodbye and promised to be home before supper, and told her not to worry about feeding the livestock.

"I'll be home in time to feed. Take care of the boys."

Cooper thought about his children for the entire drive north to the Boise. It only seemed like yesterday, or maybe the day before, that his kids were little. Now he had a growing number of grandkids, and a bunch more that Jenny had taken under her wing in the past couple of months. He hadn't been prepared for it—not taking in so many young children—but then he hadn't been prepared when his first child was born, either.

He hadn't been to Boise in several years, and he couldn't remember exactly why he was there the last time—he never had much business in the Capital. Cooper never had any use for cities. He always had trouble finding his way around in a town of more than five thousand people, and even a town that size was sometimes a challenge.

He could see the skyline of the main part of town as he drove down the hill on the southern outskirts of Boise, and made his way through the many streets and avenues on the way to his destination. He only had to stop and ask for directions once, and he nearly turned the wrong way down a one-way street, but eventually he located the building complex that he was looking for. He found a parking spot across the street from the majestic, dome-topped granite building that was his destination.

Cooper took his hat off when he walked inside and mounted the long, curved staircase to the second floor, avoiding the elevators altogether. He followed the corridor until he came to a large oak door, inset with opaque glass, and lettered with gold outlined in black. He stepped inside and waited to be acknowledged by a young woman seated at the receptionist desk. The well-groomed young woman looked up at the old rancher and smiled as she continued to speak with someone on the telephone, raising her index finger to indicate that she would only be a moment.

"Good morning—may I help you, sir?" the pleasant young woman in the crisp white blouse asked, as she returned the phone to its cradle.

"I'd like to see Owen Bryant, if it's not too much trouble," Cooper requested politely.

"He's in a meeting right now, sir. Is he expecting you?"

"No," Cooper began, regretting that he had not called first. "No, I just hoped that I might catch him in his office."

"May I have your name, sir?" the young woman inquired, making certain to demonstrate the utmost courtesy to the unknown visitor.

"I'm Cooper Barnett," he answered plainly.

"Just a moment, sir. Don't go away—I'll be right back," the receptionist said, rising quickly from her chair and rushing out through a side door that connected to an inner office. "Don't leave," she insisted again, as she disappeared through the doorway.

Seconds later the young lady reappeared on the heels of an older woman, who was neatly dressed in a fashionable suit, and wore her hair put up into a stylish, business-like coif. The woman walked directly to Cooper and introduced herself, extending a welcoming hand.

"Mr. Barnett, good morning, sir—I'm Gladys Weaver," she welcomed, shaking the old rancher's hand firmly. "The Governor is in a budget meeting with the State Comptroller and his staff right now, but if you'll just give me a minute, I'll let him know that you're here."

"You don't have to do that," Cooper said. "I can come back later—or wait until they're finished."

"Oh, no—you just have a seat, and I'll be right back, Mr. Barnett," the woman said, sounding somewhat amused. "Cynthia, don't you let him leave."

Cooper felt self-conscious about the sudden fuss that was being made, and he was a bit embarrassed as he remained on his feet, holding his well-worn old Stetson down at his side. The young receptionist stood guard next to her desk, holding her pen in front of her with both hands. She looked the old rancher up and down very carefully before she spoke.

"You look exactly the way I imagined you would," the young woman uttered aloud, as she continued to stare.

A puzzled expression crossed the old rancher's weathered face as he contemplated the receptionist's remark. The look didn't go unnoticed by the receptionist.

"Everyone in the Governor's office knows who you are, Mr. Barnett—unless they just got here yesterday. Oh, I'm sorry, I didn't mean to be rude—can I take your hat for you?"

Cooper graciously declined, wishing suddenly that he had worn the new Stetson that his daughter had given him for Christmas, instead of his dirty, sweat-stained work hat.

"Can I get you something to drink?" she offered, never taking her eyes off the man—not even for a second. "Coffee or water?"

"No, I'm fine—I'll just wait."

He shifted his weight from his left foot to his right, and looked down at the work boots that could have used an extra smudge of polish that morning. He tried to pull his suit jacket closed far enough to fasten at least one button—but without success. His stomach had grown some over the years—from age and maturity as much as his wife's cooking. He wished that the receptionist would sit down—it was beginning to unnerve him, having to stand there under the watchful gaze of a young woman no older than his daughter—one who had been told not to let him leave.

He was rescued suddenly when the door to an adjoining office burst open and Owen Bryant came through it like a gust of wind.

"Coop—you old rawhide—get yourself in here!" the Governor commanded, his voice fairly booming with authority, and brimming with good cheer. "How long has it been since the last time you've come so far from your ranch?"

Owen Bryant grasped his old friend's hand in greeting and clapped his other hand on Cooper's shoulder to guide him toward his office door. Cooper was caught off guard by such an enthusiastic welcome—especially after barging in on the Governor's busy day without any prior notice.

"I'm sorry that I didn't call, Owen," Cooper apologized, "but I just decided to make the trip this morning."

"You don't ever have to call ahead, Coop—your name is always at the top of my appointment calendar. "It's good to see you. Come on in and sit down."

"I didn't mean to pull you out of your meeting."

"What, that budget thing?" the Governor quipped, dismissively. "They'll be there when I get back—whatever they do in there, it isn't going to happen unless I sign it, so I think we'll be all right."

Owen Bryant had a powerful presence, and not only did he dominate conversations, he usually took up all the air in the room. People noticed him. The people of Idaho noticed him enough to elect him Governor of their state.

Gladys Weaver followed the two men into the Governor's office, and waited to see if she was needed.

"Cooper, you met my assistant, Gladys, didn't you? I can't get anything done around here without her—how about a cup of coffee? Gladys, would you mind asking Cynthia to bring us some black coffee?"

"Yes, sir," the prim assistant said, with an unusual eagerness to please. "I'll get it myself. No cream or sugar?"

"No, no thanks," Bryant answered quickly. "And no dainty cups and saucers—bring us some mugs—Cooper can't get his big fingers around those tiny handles."

The woman hurried out through a side door that led to her office, and came back momentarily with two steaming mugs of hot black coffee. She waited for only a moment—just to see if the Governor needed anything else.

"I'll be in my office, sir," his assistant said, as she let herself out through the side door again, and smiled at Cooper respectfully as she left, pulling the door closed behind her.

"I know you must have something on your mind, Coop," the Governor said, as he took a tentative sip of the hot liquid. "What is it?"

"I hate to bother you with this, Owen, but I didn't have anyone else to turn to for advice," Cooper began. "My Jenny got herself into some legal trouble over a custody matter with a couple of orphan girls, and I don't know where to begin to help her through it. Their folks were killed in a car crash up on White Bird Pass more than a year ago, and there's a probate lawyer here in Boise who's working on settling their grandmother's estate—she just died a few months ago. It's all kind of confusing."

"I can see that. So Jenny's been taking care of the girls?" Bryant inquired, trying to get a handle on the situation by obtaining all the preliminary information that he could.

"She rented a cottage in back of their grandmother's house, and I guess she got to know them pretty good. The woman asked Jenny to watch over her granddaughters when she was in the hospital with heart trouble, and my daughter promised that she would—she loves those two little girls and they adore her. The old woman died in the hospital, and she left a hand-written will, but it hasn't been settled yet."

"Has she contacted a family practice attorney?" the Governor asked.

"She doesn't have much money, and for now she's been putting all her trust in the probate lawyer, but I think it's going to get to be too much for him to handle alone," Cooper continued.

"That is a tough situation," Bryant agreed, "but not impossible."

"There's more," Cooper said, scowling with displeasure at having to disclose his daughter's circumstances. "Jenny's pregnant, and she's not married. I'm afraid the child services people are going to try and have her declared unfit to be given custody of those girls."

Owen Bryant was not a judgmental man. He responded quickly.

"Can they stay at your ranch until her baby comes, and until she can get back on her feet with a good-paying job?"

"Sure she can," Cooper acknowledged. "She comes down almost every weekend with the girls—all the kids love being on the ranch. But how is that going to help?"

"*All?*" the savvy Governor asked, wanting to be certain that he knew the full extent of Jenny's brood. "*All* the kids?"

"Well, there's two more boys—sons of a friend of Jenny's who lives in Twin Falls," Cooper admitted, not sure what bearing it would have on the issue of custody for Alice and June.

"Are you planning on opening an orphanage out there on the ranch, Coop?" Bryant asked with a smile.

"That's what I asked my daughter," Cooper replied, returning the wry smile. "The boys were being badly mistreated by a stepfather, and their mother asked Jenny if she would take care of them, just to keep them out of harm's way—you know?"

"Yes, I think I *do* know. And you can't stop yourself from stepping in to help when someone is in trouble."

"She's my only daughter, Owen—who else is going to help?"

"I am, Coop," Bryant said. "I can't interfere with State Child Services—they have to follow their own rules and guidelines—but I think I've heard enough to know how I can help you out. Give me a day or so to contact someone at a law firm here in town—someone who knows a lot about child custody cases."

"Does he charge a lot?" Cooper asked, unsure whether he could afford a high-priced lawyer.

"I'm sure you'll find that he's very affordable," the Governor assured his old friend. "I'll have him call you."

"I can't tell you how much I appreciate this," Cooper thanked his old friend. "And I'm sorry to lay this problem at your feet—I know how busy you must be, but I just didn't know who else to come to for advice. I'll owe you big for this."

"You'll owe *me?*" Bryant said, shrugging off any inference that it had been an imposition on him. "You'll never owe me anything, my friend. When you pulled me out of that stinkhole on the Bataan Peninsula during the war, I owed you my life—and anything else that I could give you for as long as I lived. When the other prisoners and I heard you and your Army Rangers come busting into that Japanese prison camp with bullets flying and grenades going off all around us, I thought it was Armageddon, for sure—I could have sworn that I felt the devil bite my toes. I was never so scared as I was at that instant when I thought that I might die, and at the very moment when my salvation was at hand. All of us had nearly given up hope."

"We were just doin' our job, Owen," the humble rancher said, quietly. "You know that. We were sent in there to bring you out, and that's all we did."

"You brought us out, all right—you carried my dysentery-ridden body through two miles of jungle to get to the convoy," the grateful Governor recalled. A powerful emotion built inside him from the clear memory of his days of suffering, and of the dramatic rescue that ended his imprisonment and brought him home to his wife. "You always just do your job, don't you?"

Cooper sat silently, running his hat brim through his fingers as he stared down at the floor, nodding his head slowly as he recalled with vivid clarity his memories of the war in the Philippines.

The two old friends talked for awhile about their families, and caught each other up on what was going on with their grown-up children—then the Governor buzzed his receptionist and asked her to have some lunch sent up so that they could continue their conversation for a little while longer. His assistant brought their sandwiches and hot soup into his office when it arrived, and the Governor invited her to stay and share their lunch—to take a little time to get acquainted with his friend of many years.

"Gladys, what do you think of a guy who won't even show up for his good friend's Inaugural Ball?" Bryant jabbed. "Says he didn't think he would fit in—that's the only excuse he had."

"Aw, I could never fit into a tuxedo," Cooper drawled. "And those kinds of events are for your society friends—Betty and I read all about it in the *Statesman*."

"The suit you have on is all you needed to wear to get through the door, and no one would have said a word about it, I promise you—we even had seats reserved for you and Betty at our table," he added. "Gladys, are you sure you sent Coop an invitation?"

"Oh, yes sir—and I sent out a second invitation when we didn't hear back with an RSVP on the first one," his assistant was quick to reply. She knew her boss didn't think that she was the reason his friend didn't show up for his inauguration.

"Betty thought it was a mistake when we got two of them, one after the other—she saved them both and put them in the front of one of her scrapbooks," Cooper reminisced. "We were both very proud of you."

Gladys Weaver hung on every word, delighted to be invited to sit in on the conversation and listen to the private conversation between the two men. She was now equipped with all the most recent and valuable scuttlebutt about the Governor's relationship with his old friend. She would be the star of the Capitol cafeteria for the next week, at least. The Governor was proud of his long friendship with Cooper Barnett, and didn't mind that people talked about it.

The men shook hands at the door before Cooper left the Capitol to make the drive home in time to feed his livestock before dark. Bryant knew better than to walk his friend out through the rotunda—he would have been accosted by every budget-minded legislator and lobbyist in the building on the way back to his office. He promised Cooper before he left that he would drive out to the Barnett Ranch on his next trip through Camas County, and maybe even stay for dinner.

"Cynthia, would you see if you can get Bart Crenshaw on the phone for me—or at least leave word with his office that I'd like to talk to him?" the Governor instructed.

He walked back to the solace of his huge office, and prepared to resume the meeting with his budget staff and the state comptroller. It didn't take long before he was interrupted from his meeting once again—this time with a return call from attorney Bart Crenshaw.

"Bart, I have a favor to ask of you," Bryant began. "Are you still doing some pro bono work?"

"I can if you need it," the former state attorney general offered.

"What's up?"

"There's a young woman here in Boise who's in a tight spot—she's trying to get custody of two minor girls who were orphaned a couple of months ago," Bryant explained. "Besides that, she's pregnant, and her baby is due in another month or two. Oh, by the way, she's not married—you like a challenge, don't you, Bart?"

"Yes—yes, I do," Crenshaw replied, after a short pause. "Anything else I need to know?"

"You can start by calling her father—Cooper Barnett is his name—he's a sheep rancher down in Camas County," the Governor continued. "He can fill you in with the details, and he'll put you in touch with his daughter."

"Cooper Barnett—is that the same man who brought you out of that jungle prison camp in the Philippines during the war?"

"The same," Bryant answered. "Will you help?"

"You know I will," Crenshaw answered plainly. "I'll make the call today."

"And Bart, his daughter doesn't have any money to speak of, and Cooper isn't a rich man, so take it easy on him with your fees, will you?"

"I won't hurt him," Crenshaw assured the Governor. "Maybe I'll bill him for some court costs and expenses, that's all."

'I won't forget this, Bart," Bryant said, with genuine appreciation. "Call me if you need anything."

Cooper arrived back at the ranch after Betty had picked the boys up from school, and he changed his clothes to prepare for the afternoon feeding chores with his two young helpers. He had just buttoned up his coat when the phone rang, and Betty called him into the kitchen to take the call.

Bart Crenshaw introduced himself to Cooper over the phone, and explained that the Governor had asked him to represent Jenny in her child custody case. Cooper thanked him, and told him everything he knew, then handed the phone back to his wife to give the lawyer Jenny's telephone number.

The Lamb Cart   171

"You went to see Owen Bryant today, didn't you?" Betty asked, after hanging up the phone. She was already sure that it was true.

"Yes, I did," Cooper admitted. He turned to walk out to the barn with his two eager young ranch hands. "Let's go feed the sheep and cattle, shall we, men? Then we can go check on your Mustangs."

It was still daylight when all the feeding chores were done, and they saved a little hay on the sled for the mustangs. He drove the feed team out onto the crusty snow that still covered most of the high pasture. They spotted the mustangs, banded together high on the rise above Camas Creek, where they could easily see anything that approached them from a distance. The mustangs caught the scent of hay and horses and humans, almost as soon as they noticed the feed team ascending the long slope of brushy field. Cautiously, the mustangs walked toward the approaching hay sled, nostrils flaring as they took in the tantalizing aroma of baled alfalfa. They walked a little closer, and waited.

Cooper turned the team once they got within fifty yards of the mustangs, and stopped the sled sideways to the skittish horses, so that they wouldn't be frightened away. He broke open the last bale of hay, but kept it on the sled, rather than drop it onto the ground. The mustangs would have to come close if they wanted something to eat today. He took some carrots out of the pocket of his mackinaw and gave some to each boy, cautioning them to be very careful when they offered the carrots to the horses.

"When they come up to the sled, you move real slow," he warned. "And let them come to you—if you reach out too fast, or make any sudden movements, you'll spook them."

"We will, Grandpa," Danny said, respectfully, paying close attention to all of Cooper's instructions.

"Just give them time—they'll take it from you—don't try to force it on them," he explained. "And when they take it, you let go of it—if one of them bites you, you'll know it."

Both boys nodded their understanding, and waited patiently while the Spanish Mustangs slowly approached the hay sled—step by step—as they closed the distance to the sweet-smelling alfalfa and tasty treats being held out at arm's length by the small humans.

"Don't move—just wait," Cooper continued to teach the young boys, speaking just above a whisper so that he would not startle the horses.

One of the mares—a brindle-colored beauty—was the first to stretch out her neck to reach for a carrot. Joey waited until the mare chomped down firmly on the tasty vegetable before he released it, instinctively lowering his hand very slowly so that the horses wouldn't be startled by any sudden movement.

"Good—that's good," Cooper uttered in a soft, low voice.

The big roan stallion moved up next, and gingerly took the carrot offered by Danny, turning to toss its head defiantly as quickly as it secured a good hold on the treat. The two remaining mares moved in next, less afraid to step up for their share once the stallion and the dominant mare had been successful. The carrots were consumed in a matter of minutes, and the boys pushed the alfalfa hay off the sled and onto the ground, showing the mustangs that humans were useful, and good to have around.

"Can we ride them, Grandpa?" Joey asked, as Cooper drove the feed team back down the slope toward the barn.

"Not yet, son," Cooper answered patiently. "They're not ready to have anyone on their backs yet."

"When can we ride them?" Danny asked.

"Someday—I don't know exactly when," the old rancher answered.

Cooper asked his wife to call their daughter after supper that evening, to see if she had talked with Bart Crenshaw and to find out how everything was going for the probate lawyer in his efforts to wrap up the estate of Mrs. Rolfson. Betty handed the phone over to Cooper after a few minutes, so that he could explain to his daughter what he had done.

"I talked to Governor Bryant today, Jenny, and he said he would help find a good lawyer who knew a lot about child custody law."

"I know, Dad," Jenny replied, with some self-satisfaction that she had already learned about her father's intervention. "Mr. Crenshaw already called me this afternoon—he's going to meet with me after work tomorrow, so I can tell him everything I know."

"You trust his advice, Jenny," Cooper admonished. "Owen Bryant wouldn't have referred him if he wasn't the best."

"I know, Dad," Jenny answered. "I really appreciate this."

"You're coming home this weekend again, aren't you?" Cooper asked. "Your mother is starting to get real attached to those girls, you know."

"I know what you mean, Dad," Jenny smiled into the phone. "They like you, too."

CHAPTER ELEVEN
SPRING THAW

April, 1974

Tom Benton pulled his U.S. Forest Service truck into the gas station on the corner of Main Street and Highway 20 and stopped next to one of the gas pumps. He saw Jenny Barnett coming out of the station with two little girls, and an enormous belly that signaled the arrival of another child very soon. He hadn't seen her since the month after they both graduated from high school.

"Hi, Jenny—how have you been?" he greeted, stopping to speak with his old classmate as she walked back to her car.

Jenny smiled, but didn't recognize the man. His face was vaguely familiar, but she couldn't put a name with it.

"I'm sorry," Jenny apologized. "I know that I must know you from school or somewhere, but I can't think of your name."

"I'm Tom Benton," he said, with a big smile. "I grew a couple more inches and put on some weight since high school—and I shave now."

"Oh my gosh—Tom!" Jenny was taken by surprise, and delighted to see a friendly face that wasn't likely to gossip about her. "How have you been? Got a good job with the government, I see."

"Yeah, I always wanted one of these cool Smokey Bear hats," he said, in a self-deprecating manner. "It's the only reason I took the job."

"I heard you went off to school at Boise State right after we graduated, Tom—did you get your degree?"

"Eventually—I got my draft notice after my first two years, and I had to do a four-year stint in the Army first," Tom explained.

"Dad will be impressed to hear that," Jenny said. "He wasn't very happy whenever he read about some of those boys from Portland and Seattle who wet their pants and ran away to Canada after they got their draft notices in the mail—it made him throw his newspaper in the fire."

"I finished my last two years at Utah State after I was discharged," Tom laughed. "Got my degree in Forestry."

"That would explain the cushy new job," Jenny teased. "How long have you worked for the Forest Service?"

"Just started a few months ago—I'm working up in the Sawtooth Forest above Sun Valley," he added. "What about you? It looks like you've been busy raising a family—I hadn't heard that you got married."

"I haven't," Jenny said, self-consciously. She instantly wondered what Tom must be thinking about her obvious pregnancy and the two little girls who stood next to her. "It's a long story."

"Maybe we could have lunch sometime and you can fill me in," Tom invited. "I'm already curious."

"I'll bet you are," Jenny said, playfully. "You always were inquisitive in biology class."

"Oh, Jenny, would you remind your dad that trout fishing season doesn't start for another month," Tom suggested, as he turned to go into the filling station office to pay for his gas. "I saw him with two young boys last Saturday, fishing along Camas Creek near the sheep bridge. I wouldn't want him to get cited for it."

"Tom Dalton, are you going to ticket my dad for fishing out of season?" Jenny asked in mock surprise. "That's no way to get me to have lunch with you."

"Nope," Tom answered. "It's not my job—I'm Forest Service, not Fish and Game—but you might encourage him to do his angling in one of the creeks closer to your house if he's going to ignore the calendar."

"You're a real gentleman, Tom," Jenny said, with a smirk. "I'll tell him. See you later."

"Bye, Jenny," Tom said, more curious than ever about all of Jenny's kids. He had never told her, but he always thought she was one of the prettiest girls at Camas High—and he knew for sure that she was one of the smartest. He watched through the window as she drove away.

"You'll never guess who I saw in town today," Jenny rushed to tell her mother when she came through the kitchen door with Alice and June running ahead of her. "Tom Benton—he's working for the Forest Service."

"Yes, we heard he got a job working in the Sawtooth Forest," Betty said. "His dad runs the sawmill in Fairfield, you know."

"Is there anything you don't know about people in Fairfield?" Jenny asked, exasperated that she never learned any news from town that her mother didn't already know about.

"We live here, honey," Betty said, smiling at the girls as they waited to get her attention. "It only takes about an hour, once a week, to get caught up on everybody's business—there's not more than five hundred people in the whole town, you know."

"Yeah, I guess," Jenny agreed. "Where's Dad?"

"Where he always is at this time of year—down at the lambing sheds, taking care of the newborns."

"Can we go see the lambs, Jenny?" Alice asked.

"Can we, Jenny?" June chimed in.

"You won't like the smell, June-bug," Jenny warned "It's really stinky down there—maybe we can wait a few days, until Grandpa brings some of the lambs up to the pens by the barn—then we can help bottle feed them. Would you like that?"

Alice and June didn't like the idea of waiting, but they didn't like bad smells, either. They took Jenny's word for it that the experience at the lambing sheds might be an unpleasant one for their delicate olfactory senses, and they agreed to wait until later for the opportunity to see the spring lambs.

Danny and Joey waded into the task of mucking out the lambing sheds, scooping up the manure and wet straw with square-nosed shovels and piling it into a two-wheeled cart so that it could be removed from the shed and dumped onto a pile outside the shed. They learned to ignore the stench that was trapped inside the still air of the crowded lambing sheds. The sheds were almost bursting from the large numbers of ewes and their newborns, and more were being brought in every hour.

They quickly learned that if they wanted to hang out with Grandpa Barnett and his animals, they couldn't stand idly by with their hands in their pockets—they had to jump in with both feet, ready to lend a hand and do whatever chore the old rancher gave them. The boys didn't mind—they loved living and working around the livestock every day. If they didn't work outside, then they would be helping Grandma Barnett with household chores, and neither of the brothers liked doing dishes.

More than two hundred ewes were penned in the long sheds, built end to end so that the individual pens could be accessed easily by following a center aisle, checking pen by pen to be certain the mothers and babies were doing well. The ewes and their lambs were being moved in and out every day, making room in the nursery for the newborn lambs and turning them out with their mothers as soon as they appeared healthy and steady enough on their wobbly legs to remain outside.

"Let's hitch up the mare to the lamb cart and go see if we can find any ewes that may have dropped their lambs up in the pasture or out in the brush, shall we men?" Cooper knew the boys were ready every day to go out and look for newborn lambs. Most of the time the ewe stays with its lamb, but a few were lost from time to time.

"There's one!" Danny called out from his perch in the front of the cart, from where he searched the pasture for signs of any ewes standing over their newborn lambs.

"I see it!" Joey echoed. "Go that way, Grandpa," he said, pointing in the direction of the new mother and her offspring. The lamb must have been weak and cold—it was not standing or attempting to suckle.

If a young, inexperienced or stubborn ewe didn't allow a lamb to suckle, the lamb would be put with a surrogate mother who may have lost a lamb. When that didn't work, the lamb had to be bottle fed. Sometimes, when a newborn lamb died, its skin and wool would be cut away to fashion a lamb blanket, still bearing the smell familiar to its mother, and tied onto an orphaned lamb in an attempt to get the mother of the dead lamb to accept it, and allow it to feed.

Danny and Joey learned fast, and made many trips up and down the aisles of the lambing sheds to inspect the ewes and lambs, and report back to Grandpa Barnett if a lamb was being refused a meal, or if a ewe looked sick or weak, and unable to suckle its offspring. The boys soon discovered that herd management meant having to move fast when the lambs were being born, and having to accept the fact that an occasional lamb would be lost.

"That's enough for now, boys," Cooper told the youngsters. "Why don't you go on into the house and let Grandma fix you something to eat. Wouldn't hurt you to get cleaned up a little, too—and don't forget to leave those rubber boots outside—Grandma will pitch a fit if you track that muck into her kitchen."

"Okay," both boys chorused. Their hunger overrode their desire to stay and work with the sheep, and to watch the lambs being born. They walked back to the house, talking non-stop about how much fun it was to see the newborn lambs try to stand up on their wobbly legs for the very first time, and to find their balance as they smelled their way toward a first meal under their mother's belly.

Cooper wandered into the house late, and found a note on the table, letting him know that his supper was being kept warm in the oven. He went straight to bed after he ate, turning the lights out behind him as he mounted the stairs to his bedroom. It was going to be a busy lambing season, and he was going to be working long hours for the next couple of weeks.

"Jenny's baby is due in two more weeks," Betty whispered, as Cooper slipped in under the covers and laid his head back on the pillow. "Some timing, huh?"

"Yeah, it's the lambing season," Cooper said, as he dropped into a deep sleep and immediately began to snore.

He worked every day, from before sunrise until long after dark, and before the lambs were all born, he regretted not having some extra help. Betty and the boys came out to the lambing sheds and helped every day after school, and the lamb explosion was nearly over in another week.

When Jenny came home the next weekend, Cooper had penned some bottle-fed lambs inside one of the horse stalls in the barn, and Jenny took the girls out to let them hold a bottle while the lambs filled their bellies. Betty warmed milk for the lambs in a saucepan on her stove and poured it into bottles before pulling the large rubber nipples onto the tops. Alice and June wanted to name all the lambs, and were still choosing names when Jenny told them it was time to go back inside.

"Can't we stay for a while?" Alice pleaded.

"All right—just a few minutes, though—you have homework and a reading assignment to finish this weekend."

"Can we take a lamb home with us, Jenny?" June asked.

"We don't have a place to keep it, honey. Where would it stay?"

"It could stay in our room—we'll take care of it."

"I don't think you're ready to clean up after a lamb that lives in a house, June-bug—maybe we better leave them here."

"When are we going to live here all the time?" Alice asked.

"Soon, Alice—we'll live here soon—we still have some things to do in Boise first, and you have to finish the school year."

The girls let the lambs drain the last of the bottles, then carried the empties back into the house to be washed and made ready for the next feeding.

"I don't want to go back to Boise," Alice said, as they walked toward the kitchen door. "That lady is trying to take us away and make us go to foster homes, isn't she?"

"Don't waste any more time worrying about that, Alice—I'm not going to let anybody put you in a foster home. I'm going to keep you with me, and we're getting lots of help to make sure that happens."

"Who's going to help us?" Alice wanted to know.

"A friend of Grandpa's is helping us, and so is Mr. Harker—the man we met with in Boise—remember?"

"Who is Grandpa's friend—what's he doing?"

"He's a lawyer—a very good one. And he's really smart, so we should trust him and be patient while he does his job, okay?"

"Okay," Alice replied, though not entirely convinced.

Jenny stayed up with her mother after the children were tucked in, and talked at length about the move back home to the ranch.

"Are you sure Dad is going to be okay with us living here all the time?"

"I know he's glad to have you home, and I know he loves having the kids around, so I can't see a problem," Betty assured.

"You don't think the boys are a nuisance, being under foot all the time?"

"No, of course not. Haven't you paid attention to how they shadow him, and hang on his every word? They do anything he asks them to do, and he's gotten used to having those junior-sized ranch hands around to help him out. I don't know if they make his work go any faster, but I know that he likes having them here."

"What about the girls?"

"Girls are never any trouble for your Dad—unless they start to cry, and then he wants me to handle it."

"I can't tell you how grateful I am that you're taking us in. I don't know what we would do without your help."

"You brought a lot on yourself when you took all those kids under your wing, Jenny, and your father and I are proud of you for doing it, even if he doesn't tell you so. Don't worry—we'll make it work."

"We have to get ready to go home, Alice," Jenny said, after breakfast. "We'll be able to stay longer next time we come."

Jenny turned in her two weeks notice at Idaho Joe's Cafe on her first day back at work after the weekend, much to Joe Bannock's dismay. He offered to pay for a babysitter for the new baby if Jenny would stay in Boise and agree to come back to work a few weeks after the baby came. She actually considered his offer, thinking that it would be better if she continued to bring home a paycheck after the baby was born. The last thing she wanted was to become a financial burden on her parents, even though they insisted it would be best for everyone if she stayed at the ranch.

Alice could be enrolled at the elementary school in Fairfield for the last month of the school year. It wasn't the most ideal situation, but Jenny knew Alice would like the idea. She liked school well enough, but she loved staying at the ranch—it felt more like home to the girls than anywhere else they had lived.

Bart Crenshaw swayed her decision in the end, urging her to take Alice and June to Camas County, at least until the end of the summer. For reasons Jenny didn't understand, the lawyer insisted that it would be much better if she lived with the girls at her parents' ranch—and stay there for awhile after her baby was born. She called Alex Harker and asked for his opinion, and the probate attorney strongly recommended that she heed the advice of the lawyer whose help had been arranged for by the Governor. Jenny followed Crenshaw's instructions to the letter.

She arrived at the ranch two weeks later with the back seat of the Studebaker stacked high with boxes of books, clothes, and house wares. Her mother was relieved when she arrived with the girls and all their personal belongings. It was the last weekend commute from Boise for Jenny—she was home to stay.

When the time drew near for Jenny to pack a bag and be ready on short notice to make the drive to the hospital in Hailey, she realized that she had done the right thing by moving home with the girls. She didn't wait for her water to break—when her contractions began to come with more frequency, she dressed in the middle of the night and had her mother drive her into town and drop her at the hospital. Betty parked the station wagon and went inside, waiting with Jenny until she was admitted. Five hours later she called her husband at home and gave him the news.

"We've got another Barnett girl, Coop," Betty announced, obviously pleased about the arrival of a granddaughter. "She weighs nearly seven pounds, and I counted all her fingers and toes. She's got the bluest eyes you ever saw. And Jenny's doing fine, too—just tired, that's all."

"That's just fine," Cooper said, with as much excitement in his voice as he could muster. "Just fine."

"Why don't you tell the kids," Betty advised. "I'm going to go back to Jenny's room now."

"Why don't you tell them," Cooper suggested. "You're a lot better at explaining about babies than I am."

Alice was the first to line up to take the phone from Grandpa Barnett's hand, and it was passed in turn to June, and then to Danny, and then Joey. All the kids got to hear the news first hand from Grandma Betty, and it meant a lot to them. But it didn't stop them from asking more questions after Cooper hung up the phone.

"Why did Jenny have a baby?" June asked, at almost the same instant that he placed the phone back on its hook.

"I'm not exactly sure," Cooper said, in an attempt to skate around the question. "Why don't you ask Grandma when she gets home—I have to go feed the horses now."

He pulled on his rubber boots and mackinaw and sloshed out across the muddy ground between the house and the barn, hoping to avoid more prying questions from the children, and leave them for Betty to answer when she got home. All four kids pulled on their warm coats and mud boots, and followed him out to the barn. He hoped that the roads were clear, and that Betty would drive fast and get home quickly.

"When is Jenny coming home?" Alice asked, as she walked into the barn with a list of questions in her head.

"In a couple of days, I suppose," Cooper replied. "Didn't Grandma tell you?"

"I forgot to ask her," Alice responded.

"Well, I'm sure she'll tell you when she gets home—it shouldn't be too long."

"What's the baby's name?" Joey asked.

"Yeah, what are we going to call her?" Danny chimed in.

"Jenny's going to name her Daphne," Alice answered, confidently.

Cooper stopped rearranging halters on the wall rack and turned to look at Alice, wondering for a moment if she actually had some information that he didn't, or if she was simply guessing.

"I heard Jenny and Grandma talking," Alice explained, seeing that everyone's stares were fastened on her.

"I guess that answers your question, boys," Cooper said, as he went back to the chore of coiling the halter leads. "Why don't we give some carrots to the horses?"

There was a time when Cooper was pretty good at distracting youngsters with things they liked, just to help him change the subject, but he hadn't counted on the ability of Alice and June to feed carrots to the horses and talk about the new baby at the same time.

"I wonder what color her eyes are," Alice questioned, as she held a carrot out to the huge Clydesdale mare. "I'll bet she has pretty brown hair—just like Jenny."

"I think she has blue eyes, too—just like Jenny," June ventured, as she released a big carrot immediately when the other giant Clydesdale chomped down on it.

Cooper wasn't very curious about the color of baby Daphne's hair—there would be plenty of time to coo and rave about the little girl's beauty when she was brought home. For now, Cooper only thought about what he might feed the kids if Betty didn't get home before suppertime, and decided that steak and fried potatoes would make everybody happy. He didn't know how to make macaroni and cheese.

Lucky for him, Betty got home before the children started crying and before he got cranky, so everyone got fed and no one complained.

"I don't know what I'd do without you, Betty," Cooper said, meaning it more as praise than a confession of his helplessness in the kitchen.

"You've never had to try, have you?" she answered, confirming her husband's dependence on her.

"I do all right for myself when I'm out on the sheep trail," Cooper defended. "I'm out there for a week or more at a time without your cooking."

"Maybe," Betty allowed. "But you're not doing any real cooking for yourself—your Basque shepherd is the only cook in the camp. And I don't think you've ever washed a pair of socks the whole time you're out there—or changed them, either."

"I threw a pair in the campfire once—that's almost as good. Soap and water isn't the only solution."

Betty shook her head and walked away from the conversation. She couldn't imagine how forty-five years of husband training could yield so little.

Betty left again to drive to the hospital after breakfast the next morning, and was only gone for three hours. Cooper didn't panic, knowing that the most he would be called upon to do was to apply a band-aid to a scrape, or break up a minor argument. The children usually behaved very well for him—maybe because they didn't want to see the man who was sometimes gruff become angry.

Jenny came home the following day, and everyone was outside to welcome her and see the new baby when the car came up the gravel drive. Alice and June crowded close, and the boys stood just behind them, craning their necks to get a better look as Jenny held the tiny bundle low and tugged the soft blanket away from her baby's face.

Cooper looked at the baby girl and smiled, standing a safe distance away so that his daughter wouldn't ask him if he wanted to hold his new granddaughter. The old rancher was extremely nervous around newborns—he had always believed they were far too fragile to be entrusted to his rough hands.

"Daphne—how do you spell that?" he asked his daughter, wondering where she had come up with the name for her baby.

"It's a bit tricky, Dad," she answered, good-naturedly. "It's a little different from most of the names you're familiar with, I suspect. Why don't I just let you look at the birth certificate?"

That was good enough for Cooper. He climbed the porch steps and held the back door open for everyone to go inside. The size of his family had grown considerably in the past five months, and he didn't mind. Still, he couldn't figure why his daughter would choose a name for her baby girl that no one ever heard of before.

Betty's station wagon was full of kids on Monday morning when she drove the children into Fairfield for school. Fresh rumors circulated around town that day when her makeshift school bus rolled past the

Wild Rose Hair Salon and down Main Street toward the old lava rock elementary school. She hoped that it wouldn't take more than a week or two for people to get bored, and find something else to talk about.

She had bigger things to worry about—Jenny hadn't heard from either of the Boise attorneys in almost two weeks.

Betty wondered if they were actually doing something, or simply waiting for the next phone call or letter from the child services agency. She worried all the way home, and only paid slight attention when little June asked her about Jenny's baby.

"When will Daphne be able to talk?" June asked, with genuine curiosity.

"I don't think she'll be able to say anything for awhile, June—maybe a few words next year, that's all," Betty answered. "But don't worry—in a couple of years she'll probably be talking your ear off."

Thankfully, June ended her questioning after only one inquiry about the baby's ability to communicate. The answer gave her enough to think about for the remainder of the drive home.

"I think you should call Crenshaw and ask him what's going on," Betty urged, in the first minute after she walked inside the house. "It seems like something should be happening—that child services woman is probably up to no good."

"Mom, I'll call if it will make you happy, but Mr. Crenshaw told me he would stay in touch whenever it was necessary. I don't think he's forgotten about us."

"I just don't think it would hurt to call, that's all," Betty prodded.

"Okay, Mom," Jenny agreed. "I'll call him first thing tomorrow. I'm sure to have better luck catching him in his office in the morning."

Cooper sat in his easy chair and quietly leafed through the morning paper, pretending to be deaf, and trying to remain invisible. If he had an opinion, he was too wise to voice it.

"Cooper, what do you think?" Betty asked.

Her husband was trapped, and he knew it, but he didn't give up without a struggle.

"What do I think about what?" he asked, innocently, hoping the women would pass him by and go on with their conversation without him.

"Do we have to start at the beginning? You know what I'm talking about."

He folded the paper and laid it aside, then began to get up from his chair, but changed his mind and sank back into the cushions. He drew in a deep breath and tried to think of what he might say that wouldn't alienate one or the other of the two women who were watching and waiting to hear his opinion on the matter. He thought he had come up with the perfect response.

"I don't know," he said with a shrug. "I suppose we should trust the lawyers, but maybe it wouldn't hurt to call them once, just to check in and see what's going on."

The last thing in the world he wanted to do was to interfere with Bart Crenshaw, or even to question him. He would be more likely to take the clippers away from his barber and try to give himself a haircut, even without being able to see the back of his own head. It didn't seem logical to Cooper that a sheep rancher should give legal advice to an attorney, or question his tactics and strategies.

Betty remained silent—Cooper knew her well enough to know that she would only wait until the next morning to give Jenny time to call and get an update on the progress that Harker and Crenshaw had been making on their individual cases. Cooper trusted that his old friend, Owen Bryant, would not have directed him to anyone but the very best, and he was confident that Crenshaw would do everything possible to get the best outcome for Jenny and the girls. He stayed out of the house for the rest of the day—it was the smartest way to avoid being caught up in any more women's conversations. He stayed in the barn until Danny and Joey got home from school and joined him after their afternoon snack and their report to Jenny on their day's activities. Sometimes Alice and June came out to the barn with the boys, just in case something interesting might be happening, but they usually went back into the house to be with Betty and Jenny and the baby after a few minutes of smelling hay and horse manure.

"Don't girls like horses as much as we do, Grandpa?" Joey asked, after observing the brief interest that Alice and June had in spending time in the barn and around the stables.

"Oh, they like them well enough," Cooper said. "But sometimes they don't like everything that goes with them—like cleaning up the stalls and putting up with the smell. Jenny never minded, though. She liked working in the barn more than her older brothers—she was better at it, too."

"Is that why they don't live on the ranch with you?" Danny asked.

"Because you fired them?" Joey speculated.

"No, I didn't fire them," Cooper chuckled, amused at Joey's perception of how things worked on a ranch. "You might say they quit. They went off to school, and afterwards they got married and moved to bigger towns where they could get jobs with shorter hours and better pay."

"How much does it pay to work on a ranch?" Danny inquired. "How much do you get paid to work here?"

"Nothing," Cooper answered plainly, after taking a moment or two to think it over.

"Why don't you work somewhere else?" Joey asked. "We can feed the horses for you while you go to work."

"I don't know how to do anything else," Cooper confessed. "And I don't think anyone would hire me, anyway. I've been out here working by myself too long to know how to work around other people. Besides, I've got everything I need right here—everything except enough money, that is."

Danny and Joey stopped their questions for awhile, and took some time to think about what the wise old rancher had just told them. They helped measure oats into a coffee can for the horses, making sure that the big draft horses got nearly twice as much as the smaller saddle horses.

"I still want to work on a ranch," Danny decided. "I don't care if I make any money."

"I don't care either," little Joey agreed, confident in his career decision. "I like it here."

"We better go in and see if Grandma has some supper for us, don't you think?" Cooper suggested, thinking it was about time to adjourn their discussion regarding future employment.

The boys were sometimes reluctant to leave the barn, but they never turned down food. The three ranch hands made their way back to the house, and washed up for their evening meal. Afterwards, Cooper returned to his newspaper while the boys sat at the cleared kitchen table with Alice and finished their homework with Betty's capable help. She felt like she had her own children back at the ranch again.

Jenny waited until her mom took the kids into town to drop them off at school before she called Alex Harker's office. Fortunately, he was in when she called, and was pleased to give her his progress report.

"We've published notices in the local newspapers, and no one has come forward with a claim on the estate. Just a couple of letters from local utility companies who wanted to be sure they would be paid."

"Does that mean the girls will have a trust to help pay for clothes and dentist bills and things?" Jenny asked, worried that she might not be able to afford to pay for any unforeseen expenses that may arise.

"Yes, it does," Harker answered. "And there will be a provision to take care of you, too—but only after you are appointed as their legal guardian."

"I guess I better call Mr. Crenshaw next, just to see how it's going," Jenny said, hoping that Harker might have a word or two of encouragement about her chances for a favorable outcome.

"That would be a good idea," he answered, making certain that he did not overstep his bounds and comment on the other lawyer's work.

Jenny waited for awhile before she contacted Bart Crenshaw's office. She was stalling, and only because she didn't have a good feeling about what may be going on with the child services agency. Vera Sorenson had seemed so determined to take the girls away from her, and Jenny didn't know what tricks the woman may have up her sleeve. She wanted to trust that everything would work out eventually, but a feeling in the pit of her stomach made her feel that something bad was about to happen. After a few more minutes of waiting, she decided that she should call before her mother got home, or she would have her mom standing at her side, hovering over her while she was on the phone, and pushing questions into her ear for the attorney to answer.

"Is Mr. Crenshaw in this morning?" Jenny inquired, not certain what she should ask him about the pending guardianship case.

"No, I'm sorry—he's out of the office for the next two days. May I take a message?"

"It's Jennifer Barnett. I just called to see what was happening with the guardianship matter for the Rolfson girls."

"Oh, Miss Barnett—hold on and I'll put you through to his assistant."

Jenny spoke briefly with a paralegal, and learned that Crenshaw was waiting to hear back from the State on his last request for information. No response had yet been received. It was as much a waiting game as anything, the paralegal explained—she shouldn't worry as long as she had temporary custody of the girls. If anything changed, it would have to occur through the court, and Bart Crenshaw would know about it in advance.

"I wouldn't worry about anything, Jenny," the young woman said. "I'll have Mr. Crenshaw call you when he gets back in the office."

Jenny passed the information on to her mother as soon as she got back from dropping the kids off at school.

"Bart Crenshaw's assistant said it was just one of those things that couldn't be rushed, and that in the meantime I shouldn't worry about it —nothing is going to happen without Mr. Crenshaw knowing about it."

Betty was happier with the news from the probate attorney—at least it seemed more definitive. It was a relief to know that Alice and June would be provided for financially—maybe enough for a college fund and health insurance and anything else that might become a financial burden. She wasn't worried about their day-to-day expenses, like clothing and food. An extra plate or two around the table at the Barnett Ranch was never a problem. Betty was more concerned with how her daughter would be able to take care of two girls—now three—and be able to hold down a full-time job at the same time.

"I guess that's all we can expect to hear for now," Betty allowed.

She wasn't sure if her daughter was more worried than she was about the future of Alice and June, but she suspected it. Jenny had always kept her doubts and worries to herself, even when she was young. The fact that she wasn't talking about it much told Betty that her daughter often had it on her mind. She decided not to waste any more time worrying about it—there was nothing she could do at the moment except give Jenny her support.

"The shearers are coming next week," Cooper told his wife over his first cup of morning coffee

"How long do you expect them to be here?" Betty asked.

"There should be four or five of them, and a typical shearer can do at least 150 shears in a day, so probably not more than two days, I'm thinking."

"Wool prices are still depressed, but there's nothing we can do about it—anything will help right now," Betty lamented. "We need the money."

"It's those polyesters people are wearin' now," Cooper complained. "Nobody wants to wear good wool suits or coats anymore,"

"Whatever it is that's causing it, the wool market isn't good," Betty countered.

"Well, I just *told* you what it is—everybody's wearin' polyesters now," Cooper insisted. "Folks might never go back to wearin' wool—it's the petroleum companies doin' it. I don't know how they figured a way to make clothes outta oil—everything's made of plastic or other unnatural stuff today."

"Somebody must still have a use for wool, Coop, or there wouldn't be any market for it at all."

"There purt' near ain't," Cooper concluded, sourly.

"I'm sure we'll get through it—we always do."

It rained the day that the shearers were supposed to arrive, and for most of the following day. Betty relayed the phone message to Cooper that the shearing boss called and postponed the job for three days, to allow the sheep to dry out a little before they were herded into the pens adjacent to the shearing shed. It was hard enough work without having to clip wet wool from the back and legs of a reluctant sheep.

When the shearers arrived early Friday morning, they came prepared to work through the weekend, if necessary. They didn't waste any time once they had power cords strung and connected—they kept the blades sharp in their shearing clippers, and made short work of the first 800 sheep. The remainder of Cooper's sheep were clipped by the following afternoon. It nearly cleaned out the Barnett Ranch bank account to pay for the shearing, but it had to be done.

Betty always negotiated the wool sales—it worked out better if Cooper didn't talk to the wool buyers. He had lost sales too many times in the past when he slammed the phone down after calling them a bunch of damned thieves.

CHAPTER TWELVE
MUTTON BUSTERS

"Why don't you think about getting a new pair of boots while you're in town, Coop?" Betty asked. "And you should consider wearing the new Stetson Jenny gave you—she might begin to think you don't like it.

Cooper reached up and pulled the worn and sweat-stained Stetson off his weathered brow and looked it over carefully before replacing it on his stubborn head. "I've spent the last ten years or so training this one to fit my head just right," he answered. "And I'm saving my new one for a special occasion."

"All right—I get it. You still need a new pair of boots, though."

"I'll go check out the latest models when I'm in town, if it'll make you happy," Cooper relented. "They're just gonna get dirty and worn out, though."

He brought the pickup around to the back door of the house and beeped the horn once, and two boys came bounding down the steps off the back porch and jumped into the cab of the truck with him. Cooper could hardly go anywhere lately without his junior-sized ranch hands wanting to come along. They didn't care whether it was a trip to town to buy feed or a trip to the barn to clean out the horse stalls—every trip was an excursion and every job on the ranch was an adventure for Danny and Joey.

"We're going to move most of the sheep up to their summer grazing range right after your school year ends," Cooper explained, as he turned onto the pavement and steered the truck south toward Gooding. "I'll ask Grandma and Jenny if they think it's all right for you to come along for a few days—unless you don't think you want to spend that much time away from your beds."

"We don't need to sleep in beds—we can sleep on the ground," Danny boasted. "We're not afraid."

Joey didn't say anything in support of his older brother's claim of bravery. He wanted to go, but he wasn't exactly sure that he wouldn't be just a little bit afraid to sleep outside on the ground—he had never done it before. There were coyotes, and porcupines, and other things that moved around in the dark.

"Are you sleeping on the ground, Grandpa?" Joey asked.

"Yep," he answered. "The sheep camp wagon isn't big enough for everyone, and that's where the shepherd sleeps."

"Will he let us come inside if it rains?" Joey worried.

"I think so. He might even build a fire for us in the wood stove so we can warm up a little—how would that be? And we'll cook all our meals on the campfire, if it isn't raining."

The boys were satisfied—they wanted to go. It sounded to them like the kind of place they would like to stay for the entire summer. Maybe they could talk Grandma and Jenny into letting them stay longer than a few days. They peppered Cooper with questions about what it was like to trail the sheep up to the high pastures, and how the sheep could be kept from wandering off and getting lost in the trees or tall brush.

"Who watches the sheep at night?" Danny asked.

"The dogs keep a close eye on them," Cooper assured. "And the shepherd goes out to check on them during the night if he hears a disturbance."

"What's a disturbance?" Joey asked.

"Noise—anything out of the ordinary—a ruckus. If he hears a mountain lion or coyote or anything that doesn't sound right he'll take a lantern and go out to check on the sheep," Cooper explained. "And if his big guard dogs start to bark, then he'll know something's up."

Joey rode quietly for the next few minutes, until they reached the outskirts of Gooding. He contemplated whether it was really safe to sleep outside on the ground while predators circled the band of sheep at night, looking for a vulnerable lamb, and an easy meal.

"Can I go inside the sheep wagon if there's a disturbance?" he asked.

"Don't worry about those old coyotes, men," Cooper assured, with a chuckle and a smile. "They won't want to come near the smell of men and horses, and they won't like the campfire smoke much, either."

They pulled into a parking spot at the Dairy Queen, and any thoughts of predators vanished as the boys tumbled out of the cab of the pickup and raced to the door. They held it open and waited for the man with the wallet that held the payment for their ice cream. By the time they arrived at the farm and ranch supply, their chocolate-dipped, soft ice cream cones had been swallowed, except for the small dribbles they wore on their chins and on the front of their shirts.

Cooper let the boys pick out new bandanas while he tried on two pairs of boots before they went to the back of the store to load a push cart with sacks of grain and a few grooming supplies for the horses. He stopped by the boot department again on the way out and picked up a pair of boots in his size—the first pair he tried on—and made his way back to the cash register counter at the front of the store.

"Aren't you gonna wear your new boots, Grandpa?" Joey asked, as they waited their turn at the check-out counter.

"Actually, they're for Grandma," Cooper philosophized. "But I'm gonna wear 'em, I guess."

Cooper enjoyed making runs into Gooding and Fairfield with the boys every chance he got. It helped to break up the monotony of daily life on the ranch, and he was growing accustomed to stopping for ice cream every time they came into town—something that Danny and Joey always helped him to remember. He made the drive alone after Jenny and her older brothers moved away from the ranch—most of the time, at least. Betty sometimes rode along with him, but usually one of them stayed behind, just in case something happened with the animals that needed their immediate attention. Betty had proven to be a capable animal caretaker within their first year of marriage, and she never

The Lamb Cart

shrugged off a chore that was necessary to help keep the ranch operating smoothly, if not profitably.

The next two weeks went by too quickly for Cooper. He hadn't taken the time to get a flat tire replaced on the old sheep camp wagon, and he needed to stock it with firewood and a few basic food supplies, like coffee and flour, salt and sugar, and maybe a couple of jars of honey to keep his shepherd happy. Petri's youngest son had a sweet tooth, and loved to smother his fresh, hot biscuits with butter and honey.

Those same weeks dragged on for Danny and Joey—they counted the days until school was let out for the summer. They even spent their Friday and Saturday nights in sleeping bags in the sheep wagon, and pretended that they were out on the summer grazing land in the Sawtooth Range above Sun Valley. They searched inside every compartment, box and bin, both inside and outside the old wagon, trying to figure out what was supposed to be stored inside. The firewood storage box was easy to figure out, littered on the bottom with wood chips, pieces of bark and pine cones. Some of the other nooks and hidey-holes were more mysterious, and smelled of corn meal and coffee grounds, or some other aroma or musty odor that they couldn't recognize.

Joey found a box of stick matches on top of a cupboard shelf next to the wood stove and put them in his coat pocket to take them inside for Grandma. He opened another drawer, and retrieved a small, heavy box filled with green cylindrical objects, capped with shiny gold metal. He pushed them into his vacant coat pocket while Danny was busy peering into the roomy storage space under the built-in bunk. Danny's head was stuck in as far as he could reach in an attempt to discover more interesting treasures that might be hidden in the dark corners of the storage compartment.

When they finally abandoned the sheep wagon at Grandma Betty's behest, they raced across the weed-covered ground toward the back of the house and bounded up the steps to heed the call for supper. Joey sat down at the table without removing his coat, and without stopping to wash his hands.

"Go hang up your coat and wash up first," Betty reminded him. "Danny, you go wash up, too."

Joey stood up and emptied his coat pockets onto the kitchen table, then walked to the back porch and hung up his coat. Cooper eyed the two boxes on the table in front of Joey's chair, and quickly pushed his chair back to stand, but his wife already scooped them up before little June could reach for the box of matches or get a closer look at the box of shotgun shells. Betty walked to the refrigerator, visibly annoyed with her husband, but otherwise unruffled. She had raised two boys on the same ranch without having anything blown up, and sent them away as adults, with all their body parts.

"You might want to look around in the barn and shed for anything else that could get these kids into trouble," she counseled her husband, as she opened the cabinet door above the refrigerator and put the ammunition box and matches inside.

"I'll take care of it," Cooper promised. "First thing in the morning."

"What happened to my boxes?" Joey asked when he returned to the table after washing his hands at the kitchen sink.

"Grandma put them away," Cooper quickly interjected. "Let's talk about them after we eat."

"I found them in the sheep camp," Joey explained innocently, staking a fair claim to his property.

"I know," Cooper said, spooning a large helping of mashed potatoes onto his plate. "They shouldn't have been left there—it was my mistake—they're dangerous."

Danny and Joey both had trouble absorbing the truth of Cooper's remarks, and they couldn't imagine that he was ever mistaken about anything.

Alice stared, wide-eyed, from across the table. She knew what shotgun shells were. Her father had hunted pheasant, and he kept the boxes of shells for his shotgun in a high cupboard above the kitchen sink. Both of her parents had sternly warned her never to try to climb up on the counter and get into the upper cabinet. She never did. And she never knew where her father kept his shotgun.

The following morning, before the children were awakened for breakfast, Cooper pulled his shotgun and lever-action Winchester repeater out from under his bed and took them out to the harness and tool shed, padlocked them inside a long wooden box, and locked the box up in a corner cabinet. Out of sight, out of mind—that's what his grandfather used to say. He could discuss gun safety with the boys at a better time. He questioned his own wisdom about discussing guns with them at all, but in the end, he decided they were not too young to learn about the uses and dangers of firearms—even if they were too young to handle them.

"Why don't you boys help me hook up the sheep wagon, and we'll tow it up to the summer range today," Cooper offered, over a breakfast plate of lamb chops and eggs. "Maybe we can stop in Hailey along the way."

"What's in Hailey?" Danny asked.

"I don't know," Cooper replied. "Let's look around and see, why don't we—maybe we'll find something we need."

"That's where the hospital is where Daphne was born," Alice explained to Danny. "There's a lot of people in Hailey."

"I know," Danny countered, not wanting to appear ignorant.

"How many people?" June inquired, wanting to hear specifics—even though she could barely count to ten.

"A lot more than we have here on the ranch," Jenny answered. "Now eat your breakfast before it gets cold."

"What's this?" June asked, lifting a lamb chop on the end of her fork.

"It's meat, June-bug. Just eat it—it's good for you," Jenny instructed.

"What kind of meat?" June pressed, insistent upon a clear answer to her question.

"Good meat—now eat, or Grandpa won't let us come with him when he sets up the sheep camp."

Jenny still had a clear memory of the day when her older brothers told her that mutton came from the same animals that she helped her dad feed when they were lambs. She was so upset when she first discovered that the chops she had been eating since she was old enough to chew her food came from the same sweet, woolly orphans she had bottle fed in the spring, that she came very close to becoming a vegetarian that year—and she was only four years old.

"It's lamb," Joey said.

June stopped chewing, and stared at Joey for a moment, contemplating whether or not he might be wrong about the source of the tasty breakfast meat. Somehow, she had learned to take a pragmatic view of the food sources on the ranch—a broad-minded view for a three-year-old. She resumed her chewing without further delay to insure that she wouldn't be left behind when Grandpa Barnett took the sheep camp wagon up to the mountains.

"It's good," she agreed, nodding at Jenny as she took another bite.

Cooper backed the pickup to the sheep wagon and hooked it up to the trailer hitch, then walked around the wagon to make sure that all the doors were latched and everything was secured, inside and out. He loaded up the firewood box with help from all four children, and took one final walk around the wagon to double check everything. One tire was nearly flat, and he exhaled a mild expletive under his breath. It was only a minor setback—he had replaced the old wooden axles twenty years earlier with axles from an old horse trailer, and the tires were interchangeable. He took twenty minutes to take a tire off the horse trailer and bolt it onto the axle of the sheep wagon, and then tossed the flat tire into the bed of the pickup.

"Let's load up, men," Cooper called to the boys. "We'll drop this tire off at Shorty Henderson's garage on our way through town—so he can fix it."

Betty and Jenny finished packing a lunch and loaded the girls into the station wagon, not intending to wait on Cooper.

"We'll meet you at the mercantile in Hailey," Betty called out to Cooper from the car window, as she started down the gravel drive. "I think we'll stop and say hello to my aunt while we're in town."

"Don't be late—we can't wait for you," Cooper said.

"I know where to find you," Betty called out, as she accelerated down the long drive.

Cooper followed the dust cloud set up by Betty's station wagon and towed the sheep camp wagon out to the highway and turned toward Fairfield to drop off the flat tire to be repaired. Danny and Joey kneeled up on the seat and watched the sheep wagon as it followed along behind the pickup, keeping pace with them all the way into town.

"Can you fill us up, Shorty?" Cooper asked the skinny proprietor, as he pulled onto the concrete platform and stopped next to the gas pumps. "I'll check the oil."

"Looks like you're about to set up the sheep camp again," Shorty observed. "And you've got some extra help this year, I see."

"They're pretty reliable help," Cooper agreed, wiping the oil off the dipstick with a paper towel before reinserting it to check the level. "I better have a quart of thirty weight."

"Is that a flat you need repaired?" Shorty asked, when he noticed the deflated tire in the bed of the pickup as he topped off the fuel tank.

"Yeah. If you could have it fixed by this afternoon, I'll pick it up on the way home."

Cooper dug a few coins out of his pockets and bought orange sodas for the boys from the old top-lid dispensing machine that sat outside the door to the garage office.

"Let's roll, men," Cooper called out to Danny and Joey, after signing a sales slip for Shorty. "We gotta catch up with those women before they get lost."

"Where would they get lost?" Danny wanted to know.

"In almost any store that sells baby clothes," Cooper muttered. "And once they're in—it'll be near impossible to get 'em out."

"Do baby clothes cost a lot of money, Grandpa?" Joey asked.

"Not as much as we paid for those mustangs," Cooper replied. "So I guess we got nothin' to say about what they spend on the baby—or themselves, for that matter."

"But we needed those mustangs," Danny insisted. "Who needs baby clothes?"

"Not us, that's for sure," Cooper agreed.

"Is this Hailey, Grandpa?" Joey asked, as they reached the outskirts of a small town.

"Nope—this is Bellevue. Hailey is about ten or twelve miles farther up the road—it won't be long now."

Cooper slowed the pickup as they drove through the main part of town, and he saw Betty's station wagon parked outside the mercantile. The women and girls were nowhere to be seen. The boys recognized the station wagon, too.

"I guess we've lost the ladies," Cooper said. "Maybe we better stop for some lunch in Hailey and wait for them there—unless you want to stop and help them shop for baby dresses."

The boys took a quick vote and it was unanimous—they wanted to stay with Grandpa Barnett and the sheep camp wagon. The odds were much better that they would have a new outdoor adventure if they stayed with the old sheepman. They only needed a half hour in Hailey to wolf down burgers and fries at Lucky's Cafe before they were back on the road again. They didn't see the station wagon in town, so Cooper guessed that the women were still shopping, or had driven up to Fourth Street to visit Betty's aunt.

They found the familiar campsite alongside Murdoch Creek a few miles north of Sun Valley, and Cooper got out of the truck to walk the small meadow to see if the ground was too soft from the recent spring rains to bear the weight of the pickup and sheep wagon without sinking in up to the axle.

"The ground seems firm enough over here," he called back to the boys. "You better stay in the truck until we get parked."

He walked back to the truck and pulled it ahead, stopping close to a circle of big rocks that had been arranged years earlier to contain a large campfire. Cooper was glad that he arrived ahead of Petri Beraza and his son. He disconnected the wagon from the trailer hitch, and Danny and Joey bailed out of the pickup and helped to lift the wagon tongue off the trailer hitch.

"Why don't you gather some firewood boys, and we'll build us a campfire before the ladies arrive," Cooper instructed. "There's a dead tree on the ground right over there—just pick up the broken branches and a few dry pine cones."

It didn't take long for the boys to drag and carry a large pile of firewood, and Cooper got an axe out of a box on the sheep wagon to cut up enough wood to keep a fire going until afternoon. He used dried pine needles and a few dried out pine cones for starter fuel, then added some smaller tree branches until he had a good blaze. The boys stood by the fire and watched the flames for awhile, then lost interest and walked down by the creek to explore.

"Stay out of the water—it's still too cold to go wading, and if you get your boots soaked I'll have to explain it to Grandma. Why don't you see who can find the biggest pine cone?"

It was a trick that used to work with his sons, and it still worked with Danny and Joey. They set out on a treasure hunt, each one determined to come back with the biggest pine cone in the forest.

"Stay close by so I can see you," Cooper admonished, as the boys began to wander a little too far into the trees.

It took less than five minutes for them to come running out of the trees, screaming for help.

"Grandpa! Something's in there—something's in the trees!" Danny shrilled, running up to Cooper with his little brother right on his heels.

Cooper grabbed the axe and walked toward the spot where the boys had emerged from the stand of pines.

"What was it?' Cooper called back to the boys, as he looked around in the trees at the edge of the small meadow.

"I don't know—it was big," Danny said.

"It was real big," Joey confirmed.

"Was it a coyote?" Cooper asked. "Did it look like a dog?"

"No—it looked mean," Danny worried.

Cooper looked around a few minutes more, and decided that whatever the boys had seen, their screaming must have frightened it away. He walked back toward the campfire, where the boys waited and watched to see if he had eliminated the source of their fear.

"You must have scared it off," he said. "It was afraid of you."

"There it is," Joey said, in a hoarse whisper, pointing toward a fallen tree near the creek.

Cooper chuckled as he watched a big porcupine waddle along the length of the downed tree, pausing now and then to sniff the ground and to overturn dead branches, looking for something to eat.

"I think we'll be all right—it's only a porcupine—but don't go near it unless you want some quills stuck in you."

Danny spent the next hour trying to catch ground squirrels and chipmunks, while Joey stayed close to the campfire, under Cooper's able protection. He wasn't sure he wanted to sleep on the ground when they came back later after checking on the sheep—not if porcupines and other wild animals were going to wander through camp.

Betty and Jenny finally showed up an hour later, and the girls ran down to join the boys at the creek, searching along the bank and in the shallow water for anything that swam or floated or hid under the smooth rocks on the creek bed.

"Don't fall in," Jenny called out to all four kids. "Or you'll have to ride home in the back of the pickup."

Cooper rolled two tree rounds closer to the fire—big blocks of wood from an old cottonwood trunk that had been missing their bark for several years, and recently used as chopping blocks for splitting firewood and as seats around the campfire, or as a handy table for a hot skillet. Betty sat down next to him and warmed herself by the fire. The shadows were growing longer as the afternoon crept in, and the mountain air cooled quickly as the sun dropped toward the western horizon. Jenny sat with her baby in the passenger seat of the station wagon, parked only a few feet from the campfire. She left the door open so that she could enjoy the fresh mountain air and the quiet sounds of the forest and stream. She watched her mother and father, sitting side by side next to the campfire—her mother posed with her arms folded as she stared into the campfire with a faraway look in her eyes. Her dad poked at the fire with a dead tree branch to stir the embers and move some stray pieces of wood onto the hot coals, raising the flames a little higher.

"Have you ever found that tree where you carved our initials, Coop?" Betty asked, turning for a moment to look over her shoulder to check on the children.

"It's a little farther upstream, I think," Cooper guessed. "I rode past it a couple of years back, but I don't remember exactly where."

"You carved a heart with an arrow through it, remember?" Betty reminisced. "It was our last year of high school, and I rode up here with your mom when you and your dad and grandpa trailed a band of sheep up here for the summer. You carved C.B.+ B.C. into the tree bark, and then you told me it looked like an algebra equation when you stepped back to admire your handiwork—you always were such a romantic."

"I can't help myself—I'm just a regular Casanova."

Jenny closed the passenger door and nursed her baby while the kids were distracted with their exploration of Murdoch Creek, and Betty sent her husband to retrieve the brown paper shopping bag filled with sandwiches and potato salad from the back of the station wagon.

"There's a fold-up card table there in the back if you want to use it to set the food on, and a couple of blankets to spread on the ground for the kids to sit on," Betty said.

"We're only going to be here just long enough to eat, and then we'll have to head back," Cooper replied. He carried the bag of food over to the campfire and set it on the ground next to his wife.

"That doesn't mean we have to set the food in the dirt, sheepman," she chided. "Go get the table and set it up next to the camp wagon. It wouldn't hurt to leave it here with a couple of folding chairs for your shepherd to use."

"He don't care about tables and chairs—he eats right out of his skillet most of the time. His food stays warm that way."

"I better not catch you eating out of a skillet—and I better not catch you teaching those boys to do it, either."

"You won't," Cooper said, smiling faintly as he stirred the coals and tossed another piece of wood on the fire.

Betty called the children to come and eat, then turned her attention back to her husband. She stood up and pulled his hat off and swatted him across the back of the head with it.

"Does that mean you won't do it—or you won't let me catch you doing it?"

"Either way, you won't catch me," Cooper chuckled. "Give me my hat."

It was almost dark when they arrived home, and Cooper went straight to the barn to feed the horses before going in for supper. Danny and Joey still had plenty of energy, so they followed him and helped to measure the oat rations for the horses. Everyone else went inside, tired from the day's outing. The evening ended early after Betty served up a quick meal of leftovers, and every child went to bed without a fuss. It had been a long and pleasant day. Betty had a family again.

The following morning Jenny was in hushed conversation with her mom when Cooper got back from his feeding chores. Cooper could tell something wasn't quite right. He sat down at the table and waited to see if he would get some information without having to ask.

"Jenny heard from Lorraine Fuller this morning," his wife said. "She's left her husband—took the baby and ran while he was out pretending to look for a job."

A dark look crossed Cooper's brow.

"Is she coming here to get the boys?" he asked.

It was the first concern that came to mind for the aging sheep rancher—he realized that he had allowed himself to become too attached to Danny and Joey since they came to live at the ranch. He knew that it was only intended to be temporary, but he couldn't help thinking of them as his own.

"No, Dad," Jenny responded. "She's moved to a dusty little desert town in southern Nevada—Indian Springs, I think she said. Her aunt lives there in a small trailer park, and she got a job as a waitress in a coffee shop at a small casino."

"So when's she coming to see her boys?"

"She can't, Dad—she's broke. She had just enough money to buy a bus ticket to Jackpot, and her aunt drove up there to get her. There's enough room in the travel trailer for Lorraine and the baby, but she can't take the boys in, too. The coffee shop where she works is close enough that she can walk there and back, so she's going to try to save enough money to get her own place."

Betty could tell that Cooper was visibly relieved. He had grown accustomed to having all the kids around the ranch during the past few months, and he had become especially attached to the boys. It would break his heart to see any of them leave.

"She's worried about her husband, Coop," Betty said. "He knows that she sent the boys to live with us, and she's afraid that he might come here looking for her."

"That shouldn't be a problem, if he's nothin' but a drunk. He won't be able to find his way out here unless somebody draws him a map—and what's he gonna do if he finds us, except leave with a butt full of rock salt?"

He got up and left the remainder of the conversation to the women—he had heard enough. He found the boys in the stables, trying to stand on a board rail and keep their balance while they brushed a Clydesdale's mane with a curry comb. They weren't having much success—Roadblock would only stand still for a few seconds before turning to walk to his feeder box to let the boys know it was out of oats. He excused the boys from their grooming chores, and invited them to ride along to run some fresh water into the stock pond.

Cooper drove the pickup around the barn and corrals and across the wide pasture, then stopped at the stock pond to open a valve and let water flow from an irrigation pipe. It would take awhile to raise the pond level and replenish it with fresh water, so he encouraged the boys to go wading.

"You can probably scare up a frog or two if you want to get in and wade around a little," Cooper suggested. "But take your boots off first."

The two brothers didn't have to be invited twice. It was a warm day. They stripped off shoes, socks and shirts quickly, and ran splashing into the shallow water. They only looked for frogs for a minute or two before they became distracted and began running back and forth through the water, splashing each other and stirring the murky pond into a muddy soup.

"Come on out of there boys—that pond's muddy enough now, and so are you. Let's let that mud settle back down so the livestock can drink. They won't want to swallow your bath water," Cooper ordered.

Joey stood and looked down at the unsettled brown water around his knees, suddenly feeling sorry for the sheep and cows, and wishing that he had not muddied their meager supply of drinking water. Cooper saw the dejected look on Joey's face.

"It'll be all right, son. Just climb on out of there and let it settle—it'll be clean enough to drink again in a half hour or so."

The boys stood under the fresh water flow of the irrigation pipe to wash the mud off, and then sat on the tailgate of the pickup to let their pants dry a little before they put their shirts and boots back on.

"Can we ride with you when you take the sheep up to Murdoch Creek?" Danny asked.

"Well, I've been thinking about that," Cooper answered. "I guess we can saddle old Blue and both of you can ride her—she's gentle enough—but you'll have to remember to bring plenty of carrots or she may get cranky and not want to carry you."

"We'll bring lots," Joey promised. "And some for Deuce, too."

"When are we leaving?" Danny asked, eager to get on the way.

"As soon as Tony Beraza gets here with his horse and dogs—probably tomorrow morning," Cooper explained. "The wind's picking up—we better head back to the house now—we're done here."

They drove back to the barn and saddled Deuce and Blue to go riding in the pasture. Alice and June came out of the house when they saw the horses, and Cooper put them aboard Deuce and led them around in the corral. After a few minutes, they had enough, and got down to go back inside. The girls liked feeding the horses, but weren't as interested in riding them as Danny and Joey were.

"Let's go, men," Cooper encouraged the boys as he climbed into the saddle and nudged Deuce forward with his boot heels.

Blue fell in behind Deuce and kept pace with the gelding, just as she had always done when they were out on the trail together. The old mare was better suited to pulling the lamb cart than being ridden as a saddle horse, but had equal patience for both tasks.

"Give her some rein—she knows where to go," he instructed, as Danny held on to the reins and saddle horn with one hand—just like he had seen Cooper do. Joey held on tight to Danny and watched the clouds roll by.

The boys rode double around the pasture and up the slope to the stock pond, where Cooper dismounted and shut down the water valve so the pond wouldn't overflow its banks.

Joey was content to ride behind his big brother. It felt good to be on a horse—it was as if the world had stopped for him while the big bay mare plodded around the pasture behind the lead horse, and all of life's worries were put on hold while they rode the pasture. Cowboys didn't waste their time with too much worry, he decided.

Everyone in the Barnett house was up early the next morning, and Cooper was already outside helping Tony Beraza unload his gear from his pickup and put it in the back of the station wagon. Tony had to get up at four o'clock that morning to get to the Barnett Ranch before dawn. He lowered the tailgate on his pickup to let two Great Pyrenees guardian dogs jump down, and then unloaded his paint mustang mare from the trailer while Cooper finished transferring his belongings to the other pickup.

The hooves on Tony's mustang were almost as big around as dinner plates—a sign that it may have had some draft horse somewhere in its family tree. It was steady and sure-footed on the trail, and more importantly, it knew its way home. He had given his oldest brother two hundred dollars for the nine-year-old mare three years earlier and always believed he got the best part of the bargain.

The horses were saddled and ready when the sun came up, and Betty opened the back door to release Danny and Joey before they finished their breakfast. She handed a paper bag with cinnamon rolls to Cooper after he helped the boys climb aboard the bay mare.

"Make sure they eat something, will you?" she urged.

"I wouldn't worry—they'll probably have them eaten before we get through the gate at the lower pasture."

"Are you sure it was a good idea to let those little boys go along with you? It's a long, slow ride and they're going to be awfully tired and saddle-sore."

"Do you want to tell them no?" Cooper asked, as he watched the eager boys ride the old mare around in circles near the barn. "If they have a hard time of it, Tony and I can always let the boys ride double behind us."

"We'll be waiting for you late this afternoon along the highway south of Bellevue—are you sure you'll make it that far today?"

"I think so—don't worry about it so much, Betty—I'm sure we'll be fine."

"I wasn't worried about you. You and Tony Beraza deserve what you get for choosing to be sheepherders your whole lives."

"It's what I'm good at, dear—that's why I'm so happy all the time." Cooper grinned as he turned his horse and led the other sheepmen, large and small, up the slope behind the barn to round up the band of nearly 2,000 sheep. He whistled to his dogs, but Banjo and Holly had already started up the hillside ahead of the riders, well aware of the task ahead.

Beraza's big guard dogs followed along with the men and boys, waiting until their master introduced them to the sheep and allowed them to slowly mingle with the band. He was always careful not to allow his dogs to startle or disturb the sheep. It wouldn't take long—not more than a few days—before the sheep grew accustomed to the presence of the big white dogs, and realized that they were not going to cause them any harm or herd them around like the Border Collies did.

Tony worked on his family's ranch in Carey, and hired out as a shepherd for five months of the year. He took most of his pay in trade, getting his pick of ewes and a number of spring lambs. It was an arrangement that he had worked out with Cooper years earlier, and it worked to the advantage of both men. Cooper didn't have to come up with as much cash at the end of the trailing in mid-October. Tony was able to add to the Beraza Ranch stock, and take a bigger share of his family's yearly sales. He was determined to have his own place someday, unless his older brothers gave up on ranching and ventured out to do something different with their lives.

Betty, Jenny and the girls watched from the living room window as the riders and their dogs moved the large band of sheep northwest toward Camas Creek. They disappeared from sight as they moved down below the ridgeline toward the suspension bridge that spanned the creek bed and allowed a crossing when the water in the creek was too high or moving too swiftly to cross safely.

Tony crossed the bridge first, allowing his sure-footed mare to pick its way slowly across the planks. The old horse didn't balk when it came to a place where a plank was missing—it simply slowed and stepped over the gap, then resumed its steady pace across the wide span to the other side. One of the big guardian dogs followed close behind, and the first sheep began to fall in line—cautiously at first, but in ever-increasing numbers as they crowded the bridge entrance to cross behind the horse and dog.

Cooper and the boys stayed on the ridge and watched as the herding dogs moved the band of sheep down the hillside to the stream crossing. They watched and waited for half an hour or more as the sheep moved down the hill and onto the bridge—a steady parade of woolies making their way to the far side of Camas Creek on the trail to the summer grazing range.

Danny felt uneasy about crossing the narrow suspension bridge on horseback, and he knew his little brother was nervous about it too. Joey had stopped talking ten minutes ago, and that wasn't like him.

"Does Blue know how to cross the bridge?" Danny asked, as he rode alongside Cooper and felt the fear rising in his chest.

"Don't you worry, men," Cooper assured. "Blue is steady and not afraid—she's been across that bridge many times—even on windy days when the bridge sways a little. You'll be fine."

The closer they came to the bridge, the more obvious it became to the boys that it spanned the banks high above the stream and the rocky stream bed below—perhaps not a canyon, but still frightening to novice riders so young and inexperienced. Cooper glanced at the boys from time to time, just to measure the apprehension they might be feeling about the crossing.

"You just hang onto the saddle horn and give Blue her head—don't try to rein her—you'll have an easy ride," Cooper assured again. "Trust your horse—Blue knows what to do."

Danny and Joey were both silent—they had no questions or comments—they just wanted to be on the opposite bank as quickly as possible.

The last sheep moved onto the bridge, followed closely by Banjo and Holly, and the dogs moved patiently so that the sheep would not be startled. Cooper waited until the dogs had nearly reached the other side before he urged his horse onto the bridge. Deuce lowered his head momentarily, and lifted it again, to get a good look at the bridge he was stepping onto before moving carefully across the wooden planks. Blue followed immediately behind—so close that her head nudged the rump of the horse in front. Deuce jumped a little when he felt the push from behind, and Cooper reined his horse in to keep it from breaking into a trot.

"Whoa—easy now," he soothed.

Joey panicked and began to cry—he had expected a slow and steady plod from one side of the bridge to the other—and he was startled at the sudden and unexpected movement up ahead that caused the bridge to sway slightly.

"Grandpa, Joey's crying!" Danny called out. He was on the verge of breaking down in tears himself.

Cooper turned around in his saddle to look at the boys, and saw two panic-stricken kids clinging to the saddle and each other. They looked as if they might come off the horse at the first sudden movement.

"Just stay put, boys—I'll be right there."

Cooper stepped down out of the saddle carefully, tied off his reins to the saddle horn, and moved to the side to allow Deuce to walk across the bridge without a rider. He stepped up quickly to grab Blue's reins close to the bit and keep the mare from following on the heels of the gelding as his mount reached the far side and walked out onto solid ground.

"You're okay—just hold on now—no need to cry," he calmed the boys. "Just close your eyes if you don't want to look down—I'm going to lead you across."

Cooper led the mare at a steady, even pace across the bridge, but with a temporary pause when they reached the spot where a plank was missing. Blue hesitated to make sure of the sound footing before stepping across the small gap. She gave a little jump with her hind legs as she hopped across the open space, and the boys gave a small cry in unison and gripped more tightly.

"It's okay—it's okay," Cooper calmed the young riders again. "We made it—that's the only rough spot—we're almost there."

He kept talking to Danny and Joey in a steady voice until they were safely on solid ground, then came around to the side of the horse and gave both of them a gentle slap on their boots to congratulate them for their courage.

"That wasn't so bad, was it?" he said, reassuring the boys to make them feel like it was just an everyday event on the sheep ranch.

Danny relaxed and smiled, and shook his head to agree that it wasn't so bad after all. Joey looked back over his shoulder at the narrow bridge they had just braved on horseback, and hoped that he wouldn't have to do it again.

"Do we have to go back that way?" Joey asked nervously.

"Nope—you're gonna ride home in Grandma's car. The sheep won't be coming back this way until the fall."

When the sheep bridge over Camas Creek disappeared in the distance behind them the boys' confidence returned quickly, and Joey began to serenade the sheep with his rendition of the state song—*And Here We Have Idaho*—the only song he had ever learned in its entirety. Danny tried keep up with his brother's song lyrics, and Cooper tried to stay far enough ahead of them to spare his eardrums.

By late afternoon, Cooper could see the line of trees along the banks of the Big Wood River, and could make out the border of fencing far off to the east that marked the right of way of Highway 75 leading north to Bellevue and Hailey. The afternoon shadows were lengthening, and he decided that it would be best if he and the boys rode east toward the highway, and then follow it north until they came across Betty and the girls. Banjo and Holly didn't have to be told to remain with the sheep—they had been through the routine many times. Cooper and the boys rode ahead to catch up with Tony, and to let him know where they were going, then turned east toward the highway.

It was dusk when Betty found Cooper and the boys, and exchanged a sleeping bag and sack full of food for the two tired and dusty boys. Danny and Joey climbed into the far back of the station wagon without protest, ready to go home to a warm bath and a hot meal. June peered over the back seat at the two dusty little sheepherders, and stared at their dirty faces without comment.

"Look for us not more than two or three miles up the road," Cooper suggested to his wife. "We'll settle the sheep here for the night, and we should make it to Murdoch Creek by late tomorrow."

He tied off the sleeping bag and food sack to Blue's saddle, and rode off abruptly to catch up with the sheep. He caught up with Tony and showed him the sack of food to get the shepherd's attention. He turned the lead ewes back into the band and stopped their forward progress. The sheep took advantage of the rest stop and began to graze through the brush and spring grass.

Cooper tied the horses off in a grassy area, and removed their saddles and bridles for the evening—they hadn't been ridden very hard, so the animals weren't sweat-lathered. Still, he wiped them down before he sat on the ground with Tony to eat the food that Betty had left for them. Chicken and biscuits and coleslaw and beans—packed in plastic containers for the ride—good belly filler for hungry sheepmen. They left a little chicken and a few biscuits for the dogs—nobody remembered to bring dog food for the trail up to Murdoch Creek.

They built a small campfire to warm themselves after the sun went down, but let it burn out quickly after they climbed into their sleeping bags and drifted quickly off to sleep, leaving the protection of the sheep to the big white Pyrenees dogs.

The Lamb Cart

Morning came early for the herders—before the dawn, and with a noisy yelping and growling in the dark, no more than a hundred yards from where they had camped for the night. Tony Beraza was up and had his boots on in seconds—off and running through the dark with his Winchester rifle in hand—ready for the worst. Sheep were scattering and bleating, desperate to flee the scene of the violence. Tony could barely make out the outline and light color of one of his big guard dogs in the dim light—standing over a dark shape lying on the ground. He cocked the lever action on his rifle to slide a cartridge into the chamber and advanced slowly, lowering the muzzle toward the unmoving figure that lay prone on the ground, inches away from his dog.

He poked at it with the muzzle of his rifle, hammer cocked and finger on the trigger, just in case it came to life to menace the living once again. It remained on the ground, lifeless and still. He leaned closer to get a better look at the animal in the dim light, and recognized the distinct features of a coyote—an opportunist that prowled the perimeter of the band of sheep—looking for an easy target among the smallest or the weakest among the herd. It met up with a Great Pyrenees instead, and felt the brunt of the big dog's ferocity and protective instincts.

Cooper arrived on the scene a half minute later, and witnessed the near-bloodless remains of a battle between carnivore and protector. A coyote stood little chance of success against a dog that had been bred for thousands of years to be a fearless protector—a fierce defender of the flock that would not hesitate to take on a wolf or a mountain lion—and would certainly not back down from a coyote. The would-be killer lay still—its spinal cord severed and neck broken swiftly by a crushing bite from the huge white dog.

"I'm gonna need a couple of these dogs, for sure," Cooper remarked, as he stood over the warm coyote carcass, impressed with the quickness and efficiency of the gallant guardian of the sheep.

"Yeah—they know what to do when there's trouble," Tony agreed. "Usually they just chase them off—I guess this one didn't want to leave. Dad said you were interested in having some for yourself—maybe he'll bring a couple of dogs from last year's litter up to Murdoch Creek in a few weeks, so you can see how they work after a little training. We put them in the pens with the lambs in the spring, just so they can get used to spending time with the sheep at a young age.

"I'd like that, Tony," Cooper nodded, marveling at how little blood was spilled in the quick and decisive battle between dog and coyote.

The sun was bringing light to the night horizon—slowly, but with ever-increasing visibility, and the men decided it was as good a time as any to start moving the band of sheep northward. They had moved the sheep more than three miles north by the time Betty showed up along the highway near Bellevue. Jenny and the girls decided to wait and make the afternoon trip, when provisions would be shuttled to the campsite at Murdoch Creek and everyone would be wide awake.

The boys were ready to join the trail ride again, their courage restored and their enthusiasm intact after a hot meal, a thorough wash, and a good night's rest. They were eager to get aboard Blue again and continue the ride to the campsite and summer range. A night's sleep and a full belly worked wonders. They talked with Betty about their frightening ordeal from the previous day on the suspension bridge as if it was an everyday event, and both boys proclaimed their fearlessness as they described the harrowing adventure. Danny insisted that they were not afraid when they crossed the narrow bridge on horseback.

Betty left fresh drinking water for the sheepherders, and a sack filled with scrambled egg sandwiches and cinnamon rolls they could eat along the way. The brothers mounted up for the ride north to Murdoch Creek and the grazing range, ready for a full day of herding on horseback. They were still saddle-sore from the previous day, but refused to complain for fear of being left behind to ride back to the ranch with Grandma Betty.

"Thanks, Betty," Cooper said, with genuine appreciation. "You spoil me."

"I know that," she answered. "But I don't know why. You should have to fix your own meals. You're old enough to know how."

"Too old," her sheepman answered with a grin.

As the band of sheep moved slowly northward, it neared the highway from time to time, and a few motorists honked and waved at the two boys riding double on the big bay mare. Danny and Joey were thrilled with their new status and waved at everyone they passed, including a mail truck driver and a farmer on a tractor who was moving his equipment from one field to another. The boys reveled in their newfound status and popularity.

"Everyone waves at us, Grandpa," Joey announced, when Cooper rode back to make sure the boys were keeping up.

"They must like you," he replied. "Or maybe they just think you look good on a horse."

It was late afternoon when the sheep pushed into the meadow and the wide clearing downstream from where the sheep camp wagon was parked two days earlier, and all four riders were relieved to climb down and tie up their horses. They only stopped once along the trail, just to finish what was left of the sandwiches, drink their fill of water, and wash the dust off their faces.

Betty and Jenny and the girls were already at the campsite when the herders arrived, and had a card table and folding chairs set up to serve what was likely to be the last home-cooked meal Tony Beraza would have delivered to him for the remainder of the summer. The cooking at the sheep camp would be up to him from that day on until October.

Cooper and Tony unloaded sleeping bags, a heavy quilt for those cold nights after the fire burned itself out, and a couple of feather pillows for a touch of luxury. Tony put away the iron skillet, Dutch oven, a box of cooking and dining utensils and a tray of tin dinnerware. Two cardboard boxes filled with his first supply of food and canned goods would get him by until Cooper could come back with whatever Tony wrote down on his list of necessities and foodstuffs.

Betty brought along three sleeping bags for Cooper and the boys, just in case they wanted to stay the night. It was the adventure the brothers had been waiting for—to sleep outside on the ground near the creek after driving the herd north to the summer range. They would have a lot to tell their friends and teachers at school after the summer ended.

Alice and June were eager to camp out for a night at first, but quickly changed their minds when Jenny explained that there were bugs and mosquitoes and wild things that prowled around in the night. June was undaunted, but her older sister went straight to the car and waited in the back seat until it was time to leave. She was not the outdoors type, and she was not ashamed of it.

The tired sheepmen slept soundly that night, lulled to sleep by the sounds of birds and squirrels, and water rushing over rocks in the cold mountain stream. Joey had forgotten all about the potential for trouble during the night from marauding predators and tiny camp robbers—overcome by his exhaustion and comforted by the warmth of his sleeping bag. He didn't stir until the sun came up and he heard the crackling blaze of a campfire and smelled the strong aroma of coffee that one of the men had boiling in a tin pot resting on an open grate over the fire.

Tony had already been out with the dogs to check on the sheep, and offered to share his meager breakfast of biscuits and coffee with his companions.

"Is Grandma coming with cinnamon rolls?" Danny asked.

"She'll be here," Cooper assured. "But I don't know exactly when."

The boys gave in to hunger, and accepted a breakfast of biscuits and honey before they went off to entertain themselves along the banks of the stream.

Betty arrived late with Jenny and the girls, and Jenny took her father aside to report on the morning's events.

"I got a call from Bart Crenshaw's office this morning. He said that he's attempting to get a change of venue—moving the girls' custody case from Boise to Fairfield. I don't understand what he's doing—I don't want everyone in town to have their noses in my business any more than they already do. I told him that I don't mind driving to Boise whenever it's necessary."

"Why did he say it was important to move it to our dinky little town?" Cooper asked, surprised at Crenshaw's tactics and reasoning. "Isn't it easier for him to work on it in Boise?"

"I don't know, Dad—he just told me to trust him."

Cooper stared blankly at his daughter for a moment, unable to explain what he didn't understand.

"Okay, well maybe you should." He was at a loss, but he reckoned that he would never ask Bart Crenshaw for advice on sheep ranching, so why not trust the man's judgment in matters of the law. It wasn't for him to question the lawyer's wisdom. There was a reason that Owen Bryant had sent Jenny to Bart Crenshaw, and Cooper was certain that it was a good one.

CHAPTER THIRTEEN
GARDEN HARVEST

Betty's garden usually began to yield it's bounty for the kitchen table by late May or early June, but this year it was a few days late in sprouting. A two-acre garden that usually took a week of steady work to plant with Cooper's help stretched into a two week project with the children's help.

Every tomato plant that Alice placed into the earth was painstakingly aligned with the one next to it, and the soil was lovingly pressed around the roots. Her little sister lightly caressed the radish and carrot seeds in the palm of her hand with her fingertips before she dropped them gently into the planting holes and smoothed the garden dirt over the top. The only experience the girls had with tending plants were the window sill variety that their grandmother had fussed with daily over the kitchen sink, and none of her house plants ever produced anything to eat.

Danny and Joey, meanwhile, had scattered as many corn kernels in the watering furrows as they did in the small holes that Cooper made in the evenly mounded rows intended for growing a crop of corn. The reckless planting process was beginning to wear on Cooper, and his frustration only mounted when Joey dropped a fistful of seed into a small planting pocket, tamping the soil down firmly as he proclaimed that he was going to grow the biggest corn stalk ever seen.

"Here, watch out, now," Cooper instructed the boys. "You're just wasting seed. If you plant too many together, they'll crowd each other out, and none of them will get enough water or room to grow."

Joey stared at his handiwork, stunned that his gardening theory was flawed. He continued on, planting only the amount that he had been shown, but he left his generous seed planting undisturbed, just in case Grandpa Barnett was wrong about the possibility of a giant corn stalk. Cooper hoped that the boys would lose interest soon, and wander off to spend some time with the dogs and horses, or to explore the graveyard of rusted farm implements abandoned in the tall, dead grass behind the equipment shed. But the brothers wouldn't give up—they wouldn't think of leaving a job unfinished as long as Grandpa Barnett needed their expert assistance.

In spite of all the help they received from the children, Cooper and Betty were able to finish planting the garden in two weeks. It was late in getting started, but with ample water and sunshine, they could expect to begin reaping the harvest from their two-acre cornucopia in another month.

The boys followed Cooper almost every day when he walked to the irrigation headgate to let water run into the feeder ditch at the top of the garden furrows, and they followed the path of the water as it made its way along the deep furrows toward the lower end of the garden.

Alice and June frequently checked on the growth of the tomato plants during the next few days, watching for the first evidence of tiny green fruit to emerge from the end of the stems.

"Why don't we just buy stuff at the store?" June finally questioned, impatient to see more immediate results from her efforts.

"You'll be glad that you waited when you see how good it tastes," Betty told the little girl, as she hoed a few intrusive weeds that had taken root between the plants. "And we'll be able to pick fruits and vegetables for the rest of the summer—more than we can eat."

"I told you," Alice lightly derided her little sister.

"I know," June said, dismissive of her big sister's I-told-you-so attitude. "I just want to know when we can pick something and eat it."

"Maybe we can pull a few baby carrots and have them with supper tonight," Betty proposed, quickly diffusing any concern the girls had about the long wait until harvest time.

Danny discovered a number of curved shapes cut neatly from several cabbages and lettuce leaves one afternoon, while he was pulling weeds and waiting for the water to rush down the furrows after Cooper opened the headgate near the upper end of the garden. The tiny, scalloped edges of the crescent cuts were trimmed neatly out of the leaves, and continued along the rows of leafy growth for more than twenty feet.

"What's this?" he asked, when Cooper came walking back through the garden to admire the maturing crop of vegetables.

"Interlopers," Cooper replied with a frown, as he pulled a leaf from a head of lettuce and inspected it carefully. "We've got rabbits men—they'll clean out the whole garden unless we catch them."

"Where are we going?" Joey asked, as he rushed to catch up with his big brother and to follow Cooper into the shed.

"We're going to catch interlopers," Danny explained.

Cooper considered setting a couple of old squirrel traps, and then decided against the idea when he thought one of the dogs or children might step in one accidentally and set it off. He opted for an old wooden box, propped up with a stick on one end and tied at the bottom with a long length of baling twine. It would take patience, and early morning vigilance to watch and wait for the little invaders to come out for breakfast. A small pile of fruit and vegetables placed under the open box trap may be more enticing than the fresh lettuce leaves and carrot tops the rabbits feasted upon daily without restraint. The trappers left the garden for the day, granting one more night of freedom to the trespassers, and prepared to get up extra early the following morning. It was time to catch an interloper.

"This looks like a good spot," Cooper whispered, when he spotted some fresh, loose earth protruding from under a large cabbage leaf. "Let's set it here."

He set the wooden box upside down next to a leafy cabbage, and held up one end to allow Danny to prop it with a stick. Cooper tied one end of a roll of twine to the bottom end of the stick, and Joey held a bowl filled with carrots, lettuce leaves, and sliced apples while Danny built a small mound with the delicious bait near the back of the upended box. Danny unwound the long length of twine to the edge of the garden and pulled the line taut. The trappers were ready.

"How long do we have to wait?" Joey asked in a hushed voice, but far too close to the trap to remain unheard by their prey.

"As long as we have to—let's be quiet now," Cooper said. "Those big ears on a rabbit aren't just for show. Those little cottontails can hear you real good, and from a long ways away."

Cooper lay down on his stomach in the dirt and gripped the line with Danny, just to be sure that when the moment came to drop the trap there would be no hesitation. The brothers were silent and watchful. Cooper rested his chin on his forearm and fell asleep—the weedy patch of cool earth was his cradle. He woke up when his hat was knocked off.

"We got him!" cried Danny, as he yanked hard on the line, knocking Cooper's hat off his reclining head. "Come on!"

Both boys scrambled to their feet and raced toward the wooden box trap, eager to see their trapped prey.

"Hold on, boys," Cooper called after them, slapping the dirt off his hat against his pant leg as he got to his feet. "Don't lift the box yet—it'll get away."

Cooper lifted one side of the box just enough to push his forearm under it and feel around until he was able to get a firm grip on the frantic rabbit. He overturned the box and exposed the struggling cottontail that he held firmly by the skin and fur on the furry animal's neck and shoulders.

"Can I hold it?" Danny asked.

"What are we going to do with it now?" Joey inquired.

The brothers looked to Grandpa Barnett and waited for the answer. They hadn't thought beyond the trapping of the rabbit to end its invasion of the garden.

"We're going to eat it," Cooper said plainly.

The brothers were speechless. It never occurred to them that their mission extended beyond a capture and release of the furry little varmint—somewhere far from the garden, where it wasn't likely to find its way back. Cooper could sense the hesitation in Danny and Joey to do anything quite so drastic as to end the life of a bunny, just because it ate some leafy vegetables from the garden.

"We're growing everything we need in that garden," Cooper explained. "Rabbit stew, fried rabbit with green salad and carrots, barbequed rabbit with corn on the cob—yep, everything we need is right here in the garden."

Suddenly, it made sense. The boys were satisfied with the menu, and followed Cooper to the chopping block where they witnessed the first step in the process to making good rabbit stew.

"Don't you let Alice hear you talk like that, mister," Betty scolded her husband, when he came into the kitchen with a skinned rabbit, proclaiming a victory in the garden for himself and the boys. "You'll break her little heart."

"Doesn't she like to eat?" Cooper asked. "I only said that I thought we could harvest a rabbit every day or two, along with the other things in the garden."

"Don't you have chores to do?" Betty asked her insensitive husband.

"Isn't she tired of mutton?" Cooper grumbled, on his way out the back door to join the boys in the barn. "I'm tired of mutton."

He stopped at the bottom of the porch steps and called up to his wife through the screen door.

"Why don't you tell her it's chicken?"

Jenny came into the kitchen with the baby after her mom had already started breakfast for the girls. Cooper and the boys had eaten and gone on their way an hour earlier.

"I wish we could get back to a schedule where everyone eats at the same time," Betty complained. "This isn't like any ranch I ever heard of—you'd think we were serving brunch from seven to nine at a country club."

"What's bothering you, Mom?" Jenny asked. "I know it's not about serving brunch. And I don't think they start serving brunch at a country club that early."

The Lamb Cart

"I don't understand why that city lawyer is trying to move your custody case down here to Fairfield. It just seems to me like it's going to drag it out longer than necessary—and what good will it do?"

"He said that it's better if the case is heard in the same jurisdiction where the girls are living and going to school, Mom. He said it will be easier to get written testimony from Alice's teacher, and letters from other people who know us."

"Can't her teacher send a letter to Boise? I'm just worried about that woman from the child services agency that you talk about all the time. What if she comes down here and noses around for information from the town gossips? She'll find out that you showed up with two other kids at the same time you came home with the girls, and then she might want to know all about Danny and Joey. It just seems so unnecessary, that's all."

"We've got nothing to hide, Mom," Jenny insisted. "Those boys are here with their mother's permission—and at her request."

"What if the judge in Fairfield thinks you've taken too much on yourself, and decides that it's best if the girls go to foster homes?"

"Mom, I appreciate everything you've done for us, honestly. I couldn't have done this alone—there's just no way that I could. But you have to let Mr. Crenshaw do his job—I think he knows what he's doing."

"Maybe you're right," Betty relented, pausing to reflect and consider how attorney Bart Crenshaw had become involved in the matter. "I doubt that the Governor would steer your father in the wrong direction."

"You *know* he wouldn't, Mom."

CHAPTER FOURTEEN
DOG DAYS

Alice was eager to get back to school and see the friends she had made in the brief time that she had attended Fairfield Elementary School before it was recessed for the summer in late May. But summer was going by far too quickly to suit Danny and Joey. They looked forward to every camping and fishing trip so they could stay at the sheep camp with Grandpa Barnett and Tony Beraza.

"Are we going to the sheep camp this week, Grandpa?" Danny asked.

"I think it's about time we did," Cooper responded. "Tony must be running low on provisions by now."

"We could take him some ice cream," Joey suggested. "And show him how to catch a rabbit."

"I don't think he needs our help to catch a rabbit, son," Cooper laughed. "But there's a lot of stuff he does need, so why don't we make a list tonight after supper—maybe add a couple of jars of honey to the list. He likes it, and it won't melt like ice cream before we get to Murdoch Creek."

"If it starts to melt, I could eat it," Joey giggled.

"I'm sure you could," Cooper agreed.

They made their list after supper as planned, and Cooper learned that inviting the boys to contribute wasn't a wise decision. Danny suggested taking some comic books to Tony Beraza, so that he would have something to read at night, and Joey lobbied hard to include chocolate bars and tootsie pops to the list of necessities.

Cooper hooked the horse trailer to his pickup before breakfast the following morning, and loaded Deuce and Blue before going inside to eat a quick breakfast and get the boys out to the truck. He loaded a box filled with fresh-picked ears of corn, carrots, and potatoes into the back of the truck, then called the dogs to climb aboard, and they set off for Hailey to pick up the rest of Tony's provisions before continuing on to the camp site.

Tony Beraza was as pleased to have company as he was to get fresh supplies, and he was just as happy to find a bag with some chocolate bars tucked inside, but he suspected the superhero comic book wasn't intended for him. He hadn't spoken with a human for more than three weeks, and although he loved the companionship of his dogs, he missed having a two-way conversation with a human now and then.

He helped Cooper to unload the boxes and bags of rice, flour, coffee, and other necessities, and he smiled when he found the jars of honey inside a shopping bag with a couple of boxes of oatmeal.

"Betty's coming with Jenny and the girls in a few hours," Cooper told his shepherd. "I'm sure she'll bring some lunch for us, so we'll be smart to be here at the camp when they arrive."

Cooper and Tony saddled the horses and rode with the boys to the grazing area where Tony had last left the large band of sheep. The sheep were less than a half a mile from the camp site, so they didn't really need the horses, but it gave the boys a chance to ride, and that was the main purpose of the trip as far as Danny and Joey were concerned.

Some of the sheep had wandered high up the hillside and away from the main band, so Cooper sent Banjo and Holly to round them up and bring the strays back down to join the others. They herded the band further west along the hillside, avoiding the areas that had already been grazed. Cooper didn't want any trouble with the Forest Service or Bureau of Land Management. The times were a lot different from when he herded sheep with his dad and grandfather. All they had to do was rely on their own common sense, and not let the sheep tear up the watershed on the hillsides with overgrazing, or wander onto private pasture land. He wished that the government agents he had to deal with on a regular basis understood nature conservancy half as well as sheep ranchers and their shepherds did.

"Do you think we should move the band back up behind the camp, just to start them in another direction?" Cooper asked his shepherd.

"I moved them there for a few days last week already," Tony replied. "Maybe they should keep on grazing in this direction for a little while longer."

Cooper acquiesced with a simple nod of his head. He knew that he could always rely on Tony Beraza's good judgment—the Beraza family had herded sheep on two continents for generations before the Barnett family had taken up sheep ranching in southern Idaho, and everything that Tony's father and grandfather knew about sheep had been passed on to him.

Men and boys rested quietly in their saddles and watched the sheep graze slowly along the hillside, nibbling on sweetgrass and other edibles as they tugged the blades of grass free from their roots and moved another step or two, then paused to chew and raise their heads to look in the direction of any unfamiliar or distracting sound.

"You think you want to keep these two guard dogs?" Tony asked, as they rested in their saddles and looked over the herd. "Your sheep have accepted them very fast, and they've been well trained. Your Border Collies are used to them, too."

"How old are they?" Cooper asked, only to learn how long the two guardians might live to be of service on his ranch.

"Solo is four, and Rosie is three—they're brother and sister, and they work very well together."

"How much will you want for them?" Cooper wanted to know, hoping he could afford the expense by the time he sold off all the lambs in the fall.

"Maybe we could trade for some more sheep," Tony suggested.

"One dog, one sheep?" Cooper asked, grinning big as he looked to Tony for a response.

"Oh, maybe more than that, I think," Tony laughed. "But not too many."

Tony Beraza had been working steadily to build his family's herd from several hundred to several thousand sheep, and he had a good eye for choosing healthy ewes and good breeding rams. Cooper had always been agreeable to a trade—it was something he could understand better than the value of money.

Betty's timing was perfect—Danny and Joey were trying to break their teeth on tootsie pops when she and Jenny arrived at the campsite with the girls and the baby. The girls got out of the car and aimed straight for the creek, splashing with their hands in the shallow edges along the grassy bank as they lay on their bellies to reach into the cool water.

Jenny called them to take a turn riding Blue around the small meadow, and that entertained the girls for another fifteen minutes, but they soon lost interest in that, too. What they really wanted to do was explore inside the sheep camp, but Jenny told them it was the shepherd's home for the summer, and that they would have to respect his privacy.

"It's where he lives," Jenny explained. "All of his things are in there, and he only has enough room for himself—besides, it's just a musty old trailer, and there's nothing much to see."

Danny and Joey listened to Jenny in silent disagreement. The magical old caravan was filled with cubby holes and secret hiding places everywhere a child could think to look. There were endless possibilities for adventure in a sheep camp, and both boys envied Tony Beraza for having such a perfect place to live for the summer.

The hours went by quickly for the children, and by late afternoon they had gathered two grocery bags full of the biggest pine cones they could find lying under the trees. Jenny had told the girls to find the cones and bag them so they could use them to make tree ornaments at Christmastime. Danny and Joey didn't know or care what they were going to be used for—they were happy to gather them simply for something to do.

"Look at this one, Jenny," June proclaimed, with enormous pride for having found such a large and perfectly symmetrical cone.

"I see, June-bug," Jenny praised. "It's perfect—now go and find some more. We need lots."

The children remained occupied with their cone hunt until it was time to go home. The women and girls climbed into the station wagon for the drive home, and Danny and Joey each handed one last pine cone through the car window to Jenny before saying their goodbyes. The boys watched the station wagon cross the meadow and onto the dirt road, and they continued to watch until nothing but a trail of dust was faintly visible in the distance.

Cooper helped the boys erect a canvas lean-to against one side of the sheep camp wagon, tying off the top edge above the wheels, and staking the bottom edge to the ground a few feet away. The tightly-stretched material offered a sense of security, and would serve well enough to protect from the elements if a rain cloud blew over during the night. Their shelter was ready, and the brothers were ready to brave the outdoors. Best of all, the door to the wagon would only be five feet from the spot where Joey would be sleeping, just in case there was a disturbance during the night.

"I think I'll apply for a position in Hailey with the Blaine County School District for this fall," Jenny told her mother during the drive back to the ranch. "The population is growing pretty fast because of the resort at Sun Valley and new construction in Ketchum—I should be able to find something."

"So soon? I thought you would want to take the rest of the year, until Daphne gets a little older.

"I know it would be asking a lot of you to watch the kids, Mom," Jenny said, unable to think of an alternative. "But if I don't go back to work, I don't see how I could convince a judge that I can provide for Alice and June."

"I think that's something you better discuss with Mr. Crenshaw," Betty replied thoughtfully, as she stared through the windshield and considered her daughter's dilemma. "I don't know whether it's best that you work, or stay home with the children."

"There's six of us, Mom—five kids and me. It's just too much to ask of you and Dad to take care of us unless I contribute something financially."

"Why not let your dad and I worry about that? It's not as though someone else was going to stay in your bedroom," Betty said, dismissing her daughter's concern about being a financial burden. "And it's not as though our grocery bill has gone up much—we grow almost everything we eat."

"The last of what I saved from working in Boise is gone now, Mom," Jenny confessed. "I had to give it to the hospital when Daphne came, and I still owe them money."

"We can take care of that this fall, when the lambs sell."

"I think Dad is going to get tired of having me lay around the ranch all summer, and who could blame him? If I don't find some work, he's going to be peeved."

"There was never a time when you didn't carry your weight around here, Jenny, and your father knows that better than anyone. I don't think he expects you to do anything more than you're doing for the time being," Betty insisted. "Besides, he's a changed man since you showed up with a carload of kids—he'd be lost if any of you left now."

Jenny rode awhile in silence, running ideas through her head and mulling over the assurances from her mom.

"I wonder if I could bake bread and pies and cinnamon rolls and sell them to the cafe," Jenny suggested. "I could take them into town early, so the rolls would be fresh, and then drop the kids off at school during the school year. What do you think?"

"I think you should stop worrying about that for now, and consider getting Alice signed up for a summer reading class at the school, that's what I think. They have workshops to keep kids busy during the summer, and to give them a head start on a reading program for the up coming school year. That might impress the judge when it's time, and it may even impress that child services woman."

"I'm not sure anything will impress her," Jenny began, and then stopped herself abruptly when Alice walked into the room.

Jenny kept the rest of her opinion to herself, for fear of alarming Alice. The girl didn't talk about it much, but she was keenly aware of what was going on with respect to the custody matter being reviewed by the court. She listened quietly when the adults spoke about it, and absorbed as much information as she was able to comprehend. She knew that the matter of where she and her little sister would be sent to live was not resolved, and she often worried about it without saying anything to Jenny or Grandma Barnett.

"I'll go to reading classes," Alice offered, hoping that her efforts to be a good student and a good reader would be helpful. "I like to read."

"I know you do, Alice," Jenny said with a smile, turning in her seat to give a reassuring smile to Alice and her little sister. "Maybe the school has a summer program that we can all join in, how would that be, June-bug?"

June smiled and nodded in agreement. She looked from Jenny to Alice, reading their faces to be sure everyone was happy with the idea of summer reading. The little girl didn't often understand what was being discussed, but she knew how to tell from the expression on a person's face whether there was reason to worry or not.

When the boys woke the following morning at the sheep camp on Murdoch Creek, Tony Beraza had already left camp to locate the sheep. Neither of them heard him get up and climb out of the wagon, which was probably due more to the boys being sound sleepers rather than Tony being silent when he left the camp. Cooper heard his shepherd preparing to leave, and got up with him, intending to go along on his morning rounds, but reconsidered and stayed behind so that he could wake the boys and bring them along later. He had almost forgotten that his two young helpers were still small children—too young to be left alone in camp. Even if they weren't frightened, there was no telling what mischief two young boys might get into while he was gone.

"Let's hurry, boys," Cooper urged the brothers. "We have to catch up with Tony and count our sheep."

Joey rubbed the sleep out of his eyes while his big brother pulled his boots on, ready to join the men on their daily rounds.

"How many are there?" Joey asked, yawning as he put on his coat and hat.

"More than two thousand, I think," Cooper answered, as he paused to consider the size of his band. "I hope."

Cooper regretted that he could not have split his herd into two smaller bands to make it easier to graze them and keep them under control, but he couldn't afford another shepherd, and he only had one sheep camp wagon. In years past, the Barnett Ranch herd exceeded 5,000 head of sheep, but the numbers dwindled as demand for lamb and wool diminished, and his herd grew smaller every year. He was finding it more and more difficult to compete in a declining market, and wasn't sure if it would get any better in the years ahead.

"Let's get a move on, men," Cooper prodded the brothers. "Roll up those sleeping bags and eat some oatmeal, then we'll ride out and find Tony."

He saddled the horses and rode out with the boys to find Tony Beraza and the sheep. Banjo and Holly had already gone with the shepherd—the Border Collies had a keen sense when it came to understanding who was leaving to work with the livestock, and they quickly followed after Tony when he left early. If their master had wanted them to stay in camp, he would have said something. When Cooper and the boys located the sheep, Tony and the herding dogs had the large band moving steadily along toward an area of grazing that already had a couple of months to recover from previous grazing.

"Do you want to move the camp further upstream?" Cooper asked. "We should do it while I have the pickup here if you think we should."

"No, I think it's all right where it is. It's easy enough to ride out on horseback if the sheep are more than a half mile from camp."

Cooper trusted Tony's judgment. The young Basque shepherd had herded for the Barnett Ranch for four years, and had grown up working his father's herd for at least ten years prior to that.

"I suppose we better head back to camp and get ready to go home soon, boys," Cooper said, giving advance notice to Danny and Joey that their camping expedition was nearing an end. "They'll be looking for us back at the ranch."

"Are we taking Banjo and Holly with us?" Danny queried.

"I think they're better off here for now, don't you think? They would rather stay and work with Tony than lie around by the house and barn all day with nothing to do."

"We could stay with them," Joey suggested.

"No, I think you better come home with me. I'd have more trouble with the women than I could handle if I left you up here," Cooper reasoned. "It wouldn't be safe for me to go home."

CHAPTER FIFTEEN
THE SHEEP BRIDGE

Alice could hardly contain her excitement when the library came into view. She had talked about nothing else during breakfast and the ride into town. Jenny was pleased to discover that the eight-year-old girl wanted to spend so much of her time reading.

The small-town library was a treasure trove of classical stories to pique the interest and imagination of every young and avid reader. The county's annual budget was small, but the library received a number of donations of new and used books, and the shelves were packed with good selections of reading material for young minds.

"What was your favorite book when you were in school, Jenny?" Alice asked in a whisper, as she began to prowl the aisles of the small library.

"I liked a lot of different stories, but I think I still like *Little Women* the best."

"Will you help me find it?"

"I think you may want to start with something a little easier, and save that one for later. Why don't we go and join the other kids in the reading room now, and see what they have planned for you."

Jenny left Alice with the reading group and took June to find a picture book to keep the little girl occupied for a while. They went through two books in twenty minutes, and then spent the rest of the hour looking at picture books of wild animals from the Serengeti plains of Africa. It was enough to hold June's interest for the remainder of the time her big sister was engaged with her reading group. Alice came out of the reading room—all smiles, and clutching a book that had been loaned to her for the week.

"I like coming here, Jenny—they're going to meet three times a week until school starts. Can we come again the day after tomorrow?"

"We can come as often as you like, honey," Jenny assured the little girl. "I'm really happy that you want to read more."

Jenny stopped for gas at Shorty Henderson's garage before starting back to the ranch, and bought sodas for the girls while she waited for Shorty to fill her tank and check the oil.

"A man stopped in here this morning, asking about you," Shorty said, as he replaced the oil dipstick and dropped the hood. "I told him you were in town every day or two, and he didn't say anything more—just left."

"Did you know him?"

"Nope, never saw him before. Wasn't a very friendly sort, though, if you ask me."

Jenny began to worry that someone from the State had been sent to take Alice and June. What if they just came and took the girls, she thought. No phone call, no notification to the lawyers, or any other advance warning. She was beginning to feel panicky. She rushed the girls into the car and took a side road off of Main Street, following a gravel road until she was well out of town before she turned back toward the highway. Anyone looking for her would surely be waiting at the end of Main Street near the Highway 20 intersection—it was the only paved street in town, and the only one that was well traveled—an obvious choice to look for anyone coming or going from Fairfield.

"Why are we going this way?" Alice asked. "Who's looking for you?"

"I don't know, but we're not waiting to find out," Jenny said, grimly. "We're going home."

Jenny tried to guess who else might be looking for her—someone less sinister than a state child services agent, perhaps. Maybe someone was sent to check up on the girls and to see how they were doing in their new home. An impromptu visit was the best way to learn how the girls were living every day. But why didn't they simply come to the ranch, she wondered.

"Mom, was anyone here looking for me today?" Jenny asked, as she came through the back door of the kitchen. "Anyone call, asking about the girls?"

"No, nobody was here," Betty answered, with a look of sudden concern on her face. "And no phone calls—were you expecting someone?"

"No, that's just it—somebody stopped at Shorty Henderson's this morning, asking if he had seen me. Shorty said that he had never seen him before. I don't know if it was someone from child services."

"That's strange—why wouldn't they just drive out here?"

"Maybe they didn't know how to find the ranch," Jenny said, mulling over the possibilities in her head.

Jenny called Bart Crenshaw to explain what had happened, and he promised to check into it to learn whether the state had sent someone to check on the girls.

"I'll find out what's going on," Crenshaw assured. "If it's the state, they'll tell me. In the meantime, you better stay home."

Jenny remained on the ranch for the next two days, and when she heard back from Bart Crenshaw's office that no one from child services had been sent to Fairfield, it put Jenny more at ease.

"It must have been an old friend from school in Pocatello, or somebody I knew from Boise," Jenny told her mother. "If it had been anyone from around here, Shorty would have recognized them."

"You're the one who's always telling me to relax, and trust the lawyers," Betty said. "Look at you—you're a wreck."

"I don't know what I'm so worried about, but I just don't trust that Sorenson woman. I must be getting paranoid. I wish this whole thing could be resolved right now."

"Why don't you drive the kids into Hailey this afternoon and take them to a movie?" Betty suggested. "You could pick up some things we need from the store before you come home."

"I'm almost afraid to go anywhere—I'm even nervous about taking

Alice in to join her reading group at the library."

"No one is going to bother you in Hailey," Betty reasoned.

Jenny agreed—her mother was right. She called the boys in to wash up and change clothes, and checked the Wood River newspaper to be sure a kids' movie was playing at the theater. There was almost always a different family movie at the theater every week during the summer.

"Do you want to come with us?" Jenny asked her mother.

"No, I'll stay here and take care of Daphne and your father. He'll be coming through the back door—hungry and smelly—before you get home."

Jenny and the kids enjoyed their afternoon in Hailey. The movie didn't start for another hour, so they got ice cream and sat in the park to eat it before going to the theater. They played on the swings until it was time to go.

Joey wore his dad's army hat when they went into the theater, and Jenny couldn't get him to part with it. They finished their small bags of popcorn before the prevue of coming attractions had ended, and the children remained mesmerized and entertained during full-length animated feature. June wanted to stay and watch it again.

"Is that all there is?" June asked, disappointed that it had ended so quickly as she was led by the hand through the small lobby toward the exit door.

"That's all, June-bug," Jenny affirmed. "We'll come again sometime."

It was getting late when Jenny came out of the theater with the children, but none of the kids were sleepy. It was a forty-five minute drive back to the ranch; and halfway there, Jenny regretted not stopping to find an open cafe in Hailey or Bellevue. She kept quiet, hoping that none of the children would complain of hunger before they got home. It turned out to be the least of her problems. Halfway home the oil light came on, lighting up the dashboard of the old Studebaker with its ominous red warning. A few minutes later, smoke began to rise off the motor and billow out from under the hood.

"Jenny, we're on fire!" Alice cried, sounding the alarm that they were in trouble.

"It's all right—just calm down. We just need some oil, that's all."

"But it's smoking," Alice fretted, even more urgently.

"We're less than two miles from Fairfield. We'll go slow, and I'll pull in to Mr. Henderson's garage and he'll take care of it."

"What if he's not there?" Alice continued to worry.

"Just relax everybody," Jenny urged, trying to prevent Alice from spreading panic to the other children. "He lives right behind the garage—he'll be there."

Everyone in the car remained silent for the last mile of the drive into Fairfield, and they all held their breath as Jenny steered the old sedan onto the service platform at Shorty's Garage, turning off the ignition and coasting to a stop. The garage was dark, and the overhead platform lights were turned off. Jenny hoped that Shorty hadn't gone anywhere except to bed for the night.

"You wait here, kids," Jenny instructed. "I'll go get Mr. Henderson."

Jenny prepared to exit her car just as another vehicle pulled onto the concrete gas pump platform behind her, switching its headlamps to high beam as it rolled to a stop. She was relieved to see the bright lights—probably Sheriff Gillespie or one of his deputies out on their rounds.

Her car door was pulled open and a hand grabbed her arm and yanked her out of the car. She stumbled sideways from the force, and she reached for the armrest on the door to help her to regain her balance. The stink of beer mixed with cigarette breath hit her as she stood, and her heart froze. She focused her eyes in the dim light and recognized the face of Bud Fuller looming over her in the darkness.

"Where's Lorraine?" the foul-smelling man demanded.

"I don't know," Jenny lied, as firmly and convincingly as she could. "I haven't talked to her in months."

"You're lying," Bud snarled. "She wouldn't just leave and not call to talk with her boys."

"Let go of me!" Jenny yelled, as loudly as she could, hoping to attract attention from anyone within hearing range.

She dug her fingernails into the back of Bud's hand and wrenched her arm free. He retaliated with an open-handed slap, hard to Jenny's face. Her knees buckled as she fell backwards through the open door of her car and collapsed against the side of the seat.

June released a spine-tingling scream, and Alice was frozen with fear. The boys remained silent in the back seat—trembling and too afraid to cry out. Alice suddenly reacted with an impulse prompted by a rush of adrenalin, and reached across her little sister to press the palm of her hand down hard on the car horn, gripping the steering wheel with her other hand to hold herself firmly in place while she sent out the alarm.

Bud Fuller reached to open the back door of the old Studebaker, unfazed in his drunken stupor by the blaring sound of the car horn.

"I'll just take these boys with me," he snarled, swinging the rear door open wide as he reached in to pull Joey out of the back seat. "Lorraine will turn up quick enough when she finds out I have her boys."

"No!" Jenny screamed, scrambling to her feet and throwing all of her weight against the rear car door to throw the man off balance.

"Ow! The little bugger bit me!" the stinky drunkard screamed, pulling his arm out of the car to inspect the bite mark Danny left on his forearm.

Jenny used the distraction to her advantage and leapt into action, shoving against the car door once again with all her might. Bud Fuller stumbled sideways and toppled over onto the concrete. She slammed the rear door closed and jumped into the driver's seat, pushing the lock down as she pulled the door closed.

"Lock the doors, kids! Hurry, lock the doors!" she urged frantically.

She pulled her door shut and locked it, then fired the ignition to start the overheated motor. She pumped the accelerator as the motor turned over, trying desperately to get it to start. The engine roared to life, and quickly died as she pumped the gas pedal again and flooded the engine. She pushed her foot to the floor, took a deep breath, and tried the ignition again. The engine turned over again, but just barely. It kept running, but smoke from the overheated engine block began to float up from under the hood.

Bud Fuller was on his feet and trying without success to open car doors. Jenny leaned on the car horn, hoping that Shorty would hear it and come out of his house in the rear of the garage to see what was going on.

Fuller didn't wait around any longer. Even in his drunken haze, he suspected trouble might be coming. He got back in his car and made a quick U-turn away from the garage and onto Main Street, then sped south toward the highway.

Jenny wasn't taking any chances either—she shifted into gear and sped away down Main Street into the center of the tiny town, then turned down the same gravel side road she had used earlier in the week to avoid being seen leaving town. She turned and made her way back to the highway after a mile or so on the side road. Jenny waited at Highway 20 with her headlights off, looking left and right as she strained to see any sign of headlights coming along the highway from either direction. There was nothing but darkness—she decided it was safe to go.

The old Studebaker rolled out onto the highway and turned east to avoid passing through Fairfield. She accelerated to fifty miles per hour, hoping that the engine wouldn't overheat and quit on her.

"Jenny, it's smoking again," Alice said, as quietly and calmly as she could for a frightened eight-year-old.

"I know—but we can't help it—we have to get home."

"Is Bud going to come to the ranch to get us?" Danny asked, his voice tinged with alarm.

"No, he wouldn't dare—I don't think so," Jenny's response began, but with a bravado that faded to uncertainty. "I hope not."

"I don't want to go with him," Joey began to cry.

"Just settle down now, boys," Jenny soothed. "Nobody's going to make you go with him. I won't let him take you—my dad won't let him."

Jenny saw a set of headlights approaching in her rear view mirror, and felt the fear rising in her throat again. She held her speed steady, and held her breath as the headlights overtook them, and then pulled over to pass on the left. It was a delivery van, obviously in a hurry to get to the next town. Another set of headlights appeared in Jenny's mirror, coming faster than the first. Jenny wasn't overly-concerned—they were already ten miles east of Fairfield and well on their way home. The headlights crept closer to the rear of the old Studebaker—so close that the grill and headlamps were partially obscured from view. It backed off a little, perhaps to move over and pass. Jenny focused on the road ahead, holding her speed steady. More and more smoke was pouring out from under the hood. This is not going to be good, she thought. If the engine seized up, she would be stuck on the highway with four small children. Her panic began to rise again.

A loud bang and a jolt from behind changed the course of Jenny's thoughts abruptly, and threw her forward against the steering wheel. The children had to catch themselves to keep from being thrown against the dashboard or onto the floor. Bud Fuller had found them, and from his actions, Jenny knew he was angry. She stomped her foot down hard on the gas pedal and held it there, trying to summon whatever power was left in the old V-8 motor and push the sedan down the highway as fast as it could go.

"Hang on, kids," Jenny said, grim and determined in her effort to get away.

Jenny cursed under her breath at not having kept a few extra quarts of oil and antifreeze in the trunk—her father and brothers had taught her to stop and add oil immediately whenever the oil light came on. How could she possibly be this unlucky, she thought. Smoke was billowing out from under the hood, and it was beginning to come inside the car. The engine started to make a knocking sound, and Jenny knew she was in trouble.

"Where is it—where *is* it?" she whispered hoarsely, glancing to the side of the road as she held her foot to the floor.

Bud Fuller kept pace with the speeding sedan, and began to close the distance again as the Studebaker engine began to clatter and knock more loudly, losing speed quickly as it overheated from its lack of lubrication.

"There!" Jenny said aloud. "Hang on kids—hold on to something!"

She swerved the old sedan hard to the right, slamming on the brakes as the car skidded across a wide gravel entry to a side road before it came to a stop. Bud Fuller's car flew past on the highway, and tires squealed as he slowed the car to make a U-turn. Jenny could see his headlights aiming back in the direction of the turnoff, not more than fifty yards away.

"Get out of the car kids," Jenny ordered, raising her voice to demonstrate her urgency. "Get out now!"

Jenny threw open the driver's side door and pulled June and Alice with her as she exited the car.

"Come on, boys—hurry."

The brothers didn't have to be told twice—they didn't want to be in the car, or anywhere near it, when Bud Fuller arrived. The headlights of his car were visible through the heavy brush that lined the highway right of way, and coming closer, as the car slowed and turned off the highway in their direction.

"Stay with me, kids," Jenny urged, adjusting her eyes to the darkness as she rushed toward a wide dirt trail that led away from the highway. "Hold on to me."

Jenny had followed the trail many times over the years with her father and grandfather, but never in the dark of night. Alice clutched her hand tightly, and June kept a grip on Jenny's jacket, making it difficult for her to walk. The frightened boys were both trying to hang onto Jenny's other hand. She stopped, and turned to face them.

"Danny, you and Joey came this way with Grandpa when you brought the sheep across Camas Creek—it's safe, you'll see. Alice, you hold my hand, and June-bug, you take your sister's hand and stay very quiet. You boys stay close behind us and keep up—we need to move fast."

Jenny led the children into the darkness, trying to focus in the dim light to find the high bank above Camas Creek. They were moving too slowly. She could hear tires skidding to a stop across gravel as Bud's car came to a halt. He found her car. A few seconds later, she recognized the distinctive sound of her car horn when Bud Fuller pressed and held the horn ring on the steering wheel.

"I know you're out there!" he called out into the darkness. "You got nowhere to go—I'm takin' those boys with me."

Jenny stopped, feeling dirt begin to give way under her feet where the high creek bank sloughed away and threatened to collapse under her weight. She stopped and strained again to adjust her eyes to the darkness, searching for the pathway, or anything that looked familiar.

"This way, I think," she whispered, leading the children along the high dirt bank. "We're close."

"Where are we going, Jenny," Alice worried, a little too loudly.

"Shh, we're going home," Jenny answered in a whisper. "Just stay with me—and stay together."

A wide path opened ahead of the small band of escapees, leading down into the wide gulley that had been carved out by the rushing waters from many thousands of spring rains and snow melts. Jenny led her little troupe down the incline until she heard the sound of shoe against wood, and felt a plank under her foot. It was the sheep bridge over Camas Creek, and it led to sanctuary on the other side.

The narrow suspension bridge was accessible only by foot or horseback, and Jenny was certain that Bud Fuller could not find it—even more certain that he wouldn't have the courage to cross it in the dark.

"Stay together, kids," Jenny instructed in a whisper. "Hold on to a side rail and keep up with me."

"One of the boards is gone," Danny called out to Jenny. "You have to be careful or you'll fall through."

"Where, Danny?" Jenny asked, forgetting to keep her voice low. "Where is it?"

"I don't remember—somewhere in the middle, I think."

Alice started to cry, and June quickly joined in, terrified to think that she might fall through the bridge and into the cold water below.

The three-year-old girl became even more frightened when she heard the water rushing past over the rocky creek bed in the darkness, reminding her of the danger that lurked beneath the bridge.

"Alice, stop it!" Jenny demanded, in a hoarse whisper. "You're scaring your little sister, and it's not helping."

Jenny led the children out onto the old suspension bridge. Alice clutched Jenny's arm tightly, still whimpering as she held her little sister's hand firmly in her own. The brothers followed along behind, gripping the wooden railing on one side of the bridge with both hands as they inched across the uneven wooden planks. Jenny stopped and looked back, urging the children on,

"Danny, Joey," she called in a low voice, as she tried to make out the shapes of the boys against the dark pattern of the bridge railing behind them. "Are you keeping up?"

Neither boy answered—they were concentrating on holding onto the wooden railing as they made slow progress toward the middle of the bridge. Jenny could scarcely make out their dark forms as they moved closer to her. She turned and felt her way with her foot, searching for the gap in the planks where the missing board had been knocked loose from the bridge. She was certain that Bud Fuller would not attempt to follow them if she could get the children across the bridge to the opposite bank.

"You might as well come back!" Fuller shouted into the darkness. "I'll come and get you if you don't! You've got no place to go!"

His voice was more distant and coming from a direction upstream from the bridge. A small wave of relief flooded Jenny's heart—she realized that the man had not found the path that led down to the crossing. Darkness had protected them from pursuit—at least for the moment.

Danny crossed to the opposite side of the narrow bridge, pulling his little brother with him by his shirt sleeve. They gripped the railing and moved quickly, overcoming their fear of the night crossing in the face of the fear that lay behind them—fear in the form of an evil and abusive man.

"I can find it, Jenny," Danny whispered, as he and his little brother caught up and began to pass the others. "I'll find where the board is missing."

He moved as fast as he could, sliding his hands forward along the two by four wooden railing as he stepped gingerly across the planks. He stepped off a plank and his left leg slipped through a gap, sliding through the narrow opening, and he banged his knee on a board plank as he dropped. Joey cried out as he felt his big brother's arm slip from his grasp.

"I can hear you out there!" Fuller shouted into the darkness again, laughing at the sound of the frightened boy in the distance. "Those kids are scared aren't they?"

Danny pulled himself up and rubbed his sore knee, then pulled his brother across as he alerted Jenny to the danger.

"It's here!" the boy called out in a hoarse whisper, crossing back over to the left side of the bridge in front of Jenny and the girls. "It's right here—be careful."

Jenny gripped Alice's arm and pulled her along behind as she followed Danny's voice and felt with her leading foot for the gap in the planks. She located the open space with the toe of her shoe and tested the opening to determine its width—not more than eight or ten inches, she decided. She straddled the narrow opening and pulled the girls across, one at a time.

"Are there any more?" Jenny asked, as she brought the girls up behind and caught up with the brothers. "Are there any more missing boards?"

"I don't think so," Danny whispered, anxious to get moving and put the sound of Bud Fuller's voice behind him.

Jenny felt the rising incline of the bridge planks and knew they had crossed the center of the suspension bridge, moving upwards toward the far bank.

"Keep going," Jenny encouraged in a voice just above a whisper. "Just a little farther and we'll be back on solid ground."

Danny had found his courage again—urged on by the sound of

Jenny's voice, he gripped his little brother's wrist and pulled him along toward the far side of the bridge and up onto the south bank. He knew where they were now, and he was sure that once they found their way back to the ranch, Grandpa Barnett would make sure nothing bad would happen to them.

Jenny paused on the south bank and listened, trying to hear any sound that may indicate that Bud Fuller was still in pursuit. Even if he found the sheep bridge and crossed to the other side, she was certain that he would not know what direction they had taken, making it easier to elude him on the broad expanse of brushy hillside. The darkness of night was now their protector.

"Let's go, kids. Stay together and keep moving."

She led the way up the long hillside, picking her way through the dense brush as she followed the erratic pattern of trails etched into the landscape by the migrating bands of sheep that traveled the same path year after year on their way north to the summer grazing grounds. Out of breath and panting for air, she stopped to rest near the top of a ridge and turned to wait and listen for a sound from behind them on the trail—any sign to indicate that they were being followed. All was silent, save her own audible inhaling and exhaling. The children seemed less affected by the uphill climb, but they were sure to feel the strain of exertion before they found their way home.

"I don't remember which way we came," Danny confessed, as he tried in vain to recognize any familiar landmark in the dim light. "I only remember going down the hill to the bridge."

The boys remembered their slow descent down the hillside toward the sheep bridge early in the summer, but it had been daylight then, and they were on horseback. It was a much different place in the dark of night, on foot and traveling in the opposite direction.

"No one will ever find us now." Alice whimpered. "We're lost."

"We're not lost—I know exactly where we are," Jenny said.

Jenny knew they were somewhere south of Camas Creek, and a few miles west of highway 75, but beyond that, she didn't have a clue exactly how close they were to the ranch house. The night closed around them with an inky blackness, unlit by the stars veiled with dense clouds. She drew a deep breath and started down the other side of the ridge, angling slightly to the right in a direction that she believed would lead to the Barnett Ranch.

She had no way of telling how much time had elapsed since they crossed the bridge and ascended the hill to the ridge, but she guessed that it was not more than ten or fifteen minutes. She knew that time moved slowly for the anxious mind—and she could sense a growing nervousness in the children. They were unable to walk fast, winding their way through the brush in the darkness. She was sure they had not yet covered a mile of ground since they reached the top of the ridge. They would have to move faster, or risk being exposed too long in the falling temperatures and any bad weather that may follow. Little June suddenly stopped in her tracks and began to cry.

"I'm scared, Jenny."

"There's nothing to be afraid of, June-bug. It's just dark, that's all."

Jenny kneeled down and took the three-year-old up onto her back, allowing the little girl to wrap her arms tightly around her neck as she supported the girl's tiny body with her forearms cradled under June's knees. She trudged ahead, hoping the older children would be heartened by her determination and do their best to keep up. She kept moving, hoping that she was maintaining a reasonably straight line toward the southwest.

It didn't take long before she began to feel the ever-increasing weight of the little girl on her back with every step, slowing her pace until she had to stop to rest and lower the child to the ground.

"You're going to have to walk for a little while, June—just until I catch my breath—then I'll carry you again."

"I'm thirsty, Jenny," Joey complained. "Are we going to be there soon?"

"We still have a ways to go. When we see the lights from the house, then we'll be close."

"I can't see anything," Alice fretted. "Where are we?"

"We're between the sheep bridge and the ranch, that's where we are," Jenny answered, trying to sound confident without being specific. "We'll get home faster if we keep walking, and Grandma will have supper waiting for us."

Jenny was sorry that she had mentioned food—now the children were both hungry and thirsty, and there was nothing she could do about it except keep walking. She led the way again, towing little June behind her and encouraging the others to stay close.

A sudden rush of air came down over her head, causing her to duck instinctively as she let out a startled cry. Alice screamed as June clutched Jenny's arm, and the boys stopped in their tracks, frozen with fear. Jenny heard the rush of air under the wings and caught a glimpse of a large, dark shape in the night sky as the bird coasted past—low overhead—and flapped its broad wings to lift skyward again.

"It's just an owl," Jenny soothed. "It was just coming to see what we were—it won't hurt us."

"What if it comes back?" Alice worried.

"It won't come back," Jenny assured, confidently. "It only wanted to see what was moving on the ground—it's looking for rabbits and ground squirrels and mice."

Jenny cursed under her breath. She knew that every peril—real or imagined—would unnerve the children and make it harder to control them, and harder to convince them to keep moving. She coaxed and prodded to keep the kids walking. If they stopped making progress, they were likely to become unfocused and lose their confidence in Jenny's ability to find their way home.

She glanced back to the north, hoping to see a clearing in the clouds, and praying that she might catch sight of a familiar star to help get her bearings. A break in the cloud cover far off to her right revealed a patch of stars in the night sky, but nothing that was familiar. She paused to rest again for a minute, reluctant to let the children sit down for fear of allowing exhaustion to creep in and make it impossible to get them started again. Jenny felt her own thirst begin to overwhelm her.

She breathed deep and cast a glance skyward, directly overhead, then turned her head slightly and followed a curved line of bright stars through a wide gap in the clouds. A familiar pattern emerged from the clouds—just enough to be recognizable. Jenny could make out the curved handle and ladle of the Big Dipper—the constellation of Ursa Major—almost directly overhead, and extending slightly to her right. She followed a straight line between the two bright stars that formed the lip of the Big Dipper, and although she was unable to see it behind the cloud cover, she knew that it pointed to the North Star. She had been leading the children due west, but for exactly how long she wasn't sure.

"Let's get going kids," she urged. "It can't be too much further now."

Jenny lifted June onto her back again with renewed energy and enthusiasm. She led the way, angling toward the left to change direction, and headed due south. She had no way of knowing for sure how far west they had walked, but she was certain that the only way to correct her mistake was to walk southward until they could see the lights from the ranch or stumble onto the gravel road that led from the highway to the ranch house.

"I'm really thirsty, Jenny," Danny said, in a casual way that sounded more like an observation than a complaint.

"I know—just hang on for a little while longer, kids. It can't be too much further."

She picked up the pace, hoping the children wouldn't falter or fall behind. She couldn't carry all of them, and they had to stay together. She turned to look over her shoulder frequently, checking on the position of the Big Dipper constellation so that she could keep her accurate bearing in the direction they needed to go. The clouds were steadily clearing to the north and east, allowing enough light from the stars to brighten their way. She could see the North Star clearly now—the one star in the sky that did not move from its place in the heavens as the earth rotated on its axis and revolved around the sun. It was the one star her father had taught her that she could always rely upon to be her compass if she ever lost her way at night.

Jenny could make out some shapes on the ground more easily, and was able to avoid stumbling over low brush and rocks in the dark. Her thirst was beginning to overwhelm her, and she was increasingly concerned that the children would suffer from dehydration. She stopped again to rest, and to think.

"Sit down, kids—let's rest for just a few minutes."

She looked around for an opening in the dense brush—an opening large enough to allow other vegetation to grow. She spotted a likely area a few yards to her left, and felt around on the ground for something to dig with—a sharp rock or stick would do. She found a palm-sized flat rock with a sharp edge after feeling around in the rocky soil for a few moments, and lifted it to feel its heft and size. She decided it would make a good digging tool. She got to her feet and walked toward the small clearing in the brush.

"Stay right here, kids—I'll only be a minute or two."

"Where are you going?" Alice asked, fearful that Jenny would get separated from them in the dark.

"I'm just going right over here," Jenny called back over her shoulder. "Just wait there for a minute. June, you stay with your sister."

She didn't want to tell the children she was trying to find something for them to eat—something that might also help to ease their terrible thirst. If the children knew what she was looking for, and she wasn't successful in finding it, they would probably be even thirstier and more upset than they already were. Jenny stepped into the small brush clearing and reached down to wave her hand over the ground a few inches above the earth, searching for the familiar feel of the blossom and leaf of a Camas Flower. Her hand came in contact with a cluster of plants, and she closed her fingers around it to feel its familiar shape and texture then broke some off and raised it to her nose. She had found what she was looking for. The Camas Flower was a prolific plant, and grew on the prairies all the way north to the Idaho panhandle. Its root held moisture—and it was edible.

Jenny grasped the stem and flower in her left hand and pulled upward as she dug at the earth around its base with her sharp rock. When she loosened enough soil around the root she tugged it free of the earth and brushed the dirt away, wiping it against her shirt to clean it well enough to eat without tasting a mouthful of dirt and grit.

"Jenny, where are you?" Alice called out.

"I'm right here, honey," Jenny answered, her voice full of encouragement. "I'm getting us something to eat."

"I'm thirsty," Danny reminded her.

Jenny scratched and dug with her crude tool until she had a small pile of camas roots, then stretched out the bottom of her shirt and loaded the roots into her makeshift basket, holding her shirttail up against her belly so that she wouldn't lose any as she made her way back to the children. She sat down in the dirt next to Alice, and showed her how to wipe the root on the front of her shirt and brush the last particles of sandy soil away. She took a bite out of the side of a root and chewed vigorously to release its moisture into her mouth. She handed a root to Danny and another to Joey.

"Brush it off and eat it," Jenny instructed, solemnly. "It's not Grandma's pie, but it'll fill you up, and your mouth won't dry out."

The brothers didn't hesitate to chomp down on the soft, chewy root. The root yielded its small amount of moisture, and prompted the release of saliva in their mouths, easing their thirst and overcoming their hunger as they swallowed down the less-than-tasty root.

"It don't taste like anything," Joey commented, as he munched away on his bland and meager supper.

"I know, Joey," Jenny agreed. "But you eat it—you'll feel better."

She broke off small pieces for June, and urged her to chew on the nutritious root until it was moist enough to swallow. They ate until the children didn't want any more. They hadn't eaten enough to fill their bellies, perhaps, but enough to abate their hunger and put some moisture back into their mouths.

A high-pitched yip and howl pierced the night air, causing the hair to stand up on the back of Alice's neck. The boys lifted their heads and stopped chewing, staring at Jenny through the dim light to gauge her reaction to the loud intrusion.

"Is that Banjo?" June asked, innocently.

"It's a coyote," Danny said.

"Don't be afraid, June-bug," Jenny calmed the girls, hoping that Alice would remain brave as long as her little sister didn't get frightened. "It won't want to come near us if we make noise."

The children all jumped to their feet, ready to make tracks. Alice thought the howl came from ten feet away, and it made her think she was being hunted for food. It was all she could do to keep from screaming in fear and fleeing the fearsome sound of the wild predator.

"Yell at it, Alice," Jenny encouraged. "It will be afraid of you. Joey, sing your song—I don't think the coyote will like it."

Joey took a minute to gather his composure and remember the lyrics, then began to belt out his noisy rendition of the State Song of Idaho as loudly as he could, hanging on to his big brother's shirt sleeve as he struggled to keep up with the rest of the night walkers.

Jenny checked the sky over her shoulder again, and saw the Big Dipper plainly outlined above—the North Star now clearly in view in a straight line from the lip of the dipper. She was encouraged, and began to sing along with Joey. She stopped abruptly when she felt the crunch of gravel under her feet for two or three steps. She looked down, focusing her eyesight in the dim starlight as she looked left and right down the long stretch of gravel road. She was sure they had found the road that led to the ranch from the highway south of Hailey.

"This is it, kids," Jenny announced with confidence, as she turned to the right to start them in the direction of the ranch house. "This is the way home."

"How far is it now, Jenny?" Danny asked, as his little brother continued to sing out his song lyrics at the top of his lungs.

"Not far," Jenny said. "Let's just keep walking. Joey, I think you can stop singing now."

Joey was tired of singing anyway, and didn't think anyone was listening anymore, or admiring his talent. Alice stayed close to Jenny, and picked up her pace to put the coyote as far behind her as possible. She hoped the hungry night hunter would find a rabbit or a squirrel before it caught up with them. Spirits were elevated as they followed the gravel road in the direction of home—even the children understood that they were no longer lost, if in fact, they ever were.

Jenny stopped and listened, then continued walking for a short distance, and then stopped again, cocking her head to listen for a sound she imagined coming from far behind them. She could barely make out the faint glow from a set of headlights in the distance, coming closer as it wound along the brush-lined gravel road from the east. She listened harder, and was sure she recognized the sound of the motor. She turned and began walking again toward the ranch, staying on the right side of the road as she led her dusty little troupe of hikers toward home.

The lights of the ranch house came into view a mile or so ahead, and the sound of the pickup truck grew louder as it rolled up behind Jenny and the kids and slowed to a stop.

"What the heck are you doing way out here?" Cooper Barnett called from the open window of his truck. "I drove all the way to Hailey looking for you—I couldn't find your car anywhere."

Jenny pulled the passenger door open and pushed the grateful and weary children inside, hoisting June onto her lap as the older children squeezed in tight.

"Hi, Dad," Jenny said, wearily. "Thanks for coming to look for us."

"Your mother's half sick with worry."

"My oil light came on and I drove into Fairfield to Shorty Henderson's."

"Our step-dad chased us," Danny blurted out. "And I bit him good when he tried to pull Joey out of the car." The boy was certain that retribution from the tough old rancher would soon be at hand.

"He slapped Jenny real hard and made her fall down," Alice said. She ended her explanation of the night's events with that simple comment, confident that Bud Fuller would get what was coming to him.

"A big owl flew right over my head," June added, excitedly. "And Joey sang a song to make a coyote run away."

Cooper looked at his daughter, a dark scowl on his weathered face, and waited for an explanation.

"I'll tell you about it when the kids are fed and put to bed. They're all exhausted—we've had a big day."

Cooper realized that he had too many questions to press for answers on the short drive up the gravel road to the house. Jenny was right—he could wait until the children were in bed to learn more about the day's events.

"We ate roots, Grandpa," Joey said, leaning his tired head against Cooper's arm. "They didn't taste very good, but we were hungry."

CHAPTER SIXTEEN
A FATHER'S FURY

Cooper was in the shed before daylight. He unlocked the cabinet that held the padlocked wooden box where he kept his shotgun and Winchester rifle to keep them out of the reach of curious boys. He lifted the lever-action rifle from its hiding place and removed a box of cartridges. Throwing the chamber open with a downward thrust of the lever, he loaded eight rounds plus one in the chamber. He left without saying goodbye to his wife.

He drove into Fairfield and looked for Bud Fuller's coupe—a car that his daughter tried to describe for him as best she could, even though she only saw it briefly, and in the dark of night. He drove the length of Main Street, turned around and drove back to the upper end of town, close to the highway. A car that fit Jenny's description was parked next to the gas pumps at Shorty Henderson's Garage. He pulled in behind it and shut off his motor, then walked over to where Shorty was beginning to take the lug nuts off the wheel of a farm truck.

"Coop, that fella over by the soda machine has been asking around town to find out where your daughter lives," Shorty Henderson warned. "I think he's the same one that was looking for her yesterday. I don't know him, but it seems to me like he's up to no good."

"Thanks, Shorty—I'll take care of it."

Cooper walked to the soda machine, caught Fuller by the back of his neck in the vise-like grip of his big, gnarled hand, and flung him headlong across a stack of old truck tires.

"You're making a mistake troubling my daughter and those two boys," Cooper warned, as he loomed over the sprawling man and unbuckled his belt. "Don't make it a fatal one."

He whipped his wide leather belt through the belt loops on his jeans and brought it down with all the force he could gather in his strong right arm. Fuller tried to crawl away on all fours to escape the thrashing, but the belt came down repeatedly across his back—each whack harder than the last—until it tore the fabric of his shirt and dropped the howling man flat on his stomach. He lay there, cowering, with his hands over his head as he tried in vain to protect himself from the blows inflicted by the tough old sheep rancher.

"Now you get out of here and don't you ever come back—don't you ever come back to Idaho!"

Fuller picked himself up and pushed his greasy hair out of his eyes, then walked slowly toward his car in a feeble attempt to preserve his dignity, and to make it appear like it was his own idea to leave. He glanced toward the pickup truck parked only a few feet behind his car, and spotted the rifle in the gun rack through the open window. It wasn't more than three steps away from where he stood. Cooper saw the man eyeing his Winchester.

"Are you looking at my rifle? Do you want it?" Cooper taunted, as he took one deliberate step toward the man, and then paused to give Fuller room to make his decision. "Go ahead—reach in there and take it—I won't stop you. Fetch it over here, and I'll show you how it works."

"Is that supposed to be some kind of threat?" Fuller asked nervously, as he tried to appear defiant from what he believed to be a safe distance.

"That's how I intended it," Cooper said clearly, revealing a dangerous glint in his steely gray eyes. "And I wouldn't want to be misunderstood."

"Mister, there's somethin' wrong with your head," Fuller murmured, in a barely audible voice. He thought that Jenny Barnett's father may be deranged.

"Nothin' that can't be fixed real easy," Cooper said calmly. He continued to stare the greasy-haired man down with his steely gaze. "Now go on—reach in there and get that rifle—it's already loaded for you."

Shorty Henderson stepped up behind Cooper and spoke in a low voice, leaning in close so that he could be heard.

"Coop, I wish you wouldn't try to goad that man into a gunfight so close to my gas pumps."

Cooper ignored the garage owner's plea. His focus was on his daughter's offender—the cowardly man who had made a pastime of beating one of the little boys that had since come under his protection. Fuller succumbed to the superior stature and confident attitude of the old rancher, and slid onto the driver's seat behind the wheel of his old coupe. He suspected that the rough-looking older man might have a screw loose, and he decided not to stick around to tempt fate and find out for certain. He made one last attempt to reason with the old rancher.

"Them boys don't belong to you—you got no business keepin' them here," Fuller said feebly.

"They ain't yours!" Cooper growled. "Now git!" He was growing more agitated with the young fool who seemed bent on continuing the confrontation until something blew up in his face. Cooper turned to walk away, but the fool had a final insult in his arsenal, and he used it to push the hardened old rancher one step too far.

"Your daughter ain't nothin' but a meddlin' bitch!" Fuller shouted from his open car window, as he fired the ignition and prepared to drive away.

Cooper stopped and whirled around in mid-stride, seized the tire iron from Shorty's hand, and hurled it with all his strength toward the back of Bud Fuller's car. The steel tool tumbled end-over-end, broke through the rear window and lodged tightly in the small hole that it made in the glass. It was a clear mark of Cooper Barnett's unbridled fury.

Fuller turned in his seat to look at the damage inflicted to his car window. His courage was rekindled by the sight of the broken window, and his own anger took control. He threw open the door and stepped out onto the concrete platform to confront his assailant, but back-peddled instantly when he saw the look of fury on the face of the rapidly-approaching older man.

Cooper took long, deliberate strides toward the man who was too stupid to leave when he had the chance. His fists were clenched and his jaw set like an image in stone.

"You want another sample, don't you, jackass?" the tough old rancher snarled.

Cooper Barnett was a man on fire. His eyes filled with hatred as he glared at the despicable man who had dared to harm his daughter and the boys. He crossed the short distance to the car in seconds and reached for the door handle just as the car sped away. Tires squealed and smoke spewed from beneath the spinning wheels, filling the air with the smell of burning rubber from the rear wheels. Cooper and Shorty watched as the car raced away, swerving past parked cars along Main Street and onto the highway leading west toward Mountain Home.

"I'll nail his damned hide to my barn," Cooper muttered, as he watched the car speed away.

"Who *is* that fella, Coop?" Shorty asked, unable to contain his curiosity.

"He's a jackass."

"He took my tire iron," Shorty complained.

"I'll get you another one—a bigger one—just in case he ever comes back."

Across the street from the garage, a tall man watched silently and unnoticed from the shade of a store awning, just next door to the old courthouse. He pushed his Stetson back on his forehead when the confrontation ended, and walked around the corner of the courthouse and out of sight.

Cooper arrived back at the ranch mid-morning, walked into the kitchen and sat down quietly at the table, then stood up again to get a cup of coffee from the pot on the stove.

"I'll pour it, Coop," his wife said. "Just sit down. Did you get any breakfast?"

"Uh, no," he answered, absent-mindedly. "No, I didn't."

"The boys fed your horses for you," Betty said, as she set his favorite coffee mug in front of him.

"Where are they?"

"Out in the barn, I suppose. I'm surprised they didn't hear you drive up."

"Where's Jenny?"

"In the girls' room—she's helping Alice with her reading."

Cooper nodded and sipped his coffee, reflecting on the events of the morning. He wondered if any of the townspeople witnessed what went on at Shorty's Garage. He didn't want the sheriff to get involved, but he knew that Shorty Henderson couldn't keep his mouth shut, and he believed the chances were fairly good that he would get a visit from Sheriff Gillespie or one of his deputies.

"Do you want to tell me what went on in town?" Betty asked. "Did you find who you were looking for?"

"I found him."

"In town, or on the highway near the sheep bridge?"

"He was at Shorty's Garage, getting gas."

"What did you say to him?"

"I told him that he was making a mistake to bother Jenny, and then I took my belt to him, just to be sure he understood me."

"You did *what*?"

"I told him not to come back to Idaho—I was pretty clear about it, too, I think."

Betty gave her husband a look of disbelief as she set his warmed-over breakfast plate down in front of him and rested a hand on his shoulder. She knew her husband's temper well—he kept a cool head most of the time, but when something set him off he was unstoppable.

She didn't ask any more questions

Jenny came into the kitchen with Alice and June trailing behind her, and pulled out a chair at the table.

"I thought I heard voices out here," she said, sitting down next to her father. "Do you want me to wait until after you eat before I ask you any questions?"

"No, it's okay," Cooper answered through a mouthful of buttered toast.

"Is Bud Fuller still hanging around town?"

"Not any more."

"You want to tell me anything else?"

"Nope."

"Is that man going to leave us alone now?" Alice asked, remembering the whispered conversation between Jenny and her mom. She overheard them earlier that morning, when they talked quietly about Cooper going into town to look for the man named Bud Fuller.

"I think so," the smiling old rancher nodded kindly in answer to the little girl. "I don't think he'll want to come back again."

Alice heard all that she needed to hear—she was satisfied, and didn't require any more details. It was enough for her just to feel safe again. She went back to her bedroom to continue reading.

Danny and Joey came bursting through the back door together and rushed to Cooper's side. Joey climbed into a chair next to Grandpa Barnett, and Danny stood on the other side, resting his elbows on the table, inches from the old man's plate. Cooper swallowed a mouthful of food and gulped a little coffee to wash it down.

"Something on your mind this morning?" Cooper asked his nearest sidekick.

Danny studied the old rancher's face carefully for a long moment before he asked the question that was on his mind.

"Did you shoot him?"

"No!" Cooper insisted, looking to his wife to see how much trouble he was in for leaving his Winchester in the gun rack of his pickup where the boys could see it. "No, I didn't shoot him."

"Did you punch him in the nose?" Joey asked, expecting that a broken nose and a black eye would be the very least that Grandpa Barnett would give his abusive step-father.

"No, I didn't punch him, either. But I did persuade him to leave town, and I don't think he'll be back to bother you."

Jenny knew something about her father's powers of persuasion with men he didn't like. She was dying to learn more, but decided to wait until later when the children were in bed before asking her father whether he thought Fuller might dare to come back again. She tried to imagine how the confrontation went down, but realized that her dad would probably not tell her everything.

"Why don't you see if you can find these kids a sweet roll or something while I go and lock up," Cooper suggested, looking directly at Betty as he pushed his chair back and started toward the back door to retrieve his rifle from the pickup and lock it up in the shed.

"You kids sit up at the table now, and you can have some pie and milk," Betty instructed, mainly to distract the boys from following Cooper out the door.

"I'm gonna go with Grandpa," Danny announced, turning to follow Cooper out through the back porch.

Betty caught the boy by his arm and put a hand on his shoulder to steer him back around and point him in the direction of the kitchen table.

"You sit."

"Aw, I know he's going to lock up his Winchester," the boy protested, unable to understand why he wasn't allowed to be an honor guard for his hero.

"You don't need to know any more than that," Jenny admonished. "And don't you let me catch you trying to find it, either. It's dangerous, and it's not for little boys. You'll have plenty of time to learn how to shoot when you get older."

The rest of the weekend passed uneventfully, just the way Jenny had come to like it now that she was living back on the ranch with her folks. She had all the company and all the activity she needed with a houseful of kids and a baby to care for. She felt safe staying at home with her parents, and the worry that had overwhelmed her earlier about the pending legal confrontation with the child services people seemed less ominous when she was nestled in the confines of the Barnett Ranch—protected from the outside world.

She sat up late on Sunday night and talked with her parents after the kids went to bed.

"Dad, are you going to tell me everything that went on between you and Bud Fuller in town yesterday?"

"Let's just say that rough justice was dispensed, and leave it at that." He was sure that she would hear all about it on her next trip into town.

It amazed her to think how much a person's outlook on life changed when all of the responsibilities of adulthood were brought to bear. Suddenly, it seemed that she had everything in common with the parents who had oft-times seemed boring and overbearing before she moved to Pocatello to start work and attend college. She had been excited when she was first able to live alone and enjoy her independence. She didn't miss it, though. Life with family and children was decidedly better than having every evening to herself—doing whatever she wanted, whenever she wanted. She once believed that she would never tire of that freedom and the single lifestyle.

"I might see if I can get some help to repair the shingles on the roof before the bad weather comes," Cooper proposed.

"I never knew that you asked for help to do your chores before, Dad," Jenny chided with faint smile. "Are you feeling old?"

"Aw, your mother threatens me whenever I lean a ladder up against the house."

"We don't have any insurance," Betty explained, giving her husband a disapproving sideways glance with one eyebrow raised. "I came home from town a few months ago and caught him up on the roof after I had just warned him not to do it. I told him that I'd shoot him in the leg the next time I caught him putting a ladder up against the house or barn. That seemed to be enough to convince him to get some help the next time he wanted to patch the roof."

Cooper nodded silently and obediently as he lifted his coffee mug to his lips, keeping his smart remarks to himself. He allowed a small smile to replace any words he might have been thinking while he considered his comments carefully.

"It doesn't sound like you're too concerned about my health if you're willing to shoot me in the leg to keep me from doin' my chores," Cooper grumbled. "We don't have health coverage for gunshot wounds, either."

"I can patch up a bullet wound and put a splint on a fractured leg," Betty smiled. "But I can't fix you if you break your fool neck."

Cooper excused himself and went to bed, leaving the women to talk alone. He had come to like it much better that way. Betty had often engaged him in conversations and decision-making that he wanted no part of, but now that Jenny was home, he no longer had to be asked what he thought about a dress pattern or a summer fabric, or which gift would be most appropriate for a baby shower or wedding reception. He was off the hook now that Jenny was home, and he hoped she would stick around for a long time.

It didn't take long for word of Cooper's confrontation with Bud Fuller to get around town. Shorty Henderson told the story to anybody with an ear who pulled up to his gas pumps or into his garage. The account of Cooper Barnett's ferocity became more embellished with every telling, and by the time the story began to circulate among the ladies at the Wild Rose Hair Salon, no one knew for sure whether the man had been run out of town or shot full of holes and buried under a heap of old tires behind Shorty's Garage.

"I don't think that's what happened," the county clerk told her co-workers at the Camas County Courthouse building. "Don't you think someone would have heard gunshots?"

"All I know is that the mayor's wife said that her husband said that Shorty Henderson said that Cooper Barnett nearly beat the man to death," the county records assistant insisted. "And Shorty wouldn't dare lie to the mayor."

Judge William Oakes walked through the back door of the old county court house from the small parking lot in the rear of the building and helped himself to a cup of coffee before taking the stairs up to his second floor chambers.

"Good morning, ladies," he greeted, pleasantly. "Anything new today?"

"Good morning, Judge," the prim county clerk replied. "No, nothing new—you know Fairfield."

"Uh-huh, I know Fairfield," Judge Oakes acknowledged.

Across the street at Shorty Henderson's Garage, Cooper Barnett pulled up to a gas pump to fill the tank on his pickup. Harold Henderson had carried the same nickname for as long as anyone could remember. The fact was, though, that Shorty wasn't exactly short. It's just that he grew up with three older brothers who were all considerably taller than he was. Ever since he was a kid, he had always wanted to grow up to be six feet tall. By the time he was nineteen he made it, and with an inch to spare, but his older brothers were all over six foot five by then, so the handle stuck.

"Some folks around town are saying you shot that fella that was in here lookin' for Jenny the other day," Shorty said, attempting to distance himself from the inaccuracies being peddled by the other gossip purveyors in town. "I just want you to know that I didn't say any such thing."

"I'm sure you didn't," Cooper replied.

Two local women stood at the window in the hair salon across the street, staring at Cooper between the large letters of painted signage on the thick, glass window pane as he talked to Shorty. One of them suspected he might be threatening Shorty with his life if he ever told anyone all the details about his recent confrontation with the stranger.

"I pretty much kept that whole incident to myself," Shorty continued.

"I'm sure you did, Shorty—I appreciate it."

"You need me to catch your windshield today, Coop?"

"No, it's clean enough. Have you seen Sheriff Gillespie today?"

"He had to drive over to Hill City, I think," Shorty was quick to offer. "Some motorist hit a cow and wrecked his car, I heard."

Judge Oakes sat down at his desk and went through his pile of Monday mail, giving preference to submissions that came from attorney legal filings or from courts in other jurisdictions. A change of venue filing by the Law Offices of Bartholomew Crenshaw, Esquire, and granted by the district court in Boise caught his attention. It was a child custody case captioned *The State of Idaho v. Jennifer Barnett* and the change of jurisdiction from Boise to Fairfield came as something of a surprise to the judge. His small court occasionally handled child custody cases in the event of a divorce—which didn't exactly overburden his case load in the county of fewer than 1,200 residents—or on the rare occasion when a child was orphaned or abandoned. He was aware of the children from the Barnett Ranch that had been enrolled recently at the Camas County Elementary School just down the street from the courthouse, and he was curious to learn what it was all about.

"Ethel, hold my calls for the next half hour, would you please?" he instructed his clerk. "I have some reading to do."

Cooper had learned all that he needed to know on his brief stop in town. Fairfield was bubbling over with rumors about the children and speculation about where they had come from, not to mention the unpleasant encounter he had with Bud Fuller at the garage. He sat at the lunch counter at the coffee shop and listened to the conversations going on around him, and when he had heard enough, he walked out to his truck and drove home.

"I think we would all be better off if we stayed on the ranch until it's time to enroll the kids in school again," Cooper suggested to his wife after supper.

Betty and Jenny stacked dishes in the sink while he finished his coffee, and waited for a more complete explanation.

"There's a lot of noise in town about my little dust-up with Fuller, and some rumors about the kids."

"What kind of rumors, Dad," Jenny wanted to know.

"Mostly the kind that aren't true, just like you might expect."

"I want to know."

"I don't know, Jenny," Cooper said, becoming somewhat exasperated with her questioning. "Ridiculous things, like the girls are your natural children, and you left your husband and now he's trying to get his kids back."

"That's absurd!"

"That's what I said. Why don't we let things cool down a little before you go into town?"

The time went by quickly enough for the children, and even the boys were excited to start school again at the end of August. Jenny had agonized for the past two weeks, afraid that some unforeseen legal obstacle might come up and prevent her from enrolling Alice and June in school. She was surprised that no one questioned her when she and her mom took the children into town to sign them up for the new school year. They didn't even ask for an updated temporary custody order for the girls at the elementary school—only a current letter from Lorraine to grant permission for Danny and Joey to be enrolled.

Life seemed more stable with the children back in school—it made Jenny feel that she wasn't a freak in a town full of mostly normal people, and more importantly, she felt that the kids were accepted and welcomed. Even the story that had circulated about her father giving a thrashing to Bud Fuller had lost some of its earlier intrigue, and eventually people stopped talking about it altogether. The price of gasoline was going up, and that seemed to be the new topic of concern around town.

CHAPTER SEVENTEEN
THE UMBRELLA STAND

Sheriff Sam Gillespie approached from the direction of the court house and leaned against a support column under the awning on the front of the mercantile.

"Morning, Coop," he greeted. "Waitin' on the missus?"

"Howdy, Sam. Yeah, she's got some business down at the school."

Sheriff Gillespie pulled a pouch of chewing tobacco from his hip pocket and helped himself to a hefty pinch, savoring its flavor for a moment before he continued his conversation.

"I see Jenny in town once in a while, drivin' her old lamb cart around full of little ones. She brought home a pile of kids with her last winter, didn't she?"

"Yes, she did," Cooper admitted, with a faint smile and a nod. "She did, at that."

"A new baby, too, I heard."

"A little girl," Cooper acknowledged.

"Does she look like her mother?"

"She has blue eyes," Cooper nodded, thinking about how much Daphne resembled Jenny when she was a baby.

"It sounds like everything is good at the Barnett Ranch."

"Yeah, everything's good—not much changes out there, except the head count. How about you? Any excitement in *your* job lately—round up any cattle rustlers or bank robbers?"

"We don't have a bank in Camas County, Coop—you know that. And nobody wants cows anymore—they cost too much to feed," the sheriff quipped. "The only excitement I've had this month was when I was called out to the Gilroy place to resolve a domestic dispute, but by the time I got there, Mrs. Gilroy already had it resolved."

"*Elmer* Gilroy?" Cooper asked, turning to hear an explanation from the sheriff. He was surprised that anything beyond the mundane could ever occur at the home of the meek, undersized town barber.

"He came home late one night with a snootful of whiskey—demanded his dinner like he was a real man, and told his wife to mind her own business when she asked where he had been. They made a ruckus that woke all their neighbors, then she emptied a pot of spaghetti on him and knocked him out cold with a skillet."

"That sure don't sound like Elmer. You have to take her in—his missus, I mean?"

"Naw," the sheriff scoffed. "There wouldn't have been anyone to look after old Elmer if I did. He was just lying there on the kitchen floor with his face in a mess of spaghetti and meat sauce. I could see him moving a little bit, though, so I was pretty sure he'd be all right. I stopped by the next morning, just to be sure."

"Did he have anything to say for himself?" Cooper asked, somewhat amused to learn that the old barber finally experienced a little drama in his life.

"Nope. He was just sittin' there at the kitchen table with his back to the door—wearin' the same clothes he had on the night before—sippin' on his coffee and eatin' his cold spaghetti with a spoon. I figure his wife scooped it up off the floor and made him eat it for the next three days. I don't suppose we'll see anything like that happen again—not at the Gilroy house."

"I don't suppose," Cooper agreed, chuckling a little under his breath.

The sheriff changed the tone of the conversation as he broached the subject that had been on his mind when he first approached his old acquaintance.

"I heard your daughter had a little trouble with a fella that came through town awhile back."

"She did, yes," Cooper admitted. "But I talked to him the next day, and I don't think he'll be back."

"You recall hearing his name?"

"I dunno—Fuller, I think. He wasn't from around here."

"Fuller—yeah, that sounds right," Sheriff Gillespie said. "I believe it's the same man I heard about from Sheriff Rallison over in Mountain Home."

"Did he show up over there?" Cooper asked. "I told him that I thought he should leave Idaho."

"Yeah, well it seems he went into Marvin's Garage out on the north end of town—needed to get some gas and didn't have any money to pay."

"It could have been him, I suppose—he hadn't worked for a while, I heard," Cooper said. "It follows that he'd have no money. Are you sure it was Fuller?"

"Greasy-haired guy, medium build—kept his cigarettes rolled up in the sleeve of his tee-shirt," Gillespie described briefly.

"Sounds like him."

"He drove into Marvin's with a tire iron stickin' out of a hole in his rear window."

"Yeah, that was him, all right," Cooper nodded.

"The way I heard it, he walked up to the counter, demanding all the money out of the cash register, and Marv told him to go to hell—so the man got mad and came around the counter, swinging the tire iron he had just pulled out of his rear car window."

"Was Marvin hurt?" Cooper asked, with some concern. He didn't like to think that he had provided the assault weapon to a robber.

"Yeah, he was hurt, but he gave better than he got. Marv kept a loaded 12-gauge Browning poked nose-down in an old umbrella stand behind the counter next to his cash register, just in case any trouble was to come through the door. He was suspicious when he saw that tire iron stuck in the fella's car window, so he kept his hand close to his shotgun when the man was inside. He had barely cleared the gun barrel from its holder when that tire iron came swingin' down on his shoulder and broke his collar bone," Gillespie explained. "The shotgun went off and blew that greasy fella's foot clean off—all the way to his ankle."

"The hell you say—did Fuller try to get away?" Cooper asked, with a sudden appetite for more information.

"Nope—or if he did, he didn't get very far before Sheriff Rallison and one of his deputies arrived.

"They bother to call him an ambulance?"

"Eventually they did, but first the Sheriff took the time to be certain the assailant was hurt too bad to ride in the patrol car.

"How about Marvin—is he okay?"

"Sure, he's fine—got patched up and went back to work three days after the incident. The greaser went on trial a few weeks later. Jury took nearly thirty minutes to find him guilty of armed robbery and attempted murder. The judge gave him twenty years."

"That happened fast," Cooper marveled.

"Well, everybody's entitled to a speedy trial in this country, you know." Gillespie drawled. "And Marvin was the only witness, so it didn't take long to wrap it up, given the evidence they had."

"What evidence?"

"The tire iron that broke Marv's collar bone, and Marvin's good word."

"It don't sound to me like a broken collar bone would get a fella twenty years."

"Armed robbery is armed robbery—don't matter if the weapon has bullets in it. Besides that, I'm told that Marv is pretty well liked around Mountain Home," Gillespie went on. "He's helped a lot of people out when their cars were broke down, and he always stays open late so people can get gas when they need it. Even does a few repairs if he doesn't have to work on one of those Japanese or European models—and he never overcharged anybody in his life."

"They still got Fuller in the jail in Mountain Home?"

"Naw, he's already locked up in the State Penitentiary outside of Boise. I expect that fella's hobblin' around the prison yard on his stump right now, tryin' to stay outta the way of the real tough guys. They got more than a few up there, I've heard."

"You don't suppose he'll try to appeal his case? Try to get his time shortened, maybe?" Cooper asked, eager to hear Sheriff Gillespie's professional opinion about how long the kid beater might have to spend behind bars.

"Don't matter if he does. He can appeal his sentence as much as he wants to, but he won't get his foot back—I can tell you that for nothing."

The sheriff pushed his Stetson back on his forehead, stepped down from the sidewalk, and ambled across the street toward the cafe.

"I think I'll get a cup of coffee," Gillespie said, as he began to walk away. "By the way, Coop, I'd consider it a personal favor if you wouldn't try to start any gunfights next to Shorty's gas pumps—I don't want to have to clean up your mess."

Cooper Barnett whistled a happy tune as he walked along Main Street in the direction of the old elementary school—the school where he had learned to sing off key when he was a kid. Today would be a nice day to treat Betty and Jenny to lunch at the cafe, he thought. He was going to enjoy telling his wife and daughter about Bud Fuller's missing foot, and about the dumb jackass's new accommodations in Boise.

"I thought I'd take the boys up to the sheep camp at Murdoch Creek when I take Tony Beraza's supplies up to him," Cooper suggested to his wife and daughter as they lunched at the Sagebrush Cafe. "It's the Labor Day weekend, so the boys could camp out for a couple of nights before they have to start school—what do you think?"

"I think it's a great idea, Dad," Jenny agreed. "We could drive up with you for the day and have a picnic, but I don't think the girls will want to stay the night—they don't like the mosquitoes."

Betty stopped at the post office to pick up the mail before leaving town, and discovered a letter for Jenny from Bart Crenshaw. She stayed in the small parking area without starting the car until Jenny had a chance to open the letter and read it aloud.

"The custody hearing is here in Fairfield in front of Judge Oakes. This says it's scheduled for the end of next month—I wonder if I'm supposed to do anything before then."

"Just make sure those girls look their best," Cooper advised from his thinking spot in the back seat. "And be there on time."

Betty and Jenny both turned to look over their shoulders and give him a silent stare. Cooper's advice was practical, but he rarely looked beyond the obvious.

"What?" he asked when the women wouldn't stop looking at him.

"Coop, I think what Jenny meant was do we need to get any paperwork from the school, or a health checkup from a doctor—things like that," Betty said.

"Oh, well, sure—you'll need that, too."

"I'll ask Alice's teacher to give us a letter about her progress at school, and about how well she gets along with others in her class," Jenny said. "That should be of some help if the judge knows she's well adjusted."

"Why don't you just call Bart Crenshaw and ask him to give you a list?" Cooper proposed.

"Why don't you just sit back there and be quiet?" Betty suggested.

Cooper looked around for something to read, but could only find a couple of toys, a rubber doll, and one of June's coloring books.

"I don't like riding in the back seat," he grumbled.

"You won't have to ride in the back seat tomorrow," Betty sympathized. "You can stay home."

"Fine with me," Cooper answered. "Nothing else I need from town for at least another month."

"I left an application and resume at the elementary school today, Dad," Jenny said, changing the subject to something more important than seating assignments in the family station wagon. "I told them that

I was willing to accept any position that becomes available—teacher's aide, office staff, library—any position except janitorial."

"Isn't it a bit early to start looking for work? I thought you would want to wait until the baby got a little older."

"I encouraged her to do it, Coop," Betty answered on her daughter's behalf. "I have plenty of time to watch Daphne during the day. She sleeps a lot, and we can set up a crib in the kitchen so I can work while I watch her."

"I don't know why you're in such a hurry to go to work," Cooper said, sourly.

"It's about showing the State of Idaho that I'm employable, Dad, and that I can provide for the girls financially."

"I suppose."

"In case you just forgot, there's a hearing coming up soon, Coop. Jenny needs to demonstrate that she's willing and able to do more than to simply live at home with her parents—she needs to show that she's contributing to the support and welfare of the girls. I just hope the matter of the boys doesn't come up at the hearing, too."

Cooper remained silent and sullen, wishing that he had the answers. What he really wanted was to go and have a talk with the State's attorney—just the two of them—but he knew that would only make things worse.

He spent the rest of his day getting a lasso and a halter on one of the Spanish Mustang mares, and then led her around in the corral, getting her used to being handled. She gentled fairly quick, Cooper thought, and especially with the help of a few fresh carrots. He went back to the corral every hour or so with another carrot, just to get the mare used to being led and restrained—and then rewarded her for her good behavior. The other mare and stallion remained close to the corral, drawn by their herd instincts to stay near one of their own that had been separated from them. Cooper rewarded them with carrots and hay. It was time to make the horses feel more comfortable with humans.

When Danny and Joey got older, they would need sure-footed horses to ride. It wouldn't hurt to have the mustang mare ready to take along on the sheep trail when they brought them back from their summer pasture, Cooper thought. He could let Danny ride Deuce, and Joey could hold the reins of the old bay mare, and steer her along behind. Blue had always been a good kids' horse, in addition to being a reliable cart horse during lambing season. He hoped the old mare would last a few more years.

He wondered what he might do to help persuade Jenny's girlfriend to move back to southern Idaho, now that her jackass husband was in prison. She probably didn't even know about it, he thought. If she could find a car to drive, she could work in Fairfield or Hailey or Bellevue. Maybe they could find her an old single-wide mobile home and park it on the ranch. That way, at least, she could live with her boys.

"It don't make sense for those boys to have to be uprooted again," Cooper uttered aloud to his wife, when he came back into the house and sat down at the kitchen table for a cup of coffee.

"What brought that on?" Betty asked.

CHAPTER EIGHTEEN
BUS STOP BILLY

Cooper put on his freshly-pressed suit, and waited in the kitchen for the rest of the family to get ready for the ride into town. He sat down with a cup of coffee, then got up again and climbed the stairs to his bedroom. He took a hatbox down from the closet shelf, removed his new Stetson, and snugged it down on his head. He made sure that it was a good fit, and then checked himself in the mirror.

Betty had already dropped the boys at school earlier, and left Jenny at home to get the girls dressed and ready for their court appearance. Jenny was understandably nervous about the custody hearing. She had no idea what Vera Sorenson and the State's attorney were going to attempt in court to prevent her from keeping the girls. Whatever they had up their sleeves, she hoped Bart Crenshaw had something better.

The thought struck her that the State's attorney might make a huge issue about her being single—an unwed mother, and without a job. It seemed a valid concern, and she didn't know how Crenshaw could overcome an argument like that. Whatever money was left in Dora Rolfson's estate would certainly not be enough to last forever, and the best she could hope for would be that the house and cottage in Boise could be rented for enough to help with the girls' monthly expenses.

"Now you remember to stay quiet while we're in the court house," Jenny reminded Alice and June. "And don't fidget—just sit up straight and listen to what's being said. If the judge asks you anything, don't be afraid—just answer his questions."

"What will he ask us?" Alice wanted to know, already worried.

"Nothing that you can't answer—questions about how you're doing in school and if you're happy living where you are—things like that."

"Why can't I just write him a letter?"

"We better get going, Mom," Jenny said. "The hearing starts at ten, and Bart Crenshaw said to meet him at the cafe a half hour early so we could talk about it first."

"We've got plenty of time, honey—it's only quarter to nine."

Cooper waited outside, feeling a little edgy. Hearing the women fret over something that was out of their hands made him even more anxious. He took the cotton handkerchief out of his hip pocket and gave his boots an extra wipe. He made sure to polish them better for Jenny's court hearing than he did before his trip to see the Governor. He climbed the porch steps and opened the screen door to call to the women and girls inside.

"Can we go?" he said, impatiently. "How ready do you have to be?"

Jenny sat in the back seat with the girls and Betty drove—Cooper was glad to have the passenger side so that he could do some worrying of his own without having to concentrate on driving.

He knew that Judge Oakes had to be aware of the altercation he had with Bud Fuller in front of Shorty's Garage several weeks earlier, and he wondered how that might impact his decision. He was concerned that the judge may not consider it a good idea to allow two small girls to remain in a home with a grisly old rancher who was prone to losing his temper and resorting to violence on occasion. He kept the worry to himself—it wasn't the time to bring it up with the girls in the car. Anyway, done is done, he thought—he couldn't change the past.

He stared out the window across the brush-covered prairie for most of the drive into town and reflected on how much his life had changed in the past year—all because of Jenny. He was just beginning to grow accustomed to life on the ranch with no children around when his daughter showed up with four of them and another on the way. He remembered how he was taken so much by surprise when Jenny drove up to the house in the old Studebaker, and the children all climbed out, wide-eyed and shivering in the cold. He never imagined that he could grow so fond of all of them, and now he couldn't imagine life without them.

"Do you have Alice's school records?" he asked, intending the question for anyone in the car who could answer him.

"We have everything, Coop," Betty assured quietly.

Cooper remained silent for the remainder of the drive into town. Betty pulled into the parking lot of the Sagebrush Cafe and found a spot near the front door. A late model Lincoln Town Car was parked close by, and he assumed it belonged to Bart Crenshaw—it certainly didn't belong to anyone who lived in Camas County. Betty waited in the car with the girls while Cooper and Jenny went inside to meet with the attorney.

"Good morning, Jennifer," Bart Crenshaw greeted when Jenny and her father approached the booth where he was seated.

"Good morning," Jenny returned, feeling apprehensive at the sight of the well-dressed lawyer. His presence filled her with the sudden realization of the solemn importance of the day's proceedings, and how much was hanging in the balance.

"This must be your father," Crenshaw said, extending his hand to greet Cooper in person for the first time. "You have quite a reputation, sir, and excellent character recommendations."

Cooper didn't know what to say—he simply smiled, shook the lawyer's hand, and sat down next to his daughter.

"Now then, let's talk about what will happen when we're in the courtroom," Crenshaw began. "Judge Oakes has everything he needs in order to render a decision—everything but remarks from the attorneys for the State, and from me, of course."

"I brought Alice's school records and a letter from her teacher," Jenny offered.

"We already have those, thanks—we submit those to the court in advance of the hearing, so that the judge has time to review everything first."

The Lamb Cart

"What's he going to ask me?"

"If I'm not mistaken, he's going to ask you how the girls are doing so that he can measure your enthusiasm for the job of parenting and get a feel for how much you want the girls to remain with you. He wants to learn how attached you are to them—and how much the girls have bonded with you."

"That's it?"

"No, that's not everything—he'll probably want to talk to the girls—the oldest one at least. He'll want to know that they are happy with you and with living on the ranch—he'll want to know that the girls love being where they are."

"I have to tell you that I'm really scared—I've never been more afraid in my life."

"There's a reason that we asked for a change of venue, Jenny, and I requested that the case be moved from Boise to Fairfield. It was mainly to put it in the hands of a judge who knows everything about the town where you live—a judge who has ready access to information about you and the school that the girls attend, and from people who know you. A judge in Boise could never obtain all the information he would need to make a fair decision—not like Judge Oakes can."

"I don't know if that's good or bad," Cooper interjected. "A lot of gossip gets circulated around a small town."

"I realize that, too," Crenshaw admitted. "But that doesn't mean it's all bad."

"Is there anything else my daughter needs to know?" Cooper asked, with all the concern of a protective father.

"Only this," the attorney began. "Don't say anything, and don't show any emotion or make any gestures, no matter what the State's attorney says about you. Don't react with any anger or indignation—just leave that to me—I'll do the talking for you."

Jenny and her dad left the cafe first, and moved the car across the street to park nearer to the old court house. Bart Crenshaw paid the waitress and walked across the street to join them after retrieving his briefcase from the trunk of his car. He led the Barnett family inside and up the stairs to the small courtroom.

A sheriff's deputy, acting as bailiff, ordered everyone in attendance to rise and announced that court was in session when Judge Oakes appeared through the door from his small chambers.

"Be seated," the judge said, almost as quickly as the people in the small courtroom rose to their feet.

The judge took his seat behind the bench and opened the case file that he had carried with him from his chambers. He looked around the courtroom briefly, and recognized most of those in attendance.

It was obvious from his attire that the well-dressed attorney seated next to Jennifer Barnett was Bart Crenshaw, a man who was wise enough not to overdress for his appearance in a small-town courtroom. Crenshaw didn't wear the gold cufflinks, tailored shirt, or expensive silk tie that he usually wore for court appearances in Boise or Spokane. Instead, he dressed in a plain gray suit, white shirt, and black wing-tip shoes, a style popular with everyone from bankers to car salesmen. He knew that putting on big-city airs wouldn't gain him any advantage.

Vera Sorenson was present in the courtroom, seated alongside the portly lawyer in horn-rimmed glasses who had been sent by the State Attorney's office to represent the State of Idaho Child Services Agency. The round attorney was allowed to present his remarks first, and he used a common argument that usually worked to persuade a judge to place orphaned children under the protection of the State.

"Your Honor, it is obvious that Jennifer Barnett is unable to provide for the minor children, Alice Rolfson and June Rolfson. She is currently unemployed, and has no apparent prospects for employment. The State believes that the welfare of the children would be better served if the State's Child Services Agency is allowed to place them in foster homes, toward the eventual goal of putting them up for permanent adoption."

Judge Oakes was unmoved by such common tactics. He was intent upon hearing more from the State than a one-line dismissal of a prospective guardian's worthiness, based only upon her supposed inability to care for young children.

"That's it? She doesn't have a job at the moment, so you believe she is not fit to care for these girls?" Judge Oakes asked.

Vera Sorenson sat up straight in her chair and pulled her shoulders back to reveal her indignant feelings toward the questioning directed at the State's attorney—a posture that reflected her obvious disdain for the hick-town courtroom. She glared, thin-lipped and frustrated at the small-town judge who she believed was simply wasting the State's time.

"Well, counsel?" Judge Oakes continued impatiently.

"Your Honor, the State has been reluctant to bring this up, but there is a matter of moral turpitude involved, as well. Miss Barnett is the unwed mother of an infant child—she has never been married—and the environment in which the minors are living is not a healthy one, nor is it conducive to a normal, happy life."

"They appear to be happy to me, counsel," the judge countered. "Let me hear from counsel for Jennifer Barnett."

Bart Crenshaw rose, and lifted a letter from his opened case file, then looked up at Judge Oakes with respect and made his brief request.

"Your Honor, may I approach the bench?"

Judge Oakes noticed the letter in Crenshaw's hand and gestured for him to come forward. He took the letter from the lawyer's hand and quickly read the first paragraph, then chastised Crenshaw openly.

"Counsel, I don't like last-minute surprises or theatrics of any kind in my courtroom. We may only be a small town, but we like to operate within the strict confines of procedures and the law. Why did you wait until now to give this letter to the court?"

"I apologize, Your Honor, but it was only received by my office yesterday. This morning was the first opportunity I had to present it to the court."

"I want to see counsel in my chambers," Judge Oakes ordered. He pointed in the direction of the short, round State's attorney as he rose, and the two lawyers followed him through the passage door into his chambers.

"All rise," the bailiff called to the sparsely-occupied courtroom.

"Be seated," he said, half bored as he watched Attorney Crenshaw and the fat little lawyer from Boise disappear through the side door into the judge's chambers.

"What's going on?" Betty whispered to her daughter, leaning over the railing from the court spectator section.

Jenny shook her head quietly to indicate she had no understanding of what was going on behind the closed door.

Judge Oakes sat on the edge of his desk and waited until both attorneys were in his chambers and the short one in the rear closed the door behind him. The judge extended his hand, offering the letter to the State's attorney, and gave him a moment to comprehend what he was reading. The man seemed to shrink at least one size as he focused on the Governor's seal at the top of the letterhead, and began to read the contents of the letter.

"I can save you some time, counsel," the judge said, dismissively. "The Governor of the State of Idaho is personally vouching for the character of Jennifer Barnett and the Barnett family. He says that the orphaned children would be very lucky to grow up on the Barnett Ranch. Do you have a letter from someone who says they wouldn't?"

The judge snatched the letter back from the stunned attorney and stood to leave his chambers.

"I didn't think so."

He opened his door to allow the two attorneys to return to the courtroom, and stepped back to the bench, telling the people waiting in the courtroom to be seated. He smoothed his black robe and sat down to consider his decision, then drew a deep breath and issued his order.

"I have information from the probate attorney for decedent Dora Rolfson that the handwritten will of his client is uncontested and that it has been accepted by the probate court. Mrs. Rolfson's express wish was that her granddaughters be left in the care of Jennifer Barnett, family friend and caregiver, and her estate provides adequate financial support for the minor children. School and health records show that both girls are doing well, and I have several unsolicited letters from townspeople in support of Jennifer Barnett. Other arguments to the contrary, I see no reason why Dora Rolfson's wishes should be ignored. From all credible reports, the girls are well-adjusted and happy. They appear to have a stable and healthy family environment, and they certainly have a spacious yard to play in. It is the order of this court that permanent custody of the minor children Alice Rolfson and June Rolfson is granted to Jennifer Barnett."

Judge William Oakes brought his oak gavel down with a resounding crack to signal the finality of his decision, then rose abruptly and disappeared through the side door into his chambers before another word could be uttered by the State's attorney.

Jennifer and her parents left the courtroom in a daze—bewildered and happy with the judge's hasty decision.

"What happened in there?" Vera Sorenson hissed at the short lawyer who had told her on the drive from Boise that all the arguments would be in the State's favor.

"We lost," the deflated lawyer confessed.

"What? How can that be? Didn't the judge read your brief?"

"He read everything, Vera, and he made his decision."

"Well, it's wrong," she spat furiously, as they walked the short distance to the car. "This isn't over!"

"Oh, it's over," the round lawyer insisted, as he opened the passenger door for the angry woman. "Let's just call it a day, shall we?"

Cooper took the wheel of the family station wagon for the drive back to the ranch and whistled the melody from the Idaho State Song as he motored down Highway 20 toward the turnoff for the ranch. He couldn't say why the tune was stuck in his head, but it happened. He hit a few wrong notes, and before long, Alice and June were unable to stop giggling.

"What's wrong with my whistling?" Cooper demanded, pretending to be offended.

"I think we'll drive up to Boise this weekend and pick up the rest of our things," Jenny said. "Maybe I can arrange to rent out the house and cottage while we're there."

"The sooner, the better," her mother agreed. "No reason to have them sitting there empty, and it doesn't sound like you'll be living there again—not any time soon, anyway."

Jenny took the girls with her on Saturday morning to make the trip north to clean out the cottage and place an ad in the newspaper, offering it for rent. She decided that she could go back another weekend with her dad's pickup to box up the remainder of the clothes and household items in Mrs. Rolfson's house.

The trip took most of the day, including the time it took to contact the newspaper to place an ad, clean the cottage, and stop by Idaho Joe's to say hello to Joe Bannock and ask if she could leave a key to the cottage with him.

"Of course you can leave it with me, Jenny." Joe was happy to oblige. "Are you sure you don't want your job back? I can always use a good cook."

"I've got way too many kids now, Joe—your office would be colored with crayons from floor to ceiling, and I don't think you want that."

"I wouldn't mind."

"I really appreciate you for doing this, Joe."

"It's not a problem, Jenny. I'll put the word out that the cottage is available."

It was late afternoon when Jenny and the girls left Boise to make the trip home, and it was nearly dark before they pulled into Harry's Diner at the bus stop in Mountain Home to get a drink and say hello before they finished their trip back to the ranch.

Harry was working the kitchen and filling in as a waiter, so Jenny sat at the counter with the girls and ordered sodas. A young boy in a white bib apron sat at the end of the counter, sipping a drink through a straw. He must be a kitchen helper on a break, Jenny thought, but he appeared to be far too young to be working in the diner.

"Who's your helper, Harry?" Jenny asked.

"Just a kid who got off the bus a while back and said he didn't have anyplace to go, so I put him to work and Donna fixed him up with a room. We give him enough spending money on top of room and board for him to get the things he needs, but he never seems to want anything except to go to a movie once in a while."

"Doesn't he have any family?"

"Says he doesn't. We get a lot of transients through here, but none so young, and they never stay around very long. This boy just seemed lost and in need of a place to stay."

"How long do you think he'll stick around?"

"Hard to say—as long as he wants to, I guess. He keeps showing up for work every day."

A pair of customers walked in and Harry excused himself to take water and menus to their booth.

"Let's get going, girls—it's getting late and Grandma is going to have our supper ready."

Jenny left money for the drinks on the counter and ushered the girls out the door, waving to Harry as she left.

"Say hello to Donna for me."

"I'll be sure to tell her you were here."

Jenny stared through the windshield of the old Studebaker at the glass door of the diner for a long moment, then opened her door and got out of the car to go back inside the diner.

"What did you forget, Jenny?" Alice called out from the passenger window.

"Wait there, girls—I'll be right back," Jenny said, as she walked to the door of the diner. She paused for a moment and drew in a deep breath, then pulled the door open wide. The girls watched as Jenny went inside and talked to Harry for a minute, took paper and pen out of her purse, and wrote something down to hand to Harry. He folded the paper and slipped it into his shirt pocket.

"What did you have to do, Jenny?" June asked when Jenny got back into the car.

"I'm just trying to help someone out, honey. I gave him a name and a phone number, that's all."

As usual, there was little traffic on the highway to Camas County, and they easily made it to Fairfield before six o'clock. Jenny pulled into Shorty's for gas, and Tom Benton was standing next to his Forest Service truck, watching Shorty replace a tire. He smiled and walked to the car when he recognized the old Studebaker and saw Jenny and the girls inside.

"I heard you have a new baby girl," he commented. "Congratulations."

"Is there anyone in town who doesn't know?" Jenny answered, good-naturedly.

"Of course not—anybody who didn't already know, Shorty and I told them, didn't we Shorty?"

The skinny station owner nodded as he unscrewed the gas cap on Jenny's car and pushed the nozzle into the filler tube.

"How much do you need, Jenny?"

"Five bucks worth, I guess—thanks, Shorty."

"I've been thinking that we could have that lunch soon, now that you're going to be living here full time," Tom suggested.

"Is there anything that you don't know about me, Tom Benton?"

"A guy has to keep track of a girl's whereabouts if he ever expects to get a chance to ask her out, and keeping track of everything you've been up to lately hasn't been easy. So, how about that lunch? Is tomorrow good?"

"I have a better idea—why don't you follow us out to the place and have supper with us tonight?"

Tom was caught off guard by the sudden offer from the freckle-nosed young woman with brilliant blue eyes and pretty brown hair—he wasted no time in accepting.

"Are you sure you're folks won't mind?"

"There's always enough food to feed a platoon of men at our place, and my dad will be glad to see you. Just expect to talk to him about your time in the army for an hour."

"I won't mind. And I am kind of hungry."

Alice and June giggled as Jenny and Tom looked at each other for a long time without speaking.

"Well, let's go then, if you're ready," Jenny said, interrupted by the twittering girls.

"I'll be right behind you."

Governor Owen Bryant sat down in his tall leather swivel chair and picked up a hand-addressed envelope that his assistant had placed in the center of his large desk blotter—a spot that was certain to catch his attention. It was addressed to him and marked *Personal and Confidential*. The envelope didn't contain a return address, but the postmark revealed that it had been mailed from Fairfield, Idaho two days earlier. He pulled open his center desk drawer, retrieved a silver letter opener, and sliced through the flap to remove the hand-written letter. He leaned back in his chair and put his feet up on his desk as he unfolded the simple, two-page letter and began to read. After a minute or two, he dropped the letter to his chest and held it for a moment as he reflected on the message he had just read.

The door from the adjoining office opened and his assistant stuck her head inside.

"Will you be needing anything else before I leave for the day, sir?" Mrs. Weaver asked.

"No thank you, Gladys—I'm fine—you go on home now," he replied. "Oh, hold on a second—would you call my wife and tell her I'll be home in half an hour? I appreciate it."

Gladys Weaver smiled as she pulled the door closed behind her, but not before she noticed the opened letter the Governor held in his hand. He lifted the letter and read it a second time.

My old friend,

I realize that it's been awhile since we last spoke, but I'm sure you must know that you are often on my mind and that my wife and I speak of you and Janet frequently. I understand that your responsibilities must keep you constantly occupied—even more than I can imagine. Still, I hope that someday soon you might find the time to stop and visit us on one of your next trips through Camas County.

The letter you wrote in support of the Barnett family came as no surprise to me—I have known for many years that you are a man of true compassion, and that you have a sincere belief in justice and the law. It is one of many reasons that I have always regarded you so highly.

Had it not been for you and your family, I would not have made it through those most difficult times during the Great Depression, when you found me rifling through the garbage cans that day behind the bus depot, looking for something to eat. I have not forgotten that when you learned that I slept on the benches and baggage carts at the bus stop every night, you took me home with you— to the protection of your father, and the loving care of your sweet, saintly mother. I could not remember a time when I had such a safe and loving home. You even fought my battles for me at school when the other kids teased me for my shabby clothes and taunted me with names like "Bus Stop". Somehow, you convinced me that it was a good nickname for a boy, and a better one than most.

Had I not been given that chance for a new life, I would never have had the opportunity to finish school, or to go on to college and obtain a law degree, and eventually, to be appointed to the bench. I have truly enjoyed my career as a judge, and although it has had its difficult times, I am most grateful to have the opportunity to make decisions that affect people's lives in a positive way. Mildred and I will look forward to seeing you—hopefully one day in the not-too-distant future.

Your loyal friend, always

Bus Stop Billy

The Governor lowered his feet to the floor, folded the letter and slid it back into its envelope, then picked up the telephone and dialed his home number.

"What do you have planned for dinner tonight, Janet?" he asked his wife.

"I took a roast out of the freezer this afternoon—why, do you have something better in mind?"

"Maybe we could go out for a steak dinner—I've been thinking about a big, juicy ribeye and baked potato all afternoon," he suggested, offering to save his wife from preparing dinner at home.

"Sounds good to me, Governor—what's the occasion?"

"I thought we could talk about taking some time off and driving down to Burley to visit our daughter and grandkids—maybe I could get in a round or two of golf with my son-in-law."

"This is sudden. You haven't taken any time off in two years. What have you done with my workaholic husband?"

"I'm not a workaholic—I'm just busy. We're due for some time off, and I think I can clear my calendar for a few days next week. We can even stop in Fairfield on the way and visit some old friends, if you like."

"I'd love to, Owen. You won't back out at the last minute, will you?"

"No, I won't back out."

"Do you promise?"

"Of course I promise—they don't call me The Honorable Owen Bryant for nothing."

EPILOGUE

The era of the western ranch has become little more than a footnote in American history—a lifestyle that once thrived in a time long past. But there still exists in rural America a way of life that has held fast for generations. It is where strong women and men of honor forge their lives from a hard land and lay claim to what is rightfully theirs—it is the place they call home.

The Keeper

A woman waited sadly in the dim and waning light
How she came to be alone no one could say
But there were whispers in the depot
On that cold and rainy night
And while strangers watched she bowed her head to pray

"What will I do, where can I go?"
She mourned and tried to find a way
With a desperate, aching heart and spirits low
And the bitter, chilling winter grew much colder every day
Soon to turn from freezing rain to drifting snow

Her choice was made, she went alone
And as she sojourned to the north
To make a new life in a city far away
She knew the odds were stacked against her,
Her proud spirit nearly broken
And she knew an infant child was on the way

There's a feeling in the soul
That makes a body quake with fear
And dread the sentence of a lifetime spent alone.
It robs the heart of hope and courage
As the weeping time draws near
And sends a numbing chill down to the bone

When she thought no more could happen
In her world so filled with strife
Four more children came to be within her care
To test her will and mettle as she struggled with her life
So she humbly traveled home with soul laid bare

Help was waiting on the ranch where she spent her younger days
From a loving mom and disapproving dad
There to help, but not to judge her for the error of her ways
A man of honor and a mother who was glad

Jenny's baby cried its greeting in the middle of the night
As it awakened to a world so vast and new,
And a mother who was waiting with a face that shone so bright
When she saw her infant daughter's little eyes of brilliant blue

There's a hard path must be followed
When all the chips are down
One more test that must be passed before it's done
She'll be judged for her compassion
When the Keeper makes her rounds
She'll need all her strength before her race is run

Cold wind blowing down the prairie lifts the night bird on the wing
Lonely land where feathered hunter seeks its prey
Children huddled in the twilight beg the meadowlark to sing
And the stars come out to light their lonely way

Broken silence in the darkness when the coyote howls at night,
Sending chills through little hearts and little bones
But the Keeper guards her flock, erasing traces of their fright
And every child yearns to journey home

Richard Hooton

So she gathered all her cubs
She was a lioness on the prowl
Little Joseph wore a hat
And Brother Danny wore a scowl

Mother Jenny led the way
As they walked out into the night
Fretful Alice stayed the course
And tiny June just held on tight

'cross the sheep bridge there was refuge
'cross the bridge and homeward bound
Every child will be protected
When the Keeper comes around

Richard Hooton

See 1stWorld Books at:

www.1stWorldPublishing.com

See our classic collection at:

www.1stWorldLibrary.com